John Delaware Lewis

Satirae

with a literal English prose translation and notes by John Delaware Lewis - Vol. 1

John Delaware Lewis

Satirae
with a literal English prose translation and notes by John Delaware Lewis - Vol. 1

ISBN/EAN: 9783337367572

Printed in Europe, USA, Canada, Australia, Japan

Cover: Foto ©Andreas Hilbeck / pixelio.de

More available books at **www.hansebooks.com**

D. IUNII IUVENALIS

SATIRAE

WITH

A LITERAL ENGLISH PROSE TRANSLATION AND NOTES

BY

JOHN DELAWARE LEWIS, M.A.

TRIN. COLL. CAMB.

Second Edition, Revised

VOL. I.

LONDON
TRÜBNER & CO., LUDGATE HILL

1882

ADVERTISEMENT TO THE SECOND EDITION.

In this edition, the Notes have been considerably enlarged, and some errors have been corrected. George Long somewhere says that the greatest scholar in Europe will occasionally be guilty of mistakes, which a schoolboy will be able to point out. If this be true, as I believe it to be, Editors of modest pretensions have some excuse to offer for their lapses.

At any rate, I must confess to having discovered a few blunders in my first edition, which will not disfigure this one. Those which are left are not, I hope, very numerous or very serious.

I have also subjoined the most important of the " various readings."

April 1882.

PREFACE.

—◆◆—

THE accompanying translation of Juvenal, originally
made for my own amusement, and which has been lying
by me in manuscript for some years, is not sent to
press without a certain degree of hesitation. I have
been induced to publish it, principally from the belief
that there is not in the English language any literal
prose translation of the great Satirist of a character to
be entirely satisfactory to the scholar. Madan's is literal
enough, but almost unintelligible to any one who is unable
to read Latin. That of Mr. Evans, in " Bohn's Classical
Library," is an excellent and spirited rendering, well
adapted to the series of which it forms a volume—that
is to say, well qualified to convey the general meaning
of Juvenal to the English reader. Perhaps a still higher
character, from the scholar's point of view, might fairly
be assigned to it. But, at any rate, I differ from Mr.
Evans so frequently that I do not think his perform-
ance any bar to my attempt.* These two are the only

---

* For example, in the first page (14) at which I open by chance—it is
only a half-page, containing a version of twenty lines of the original, at
the end of Satire ii—there are three considerable differences between Mr.
Evans and myself. He translates *Sed tu vera puta*, " but do thou believe
them true ; " *Hic fiunt homines*, " here they learn to be men ; " *Sic praetextatos referunt Artaxata mores*, " thus it is the vices of our young nobles

prose versions in English, as far as I know, which have any pretensions to be called literal ones.

Whatever may be the shortcomings and faults of this version (and I am conscious that they may be many), I have endeavoured, throughout, to give, as nearly as possible, the exact sense of the original, as it was understood by me. Whenever the choice presented itself to me—as it necessarily did, at almost every line—between a literal, and, it may be thought, a somewhat tame and bald version, and what is called " a spirited rendering," I have deliberately preferred the former; my object being to translate, as a help to those who wish to make acquaintance with the original, not to paraphrase for the benefit of what is called " the English reader."

I have added some Notes—they should perhaps rather be described as the materials and memoranda for notes— which were collected by me with the view of carrying out a project which occurred to me, on the completion of the translation, that of attempting a completely new edition (as I understand the word " edition ") of this poet. But circumstances compelled me to abandon this project shortly after it was conceived, without much hope of being able at any future time to take it seriously in hand. I have accordingly printed my Notes as they stand; and it is my hope that, even in their present state, they may be found to contain some useful hints and helps towards a correct understanding of a difficult author.

---

are aped even at Artaxata." Often, *ex gr.*, . . . iii 61 186 319, iv 57, vi 153 413 426 454 (450), &c. &c., he seems to me to commit serious errors in translating.

Every illustrative passage quoted by me has been collected in the course of my own reading; or, in the few cases where I have taken from another editor, he is scrupulously named. But where so many have been over the ground before me, it must of course follow that a great number of these passages have appeared in previous editions. I have selected these illustrations almost exclusively from the books of Roman authors, and in preference from such as flourished in or near the time of Juvenal, as Martial and the younger Pliny; and I hope they will generally be found pertinent. By bringing together everything which might be forced into a connection, however remote, with our author, from every one who ever wrote in Greek as well as in Latin—down to Fulgentius, Johannes Sarisburensis, and, possibly, Erasmus—it would have been easy to swell these Notes into twelve times their present dimensions. My only fear, however, is that I may have quoted too much, as it is.

Much that will be found in the Notes will be A B C to scholars. But I was anxious to make them sufficient for the student, and the ordinary reader. The course I have adopted with regard to well-known subjects is simply to give a few words of explanation,—*ex gr.,* . . . *Chrysippus,* the Stoic philosopher; *Electra,* the sister of Orestes; *Infamia* imposed certain legal disabilities . . . referring to the generally accessible Dictionaries of Dr. Smith for fuller information. To go more into detail would be mere book-making: on the other hand, it is not agreeable to a reader, who merely wants enough explanation to help him on, to be driven off straightway to a book of reference.

The English editions of Juvenal which have come under my notice are that of Mr. Macleane, and three school-books by Messrs. Escott, Prior, and Simcox, respectively. Macleane is an editor of masculine judgment, hardly inferior to that of Heinrich, whose commentary he with justice admires. I have sometimes, in my translation, borrowed a word or a turn of expression from him, owing to the fact that it lingered in my memory, and that I could not find anything better to replace it. His failing is in being at times too dogmatic. Mr. Escott and Mr. Prior have published two excellent school-books. Mr. Simcox, whose Juvenal forms part of the "Catena Classicorum," offers some acute suggestions: but his vice is precisely over-acuteness, a perpetual straining after some meaning, other than the apparent one, of a word or a passage, which at times makes his notes very misleading to the school-boy, or else absolute nonsense.*

Mr. Mayor's Juvenal I have not had the advantage of seeing, except the text and the notes to Satire i and Satire iii 1–9. I have frequently inquired for the entire work, and have always been told that it was out of print,

---

* *Ex gr.,* Notes to i 59-62, iii 34-36 (*quemlibet,* "the most expensive gladiators"), 221, iv 48 104, v 5 33 104, vii 193 194, viii 162, x 18 21, xi 6 203, xiii 28, xiv 2-9 102 133 217 253-254 257 298, xv 117, and the exquisitely ridiculous note at xvi 46. Mr. Simcox's Introduction commences in these words, "About the life of Juvenal, only three things can be said to be known : that he was the heir of a freedman, that he practised declamation, and that he was banished for affronting an actor." This is not a proper way of introducing the Author to the school-boy's notice. None of these things are *known.*

and that a second edition would shortly appear. The
portion just alluded to is Part I of this second edition.
Sheridan, if I remember rightly, speaks somewhere of a
rivulet of text meandering through a meadow of margin.
If this part be a fair specimen of the whole work, it
might be described as a thin stream of commentary on
Juvenal running under the surface of a vast sea of citations and excursuses. Thus, for instance, on *hortos*, i
75, we have an essay of more than two closely-printed
pages, and with over one hundred and fifty citations on
the subject, bringing in almost everything that every
ancient author has said about gardens, from Naboth's
vineyard downwards. On iii 9, we have an excursus of
several pages—how many, I do not know; Part I ends
with the fourth—on recitations. In other places, *ex gr.*,
i 74 *laudatur*, 75 *debent*, 77 *dormire*, we have passages
quoted apparently for no other reason than because they
contain the same word. All this, which is very well in
its proper place, is not to edit an author, but to smother
him; to put not his meaning but one's own erudition
before the world; to make him not the editor's chief
consideration, but merely a peg on which to hang the
signs of the editor's learning. Mr. Mayor has edited only
thirteen of Juvenal's Satires, the sixth (the longest and,
in many respects, the most important) not being included
in his work.

In the text, I have not followed any editor exclusively,
but, where different readings occur, have selected that
which seemed to me the best. I had thought of saying
something about the MSS. of Juvenal, but to do so hardly
seems within the scope of this volume, which has already

reached to larger limits than I had expected. The most
important of the "various readings" are given in Jahn's
edition. One MS. only is alluded to in these Notes, the
Codex Pithoeanus, under the usual abbreviation (P). It
is generally considered the most ancient and valuable
extant (if it be still extant)* MS. of Juvenal, but its
readings are often hopelessly corrupt, and some editors
seem to me not to have evinced sound judgment in relying,
as they have done, almost exclusively upon it.

WESTBURY HOUSE, PETERSFIELD,
April 1873.

* It is, I believe, in the Library of Montpellier.

CORRIGENDA.

VOL. I.

Page 19, last line but one (translation), *for* "*have better* arranged,"
  read "have better *arranged.*"

  45, line 10 (translation), *for* "the pallor of a wretched, exalted
    friendship," *read* "the pallor of a friendship, distin-
    guished and miserable."

  88. lines 12, 13 (translation), *for* "her female secretary is un-
    done," *read* "it is all up with her female secretary."

Shall one, then, have recited to me his comedies, and another
his elegies, with impunity? Shall huge "Telephus" with
impunity have consumed a whole day, or—with the margin to
the end of the book already filled—"Orestes" written on the
very back, and yet not concluded? To no one is his own house
more familiar than are to me "the grove of Mars" and "the
cave of Vulcan neighbouring on the Aeolian rocks." What the
winds are about, what shades Aeacus is torturing, from what

reached to larger limits than I had expected. The most important of the " various readings " are given in Jahn's edition. One MS. only is alluded to in these Notes, the Codex Pithocanus, under the usual abbreviation (P). It

D. IUNII IUVENALIS

S A T I R A E.

SATIRA I.

SEMPER ego auditor tantum ? numquamne reponam,
  vexatus toties rauci Theseide Codri ?
impune ergo mihi recitaverit ille togatas,
hic elegos ? impune diem consumpserit ingens
Telephus, aut summi plena iam margine libri   5
scriptus et in tergo nec dum finitus Orestes ?
nota magis nulli domus est sua, quam mihi lucus
Martis et Aeoliis vicinum rupibus antrum
Vulcani.   quid agant venti, quas torqueat umbras
Aeacus, unde alius furtivae devehat aurum   10

2. Cordi.   3. cantaverit.   10. furtive.

SATIRE I.

Am I always to be a hearer only?   Shall I never retaliate,
though tormented so often by the "Theseis" of husky Codrus?
Shall one, then, have recited to me his comedies, and another
his elegies, with impunity?   Shall huge "Telephus" with
impunity have consumed a whole day, or—with the margin to
the end of the book already filled—"Orestes" written on the
very back, and yet not concluded?   To no one is his own house
more familiar than are to me "the grove of Mars" and "the
cave of Vulcan neighbouring on the Aeolian rocks."   What the
winds are about, what shades Aeacus is torturing, from what

pelliculae, quantas iaculetur Monychus ornos,
Frontonis platani convulsaque marmora clamant
semper et assiduo ruptae lectore columnae:
exspectes eadem a summo minimoque poeta.
et nos ergo manum ferulae subduximus, et nos   15
consilium dedimus Sullae, privatus ut altum
dormiret; stulta est clementia, cum tot ubique
vatibus occurras, periturae parcere chartae.
cur tamen hoc potius libeat decurrere campo,
per quem magnus equos Auruncae flexit alumnus,   20
si vacat ac placidi rationem admittitis, edam.
     Cum tener uxorem ducat spado, Mevia Tuscum
figat aprum et nuda teneat venabula mamma,
patricios omnes opibus cum provocet unus,
quo tondente gravis iuveni mihi barba sonabat,   25
cum pars Niliacae plebis, cum verna Canopi

25. juvenis.

---

quarter another *character* carries off the gold of the stolen little
fleece, what vast mountain-ashes Monychus hurls, *all this* the
plane-trees and the quivering marbles of Fronto are for ever
echoing, and the columns riven by the eternal reader. You
may look for the same things from the greatest and the smallest
poet. Well, then, I too have slipped away my hand from under
the *schoolmaster's* ferule; I too have given advice to Sulla to
sleep soundly in a private station. It is a foolish act of
clemency, when you run up against so many bards in all directions, to spare ·paper which is sure to be wasted. Why, however, I choose rather to run my course on the same plain as that
along which the great foster-son of Aurunca drove his steeds, if
you are at leisure, and can lend a quiet ear to the reason, I will
tell you.
     When an effeminate eunuch marries a wife, when Mevia
transfixes a Tuscan boar, and with naked breasts grasps the
hunting-spears, when a single individual vies with the whole
body of patricians in wealth, under whose razor my heavy beard
used to sound when I was a young man, when Crispinus, one

Crispinus, Tyrias humero revocante lacernas,
ventilet aestivum digitis sudantibus aurum,
nec sufferre queat maioris pondera gemmae,
difficile est satiram non scribere.◁ nam quis iniquae   30
tam patiens urbis, tam ferreus, ut teneat se,
causidici nova cum veniat lectica Mathonis
plena ipso, post hunc magni delator amici
et cito rapturus de nobilitate comesa
quod superest, quem Massa timet, quem munere palpat 35
Carus et a trepido Thymele summissa Latino ;
cum te summoveant qui testamenta merentur
noctibus, in coelum quos evehit optima summi
nunc via processus, vetulae vesica beatae ?
unciolam Proculeius habet, sed Gillo deuncem,   40
partes quisque suas ad mensuram inguinis heres.
accipiat sane mercedem sanguinis et sic
palleat, ut nudis pressit qui calcibus anguem,
aut Lugdunensem rhetor dicturus ad aram.

---

of the rabble of the Nile, the born slave of Canopus, with his
shoulder hitching up his Tyrian cloak, airs his summer gold
ring on his sweaty fingers, and is unable to support the weight
of a heavier gem, it is difficult not to write Satire. For who so
tolerant of the injustices of the town, so steeled, as to contain
himself when the new litter of Matho the lawyer comes up,
filled by the great man, *and* after him he that informed upon
his powerful friend, and who will soon clutch all that remains
of the devoured nobility, whom Massa *himself* fears, whom
Carus tries to wheedle with a bribe, and Thymele sent privately
by the trembling Latinus ; when men elbow you out of the way
who earn legacies by night work, who are raised to the skies by
what is now the best road to the highest advancement—the
letch of some rich old hag? Proculeius gets a paltry twelfth
of the property, but Gillo eleven-twelfths; each inherits his share
in proportion to his powers. Let him receive, for what I care,
the price of his life-blood, and be just as pale as one who has
trodden bare-footed on a snake, or a rhetorician about to speak

quid referam quanta siccum iecur ardeat ira,   45
cum populum gregibus comitum premit hic spoliator
pupilli prostantis, et hic damnatus inani
iudicio (quid enim salvis infamia nummis?)
exsul ab octava Marius bibit et fruitur dis
iratis, at tu victrix provincia ploras?   50
haec ego non credam Venusina digna lucerná?
haec ego non agitem? sed quid magis Heracleas
aut Diomedeas aut mugitum labyrinthi
et mare percussum puero fabrumque volantem,
cum leno accipiat moechi bona, si capiendi   55
ius nullum uxori, doctus spectare lacunar,
doctus et ad calicem vigilanti stertere naso;
cum fas esse putet curam sperare cohortis,
qui bona donavit praesepibus et caret omni
maiorum censu, dum pervolat axe citato   60
Flaminiam puer? Automedon nam lora tenebat,

   46. premat.   58. spectare.   60. rotato.

at the altar of Lyons. Why relate with what ire my parched entrails burn when here the plunderer of his ward, reduced to prostitution, presses on the people with his crowds of hangers-on, and here, condemned by an empty sentence (for what matters infamy when the money is safe?) Marius in exile drinks from the eighth hour and enjoys the anger of the gods; but thou, O Province! victorious *in the suit*, art in tears? Shall I not deem such things worthy of the lamp of Venusia? Shall I not assail these things? But why rather *treat of fables* about Hercules, or Diomed, or the bellowing of the Labyrinth, and the sea struck by the boy *Icarus* and the flying artificer, when the pander inherits the adulterer's fortune (if there be no legal right to take, in the wife), practised in gazing at the ceiling, and practised in snoring over his cups, with a wide-awake nose; when that man thinks he is entitled to look for the command of a cohort who has spent his fortune on his stables, and has lost all his ancestral property, while yet a boy, flying along the Flaminian Way with rapid chariot—for he held the reins as

ipse lacernatae cum se iactaret amicae.
nonne libet medio ceras implere capaces
quadrivio, cum iam sexta cervice feratur
hinc atque inde patens ac nuda paene cathedra   65
et multum referens de Maecenate supino
signator falso, qui se lautum atque beatum
exiguis tabulis et gemma fecerat uda?
occurrit matrona potens, quae molle Calenum
porrectura viro miscet sitiente rubetam,   70
instituitque rudes melior Locusta propinquas
per famam et populum nigros efferre maritos.
aude aliquid brevibus Gyaris et carcere dignum,
si vis esse aliquis.   probitas laudatur et alget.
criminibus debent hortos praetoria mensas   75
argentum vetus et stantem extra pocula caprum.
quem patitur dormire nurus corruptor avarae,
quem sponsae turpes et praetextatus adulter?

74. aliquid.

Automedon when the great man was showing himself off to his cloaked *boy*-mistress. Does not one feel inclined to fill one's capacious tablets in the very middle of the cross-ways, when there comes, borne on the shoulders of positively six *slaves*, exposed to view on both sides, and with litter almost uncovered, and reminding one a good deal of the listless Maecenas, the forger who has made himself genteel and wealthy by *a few* small tablets and a moistened seal? *Then* there meets you the imperious matron, who, when her husband is thirsty, will hand him the mellow wine of Cales, in which she mixes the toad's poison, who, improving on Locusta, has taught her simpler kinswomen to carry out to burial their livid husbands in defiance of rumour and the public gaze. Dare something deserving of small Gyarus and the gaol, if you wish to be somebody; honesty is praised and starves. To their crimes they are indebted for their gardens, palaces, *costly* tables, old plate, and the goat standing out in relief from the cup. Whom does the seducer of his own daughter-in-law, greedy *for gold*, permit to sleep?

si natura negat, facit indignatio versum
qualemcumque potest, quales ego vel Cluvienus.   80
   Ex quo Deucalion nimbis tollentibus aequor
navigio montem ascendit sortesque poposcit,
paulatimque animá caluerunt mollia saxa,
et maribus nudas ostendit Pyrrha puellas,
quidquid agunt homines, votum timor ira voluptas   85
gaudia discursus nostri est farrago libelli.
et quando uberior vitiorum copia? quando
maior avaritiae patuit sinus? alea quando
hos animos? neque enim loculis comitantibus itur
ad casum tabulae, posita sed luditur arca   90
proelia quanta illic dispensatore videbis
armigero? simplexne furor sestertia centum
perdere et horrenti tunicam non reddere servo?
quis totidem erexit villas, quis fercula septem
secreto coenavit avus? nunc sportula primo   95

---

whom the unnatural brides and the stripling adulterer? If
nature denies the power, indignation produces verse, of whatever kind it is capable, such as I or Cluvienus *make*.

   From the time when Deucalion, while the storms upheaved
the sea, ascended the mountain in his ship and consulted the
oracle, the softening stones warming by degrees into life, as
Pyrrha showed to the males the naked virgins, whatever men
are engaged in, their wishes, fears, anger, pleasures, joys, run-
nings to and fro, form the medley of my book. And when
was the supply of vices more fruitful? When did the pocket
of avarice gape wider? When had gambling such vitality as
now? For, indeed, not with their purses about them do people
go to the chances of the gaming-table, but they play with their
cash-box for a stake. How sharp the battles you will see there,
with the steward for arm-bearer! Is it not something more
than madness to lose a hundred sestertia and not restore his
tunic to the shivering slave? Which of our forefathers erected
so many villas? which of them supped by himself on seven
courses? Nowadays the tiny "dole" occupies a place on the

limine parva sedet turbae rapienda togatae.
ille tamen faciem prius inspicit et trepidat, ne
suppositus venias ac falso nomine poscas.
agnitus accipies; iubet a praecone vocari
ipsos Troiugenas; nam vexant limen et ipsi   100
nobiscum. "da praetori, da deinde tribuno."
sed libertinus prior est. "prior," inquit, "ego adsum.
cur timeam, dubitemve locum defendere, quamvis
natus ad Euphraten, molles quod in aure fenestrae
arguerint, licet ipse negem ? sed quinque tabernae 105
quadringenta parant.   quid confert purpura maior
optandum, si Laurenti custodit in agro
conductas Corvinus oves ? ego possideo plus
Pallante et Licinis."   exspectent ergo tribuni,
vincant divitiae, sacro nec cedat honori,   110
nuper in hanc urbem pedibus qui venerat albis,
quandoquidem inter nos sanctissima divitiarum

106. majus.

---

outer threshold, to be pounced upon by the toga-clad crowd.
Yet the master looks into your face beforehand and is alarmed
lest you come in the place of some one else, and apply under a
false name. When you are identified you will be served ; he
orders the Trojugenae themselves to be summoned by his crier ;
for even such as they infest the threshold with us. " Help the
Praetor, then help the Tribune." But a freedman has the precedence. "I am the first-comer," he says ; "why should I
fear, or hesitate, to stand up for my turn, although born near
the Euphrates, which the effeminate openings in my ears would
attest, though I denied the fact myself? But *for all that* the
five tabernae are worth four hundred sestertia *to me*. What so
desirable does the Laticlave confer, if Corvinus keeps sheep for
hire in the Laurentine country? I possess more than Pallas
and the Licini." Let the Tribunes wait then ; let riches carry
the day, nor let him give place to the inviolable magistrate,
who not long ago came into this city with whitened feet, since
among us the most sacred majesty is that of riches, although,

maiestas, etsi funesta pecunia templo
nondum habitas, nullas nummorum creximus aras,
ut colitur Pax atque Fides Victoria Virtus　　　　115
quaeque salutato crepitat Concordia nido.
sed cum summus honor finito computet anno,
sportula quid referat, quantum rationibus addat,
quid facient comites, quibus hinc toga, calceus hinc est
et panis fumusque domi ? densissima centum　　　　120
quadrantes lectica petit, sequiturque maritum
languida vel praegnans et circumducitur uxor.
hic petit absenti nota iam callidus arte,
ostendens vacuam et clausam pro coniuge sellam.
" Galla mea est," inquit, " citius dimitte.　moraris."　　125
" profer Galla caput ! "　" noli vexare, quiescit."
　　Ipse dies pulchro distinguitur ordine rerum :
sportula, deinde forum iurisque peritus Apollo
atque triumphales, inter quas ausus habere

---

as yet, pernicious money, you do not dwell in a temple *of your
own*, nor have we erected altars to coin, in the same way as
Peace is worshipped, and Faith, Victory, Virtue, and Concord,
which twitters when the nest *of her sacred birds* is saluted.
But when the highest magistrate computes at the end of the
year what the " dole " brings in, how much it adds to his income, what will the dependants do who derive from this source
their toga, their shoes, and bread, and firing for their house-
holds ?　A dense crowd of litters comes in search of the
hundred quadrantes; and the wife, though sick, or in the
family way, follows her husband, and is carried the round.
One, grown cunning at an old trick, asks for *the share of* his
wife, though absent, exhibiting an empty and closed *sedan-
chair* in the place of his spouse.　" It is my Galla," he says ;
" dismiss us as soon as you can ; you are detaining us."　" Put
out your head, Galla."　" Don't disturb her, she's asleep."
　　The day itself is portioned out with a beautiful ordering of
events : the " dole," then the Forum and Apollo learned in the
law, and the triumphal statues, among which I know not what

nescio quis titulos Aegyptius atque Arabarches,   130
cuius ad effigiem non tantum meiere fas est.
vestibulis abeunt veteres lassique clientes,
votaque deponunt, quamquam longissima coenae
spes homini : caulis miseris atque ignis emendus.
optima silvarum interea pelagique vorabit   135
rex horum, vacuisque toris tantum ipse iacebit.
nam de tot pulchris et latis orbibus et tam
antiquis una comedunt patrimonia mensá.
nullus iam parasitus erit.   sed quis ferat istas
luxuriae sordes ? quanta est gula, quae sibi totos   140
ponit apros, animal propter convivia natum !
poena tamen praesens, cum tu deponis amictus
turgidus et crudum pavonem in balnea portas.
hinc subitae mortes atque intestata senectus ;
it nova nec tristis per cunctas fabula coenas,   145
ducitur iratis plaudendum funus amicis.

143. crudus.

" Aegyptius and Arabarches " has dared to place his titles of
honour, at whose image one may, without sacrilege, commit
more than one kind of nuisance.   The old and wearied clients
leave the porch and give up their hopes, though the expectation
of a dinner is the most long-lived *of all* in man : the poor
fellows must buy their pot-herbs and firing.   In the meanwhile
their patron will devour the choicest produce of forests and
sea, and will recline in solitary state on the couches empty *of
all but himself;* for off so many beautiful and broad and antique
round tables, these people devour their patrimonies at a single
course.   Soon there will be no parasite ; but who will bear such
sordid luxury as this ?   What gluttony is that which serves up
for itself whole boars, an animal created for banquets !   Yet
the penalty is at hand when you lay aside your clothes, gorged
with food, and carry an undigested peacock to the bath.   Hence,
sudden deaths and intestate old age.   The new but not sorrowful
tidings go the round of all the dinner-tables, and your funeral
comes forth amidst the applause of disappointed friends.

Nil erit ulterius, quod nostris moribus addat
posteritas; eadem cupient facientque minores;
omne in praecipiti vitium stetit, utere velis,
totos pande sinus. dicas hic forsitan "unde   150
ingenium par materiae? unde illa priorum
scribendi, quodcumque animo flagrante liberet,
simplicitas, cuius non audeo dicere nomen?
quid refert dictis ignoscat Mucius an non?
pone Tigellinum, taeda lucebis in illa,   155
qua stantes ardent, qui fixo gutture fumant,
et latum media sulcum deducis arena."
qui dedit ergo tribus patruis aconita, vehatur
pensilibus plumis, atque illinc despiciat nos?
"cum veniet contra, digito compesce labellum.   160
accusator erit, qui verbum dixerit 'hic est.'
securus licet Aeneam Rutulumque ferocem
committas, nulli gravis est percussus Achilles

156. pectore.   157. diducit.

There will be nothing further for posterity to add to our
manners; our descendants will wish for and do the same things;
every vice has reached its culminating point. Take to your
sails. Crowd all canvas. Perhaps you will say at this point,
"Whence *is to come* the talent equal to the subject? Whence
that straightforwardness of the ancients in writing whatever
their burning impulses inclined them to, the *very* name of which
I dare not utter? What does it matter whether a Mucius forgive your words or not? Portray Tigellinus: you will shine
in the midst of those faggots in which they blaze, standing, who
smoke with throat fixed *to the stake*, and you will draw a broad
furrow in the midst of the sand." He, then, who has given
aconite to his three uncles is to be carried on suspended down-
cushions, and thence look down on us? "When he comes in
your way, close your lip with your finger. He who *simply* says
the words, 'That's he,' will be *looked upon as* his accuser. You
may safely pit together Aeneas and the fierce Rutulian: Achilles,
though struck down, will harm no one; nor Hylas, long sought

aut multum quaesitus Hylas urnamque secutus;
ense velut stricto quoties Lucilius ardens   165
infremuit, rubet auditor, cui frigida mens est
criminibus, tacitâ sudant praecordia culpa :
inde irae et lacrimae.   tecum prius ergo voluta
haec animo ante tubas.   galeatum sero duelli
poenitet." experiar quid concedatur in illos,   170
quorum Flaminia tegitur cinis atque Latina.

— — —

SATIRA II.

ULTRA Sauromatas fugere hinc libet et glacialem
Oceanum, quoties aliquid de moribus audent
qui Curios simulant et Bacchanalia vivunt.
indocti primum : quamquam plena omnia gypso
Chrysippi invenies ; nam perfectissimus horum est,   5

5. invenias.

for and gone after his pitcher.   *But* as often as Lucilius has
raged in his fury, as though with drawn sword, the hearer grows
red whose conscience is chilled with the sense of crime, his
innermost parts are clammy with concealed guilt.   Hence rage
and tears.   Turn over, therefore, first these things in your mind
before the *sound of the* trumpet : when the helmet is on, it is
too late to repent of the fight." I will try, *then*, what I may
be permitted to do against those whose ashes are covered by the
Flaminian and the Latin roads.

SATIRE II.

ONE feels inclined to fly from here beyond the Sarmatians and
the Frozen Ocean, whenever those *fellows* dare *to say* anything
about morals who ape the Curii and live like Bacchanals.
Ignoramuses, to begin with, though you will find all their pre-
mises full of plaster-casts of Chrysippus; for the most accom-

si quis Aristotelem similem vel Pittacon emit,
et iubet archetypos pluteum servare Cleanthas.
fronti nulla fides; quis enim non vicus abundat
tristibus obscenis? castigas turpia, cum sis
inter Socraticos notissima fossa cinaedos.   10
hispida membra quidem et durae per brachia setae
promittunt atrocem animum, sed podice levi
caeduntur tumidae medico ridente mariscae;
rarus sermo illis et magna libido tacendi
atque supercilio brevior coma. verius ergo   15
et magis ingenue Peribomius. hunc ego fatis
imputo, qui vultu morbum incessuque fatetur.
horum simplicitas miserabilis, his furor ipse
dat veniam: sed peiores, qui talia verbis
Herculis invadunt et de virtute locuti   20
clunem agitant. "ego te ceventem, Sexte, verebor?"

8. frontis.

---

plished of these is he that has bought a likeness of Aristotle or
Pittacus, and bids his bookcase hold originals of Cleanthes.
There is no trusting the outside; for what street is there that
does not abound in debauchees of severe aspect? You rebuke
abominations, while you *yourself* are the most notorious sink
among the unnatural creatures *who call themselves* followers of
Socrates. The shaggy limbs, indeed, and the stiff bristles on
the arms give promise of an intrepid soul: but on the hairless
posteriors, the surgeon, with a smile, lances the swollen piles.
These fellows speak but seldom, they have a great fancy for
holding their tongues, and their hair is *cut* shorter than their
eyebrows. Peribomius, then, *acts* more truthfully and more
ingenuously: I lay that man to the account of the Fates who
by his look and gait avows his diseased tastes. The frankness
of such persons is *simply* pitiable: to such their very madness
furnishes an excuse. But they are worse who attack such vices
in the words of a Hercules, and act the wanton after talking of
virtue. "Shall I stand in awe of you, Sextus, who exhibit
your lewdness?" says the notorious Varillus. "In what am I

infamis Varillus ait, " quo deterior te ?
loripedem rectus derideat, Aethiopem albus."
quis tulerit Gracchos de seditione querentes ?
quis coelum terris non misceat et mare coelo,   25
si fur displiceat Verri, homicida Miloni,
Clôdius accuset moechos, Catilina Cethegum,
in tabulam Sullae si dicant discipuli tres ?
qualis erat nuper tragico pollutus adulter
concubitu, qui tunc leges revocabat amaras   30
omnibus atque ipsis Veneri Martique timendas,
cum tot abortivis fecundam Iulia vulvam
solveret et patruo similes effunderet offas.
nonne igitur iure ac merito vitia ultima fictos
contemnunt Scauros et castigata remordent ?   35
    Non tulit ex illis torvum Lauronia quemdam
clamantem toties " ubi nunc lex Iulia ? dormis ? "
ad quem subridens " felicia tempora, quae te
moribus opponunt ! habeat iam Roma pudorem.

---

worse than you ? Let a straight-limbed man jeer at one who is
club-footed, a white man at a blackamoor." Who would stand
the Gracchi complaining of sedition ? Who would not confound heaven with earth and sea with heaven, if a thief were
displeasing to Verres, a murderer to Milo, if Clodius were to
impeach adulterers, or Cataline Cethegus, if Sulla's proscription-
list were inveighed against by his three disciples ? Of such a
kind was the adulterer, lately defiled by a tragical amour, who,
at that very time, was reviving bitter laws, which all might
tremble at, even Venus and Mars themselves, while Julia was
opening her fruitful womb by so many abortives, and giving
vent to embryos resembling her uncle. Is it not then lawfully
and deservedly that *even* the most vicious despise these sham
Scauri, and, when rebuked, return the bite ?
    Lauronia would not suffer a certain grim-looking fellow of
this class, continually crying out, " Where are you now, Julian
law ? Are you asleep ? " To whom, with a smile, " Happy the
times," *said she,* " which oppose you to our manners ! Let

tertius e coelo cecidit Cato.   sed tamen unde   , 40
haec emis, hirsuto spirant opobalsama collo
quae tibi? ne pudeat dominum monstrare tabernae.
quod si vexantur leges ac iura, citari
ante omnes debet Scantinia.   respice primum
et scrutare viros.   faciunt hi plura, sed illos   45
defendit numerus iunctaeque umbone phalanges :
magna inter molles concordia.   non erit ullum
exemplum in nostro tam detestabile sexu.
Tedia non lambit Cluviam nec Flora Catullam,
Hispo subit iuvenes et morbo pallet utroque.   50
numquid nos agimus causas, civilia iura
novimus, aut ullo strepitu fora vestra movemus ?
luctantur paucae, comedunt coliphia paucae.
vos lanam trahitis calathisque peracta refertis
vellera, vos tenui praegnantem stamine fusum   55
Penelope melius, levius torquetis Arachne,

43. ac jure : at jure (Jahn).

Rome begin to have a sense of shame : a third Cato has fallen
from the sky.   But, nevertheless, where do you buy these perfumes of yours, which exhale from your hairy neck ? Don't be
ashamed to name the owner of the shop.   Now, if laws and
statutes are to be disturbed *from their sleep,* before all others
the Scantinian ought to be called up.   First look to the men
and observe them ; they do worse *than we ;* but *as to* these,
their number protects them, and their phalanxes closed up
shield to shield.   Great is the concord between effeminates.
There will not be *found* any such execrable example in our sex.
Tedia does not caress Cluvia, nor Flora Catulla : Hispo submits
himself to young men, and is pale with a doubly unnatural
taste.   Pray, do we plead causes, are we acquainted with the
laws of the state, or do we disturb your courts with any clamour
of ours ? There are few women who wrestle, few who eat the
food of athletes : *while* you card wool, and bear back in baskets
the completed fleeces : you twist the distaff pregnant with slender thread better than Penelope, more nimbly than Arachne,

horrida quale facit residens in codice pellex.
notum est, cur solo tabulas impleverit Hister
liberto, dederit vivus cur multa puellae.
dives erit magno quae dormit tertia lecto.   60
tu nube atque tace, donant arcana cylindros.
de nobis post haec tristis sententia fertur ;
dat veniam corvis, vexat censura columbas."

Fugerunt trepidi vera ac manifesta canentem
stoicidae ; quid enim falsi Lauronia ? sed quid   65
non facient alii, cum tu multicia sumas,
Cretice, et hanc vestem populo mirante perores
in Proculas et Pollitas ? est moecha Fabulla ;
damnetur, si vis, etiam Carfinia, talem
non sumet damnata togam. " sed Iulius ardet,   70
aestuo." nudus agas, minus est insania turpis.
en habitum, quo te leges ac iura ferentem
vulneribus crudis populus modo victor et illud

71. infamia.

---

work such as a dirty *slave*-concubine has to do, sitting on the log
she is tied to. It is notorious why Hister filled up his will in
favour of his freedman alone, why, during his life, he gave so
many presents to his virgin-wife. She will be rich who sleeps
third in a large bed. Do you get married and hold your tongue :
secrets confer cut jewels. *Yet,* after this, a harsh verdict is
passed upon us *women.* Judgment pardons the ravens and
harasses the doves."

The Stoicidae fled in confusion from her as she gave utterance to these true and palpable things. For what had Lauronia
said that was false ? But what will not others do, when you,
Creticus, put on gauze dresses, and, with the people astonished
at such attire, hold forth against the Proculas and the Pollitae ?
Fabulla is an adulteress ; let Carfinia be condemned, if you
please, into the bargain : yet, though condemned, she will not
put on such a toga as that. " But July rages ; I am on fire."
Plead stark naked, *then ;* insanity would be less disgraceful. A
pretty dress for the people, but recently victorious, with their

montanum positis audiret vulgus aratris !
quid non proclames, in corpore iudicis ista   75
si videas ? quaero an deceant multicia testem ?
acer et indomitus libertatisque magister,
Cretice, perluces.   dedit hanc contagio labem
et dabit in plures, sicut grex totus in agris
unius scabie cadit et porrigine porci,   80
uvaque conspecta livorem ducit ab uva.
foedius hoc aliquid quandoque audebis amictu,
nemo repente fuit turpissimus ; accipient te
paulatim, qui longa domi redimicula sumunt
frontibus et toto posuere monilia collo   85
atque bonam tenerae placant abdomine porcae
et magno cratere deam ; sed more sinistro
exagitata procul non intrat femina limen,
solis ara deae maribus patet.   " ite profanae ! "

81. contacta.   83. venit.

wounds yet green, and that *old* mountain populace, after laying
down their ploughs, to hear you proposing laws and statutes in!
What would you not exclaim if you saw such clothes on the
person of a Judex!   I ask whether gauze dresses would become
even a witness?   *And yet* you, stern unbending man, master
of your freedom, *you*, Creticus, are showing your nakedness.
Contagion has given *us* this plague-spot, and will pass it on to
many more, just as a whole herd in the fields perishes through
the mange and scurf of a single pig, and one grape acquires a
taint from the *mere* sight of *another* grape.   You will, one day
or other, venture on something yet more disgraceful than this
dress.   No one reaches the height of infamy at a step : by
degrees, people will take you into their company, who, in their
houses, wear long fillets on their brows, and put chains all over
their necks, and propitiate Bona Dea with the belly of a young
sow and a huge bowl ; but, by a perverted usage, woman, driven
far away, does not cross the threshold.   To males alone is the
altar of the goddess open.   " Hence, ye profane fair ! " is the cry.
" Here no female piper sounds her plaintive horn instrument."

clamatur, "nullo gemit hic tibicina cornu." 90
talia secreta coluerunt orgia taeda
Cecropiam soliti Baptae lassare Cotytto.
ille supercilium madidá fuligine tactum
obliqua producit acu pingitque trementes
attollens oculos, vitreo bibit ille Priapo 95
reticulumque comis auratum ingentibus implet
caerulea indutus scutulata aut galbina rasa,
et per Iunonem domini iurante ministro.
ille tenet speculum, pathici gestamen Othonis,
Actoris Aurunci spolium, quo se ille videbat 100
armatum, cum iam tolli vexilla iuberet.
res memoranda novis annalibus atque recenti
historiá, speculum civilis sarcina belli.
nimirum summi ducis est occidere Galbam
et curare cutem, summi constantia civis 105
Bebriaci campo spolium affectare Palati
et pressum in faciem digitis extendere panem,

93. tinctum.

Such orgies as these the Baptae celebrated with secret torch, who
were wont to weary out even the Athenian Cotytto. One, with
slanted needle, lengthens his eyebrows, touched with damp soot,
and raising *the lids*, paints his quivering eyes: another drinks
out of a Priapus-shaped glass, and fills a net of gold thread with
his bushy hair, dressed in blue checks, or pale green stuffs, shorn
of their pile, while the servant too swears by the Juno of his
master. Another holds a mirror, the object wielded by pathic
Otho, "the spoil of Auruncan Actor," in which he used to
behold himself accoutred at the moment of ordering the standards to be taken up. A thing to be commemorated in our new
annals and recent history, a mirror, the baggage of a civil war!
Doubtless it showed a consummate general to slaughter Galba,
and to pamper his own skin: the energy of a great citizen to
aim at the spoils of the Palace on the field of Bebriacum, and
to spread with his fingers the bread-poultice pressed upon his
face: an act which neither the quivered Semiramis perpetrated

quod nec in Assyrio pharetrata Semiramis orbe,
maesta nec Actiacá fecit Cleopatra cariná.
hic nullus verbis pudor aut reverentia mensae,   110
hic turpis Cybeles et fracta voce loquendi
libertas, et crine senex fanaticus albo
sacrorum antistes, rarum ac memorabile magni
gutturis exemplum conducendusque magister.
quid tamen exspectant, Phrygio quos tempus erat iam 115
more supervacuam cultris abrumpere carnem?
quadringenta dedit Gracchus sestertia dotem
cornicini, sive hic recto cantaverat aere: ·
signatae tabulae, dictum "feliciter!" ingens
coena sedet, gremio iacuit nova nupta mariti.   120
o proceres, censore opus est an haruspice nobis?
scilicet horreres maioraque monstra putares,
si mulier vitulum vel si bos ederet agnum?
segmenta et longos habitus et flammea sumit,

116. abscindere.   118. cantaverit.

in the Assyrian world, nor sorrowing Cleopatra in her Actian
ship. Here is no shame in their language, nor respect for the
decorum of the table. Here is the foul license of Cybele, and
of speaking in effeminate tones, and the phrenzied old man, with
white hair, the chief priest of the rites, a rare and notable
example of monstrous gluttony, who might be engaged to teach
the science. *Yet* what are they waiting for, since the time has
long since come for them to cut off with knives, after the Phrygian fashion, their superfluous parts? Gracchus has brought a
dowry of four hundred sestertia to a cornet-player—or it may
have been on a straight horn that he had performed: the contract has been signed; felicitations offered; a dinner on a large
scale is set out; the new-made bride has reclined on the bosom
of his husband. O nobles! is it a censor we need, or an arus-
pex? Would you, forsooth, be *more* horrified, would you deem
it a greater prodigy, if a woman gave birth to a calf or an ox to
a lamb? That man puts on flounces and long dresses and
bridal-veils who has borne the sacred *emblems* swinging from

arcano qui sacra ferens nutantia loro 125
sudavit clipeis ancilibus. o pater urbis,
unde nefas tantum Latiis pastoribus ? unde
haec tetigit, Gradive, tuos urtica nepotes ?
traditur ecce viro clarus genere atque opibus vir :
nec galeam quassas, nec terram cuspide pulsas, 130
nec quereris patri ? vade ergo et cede severi
iugeribus campi, quem negligis. "officium cras
primo sole mihi peragendum in valle Quirini."
quae causa officii ? "quid quaeris ? nubit amicus,
nec multos adhibet." liceat modo vivere, fient, 135
fient ista palam, cupient et in acta referri.
interea tormentum ingens nubentibus haeret,
quod nequeunt parere et partu retinere maritos.
Di melius, quod nil animis in corpora iuris
natura indulget; steriles moriuntur, et illis 140

139. sed melius.   140. morientur.

the mystic thong, who has sweated beneath the shields of Mars!
O father of the city ! whence *has come* such monstrous impiety
to the shepherds of Latium ? Whence, O Gradivus ! has this
stinging itch seized your descendants? See now, a man illustrious in family and fortune is handed over *in marriage* to
another man ; and you do not shake your helmet, nor strike the
earth with your spear, nor complain to your father. Be off,
then, and retire from the soil of that stern field which you
neglect. "I have a visit of ceremony to go through at sunrise
to-morrow, in the valley of Quirinus." "What is the occasion
of the visit ?" "Why ask ? A male friend is to be taken to
wife. He invites but a small party." Let us only live *a little
longer ;* these sort of things will be done, yes, will be done
openly, and will be for getting themselves recorded in the
gazette. Meanwhile, there is one great cause of torment which
sticks to these male brides—that they are unable to bear, and
by means of offspring to retain *the affections of* their husbands.
But the gods *have better* arranged, that nature should vouchsafe
to their wills no power over their bodies. They die barren, and

turgida non prodest condita pyxide Lyde,
nec prodest agili palmas praebere Luperco.
vicit et hoc monstrum tunicati fuscina Gracchi,
lustravitque fuga mediam gladiator arenam
et Capitolinis generosior et Marcellis   145
et Catulis Paulique minoribus et Fabiis et
omnibus ad podium spectantibus, his licet ipsum
admoveas, cuius tunc munere retia misit.
    Esse aliquos manes et subterranea regna,
et contum et Stygio ranas in gurgite nigras,   150
atque una transire vadum tot millia cymba,
nec pueri credunt, nisi qui nondum aere lavantur,
sed tu vera puta: Curius quid sentit et ambo
Scipiadae, quid Fabricius, manesque Camilli,
quid Cremerae legio et Cannis consumpta iuventus,   155
tot bellorum animae, quoties hinc talis ad illos
umbra venit? cuperent lustrari, si qua darentur

149. aliquid.

---

to them bloated Lyde is of no help with her medicated box,
nor does it help them to hold out their hands to the nimble
Lupercus. Yet even this monstrosity was surpassed by the
trident of Gracchus, clad in a tunic, when a gladiator traversed
in flight the middle of the arena, who was more nobly born
than the Capitolini, and the Marcelli, and the Catuli, and the
descendants of Paulus, and the Fabii, and all the spectators in
the front seats, even though you add to these the man himself
at whose show he then threw the nets.
    That there exist certain Manes and underground kingdoms,
and a punt-pole and black frogs in the Stygian whirlpool, and
that so many thousands pass over the waters in a single bark,
not even boys believe, unless it be those who are not yet washed
for money *at the baths*. But suppose these things to be true.
What must Curius feel, and the two Scipiones? What Fabricius
and the Manes of Camillus? What the legion of Cremera and
the youth exterminated at Cannae, souls from so many wars,
when such a shade as this reaches them from here? They

sulfura cum taedis et si foret humida laurus.
illuc heu miseri traducimur! arma quidem ultra
litora Iuvernae promovimus et modo captas 160
Orcadas ac minima contentos nocte Britannos,
sed quae nunc populi fiunt victoris in urbe,
non facient illi quos vicimus. " et tamen unus
Armenius Zalates cunctis narratur ephebis
mollior ardenti sese indulsisse tribuno." 165
aspice quid faciant commercia: venerat obses
hic fiunt homines! nam si mora longior urbem
indulsit pueris, non umquam deerit amator,
mittentur braccae cultelli frena flagellum;
sic praetextatos referunt Artaxata mores. 170

159. illic.

---

would wish to be purified, if sulphur could be anyhow procured, with pine-torches, or if there were any moistened laurel there. To such an exhibition of ourselves, alas, are we poor wretches brought! Our arms, indeed, we have advanced beyond the shores of Iuverna and the lately conquered Orcades, and the Britons contented with very short nights: but the things which are now done in the city of the victorious people, those whom we have vanquished will not do. "And yet one of them, the Armenian Zalates, more effeminate than all the young men *his companions*, is said to have yielded his person to the burning Tribune." See what the intercourse *of nations* can do. He had come as a hostage; here it is that men are made! For if a longer stay in the city be permitted the boys, they will never be in want of a lover. Their trousers, their knives, their bridles, their whips will be cast aside; thus it is that they carry back to Artaxata the manners of the young Romans.

SATIRA III.

QUAMVIS digressu veteris confusus amici
   laudo tamen, vacuis quod sedem figere Cumis
destinet atque unum civem donare Sibyllae.
ianua Baiarum est et gratum litus amoeni
secessus. ego vel Prochytam praepono Suburae.   5
nam quid tam miserum, tam solum vidimus, ut non
deterius credas horrere incendia, lapsus
tectorum assiduos ac mille pericula saevae
urbis et Augusto recitantes mense poetas?
sed dum tota domus reda componitur una,   10
substitit ad veteres arcus madidamque Capenam.
hic, ubi nocturnae Numa constituebat amicae,
nunc sacri fontis nemus et delubra locantur
Iudaeis, quorum cophinus foenumque supellex;
omnis enim populo mercedem pendere iussa est   15

SATIRE III.

ALTHOUGH distressed at the departure of my old friend, yet I
commend him for determining to fix his abode at unfrequented
Cumae, and to give one citizen to the Sibyl. It is the way of
approach to Baiae, and a pleasant sea-shore agreeable to retire
to. I prefer even Prochyta to the Suburra. For what *place*
have we seen so wretched, so lonely, that you would not think
it worse to be in dread of fires, the perpetual falling-in of houses,
the thousand dangers of the cruel city,—and poets reciting in
the month of August? But while all his household was being
stowed in a single carriage, he (*i.e., my friend Umbricius*) halted
at the old triumphal arches and the wet *gate of* Capena. Here,
where Numa used to make assignations with his nocturnal
mistress, nowadays the grove of the holy fountain and the
sacred precincts are let out to the Jews, whose furniture is a
basket and *some* hay; for every tree is bidden to pay rent to

arbor, et eiectis mendicat silva Camenis.
in vallem Egeriae descendimus et speluncas
dissimiles veris.   quanto praesentius esset
numen aquae, viridi si margine clauderet undas
herba, nec ingenuum violarent marmora tophum !   20
hic tunc Umbricius, "quando artibus" inquit "honestis
nullus in urbe locus, nulla emolumenta laborum,
res hodie minor est, here quam fuit, atque eadem cras
deteret exiguis aliquid, proponimus illuc
ire, fatigatas ubi Daedalus exuit alas,   25
dum nova canities, dum prima et recta senectus,
dum superest Lachesi quod torqueat, et pedibus me
porto meis nullo dextram subeunte bacillo.
cedamus patria.   vivant Artorius istic
et Catulus, maneant qui nigrum in candida vertunt,   30
quis facile est aedem conducere flumina portus,
siccandam eluviem, portandum ad busta cadaver,

---

the people, and the Camenae having been turned out, the wood
is a mass of beggars.   We descend into the valley of Egeria
and the grottoes unlike natural ones.   How much more present
to us would the divinity of the spring be, if turf enclosed the
waters with its margin of green, and marble did not do violence
to the native tufa-stone !   Here, then, Umbricius—" Since,"
said he, " there is no place in the city for honest employments,
no return for industry, *since* to-day my means are smaller than
they were yesterday, and those same means will to-morrow wear
away somewhat from their scanty residue, I propose to go to
the spot where Daedalus put off his wearied wings, while my
hair is *but* recently grizzled, while my old age is *but* beginning
and *still* erect, while there remains something for Lachesis to
spin, and I bear myself on my own feet with no staff supporting
my right hand.   I must leave my country : let Artorius and
Catulus live there ; let those remain who turn black into white,
to whom it comes easy to take contracts about temples, rivers,
harbours, cleansing a sewer, carrying a corpse to the funeral-

et praebere caput domina venale sub hasta.
quondam hi cornicines et municipalis arenae
perpetui comites notaeque per oppida buccae   35
munera nunc edunt, et verso. pollice vulgi
quem libet occidunt populariter, inde reversi
conducunt foricas, et cur non omnia? cum sint
quales ex humili magna ad fastigia rerum
extollit, quoties voluit Fortuna iocari.   40
quid Romae faciam? mentiri nescio, librum,
si malus est, nequeo laudare et poscere, motus
astrorum ignoro, funus promittere patris
nec volo nec possum, ranarum viscera numquam
inspexi, ferre ad nuptam quae mittit adulter,   45
quae mandat, norint alii, me nemo ministro
fur erit, atque ideo nulli comes exeo, tamquam
mancus et exstinctae corpus non utile dextrae.
quis nunc diligitur, nisi conscius, et cui fervens

---

pile, and to put up a man for sale under the mistress-spear.
These men, who were formerly horn-blowers, and constant
attendants at the amphitheatres of country places, *with their*
puffed-out cheeks ,well-known from town to town, now give
shows of gladiators, and, when the vulgar turn up their thumbs,
kill off any one you like to please the people : returned thence,
they farm the public privies, and why not everything, since
they are men such as Fortune raises up from obscurity to the
highest summits of affairs, whenever she chooses to be sportive ?
What should I do in Rome ? I know not how to lie ; if a
book is a bad one, I cannot praise it and ask for a copy ; I am
ignorant of the motions of the stars ; I neither will nor can
promise the death of a father ; I never inspected the entrails
of frogs ; let others know how to carry to a married woman the
presents and the messages of her lover—nobody shall be a thief
by my aid, and therefore I am not going out in the suite of
any one, as though I were maimed and a useless trunk with
right hand destroyed. Who nowadays is cherished except the

aestuat occultis animus semperque tacendis ?   50
nil tibi se debere putat, nil conferet. umquam,
participem qui te secreti fecit honesti ;
carus erit Verri, qui Verrem tempore quo vult
accusare potest. tanti tibi non sit opaci
omnis arena Tagi quodque in mare volvitur aurum,   55
ut somno careas ponendaque praemia sumas
tristis et a magno semper timearis amico !
   Quae nunc divitibus gens acceptissima nostris
et quos praecipue fugiam, properabo fateri,
nec pudor obstabit. non possum ferre, Quirites,   60
Graecam urbem. quamvis quota portio faecis Achaei !
iam pridem Syrus in Tiberim defluxit Orontes,
et linguam et mores et cum tibicine chordas
obliquas, nec non gentilia tympana secum
vexit, et ad circum iussas prostare puellas :   65
ite quibus grata est picta lupa barbara mitra !

---

accomplice, he whose raging mind boils with hidden things
which must ever be kept unrevealed? Nothing does that man
think he owes you, nothing will he ever bestow *on you*, who
has made you the sharer in an honourable secret. He will be
dear to Verres who can accuse Verres at any time he pleases.
Let not all the sands of shady Tagus, and all the gold that is
rolled into the sea, be of such account to you as that you
should lose your sleep, and sorrowfully take bribes which will
have to be disgorged, and always be feared by your powerful
friend.

   What race, is now most in favour with our rich men, and
what people I would particularly shun, I will hasten to tell you,
nor shall shame prevent me. I cannot bear, Romans, a Greek
city ; and yet, how small a portion of our dregs is from Greece !
Long since, Syrian Orontes has flowed into the Tiber, and has
brought with it its language and manners, and with the piper the
oblique chords, and the national tambourines, and the girls
made to stand for hire at the circus. Hie thither, ye who have
a fancy for a foreign harlot in an embroidered turban ! That

rusticus ille tuus sumit trechedipna, Quirine,
et ceromatico fert niceteria collo !
hic alta Sicyone, ast hic Amydone relicta,
hic Andro, ille Samo, hic Trallibus aut Alabandis ·   70
Esquilias dictumque petunt a vimine collem,
viscera magnarum domuum dominique futuri.
ingenium velox, audacia perdita, sermo
promptus et Isaeo torrentior.   ede, quid illum
esse putes ? quem vis hominem secum attulit ad nos,   75
grammaticus rhetor geometres pictor aliptes
augur schoenobates medicus magus, omnia novit.
Graeculus esuriens, in coelum, iusseris, ibit ;
ad summam, non Maurus erat neque Sarmata nec Thrax,
qui sumpsit pennas, mediis sed natus Athenis.   80
horum ego non fugiam conchylia ? me prior ille
signabit fultusque toro meliore recumbet,
advectus Romam quo pruna et cottana vento ?

79. in summa.

---

once rustic *son* of yours, Quirinus, adopts Greek slippers and
wears Greek prizes of victory on his neck anointed with Ceroma.
This one who has left steep Sicyon, and this Amydon, this one
from Andros, and that from Samos, another from Tralles or
Alabanda, seek the Esquiline and the hill named from its osiers,
the vitals of great houses and their future masters.   Their wit
is quick, their impudence desperate, their speech ready, and
more fluent than *that of* Isaeus.   Tell us what you take one of
these fellows to be?   He has brought us a Jack-of-all-trades
in his person—grammarian, rhetorician, geometrician, painter,
anointer, augur, tight-rope dancer, physician, magician : he
knows everything.   Bid the hungry Greekling go to heaven,
he will go.   In short, it was not a Moor, nor a Sarmatian, nor
a Thracian who put on wings, but one born in the heart of
Athens.   Shall I not shun the purple robes of these fellows?
Shall such an one sign his name before me, and recline at table
propped on a more honourable couch, though imported to Rome
by the same wind as plums and figs ?   Is it then so absolutely

usque adeo nihil est, quod nostra infantia coelum
hausit Aventini bacca nutrita Sabina?   85
quid quod adulandi gens prudentissima laudat
sermonem indocti, faciem deformis amici,
et longum invalidi collum cervicibus aequat
Herculis Antaeum procul a tellure tenentis,
miratur vocem angustam, qua deterius nec   90
ille sonat, quo mordetur gallina marito.
haec eadem licet et nobis laudare, sed illis
creditur. an melior, cum Thaida sustinet, aut cum
uxorem comoedus agit vel Dorida nullo
cultam palliolo? mulier nempe ipsa videtur,   95
non persona loqui, vacua et plana omnia dicas
infra ventriculum et tenui distantia rima.
nec tamen Antiochus, nec erit mirabilis illic
aut Stratocles aut cum molli Demetrius Haemo,
natio comoeda est. rides, maiore cachinno   100
concutitur; flet, si lacrimas conspexit amici,

---

nothing that my infancy drank in the air of the Aventine,
nourished on the Sabine olive? Why add that the race so
cunning in flattery praises the conversation of an ignorant and
the face of a hideous friend, and compares the long throat of
a puny fellow to the neck of a Hercules holding Antaeus far
from the earth, or admires the squeaking voice than which
nothing worse comes even from the male bird which pecks at
the hen? We too have it in our power to praise these same
things, but then they are believed. Can any one be better than
he when he sustains the part of Thais, or when he acts the wife
in a comedy, or Doris unattired in a mantle? To be sure a
woman in person seems to speak, and not a mask *merely:* you
would declare it was a woman perfect in all respects. And yet
Antiochus, or Stratocles, or Demetrius, and the effeminate
Haemus, would be no marvels in their own country. The
nation is one of comedians. Do you laugh, he is convulsed
with a louder guffaw; he weeps if he has seen the tears of a
friend, without feeling any grief; if you should ask for a trifle

nec dolet; igniculum brumae si tempore poscas,
accipit endromidem; si dixeris ' aestuo,' sudat.
non sumus ergo pares: melior, qui semper et omni
nocte dieque potest alienum sumere vultum,   105
a facie iactare manus, laudare paratus,
⟨si bene ructavit, si rectum minxit amicus,
si trulla inverso crepitum dedit aurea fundo.
praeterea sanctum nihil est nec ab inguine tutum,
non matrona laris, non filia virgo, neque ipse   110
sponsus levis adhuc, non filius ante pudicus;
horum si nihil est, aviam resupinat amici.
scire volunt secreta domus atque inde timeri.]
  Et quoniam coepit Graecorum mentio, transi
gymnasia atque audi facinus maioris abollae.   115
stoicus occidit Baream, delator amicum,
discipulumque senex, ripa nutritus in illa,
ad quam Gorgonei delapsa est pinna caballi.
non est Romano cuiquam locus hic, ubi regnat

105. aliena.   107. lectum.   118. penna.

of fire in winter time, he accepts a wrapper; if you say, ' I am
hot,' he sweats. We are not equally matched, then; he has
the advantage of me, who, at all times, and every day and night,
is able to assume a countenance which is not his own, to wave
his hands from his face, prepared to express his approval if his
friend has belched freely, or successfully performed other natural
acts. Moreover, nothing is sacred to him or safe from his lust:
not the mistress of the house, not the virgin daughter, nor the
betrothed bridegroom himself, still beardless, nor the son,
hitherto chaste. If there be none of these, he lays hold of his
friend's grandmother. They seek to know the secrets of the
house, and so to be feared.
  And since we have begun to mention the Greeks, pass by
their training-schools, and hear a crime of the larger cloak. A
stoic killed Bareas, the informer his friend, an old man brought
up on that shore on which the pinion of the Gorgonean steed
lighted, his own disciple. There is not place for any Roman

Protogenes aliquis vel Diphilus aut Erimarchus,   120
qui gentis vitio numquam partitur amicum,
solus habet; nam cum facilem stillavit in aurem
exiguum de naturae patriaeque veneno,
limine summoveor, perierunt tempora longi
servitii; nusquam minor est iactura clientis.   125
    Quod porro officium, ne nobis blandiar, aut quod
pauperis hic meritum, si curet nocte togatus
currere, cum praetor lictorem impellat et ire
praecipitem iubeat, dudum vigilantibus orbis,
ne prior Albinam et Modiam collega salutet?   130
divitis hic servi claudit latus ingenuorum
filius; alter enim quantum in legione tribuni
accipiunt donat Calvinae vel Catienae,
ut semel atque iterum super illam palpitet, at tu,
cum tibi vestiti facies scorti placet, haeres   135
et dubitas alta Chionen deducere sella.

---

here, where reign some Protogenes or Diphilus or Erimarchus,
who, with the vicious propensity of his race, never shares a
friend, *but* keeps him to himself; for when he has instilled into
his ready ear a particle of the poison of his own nature and
country, I am elbowed away from the threshold, my long period
of servitude has been thrown away. Nowhere is the pitching
overboard of a client of less account.

    What, moreover, are the services of the poor man—to speak
plain truth—what are his good turns *worth* here, if he makes
it his business to hurry in his toga before daybreak, when the
praetor *himself* is urging on his lictor, and bidding him go with
all speed, since the childless matrons have been long awake, for
fear his colleague be beforehand in paying his respects to Albina
and Modia? Here the son of free-born parents gives the wall
to the wealthy man of servile birth; for the latter gives to
Calvina or Catiena, to enjoy her favours once and again, as
much as the tribunes in the legion receive; but you, when the
face of a dressed-up harlot pleases you, hesitate and are doubtful
about handing down Chione from her lofty seat. Produce at

da testem Romae tam sanctum, quam fuit hospes
numinis Idaei, procedat vel Numa vel qui
servavit trepidam flagranti ex aede Minervam:
protinus ad censum, de moribus ultima fiet   140
quaestio, 'quot pascit servos? quot possidet agri
iugera? quam multa magnaque paropside coenat?'
quantum quisque sua nummorum servat in arca,
tantum habet et fidei.   iures licet et Samothracum
et nostrorum aras, contemnere fulmina pauper   145
creditur atque deos, dis ignoscentibus ipsis.
quid quod materiam praebet causasque iocorum
omnibus hic idem, si foeda et scissa lacerna,
si toga sordidula est et rupta calceus alter
pelle patet, vel si consuto vulnere crassum   150
atque recens linum ostendit non una cicatrix.
nil habet infelix paupertas durius in se,
quam quod ridiculos homines facit.   'exeat,' inquit,

Rome a witness as virtuous as was the host of the Idaean deity ;
let Numa stand forth, or he who saved the trembling Minerva
from the burning temple, forthwith the inquiry will be as to
his property, and last of all as to his character. 'How many
slaves does he keep? How many acres of land does he possess?
How numerous and how large the dishes at his dinners?' In
proportion to the amount of money each man keeps in his
strong-box, so much belief does he obtain.   Though you swear
by the altars of the Samothracian and our own *divinities*, the
poor man is supposed to contemn thunderbolts and gods, with
the connivance of the gods themselves.   Why add that this
same *poor man* furnishes everybody with material and subjects
for jests, if his cloak is dirty and torn, if his toga is a trifle
shabby and one of his shoes shows an opening with a slit in
the leather, or if more than one seam exhibits the coarse and
recently applied thread, where the rent has been sewn together?
There is nothing which unhappy poverty has in itself harder
than this, that it makes men ridiculous. 'Let him be off,'
says *the usher*, 'if he has any shame, and rise from the cushions

'si pudor est, et de pulvino surgat equestri,
cuius res legi non sufficit, et sedeant hic'—   155
lenonum pueri quocumque in fornice nati,
hic plaudat nitidi praeconis filius inter
pinnirapi cultos iuvenes iuvenesque lanistae ;
sic libitum vano, qui nos distinxit, Othoni.
quis gener hic placuit censu minor atque puellae   160
sarcinulis impar ? quis pauper scribitur heres ?
quando in consilio est aedilibus ? agmine facto
debuerant olim tenues migrasse Quirites !
haud facile emergunt, quorum virtutibus obstat
res angusta domi, sed Romae durior illis   165
conatus, magno hospitium miserabile, magno
servorum ventres et frugi coenula magno.
fictilibus coenare pudet, quod turpe negavit
translatus subito ad Marsos mensamque Sabellam
contentusque illic veneto duroque cucullo.   170

---

170. culullo (Ruperti).

---

of the knights, whose property does not satisfy the law, and let
there sit here'—the sons of pimps, in whatever brothel born ;
here let the son of the sleek crier applaud among the gladiator's
dandy youths and the youths of the trainer.   Such was the
fancy of idle Otho, who made the distinction between us.
Who is acceptable here as a son-in-law whose means are inferior,
and who is unequal to *furnishing* a trousseau for the young
lady ? What poor man is put down for a legacy ? When is
he called into counsel *even* by the aediles ? The poor among
the Romans ought long ago to have emigrated in a body.   Not
easily do those emerge from obscurity whose noble qualities are
cramped by domestic poverty ; but at Rome the attempt is still
harder for them ; a great price *must be paid* for a wretched
lodging, a great price for slaves' keep, a great price for a modest
little dinner.   A man is ashamed to dine off earthenware, which
he would not think discreditable if he were suddenly transported
to the Marsians and a Sabine repast, and contented there with
wearing a sea-green and thick capote.

Pars magna Italiae est, si verum admittimus, in qua
nemo, togam sumit nisi mortuus. ipsa dierum
festorum herboso colitur si quando theatro
maiestas, tandemque redit ad pulpita notum
exodium, cum personae pallentis hiatum   175
in gremio matris formidat rusticus infans,
aequales habitus illic similesque videbis
orchestram et populum, clari velamen honoris
sufficiunt tunicae summis aedilibus albae.
hic ultra vires habitus nitor, hic aliquid plus   180
quam satis est interdum aliena sumitur arca.
commune id vitium est, hic vivimus ambitiosa
paupertate omnes. quid te moror? omnia Romae
cum pretio. quid das, ut Cossum aliquando salutes,
ut te respiciat clauso Veiento labello?   185
ille metit barbam, crinem hic deponit amati,
plena domus libis venalibus. accipe et istud

177. similemque.

There is a great part of Italy, if we accept the truth, in which
no one wears a toga but the dead. Whenever even the majesty
of festive days is celebrated in a grassy theatre, and at length
the well-known interlude reappears on the stage, when the
rustic infant in its mother's lap is frightened at the gaping of
the ghastly mask, there you will see an equality in dress,
the orchestra-stalls and the people alike; and, as the garb of
their high office, white tunics are sufficient for the highest
aediles. Here splendour of dress is *carried* beyond people's
means; here something more than is enough is occasionally
taken out of another man's strong-box. This vice is common
to us all; here all of us live in *a state of* pretentious poverty.
Why detain you *further?* In Rome, everything costs a price.
What *fee* do you give to be able to pay your respects sometimes
to Cossus? for Veiento to bestow a look on you, without
opening his lips? One *patron* shaves the beard, another cuts
off the hair of a favourite; the house is full of cakes for sale.
Take this and let it stir up your bile; we clients are obliged to

fermentum tibi habe: praestare tributa clientes
cogimur et cultis augere peculia servis.

Quis timet aut timuit gelida Praeneste ruinam,   190
aut positis nemorosa inter iuga Volsiniis, aut
simplicibus Gabiis, aut proni Tiburis arce ?
nos urbem colimus tenui tibicine fultam
magna parte sui; nam sic labentibus obstat
villicus, et veteris rimae cum texit hiatum,   195
securos pendente iubet dormire ruina.
vivendum est illic, ubi nulla incendia, nulli
nocte metus. iam poscit aquam, iam frivola transfert
Ucalegon, tabulata tibi iam tertia fumant,
tu nescis; nam si gradibus trepidatur ab imis,   200
ultimus ardebit, quem tegula sola tuetur
a pluvia, molles ubi reddunt ova columbae.
lectus erat Codro Procula minor, urceoli sex,
ornamentum abaci, nec non et parvulus infra

195. contexit.

---

pay tribute and to increase the perquisites of *these* dandified
slaves.

Who fears, or *ever* has feared, the falling of a house at cool
Praeneste, or at Volsinii seated among the wooded hills, or
at primitive Gabii, or on the heights of sloping Tibur? We
inhabit a city propped up to a great extent by thin buttresses;
for in this way the steward prevents the houses from falling;
and when he has plastered over the gaping of an old crack, he
bids us sleep secure, with ruin overhanging *us*. The place to
live in is where there are no fires, no nocturnal alarms. Already
Ucalegon is calling for water, already he is removing his chattels,
already your third story is smoking: you yourself know nothing
about it; for if the alarm begins from the bottom of the stairs,
he will be the last to burn whom the tiling alone protects from
the rain, where the soft doves lay their eggs. Codrus had a
couch too small for *his* Procula, six little jugs, the ornament of
his sideboard, and a tiny drinking-cup beneath it into the
bargain, and a *figure of* Chiron reclining under the same marble:

cantharus et recubans sub eodem marmore Chiron, 205
iamque vetus Graecos servabat cista libellos,
et divina opici rodebant carmina mures.
nil habuit Codrus, quis enim negat? et tamen illud
perdidit infelix totum nihil; ultimus autem
aerumnae est cumulus, quod nudum et frusta rogantem 210
nemo cibo, nemo hospitio tectoque iuvabit.
si magna Asturici cecidit domus, horrida mater,
pullati proceres,. differt vadimonia praetor;
tunc gemimus casus urbis, tunc odimus ignem.
ardet adhuc, et iam accurrit qui marmora donet, 215
conferat impensas; hic nuda et candida signa,
hic aliquid praeclarum Euphranoris et Polycleti,
haec Asianorum vetera ornamenta deorum,
hic libros dabit et forulos mediamque Minervam,
hic modium argenti: meliora ac plura reponit 220
Persicus orborum lautissimus et merito iam
suspectus, tamquam ipse suas incenderit aedes.

214. geminus. 215. occurrit. 218. Phaecasianorum.

a chest, old by this time, contained some Greek books, and
barbarians of mice were gnawing the divine poems.   Codrus
had nothing: who indeed denies this? and yet the wretched
man lost all that nothing: but the crowning point of his misery
is, that though naked and begging for broken scraps, no one
will help him with food, no one with shelter or a roof.   If the
great house of Asturicus has been destroyed, *we have* the matrons
dishevelled, the nobles in mourning, the praetor adjourns his
court; then we groan over the accidents of the town, then we
detest fire.   The fire is still burning, and already some one
runs up to make a present of marbles, and share in the expenses
of rebuilding.   One will contribute nude and white statues,
another some masterpiece of Euphranor or Polycletus; some
lady *will give* antique ornaments of Asiatic gods, another *man*
books and bookcases and a bust of Minerva, another a bushel
of silver: Persicus replaces *what is lost by* choicer and more
numerous objects, most sumptuous of childless men, and sus-

si potes avelli circensibus, optima Sorae
aut Fabrateriae domus aut Frusinone paratur,
quanti nunc tenebras unum conducis in annum.   225
hortulus hic, puteusque brevis nec reste movendus
in tenues plantas facili diffunditur haustu.
vive bidentis amans et culti villicus horti,
unde epulum possis centum dare Pythagoreis :
est aliquid, quocumque loco, quocumque recessu   230
unius sese dominum fecisse lacertae.

Plurimus hic aeger moritur vigilando ; sed ipsum
languorem peperit cibus imperfectus et haerens
ardenti stomacho ; nam quae meritoria somnum
admittunt ?' magnis opibus dormitur in urbe ;   235
inde caput morbi ; redarum transitus arcto
vicorum in flexu et stantis convicia mandrae
eripient somnum Druso vitulisque marinis.

232. illum.   238. eripiunt.

pected with reason of having himself set fire to his own house.
If you are capable of being torn away from the games of the
Circus, an excellent house can be procured at Sora, or Fabra-
teria, or Frusino, for the same price at which you now hire a
dark hole for a single year.   There *you have* a little garden,
and a shallow well, that does not require to be worked with
a rope, irrigates your tender plants with easy draught.   Live
enamoured of your hoe, and the overseer of your own trim
garden, from which you could furnish a banquet for a hundred
Pythagoreans.   It is something, in whatever place, in whatever retreat, to have made one's self owner of a single lizard.

Many a sick man dies here from want of sleep, the indispo-
sition itself having been produced by food undigested, and
clinging to the fevered stomach.   For what hired lodgings allow
of sleep?   Rich men *alone* can sleep in the city.   Hence the
origin of the disease.   The passage of carriages in the narrow
windings of the streets, and the abuse *of the drovers* from the
herds brought to a stand, would rob of sleep *even* Drusus and
sea-calves.

Si vocat officium, turba cedente vehetur
dives et ingenti curret super ora Liburno   240
atque obiter leget aut scribet vel dormiet intus,
namque facit somnum clausa lectica fenestra.
ante tamen veniet; nobis properantibus obstat
unda prior, magno populus premit agmine lumbos
qui sequitur, ferit hic cubito, ferit assere duro   245
alter, at hic tignum capiti incutit, ille metretam;
pinguia crura luto, planta mox undique magna
calcor, et in digito clavus mihi militis haeret.
   Nonne vides, quanto celebretur sportula fumo?
centum convivae, sequitur sua quemque culina.   250
Corbulo vix ferret tot vasa ingentia, tot res
impositas capiti, quot recto vertice portat
servulus infelix et cursu ventilat ignem.
scinduntur tunicae sartae modo, longa coruscat

246. lignum.

If a complimentary attendance calls him, the rich man will
be carried through the yielding crowd, and will speed over their
heads on his huge Liburnian *bearers*, and will read on his way,
or write, or even sleep inside; for a litter with closed windows
is productive of sleep. Yet he will arrive before us: we, in our
hurry, are impeded by the wave in front, *while* the multitude
which follows us presses on our loins in dense array; one strikes
me with his elbow, another with a hard pole, one knocks a
beam against my head, another a wine-jar. My legs are sticky
with mud; before long I am trodden on upon all sides by large
feet, and the hobnails of a soldier stick into my toe.

Do you not see with how great *an accompaniment of* smoke
the Sportula is frequented? A hundred guests: every one is
followed by his own *portable* kitchen. Corbulo could scarcely
bear so many huge vessels, so many things placed on his head,
as the unfortunate little slave carries with upright summit, while
he fans the fire by his rapid motion. Tunics that have only
just been patched are torn; the long fir-trunk vibrates in the
approaching waggon, and other carts convey the pine-tree; they

sarraco veniente abies, atque altera pinum   255
plaustra vehunt, nutant alte populoque minantur.
nam si procubuit qui saxa Ligustica portat
axis et eversum fudit super agmina montem,
quid superest de corporibus? quis membra, quis ossa
invenit? obtritum vulgi perit omne cadaver   260
more animae.   domus interea secura patellas
iam lavat et bucca foculum excitat et sonat unctis
striglibus et pleno componit lintea gutto.
haec inter pueros varie properantur, at ille
iam sedet in ripa tetrumque novicius horret   265
porthmea, nec sperat coenosi gurgitis alnum
infelix, nec habet quem porrigat ore trientem.

    Respice nunc alia ac diversa pericula noctis,
quod spatium tectis sublimibus, unde cerebrum
testa ferit, quoties rimosa et curta fenestris.   270
vasa cadunt; quanto percussum pondere signent

     256. altae.   261. morte.

---

oscillate on high, and threaten the people; for if the vehicle
which carries Ligurian stone blocks has *once* upset, and poured
its overturned mountain-load upon the troops *of passers-by*, what
will remain of their bodies? who will find their limbs, who their
bones? All the carcases of the vulgar, crushed to atoms, will
perish like a breath. The unsuspecting household, in the meanwhile, are by this time washing the dishes, and blowing up the
fire with their mouths, and resounding with the oiled scrapers,
and arranging the towels, with the full oil-flask. These are the
bustling occupations of the slaves, in their various ways : but
he (*the victim*) is already seated on the banks *of the Styx*, and,
novice as he is, dreads the grim ferryman, nor does he hope for
the boat *to make the passage* of the muddy abyss, nor has he a
triens in his mouth to offer, *as a fee*.

    Observe now the different and distinct dangers of the night;
what a height it is to the lofty house-tops, from which a potsherd
strikes your pate as often as cracked and broken utensils fall
from the windows; with what a weight they dint and damage

et laedant silicem. possis ignavus haberi
et subiti casus improvidus, ad coenam si
intestatus eas: adeo tot fata, quot illa
nocte patent vigiles te praetereunte fenestrae. 275
ergo optes votumque feras miserabile tecum,
ut sint contentae patulas defundere pelves.
ebrius ac petulans, qui nullum forte cecidit,
dat poenas, noctem patitur lugentis amicum
Pelidae, cubat in faciem, mox deinde supinus. 280
ergo non aliter poterit dormire? quibusdam
somnum rixa facit; sed quamvis improbus annis
atque mero fervens, cavet hunc, quem coccina laena
vitari iubet et comitum longissimus ordo,
multum praeterea flammarum et aenea lampas. 285
me, quem luna solet deducere vel breve lumen
candelae, cuius dispenso et tempero filum,
contemnuit. miserae cognosce prooemia rixae,

297. diffundere, effundere.

the flint-*pavement* when they strike it. You may *well* be
accounted remiss and improvident about a sudden accident, if
you go out to supper without having made a will. Just so
many fatal chances there are, as there are wakeful windows open
on the night when you are passing by. Hope then, and bear
this pitiable prayer about with you, that they may be content
to empty out flat-pans *over you*. The drunken and insolent
fellow, who has not chanced to pummel anybody, suffers tortures;
he undergoes a night like that of Achilles mourning for his
friend; he lies *first* on his face, and directly afterwards on his
back. Won't he then be able to sleep otherwise? *No;* it is a
quarrel that makes some people sleep: but though wanton from
his years and heated with wine, he keeps clear of him whom
the scarlet cloak and the very long train of attendants, and
moreover the multitude of torches and the bronzed candelabrum,
point out as one to be avoided: me, whom the moon is wont to
escort home, or the brief light of a candle, whose wick I regu-
late and husband, he despises. Mark the preliminaries of the

si rixa est, ubi tu pulsas, ego vapulo tantum.
stat contra starique iubet. parere necesse est, 290
nam quid agas, cum te furiosus cogat et idem
fortior ? ' unde venis ? ' exclamat ' cuius aceto,
cuius conche tumes ? quis tecum sectile porrum
sutor et elixi vervecis labra comedit ?
nil mihi respondes ? aut dic, aut accipe calcem ! 295
ede, ubi consistas ! in qua te quaero proseucha ? '
dicere si tentes aliquid tacitusve recedas,
tantumdem est, feriunt pariter, vadimonia deinde
irati faciunt.   Libertas pauperis haec est :
pulsatus rogat et pugnis concisus adorat, 300
ut liceat paucis cum dentibus inde reverti.
nec tamen haec tantum metuas, nam qui spoliet te
non deerit, clausis domibus, postquam omnis ubique
fixa catenatae siluit compago tabernae ;
interdum et ferro subitus grassator agit rem, 305

---

wretched brawl, if brawl it be, where you strike and I am
beaten only. He stands facing you, and orders you to stand ;
you must needs obey, for what are you to do when a madman
forces you, and he too stronger than yourself ? 'Whence do
you come ?' he exclaims. 'With whose vinegar, with whose
beans are you gorged ? What cobbler has been devouring with
you cut leeks or sodden sheep's-head ? Do you answer me
nothing ? Speak or be kicked ! Tell me where you take up
your begging-stand : in what synagogue am I to look for you ?'
It is all one whether you try to say anything, or draw back in
silence ; they beat you just the same ; then, *as if* in a passion,
they are for making you give bail. This is the liberty of a poor
man ; after being beaten, he prays, and after being thrashed
with fisty-cuffs, he entreats, to be allowed to retire from the
scene with a few teeth *left him*. Nor yet are such things all
you have to fear : for there will not be wanting he who will
plunder you after the houses are closed, and in all directions the
fastenings of the chained-up shops are fixed and at rest. Sometimes, too, the swift footpad plies his business with the steel, as

armato quoties tutae custode tenentur
et Pomptina palus et Gallinaria pinus;
sic inde huc omnes tamquam ad vivaria currunt.
qua fornace graves, qua non incude, catenae?
maximus in vinclis ferri modus, ut timeas, ne   310
vomer deficiat, ne marrae et sarcula desint.
felices proavorum atavos, felicia dicas
secula, quae quondam sub regibus atque tribunis
viderunt uno contentam carcere Romam.

    His alias poteram et plures subnectere causas,   315
sed iumenta vocant, et sol inclinat, eundum est;
nam mihi commota iamdudum mulio virga
annuit. ergo vale nostri memor, et quoties te
Roma tuo refici properantem reddet Aquino,
me quoque ad Helvinam Cererem vestramque Dianam   320
convelle a Cumis; satirarum ego, ni pudet illas,
adiutor gelidos veniam caligatus in agros."

321. converte.   322. auditor.

---

often as the Pomptine marshes and the Gallinarian forest are
kept safe by an armed guard: all these fellows run from there
to this place just as to a game-preserve. What forge is there,
what anvil, on which chains are not *lying* heavy? The greatest
proportion of iron is *used* in *making* fetters, so that one may
well fear that ploughs will fail, that mattocks and hoes will run
short. Happy our remote ancestors! happy one may call the
ages which of yore, under kings and tribunes, beheld Rome
contented with a single prison.

    To these I had it in my power to add other and many
reasons; but my steeds summon me, and the sun is declining.
I must be off. For the muleteer has been signalling to me for
some time by a movement of his whip. Good-bye, then, and
remember me, and as often as Rome shall restore you, eager to
recruit yourself, to your *favourite* Aquinum, do you tear me
away too from Cumae to Helvine Ceres and your Diana. I will
come, in my hobnailed shoes, to that cool country to assist you
in your Satires, if they be not ashamed *of my aid.*"

E CCE iterum Crispinus, et est mihi saepe vocandus
ad partes, monstrum nulla virtute redemptum
a vitiis, aegrae solaque libidine fortes
deliciae; viduas tantum aspernatur adulter.
quid refert igitur, quantis iumenta fatiget   5
porticibus, quanta nemorum vectetur in umbra,
iugera quot vicina foro, quas emerit aedes?
nemo malus felix, minime corruptor et idem
incestus, cum quo nuper vittata iacebat
sanguine adhuc vivo terram subitura sacerdos.   10
sed nunc de factis levioribus; et tamen alter
si fecisset idem, caderet sub iudice morum.
nam quod turpe bonis, Titio Seioque, decebat
Crispinum; quid agas, cum dira et foedior omni

3. aeger; fortis.   4. delicias; viduae; spernatur.
9. vitiata.

SATIRE IV.

WHAT, Crispinus again! and I shall often have to summon him
to play his part; a monster redeemed by no one virtue from his
vices; a minion, feeble *in all else*, and strong in his lusts alone.
It is only single women that this adulterer turns up his nose at.
What matters it then in what vast colonnades he wearies his
steeds, in what vast shade of groves he is carried, how many
acres in the neighbourhood of the Forum, what houses he has
bought? No bad man is happy, least of all a seducer who is at
the same time incestuous, with whom not long ago there lay a
filleted priestess, destined to be put under the ground with her
life-blood still warm. But now of lighter deeds: and yet
another, if he had done the same, would have been condemned
by *our* censor. For what would be disgraceful for good men,
for Titius and Seius, was becoming to Crispinus. What are you

crimine persona est? mullum sex millibus emit,   15
aequantem sane paribus sestertia libris,
ut perhibent qui de magnis maiora loquuntur.
consilium laudo artificis, si munere tanto
praecipuam in tabulis ceram senis abstulit orbi;
est ratio ulterior, magnae si misit amicae,   20
quae vehitur clauso latis specularibus antro.
nil tale exspectes, emit sibi.   multa videmus,
quae miser et frugi non fecit Apicius.   hoc tu
succinctus patriâ quondam, Crispine, papyro,
hoc pretio squamae! potuit fortasse minoris   25
piscator, quam piscis, emi; provincia tanti
vendit agros, sed maiores Appulia vendit.
    Quales tunc epulas ipsum glutisse putemus
induperatorem, cum tot sestertia partem
exiguam et modicae sumptam de margine coenae   30

28. nunc; putamus.

---

to do when the person himself is *more* loathsome and more foul than any accusation *can represent him?* He bought a mullet for six thousand sesterces, equalling, forsooth, the sestertia by as many pounds in weight, as they relate, who, about big things, talk still bigger. I praise the design of the contriver, if by a present of such value he ;carried off the principal place in the will of some childless old man. There is a further way of accounting for it, if he sent it to some mistress of rank who is carried about in her closed-up den, with its broad windows. Don't anticipate anything of the kind; he bought it for himself. We see many things such as Apicius, poor frugal man, never did. Did you *do* this, Crispinus, when girt about in days of yore with the papyrus of your country? Were fish scales *sold* at this price? The fisherman himself might, perhaps, have been bought for less than your fish. The provinces sell estates for this sum; and Apulia still larger ones.

    What sort of banquets must we suppose the Emperor himself to have gorged at that time, when so many sestertia, *representing* but a small portion, and one taken from among the side-dishes

purpureus magni ructarit scurra Palati,
iam princeps equitum, magna qui voce solebat
vendere municipes fracta de merce siluros!
incipe Calliope! licet et considere; non est
cantandum, res vera agitur.   narrate puellae   35
Pierides; prosit mihi vos dixisse puellas!
   Cum iam semianimum laceraret Flavius orbem
ultimus, et calvo serviret Roma Neroni,
incidit Adriaci spatium admirabile rhombi
ante domum Veneris, quam Dorica sustinet Ancon,   40
implevitque sinus; nec enim minor haeserat illis,
quos operit glacies Maeotica, ruptaque tandem
solibus effundit torpentis ad ostia Ponti,
desidia tardos et longo frigore pingues.
destinat hoc monstrum cymbae linique magister   45
pontifici summo.   quis enim proponere talem
aut emere auderet, cum plena et litora multo

33. pacta, facta, fricta, Pharia.   43. effudit.

---

of an ordinary dinner, were belched forth by this purple-clad
buffoon of the great palace, now at the head of the knights, but
who used with loud voice to sell his compatriot shad-fish, part
of his damaged wares! Begin Calliope; you may sit down
too; it is not a case for singing; we are dealing with a real
occurrence.   Narrate, maiden Pierides; and may I have the
benefit of having called you " maidens."

While the last of the Flavii was mangling the world, half
dead by this time, and Rome was in slavery to a bald Nero, a
wonderful-sized Adriatic turbot fell *into the net* before the temple
of Venus which Doric Ancon supports, and filled its folds; nor,
indeed, when it stuck there, was it smaller than those which the
ice of the Maeotis encloses, and which, when it is at length
broken up by the sun's rays, it pours forth to the outlets of the
sluggish Euxine, heavy from rest, and fat from the long cold.
This prodigy the owner of the boat and net destines for the
chief pontiff.   For who would dare set up for sale or buy such
a fish, when even the shores were full of a crowd of informers?

delatore forent? dispersi protinus algae
inquisitores agerent cum remige nudo,
non dubitaturi fugitivum dicere piscem   50
depastumque diu vivaria Caesaris, inde
elapsum veterem ad dominum debere reverti.
si quid Palfurio, si credimus Armillato,
quidquid conspicuum pulchrumque est aequore toto,
res fisci est, ubicumque natat; donabitur ergo,   55
ne pereat. iam letifero cedente pruinis
autumno, iam quartanam sperantibus aegris,
stridebat deformis hiems praedamque recentem
servabat; tamen hic properat, velut urgeat auster.
utque lacus suberant, ubi quamquam diruta servat   60
ignem Troianum et Vestam colit Alba minorem,
obstitit intranti miratrix turba parumper;
ut cessit, facili patuerunt cardine valvae,
exclusi spectant admissa opsonia patres.
itur ad Atriden. tum Piccus "accipe," dixit,   65

64. exspectant.

These inspectors of seaweed, dispersed about, would forthwith
have called the helpless boatman to account, and would not have
hesitated to declare the fish a stray, and one that had long been
fed in the preserves of Caesar, *and*, that having escaped thence,
it ought to return to its old master. If we give any credence
to Palfurius or Armillatus, whatever is remarkable or fine in the
whole sea is the property of the privy-purse, wherever it swims.
It must be made a present of, therefore, lest it be wasted. With
deadly autumn already giving place to the hoar-frosts, and sick
people already hoping for the quartan, grim winter was raging
and preserving the recent capture; yet our man hurries on as if
the south wind impelled him; and when the lakes were near at
hand, where Alba, although in ruins, still preserves the Trojan
fire and worships the lesser Vesta, the wondering crowd prevented his entrance for a short time. As it gave way, the folding-
doors opened with ready hinge. The senators, shut out, behold
the dainty admitted. He makes his way to Atrides. Then says

" privatis maiora focis, genialis agatur
iste dies, propera stomachum laxare saginis
et tua servatum consume in secula rhombum.
ipse capi voluit."   quid apertius? et tamen illi
surgebant cristae; nihil est quod credere de se   70
non possit, cum laudatur dis aequa potestas.
sed deerat pisci patinae mensura. vocantur
ergo in consilium proceres, quos oderat ille,
in quorum facie miserae magnaeque sedebat
pallor amicitiae. primus, clamante Liburno,   75
" currite, iam sedit!" raptâ properabat abolla
Pegasus, attonitae positus modo villicus urbi.
anne aliud tunc praefecti? quorum optimus atque
interpres legum sanctissimus, omnia quamquam
temporibus diris tractanda putabat inermi   80
iustitiā. venit et Crispi iucunda senectus,
cuius erant mores qualis facundia, mite

---

the Picenian, " Accept what is too great for a private kitchen ;
let this day be devoted to your genius ; hasten to distend your
stomach with good things, and consume a turbot reserved for
your epoch. The fish got himself caught of his own accord."
What could be more glaring? And yet his (*the Emperor's*) crest
was rising. There is nothing which power is not able to believe
of itself when it is extolled as being equal to the gods. But
there was wanting a dish to the measure of the fish. So
the chiefs are called into counsel, whom he hated, on whose
faces sat the pallor of a wretched, exalted friendship. First
of all, at the cry of the Liburnian *slave*, " Make haste ; he is
already seated!" there hurried along, snatching up his cloak,
Pegasus, who had recently been set as bailiff over the awestruck
city—were the Praefects anything else at that period? of whom
he was the best and the most righteous interpreter of the laws,
although, in *such* dreadful times, he thought everything was to
be administered by justice unarmed. There came, too, pleasant
old Crispus, whose moral character was of the same kind as his
eloquence, a gentle nature. Who *could have been* a more useful

ingenium.   maria ac terras populosque regenti
quis comes utilior, si clade et peste sub illâ
saevitiam damnare et honestum afferre liceret   85
consilium ?   sed quid violentius aure tyranni,
cum quo de pluviis aut aestibus aut nimboso
vere locuturi fatum pendebat amici ?
ille igitur numquam direxit brachia contra
torrentem, nec civis erat, qui libera posset   90
verba animi proferre et vitam impendere vero :
sic multas hiemes atque octogesima vidit
solstitia, his armis illâ quoque tutus in aulâ.
proximus eiusdem properabat Acilius aevi
cum iuvene, indigno quem mors tam saeva maneret   95
et domini gladiis tam festinata ; sed olim
prodigio par est cum nobilitate senectus,
unde fit ut malim fraterculus esse gigantis.
profuit ergo nihil misero, quod cominus ursos
figebat Numidas Albanâ nudus arenâ   100

96. jam destinata.   97. in nobilitate.

---

minister to one ruling over seas and lands and peoples, if, under
that scourge and pest, he had been allowed to condemn his
violence, and to offer honest advice ? But what more ruthless
than the car of a tyrant, with whom hung suspended the fate
of a friend, about to talk *merely* of the showers, or the heats, or
the rainy spring ? He, then, never directed his arms against the
torrent, nor was he a citizen who could give utterance to the
free sentiments of his soul, and stake his life on the truth. In
this way he saw many winters and eighty summers ; with such
armour, safe even in that court. Next to him hurried Acilius,
of the same age, with a young man who did not deserve that a
death so cruel should await him, and one so prematurely inflicted
by the despot's swords : but for a long time past, old age, coupled
with nobility, is as good as a prodigy ; whence it happens that I
would prefer to be the small brother of a giant. It availed the
wretched man nothing, then, that he used to transfix Numidian
bears in hand-to-hand fight, a naked huntsman on the arena of

venator. quis enim iam non intelligat artes
patricias ? quis priscum illud miratur acumen,
Brute, tuum ? facile est barbato imponere regi.
nec melior vultu, quamvis ignobilis, ibat
Rubrius, offensae veteris reus atque tacendae,   105
et tamen improbior satiram scribente cinaedo.
Montani quoque venter adest abdomine tardus,
et matutino sudans Crispinus amomo,
quantum vix redolent duo funera, saevior illo
Pompeius tenui iugulos aperire susurro,   110
et qui vulturibus servabat viscera Dacis
Fuscus, marmorea meditatus proelia villa,
et cum mortifero prudens Veiento Catullo,
qui numquam visae flagrabat amore puellae ;
grande et conspicuum nostro quoque tempore monstrum, 115
caecus adulator dirusque a ponte satelles,
dignus Aricinos qui mendicaret ad axes
blandaque devexae iactaret basia redae.

101. intelligit.   102. miretur.

Alba. For who by this time does not understand the artifices
of the patricians? Who marvels at that old-world craftiness of
yours, Brutus? It is easy to impose on a king with a beard.
Nor, with more cheerful looks, though not one of the nobility,
went Rubrius, guilty of an old offence, and one not to be spoken
of, and yet more impudent than the pathic satirist. Fat-bellied
Montanus is present, too, unwieldy with his paunch ; and Crispinus, reeking with his morning perfume to a degree that two
funerals would hardly smell of ; and Pompeius, still more ruthless than he at slitting throats by a gentle whisper ; and he
who was preserving his entrails for the Dacian vultures, Fuscus,
who had studied battles in his marble villa ; and wary Veiento,
with the deadly Catullus, who was burning with lust for a girl
whom he could not see, a great and conspicuous prodigy even
in our time, a blind flatterer, and horrible satellite of the bridge
kind, worthy to beg beside the vehicles on the Arician *hill*, and
to throw sweet kisses to the carriage on its way down. No one

nemo magis rhombum stupuit, nam plurima dixit
in laevum conversus, at illi dextra iacebat   120
bellua.   sic pugnas Cilicis laudabat et ictus
et pegma et pueros inde ad velaria raptos.
non cedit Veiento, sed ut fanaticus oestro
percussus Bellona tuo, divinat et " ingens
omen habes," inquit, " magni clarique triumphi.   125
regem aliquem capies, aut de temone Britanno
excidet Arviragus.   peregrina est bellua, cernis
erectas in terga sudes ? " hoc defuit unum
Fabricio, patriam ut rhombi memoraret et annos.
" quidnam igitur censes ? conciditur ? " " absit ab illo   130
dedecus hoc ! " Montanus ait, " testa alta paretur,
quae tenui muro spatiosum colligat orbem ;
debetur magnus patinae subitusque Prometheus.
argillam atque rotam citius properate ! sed ex hoc
tempore iam, Caesar, figuli tua castra sequantur."   135

---

was more struck with the turbot; for he made many remarks
turning to the left, whereas the monster was lying to his right.
In the same way he used to praise the fighting of the Cilician
gladiator, and his thrusts, and the stage-machine, and the boys
caught up by it to the awnings.   Veiento is not to be outdone,
but, like one frenzied and stung by thy gadfly, Bellona, he
bursts into prophecy, and, " You have *there* a mighty omen,"
he says, " of a great and glorious triumph : you will capture
some king, or Arviragus will tumble out of his Britannic chariot : the monster is a foreigner; do you perceive the bristles
erect on his back ? "   In one thing alone was Fabricius at fault,
in mentioning the country and age of the turbot.   " What then
do you opine for ?   Is it to be cut up ? "   " Far from it be such
a disgrace as this," says Montanus ; " let a deep vessel be prepared to contain the spacious circumference between its thin
sides.   Some great Prometheus, and a speedy one, is required
for the dish.   Quick with the clay and the wheel; but now
from this time forth, Caesar, let potters follow your camp." This
proposal, worthy of the man, carried the day ; he was versed in

vicit digna viro sententia; noverat ille
luxuriam imperii veterem noctesque Neronis
iam medias aliamque famem, cum pulmo Falerno
arderet. nulli maior fuit usus edendi
tempestate mea; Circeis nata forent an   140
Lucrinum ad saxum Rutupinove edita fundo
ostrea, callebat primo deprendere morsu,
et semel aspecti litus dicebat echini.
surgitur, et misso proceres exire iubentur
consilio, quos Albanam dux magnus in arcem   145
traxerat attonitos et festinare coactos,
tamquam de Cattis aliquid torvisque Sicambris
dicturus, tamquam diversis partibus orbis
anxia praecipiti venisset epistola pennâ.

Atque utinam his potius nugis tota illa dedisset   150
tempora saevitiae, claras quibus abstulit urbi
illustresque animas impune et vindice nullo !

---

the old debauchery of the imperial court, and Nero's midnights,
and that second appetite when the lungs were fired by Falernian
wine. No one had greater experience in eating in my time :
he was skilled in detecting at the first bite whether oysters
were natives of Circeii or the Lucrine rocks, or produced from
the depths of Rutupiae ; and he could tell the shore a sea-
urchin came from the moment he saw him. They rise, and,
the council dismissed, the nobles are ordered to retire, whom
the great chief had dragged to his Alban citadel, bewildered and
forced to hurry, as though he had been about to make some
communication to them concerning the Catti or the fierce
Sicambri, as though from the opposite end of the world an
anxious express had come with dashing wing.

And *yet*, I would that he had rather devoted *even* to such
trifles *as these* the whole of that period of violence in which he
deprived the city of noble and illustrious spirits with impunity,
and with none to avenge them. But he perished as soon as
he had begun to be an object of fear to the rabble. This it

sed periit, postquam cerdonibus esse timendus
coeperat; hoc nocuit Lamiarum caede madenti.

SATIRA V.

SI te propositi nondum pudet atque eadem est mens,
   ut bona summa putes alienā vivere quadra,
si potes illa pati, quae nec Sarmentus iniquas
Caesaris ad mensas nec vilis Galba tulisset,
quamvis iurato metuam tibi credere testi.   5
ventre nihil novi frugalius.   hoc tamen ipsum
defecisse puta, quod inani sufficit alvo;
nulla crepido vacat? nusquam pons et tegetis pars
dimidia brevior? tantine iniuria coenae?
tam ieiuna fames, cum possit honestius illic   10
et tremere et sordes farris mordere canini?

10. cum Pol sit; possis cum.

was that was fatal to one reeking with the slaughter of the
Lamiae.

SATIRE V.

IF you are not yet ashamed of your course of life, and are of
the same mind, so as to think it the chief good to live on
another man's crumbs, if you can put up with such things as
not even Sarmentus at the unequal board of Caesar, nor vile
Galba, would have borne, I should be afraid to believe your
evidence, even though you were on oath.   I know of nothing
more frugal than the belly.   Suppose, however, even that *little*
to be wanting which suffices to an empty stomach, is there no
raised footpath vacant? is there nowhere a bridge or a bit of
mat, short of its half, *to beg on?* Is the insult of a dinner
worth such a price?   Is your hunger so craving, when it might
more honourably be shivering there and gnawing dirty scraps of
dog-biscuit?

Primo fige loco, quod tu discumbere iussus
mercedem solidam veterum capis officiorum.
fructus amicitiae magnae cibus, imputat hunc rex,
et quamvis rarum tamen imputat. ergo duos post 15
si libuit menses neglectum adhibere clientem,
tertia ne vacuo cessaret culcita lecto,
" una simus " ait. votorum summa, quid ultra
quaeris? habet Trebius, propter quod rumpere somnum
debeat et ligulas dimittere, sollicitus ne 20
tota salutatrix iam turba peregerit orbem,
sideribus dubiis, aut illo tempore, quo se
frigida circumagunt pigri sarraca Bootae.
qualis cocna tamen! vinum, quod sucida nolit
lana pati; de conviva Corybanta videbis. 25
iurgia proludunt, sed mox et pocula torques
saucius et rubra deterges vulnera mappa,

12. finge.

Impress this on yourself in the first place, that you, when
bidden to recline at table, are receiving payment in a lump for
your old services. The return for this lofty connection is food ;
this the great man sets down to your account, and, rare though
it be, still he sets it down. If, therefore, after the lapse of two
months, it has pleased him to invite his neglected client, that a
third cushion might not go a-begging on some couch not yet
filled up, " Let us dine together," he says. The summit of your
wishes *is attained :* what more do you ask for? Trebius has
got that for the sake of which he is bound to break his sleep,
and to leave his shoes untied, in his solicitude lest the whole
crowd of visitors should already have accomplished their round,
while the stars are growing dim or *even* at the time when the
cold wain of sluggish Bootes is wheeling round. Yet what a
dinner it is ! Wine, which newly-shorn wool would not imbibe :
you will see the guest turn into one of the Corybantes. Wrang-
lings form the prelude : but soon you hurl even your cups when
you have been struck, and wipe your wounds with reddened

inter vos quoties libertorumque cohortem
pugna Saguntina fervet commissa lagena.
ipse capillato diffusum consule potat   30
calcatamque tenet bellis socialibus uvam,
cardiaco numquam cyathum missurus amico;
cras bibet Albanis aliquid de montibus aut de
Setinis, cuius patriam titulumque senectus
delevit multa veteris fuligine testae;   35
quale coronati Thrasea Helvidiusque bibebant
Brutorum et Cassi natalibus. ipse capaces
Heliadum crustas et inaequales beryllo
Virro tenet phialas ; tibi non committitur aurum,
vel si quando datur, custos affixus ibidem,   40
qui numeret gemmas, ungues observet acutos.
" da veniam, praeclara illic laudatur iaspis."
nam Virro, ut multi, gemmas ad pocula transfert
a digitis, quas in vaginae fronte solebat
ponere zelotypo iuvenis praelatus Iarbae.   45

---

towel, as often as between you and the cohort of freedmen
rages a fight waged with Saguntine pitchers. The host swills
wine bottled under some long-haired Consul, and keeps to himself *the juice of* the grape trodden during the social wars, of
which he will never send even a small cup to a friend with the
cardiac disease. To-morrow he will drink something from the
Alban or Setine hills, whose country and label old age has
effaced by the quantity of smoke undergone by the ancient
wine-jar,—such *wine* as Thrasea and Helvidius, with chaplets
on their heads, used to drink on the birthdays of the Bruti and
Cassius. Virro himself retains the capacious embossed cups of
amber, and the drinking vessels rough with beryl; the gold is
not entrusted to you, or, if at any time it is handed you, a
guardian is attached to its company to count the gems and
observe your sharp nails. "Pray excuse me; there is a splendid
jasper there which is *much* admired !" For Virro, like many,
transfers from his fingers to his drinking cups the gems which
the youth preferred to jealous Iarbas was wont to set at the top

tu Beneventani sutoris nomen habentem
siccabis calicem nasorum quatuor ac iam
quassatum et rupto poscentem sulfura vitro.
si stomachus domini fervet vinoque ciboque,
frigidior Geticis petitur decocta pruinis ;   50
non eadem vobis poni modo vina querebar,
vos aliam potatis aquam.   tibi pocula cursor
Gaetulus dabit, aut nigri manus ossea Mauri,
et cui per mediam nolis occurrere noctem,
clivosae veheris dum per monumenta Latinae.   55
flos Asiae ante ipsum pretio maiore paratus,
quam fuit et Tulli census pugnacis et Anci
et, ne te teneam, Romanorum omnia regum
frivola.   quod cum ita sit, tu Gaetulum Ganymedem
respice, cum sities.   nescit tot millibus emptus   60
pauperibus miscere puer, sed forma, sed aetas
digna supercilio.   quando ad te pervenit ille ?

---

of his scabbard. You will drain a beaker bearing the name
of the cobbler of Beneventum, with four spouts, and already
cracked, and calling for sulphur-*matches* in exchange for broken
glass.   If the stomach of my lord is heated with wine and food,
he calls for *water*, boiled down, and cooled with the snow of
Scythia. Was I complaining just now that the same wines are
not set before you ? You drink a different water. Your cups
will be served to you by a Gaetulian lackey, or the bony hand
of a black Moor, one whom you would not like to run against
in the middle of the night, while you are being conveyed
through the tombs on the steep Latin way. Before the master
stands the flower of Asia, purchased at a price larger than made
up the fortune of either warlike Tullus or Ancus ; and, in
short, all the goods and chattels of the Roman kings. Such
being the case, do you look to your Gaetulian Ganymede
when you are thirsty. A boy bought for so many thousands is
incapable of mixing for poor people : yet his beauty, his age,
justify his pride. When does the former reach you ? When

quando vocatus adest calidae gelidaeque minister ?
quippe indignatur veteri parere clienti,
quodque aliquid poscas, et quod se stante recumbas.   65
maxima quaeque domus servis est plena superbis.
ecce, alius quanto porrexit murmure panem
vix fractum, solidae iam mucida frusta farinae,
quae genuinum agitent, non admittentia morsum ;
sed tener et niveus mollique siligine factus   70
servatur domino.   dextram cohibere memento,
salva sit artoptae reverentia ! finge tamen te
improbulum, superest illic qui ponere cogat.
" vis tu consuetis audax conviva canistris
impleri, panisque tui novisse colorem ?"   75
" scilicet hoc fuerat, propter quod saepe relictâ
coniuge per montem adversum gelidasque cucurri
Esquilias, fremeret saeva cum grandine vernus
Iuppiter et multo stillaret paenula nimbo !"
aspice, quam longo distendat pectore lancem,   80

63. rogatus.   72. artocopi.

---

does he come at your call to serve hot and cold water ?   He is
indignant forsooth at *the idea of* obeying an old client, and at
your asking for anything, and at your reclining while he stands.
Every great house is full of supercilious slaves.   See with what
grumbling another fellow has handed you the bread, broken
with difficulty, scraps of solid flour, mouldy by this time, so as
to irritate your grinders by not admitting of a bite.   But *bread*
tender and snow-white and made of soft grain is kept for my lord.
Be sure you restrain your right hand : respect for the bread-pan
must be maintained.   Imagine yourself, however, to be a trifle
impudent, there is one standing above you there to make you hand
over.   "Will you, you audacious guest, fill yourself from your usual
basket, and know the colour of your own bread?"   "Forsooth, this
it was for the sake of which I often left my wife and ran up the
opposite hill, the cold Esquiline, when the vernal sky sounded
with the pitiless hail, and my cloak dripped with the frequent
showers !"   See with how long a breast the lobster which is

quae fertur domino squilla, et quibus undique septa
asparagis, qua despiciat convivia cauda,
dum venit excelsi manibus sublata ministri.
sed tibi dimidio constrictus cammarus ovo
ponitur exiguâ feralis coena patellâ.   85
ipse Venafrano piscem perfundit, at hic, qui
pallidus affertur misero tibi caulis, olebit
laternam; illud enim vestris datur alveolis, quod
canna Micipsarum prora subvexit acuta,
propter quod Romae cum Bocchare nemo lavatur,   90
quod tutos etiam facit a serpentibus Afros.
mullus erit domino, quem misit Corsica vel quem
Tauromenitanae rupes, quando omne peractum est
et iam defecit nostrum mare, dum gula saevit,
retibus assiduis penitus scrutante macello   95
proxima, nec patimur Tyrrhenum crescere piscem.
instruit ergo focum provincia, sumitur illinc

91. **Afris, atris.**   92. domini.   96. patitur.

carried to my lord distends, *as it were*, the dish, and with what
asparagus it is fenced in on all sides, with what a tail it looks
down upon the company, while it comes borne aloft by the
hands of a tall attendant! But to you a common crab, scantily
garnished with half an egg, is served,—a funereal supper on a
tiny dish. The host pours over his fish oil from Venafrum;
but this sickly cabbage which is brought to you, poor man!
will smell of the lamp: for that *oil* is served in your sauce-boats
which the canoe of the Micipsae has imported with its sharp
prow, for fear of which no one in Rome bathes with Bocchar,
which even makes the Africans safe from serpents. There will
be a mullet for my lord, which Corsica has sent, or the rocks of
Tauromenium, since all our seas have been ransacked and have
failed by this time, while gluttony rages, the market with unceasing nets searching to the bottom the neighbouring *seas*, and
we do not even allow the Tyrrhenian fish to grow. So the provinces supply our kitchen; thence we are furnished with what

quod captator emat Laenas, Aurelia vendat.
Virroni muraena datur, quae maxima venit
gurgite de Siculo; nam dum se continet Auster,   100
dum sedet et siccat madidas in carcere pennas,
contemnunt mediam temeraria lina Charybdim.
vos anguilla manet longae cognata colubrae,
aut glacie aspersus maculis Tiberinus, et ipse
vernula riparum, pinguis torrente cloaca,   105
et solitus mediae cryptam penetrare Suburae.
    Ipsi pauca velim, facilem si praebeat aurem.
nemo petit, modicis quae mittebantur amicis
a Seneca, quae Piso bonus, quae Cotta solebat
largiri (namque et titulis et fascibus olim   110
maior habebatur donandi gloria), solum
poscimus ut coenes civiliter; hoc face et esto,
esto, ut nunc multi, dives tibi, pauper amicis.
    Anseris ante ipsum magni iecur, anseribus par

101. pinnas.   105. torpente.

---

the fortune-hunter Laenas may buy, and Aurelia sell *again*.
To Virro a lamprey is served, of huge size, which has come from
the Sicilian whirlpool; for while Auster contains himself, while
he sits and dries his humid pinions in prison, the adventurous
fishing-nets make light of the very centre of Charybdis.   An
eel awaits you folks, a relative of the long snake, or a Tiburine
pike, sprinkled with frost-spots, and even the low native of the
river banks, fattened by the gushing sewer, and wont to pene-
trate the drains under the very middle of the Suburra.
    I should like a few words with the host, if he would lend me
a favourable ear.   Nobody asks for the gifts which used to be
sent to his humble friends by Seneca, which worthy Piso, which
Cotta was in the habit of dispensing : for in old times the glory
of giving was held to be greater than even inscriptions of nobility
or fasces : all we ask is that you dine with common courtesy.
Do this and be—be, as many are nowadays—a rich man for
yourself, a poor man for your friends.
    Before the host, the liver of a huge goose, fatted poultry the

altilis, et flavi dignus ferro Meleagri   115
fumat aper, post hunc tradentur tubera, si ver
tunc erit et facient optata tonitrua coenas
maiores.   "tibi habe frumentum" Allidius inquit,
"o Libye, disiunge boves, dum tubera mittas."
structorem interea, ne qua indignatio desit,   120
saltantem spectas et chironomunta volanti
cultello, donec peragat dictata magistri
omnia ; nec minimo sane discrimine refert,
quo gestu lepores et quo gallina secetur.
duceris planta velut ictus ab Hercule Cacus,   125
et ponere foris, si quid tentaveris umquam
hiscere, tamquam habeas tria nomina.   quando propinat
Virro tibi sumitque tuis contacta labellis
pocula ? quis vestrum temerarius usque adeo, quis
perditus, ut dicat regi "bibe"? plurima sunt, quae   130
non audent homines pertusa dicere laena.

116. spumat; radentur.

---

size of geese, and a boar smokes worthy of the steel of yellow-
haired Meleager; after which truffles will be served, if it should
then be spring-time, and the wished-for thunder increases the
bill of fare. "Keep your corn to yourself, O Libya!" says
Allidius; "unyoke your oxen, provided you send us truffles."
Meanwhile, that no *cause for* indignation may be wanting, you
behold the carver skipping and waving his hands with flourishes
of the knife, until he has gone through all the directions of his
professor. Nor, in truth, does it make a trifling difference with
what gestures hares, and with what fowls, are cut up. You
will be dragged by the heels, like a Cacus knocked on the head
by Hercules, and thrust out of doors, if you should ever attempt
to open your mouth about anything, as though you had three
names! When does Virro drink with you, or take the cup con-
taminated by your lips? Which of you is so utterly foolhardy,
or so lost to shame, as to say to the great man, "Drink"?
There are very many things which men dare not say when their

quadringenta tibi si quis deus aut similis dis
et melior fatis donaret homuncio, quantus
ex nihilo fieres, quantus Virronis amicus!
"da Trebio! pone ad Trebium! vis, frater, ab ipsis   135
ilibus?" o nummi, vobis hunc praestat honorem,
vos estis fratres.   dominus tamen et domini rex
si vis tu fieri, nullus tibi parvulus aula
luserit Aeneas nec filia dulcior illo.
iucundum et carum sterilis facit uxor amicum.   140
sed tua nunc Migale pariat licet et pueros tres
in gremium patris fundat simul, ipse loquaci
gaudebit nido, viridem thoraca iubebit
afferri minimasque nuces assemque rogatum,
ad mensam quoties parasitus venerit infans.   145
vilibus ancipites fungi ponentur amicis,
boletus domino, sed quales Claudius edit
ante illum uxoris, post quem nil amplius edit.

142. semel.   146. portentur.

---

cloaks have got holes in them.   If some god, or some little man
like to the gods, and better than the Fates, were to give you
four hundred *sestertia*—from a nobody, what a great man you
would become, what a great friend of Virro's.   "Serve Trebius!
Set before Trebius!   May I help you, *dear* brother, to some of
the tit-bits of the inside?"   O money! it is to you he pays this
honour; it is you who are his brother.   If, however, you wish
to become the lord and king of your lord, let no little Aeneas
play in your halls, nor a daughter yet more endearing than he:
a barren wife makes an agreeable and valued friend.   But, now,
though your Migale should bring forth, and pour three boys at
a birth into the lap of their father, your patron himself will
rejoice in the twittering nest, and will order the green doublet
to be brought in, and the filberts, and the small coin begged for,
as often as the infant parasite shall come to the table.   To his
friends of small account, doubtful-looking funguses will be
served,—a mushroom to my lord; aye, such as Claudius ate
before that one of his wife's, after which he ate nothing more.

Virro sibi et reliquis Virronibus illa iubebit
poma dari, quorum solo pascaris odore,   150
qualia perpetuus Phaeacum autumnus habebat,
credere quae possis surrepta sororibus Afris;
tu scabie frueris mali, quod in aggere rodit
qui tegitur parmá et galeá metuensque flagelli
discit ab hirsutá iaculum torquere capellá.   155
forsitan impensae Virronem parcere credas;
hoc agit, ut doleas; nam quae comoedia, mimus
quis melior plorante gulá? ergo omnia fiunt,
si nescis, ut per lacrimas effundere bilem
cogaris pressoque diu stridere molari.   160
tu tibi liber homo et regis conviva videris;
captum te nidore suae putat ille culinae,
nec male coniectat.   quis enim tam nudus, ut illum
bis ferat, Etruscum puero si contigit aurum
vel nodus tantum et signum de paupere loro?   165
spes bene coenandi vos decipit.   "ecce dabit iam

Virro will order such apples to be handed to himself and the
rest of the Virros as will feast you with their odour alone, such
as the eternal autumn of the Phaeacians possessed, which you
might believe to have been pilfered from the African sisters.
You will enjoy a scabby apple, such as on the rampart he (*the
monkey*) gnaws who is dressed up with a shield and helmet, and,
in dread of the whip, is taught to throw his dart from *the back
of* a shaggy goat. Perhaps you believe Virro to be practising
economy. *No;* he is acting on purpose to annoy you; for
what comedy, what farce is better than disappointed gluttony?
So everything is done, if you do not know it, to compel you to
give vent to your bile by tears, and gnash long with compressed
teeth. You appear to yourself to be a free man, and the great
lord's guest. He thinks you are caught by the savour of his
kitchen; nor does he conjecture amiss; for who so destitute as
to put up with the man a second time if the Etruscan gold *bulla*
has fallen to his lot in boyhood, or even a knot merely, and
a symbol *of freedom* made of humble leather? The hope of

semesum leporem atque aliquid de clunibus apri ;
ad nos iam veniet minor altilis."   inde parato
intactoque omnes et stricto pane tacetis.
ille sapit, qui te sic utitur.   omnia ferre   170
si potes, et debes ; pulsandum vertice raso
praebebis quandoque caput, nec dura timebis
flagra pati his epulis et tali dignus amico.

SATIRA VI.

CREDO Pudicitiam Saturno rege moratam
    in terris visamque diu, cum frigida parvas
praeberet spelunca domos, ignemque laremque
et pecus et dominos communi clauderet umbra,
silvestrem montana torum cum sterneret uxor   5

168. vos.

dining well deceives you.   "See, he is just going to give us a
half-eaten hare and a trifle from the haunch of a boar ; some
of the inferior poultry will be coming to us directly."   For this
reason you are all silent, with your bread ready and untasted,
and grasped *in your hands*.   He is wise who so uses you.   If
you are able to bear everything, you ought *to bear everything*.
Some day or other you will be holding out your head with
shaven crown to be thumped, and won't hesitate to submit to
the sharp whip, *showing yourself* worthy of such a banquet and
of such a friend !

SATIRE VI.

I CAN believe that chastity tarried on earth, and was long seen
in the time of King Saturn ; when the cool cave furnished a
small dwelling, and enclosed fire and household gods, the herd
and its masters in a common shade ; when the mountain wife
spread a rustic couch with leaves and straw, and the skins of

frondibus et culmo vicinarumque ferarum
pellibus, haud similis tibi, Cynthia, nec tibi, cuius
turbavit nitidos exstinctus passer ocellos,
sed potanda ferens infantibus ubera magnis
et saepe horridior glandem ructante marito.   10
quippe aliter tunc orbe novo coeloque recenti
vivebant homines, qui rupto robore nati
compositive luto nullos habuere parentes.
multa pudicitiae veteris vestigia forsan
aut aliqua exstiterint et sub Iove, sed Iove nondum   15
barbato, nondum Graecis iurare paratis
per caput alterius, cum furem nemo timeret
caulibus et pomis, et aperto viveret horto.
paulatim deinde ad superos Astraea recessit
hac comite, atque duae pariter fugere sorores.   20
antiquum et vetus est alienum, Postume, lectum
concutere atque sacri genium contemnere fulcri;
omne aliud crimen mox ferrea protulit aetas,
viderunt primos argentea secula moechos.

---

wild beasts of the neighbourhood; not like to you, Cynthia,
nor to you whose bright eyes the death of a sparrow clouded;
but bearing breasts to be quaffed by her huge infants, and often
more uncouth than her acorn-belching husband.   For indeed
men were living differently then, with a new world and sky
fresh-made, who, born from the riven oak or compounded of
clay, had no parents. Many vestiges of old-world chastity, or
some *at least*, may perhaps have existed even under Jove, but
Jove not yet bearded, when Greeks were not yet prepared to
swear by another's head, when no one feared a thief for his
cabbages and apples, and *every one* lived with an unenclosed
garden. By degrees afterwards Astraea withdrew to the gods
above, with her for a companion, and the two sisters fled at the
same time.   It is *an* ancient and old-world *practice*, Postumus,
to trespass on another's bed, and to contemn the genius of the
sacred couch. Every other crime the period of iron soon produced; the silver age beheld the first adulterers.

Conventum tamen et pactum et sponsalia nostra   25
tempestate paras, iamque a tonsore magistro
pecteris et digito pignus fortasse dedisti.
certe sanus eras. uxorem, Postume, ducis?
dic, qua Tisiphone, quibus exagitare colubris?
ferre potes dominam salvis tot restibus ullam,   30
cum pateant altae caligantesque fenestrae,
cum tibi vicinum se praebeat Aemilius pons?
aut si de multis nullus placet exitus, illud
`nonne putas melius, quod tecum pusio dormit,
pusio, qui noctu non litigat, exigit a te   35
nulla iacens illic munuscula, nec queritur quod
et lateri parcas nec quantum iussit anheles?
sed placet Ursidio lex Iulia, tollere dulcem
cogitat heredem, cariturus turture magno
mullorumque iubis et captatore macello.   40
quid fieri non posse putes, si iungitur ulla
Ursidio, si moechorum notissimus olim
stulta maritali iam porrigit ora capistro,

Yet you are preparing a marriage covenant and settlements
and a betrothal in our time, and are already having your hair
dressed by a master barber, and have perhaps given a pledge for
her finger. Assuredly you used to be sane. Are you taking to
yourself a wife, Postumus? Say by what Tisiphone, by what
snakes are you driven wild? Are you able to bear any lady
paramount when there are so many ropes still in existence;
when high and dizzy windows are open; when the Aemilian
bridge offers itself close at hand to you? Or if, out of *so* many
modes of exit, none pleases you, do you not think this preferable
that a boy sleeps with you; a boy who does not dispute at
night, exacts from you, as he lies there, no little presents, and
does not complain that you neglect him? But the Julian law
pleases Ursidius; he thinks to rear a sweet heir, though he will
lose the fine turtle-dove, and the bearded mullets, and *the produce of* the fortune-hunting market. What can you suppose
impossible, if any woman is coupled to Ursidius, if that once

quem toties texit perituri cista Latini ?
quid, quod et antiquis uxor de moribus illi   45
quaeritur.   o medici, mediam pertundite venam !
delicias hominis !   Tarpeium limen adora
pronus et auratam Iunoni caede iuvencam,
si tibi contigerit capitis matrona pudici.
paucae adeo Cereris vittas contingere dignae,   50
quarum non timeat pater oscula.   necte coronam
postibus et densos per limina tende corymbos !
unus Hiberinae vir sufficit !   ocius illud
extorquebis, ut haec oculo contenta sit uno.
magna tamen fama est cuiusdam rure paterno   55
viventis.   vivat Gabiis, ut vixit in agro,
vivat Fidenis, et agello cedo paterno.
quis tamen affirmat nil actum in montibus aut in
speluncis ? adeo senuerunt Iuppiter et Mars ?

46. nimiam.

most notorious of adulterers, whom the chest of Latinus in danger of his life has so often concealed, is now offering his foolish
head to the matrimonial halter?   Nay, more, he is looking out
for a wife of even antique morality.   Oh ! doctors, lance him
through the middle vein !   A pretty fellow !   Adore, prostrate,
the Tarpeian threshold, and sacrifice a gilded-*horned* heifer to
Juno, if a matron of modest person has fallen to your happy lot.
So few there are worthy to handle the fillets of Ceres, whose
own fathers do not shrink from their kisses.   Bind the garland
. to your doorposts, and hang thick bunches of flowers across your
gateways.   A single husband satisfies Hiberina !   You will more
readily extort this from her, that she should be content with a
single eye.   However, great is the reputation of a certain some
one living on her father's estate.   Let her live at Gabii as she
has lived in the country, let her live at Fidenae, and I give up
the paternal farm.   And yet who assures us that nothing has
taken place on the hills or in the caves?   Have Jupiter and
Mars grown so old?

Porticibusne tibi monstratur femina voto　　　　　　60
digna tuo, cuneis an habent spectacula totis
quod securus ames quodque inde excerpere possis?
chironomon Ledam molli saltante Bathyllo,
Tuccia vesicae non imperat, Appula gannit
sicut in amplexu subitum et miserabile longum,　　65
attendit Thymele; Thymele tunc rustica discit.
ast aliae, quoties aulaea recondita cessant,
et vacuo clausoque sonant fora sola theatro,
atque a plebeiis longe Megalesia, tristes
personam thyrsumque tenent et subligar Acci.　　70
Urbicus exodio risum movet Atellanae
gestibus Autonoes, hunc diligit Aelia pauper.
solvitur his magno comoedi fibula, sunt quae
Chrysogonum cantare vetent, Hispulla tragoedo
gaudet: an exspectas ut Quintilianus ametur?　　75

75. exspectes.

In *all* the piazzas can a woman be shown you who comes up
to your wishes, or do the public shows contain in all their com-
partments of seats a being whom you might love in security and
thence select? While the effeminate Bathyllus is dancing *the
part of* the pantomimic Leda, Tuccia cannot command her
passions; Appula gives a gasp, as though in a sexual embrace,
sudden and pitiable and long; Thymele watches her, then it is
that Thymele *herself*, rustic that she is *in comparison*, learns
something. But other ladies, whenever the drop-scene is packed
away and at rest, and the law-courts alone resound, while the
theatre is empty and closed, and the Megalesia are *still* a long
way from the Plebeian games, in their dulness handle the mask
and thyrsus and drawers of Accius. Urbicus raises a laugh in
the interlude by the gesticulations of Autonoe of the Atellan
farce; and the poor Aelia is in love with him. For others, the
fibula of the comedian is loosened at a great price: there are
some who prevent Chrysogonus from singing: Hispulla delights
in a tragedian. Do you suppose that Quintilian will be fallen

accipis uxorem, de qua citharoedus Echion
aut Glaphyrus fiat pater Ambrosiusque choraules.
longa per angustos figamus pulpita vicos,
ornentur postes et grandi ianua lauro,
ut testudineo tibi, Lentule, conopeo   80
nobilis Euryalum mirmillonem exprimat infans.
    Nupta senatori comitata est Hippia ludium
ad Pharon et Nilum famosaque moenia Lagi,
prodigia et mores urbis damnante Canopo.
immemor illa domus et coniugis atque sororis   85
nil patriae indulsit, plorantesque improba natos,
utque magis stupeas, ludos Paridemque reliquit.
sed quamquam in magnis opibus plumaque paterna
et segmentatis dormisset parvula cunis,
contempsit pelagus; famam contempserat olim,   90
cuius apud molles minima est iactura cathedras.
Tyrrhenos igitur fluctus lateque sonantem

---

in love with? You receive a wife, by whom the harper Echion,
or Glaphyrus, and Ambrosius, the choral flute-player, may become a father. Let us erect long scaffoldings along the narrow
streets, let the doorposts and gate be adorned with a huge bay,
in order that, in your bed inlaid with tortoise-shell, O Lentulus! your noble infant may present the image of Euryalus, the
gladiator!

    Hippia, married to a senator, accompanied a gladiator to Pharos
and the Nile, and the infamous walls of Lagus,—Canopus *itself*
condemning the portentous exhibitions, and manners of our city.
This woman, unmindful of her home and her husband and her
sister, showed no regard for her country, and shamelessly deserted
her weeping children, and, to amaze you still more, Paris and
the public games. But though, as a child, she had slept in great
luxury, on the soft down of her father's house, and in a cradle
decked with fringes, she made light of the sea; her reputation
she had long made light of, the loss of which is *held to be*
very trifling among the soft litters of the ladies. So then she
bore up against the Tuscan waves and the wide-sounding Ionian,

pertulit Ionium constanti pectore, quamvis
mutandum toties esset mare.   iusta pericli
si ratio est et honesta, timent pavidoque gelantur   95
pectore, nec tremulis possunt insistere plantis :
fortem animum praestant rebus, quas turpiter audent.
si iubeat coniux, durum est conscendere navem ;
tunc sentina gravis, tunc summus vertitur aer :
quae moechum sequitur, stomacho valet.   illa maritum 100
convomit, haec inter nautas et prandet et errat
per puppem et duros gaudet tractare rudentes.
qua tamen exarsit forma, qua capta inventa
Hippia, quid vidit, propter quod ludia dici
sustinuit ? nam Sergiolus iam radere guttur   105
coeperat et secto requiem sperare lacerto ;
praeterea multa in facie deformia, sicut
attritus galea mediisque in naribus ingens
gibbus, et acre malum semper stillantis ocelli.

108. galeae (H. Vales).

with undaunted breast, although the sea had to be changed so
many times.   If there be a reason for incurring danger which is
just and honourable, they are frightened, and turn ice-cold in
their fainting hearts, and cannot stand upon their tottering feet.
They bestow their fortitude of soul upon the things which they
dare *to do* disgracefully.   When the husband bids, it is a dreadful
thing to embark in a ship ; then the bilge-water is offensive,
then the sky is turning upside down : she who follows an adulterer is strong in her stomach.   The former is sick all over her
husband : the latter dines among the sailors, and strolls about
the deck and delights to handle the hard ropes.   Yet by what
personal beauty was Hippia inflamed, by what youthfulness was
she captivated ? what did she see for the sake of which she
endured to be called the gladiator's woman ? For darling Sergius
had already begun to shave his throat, and to hope for repose for
his wounded arm.   Moreover, there were many disfigurements
in his face ; as, for instance, a place worn by his helmet, and a
huge wen in the middle of his nose, and the acrid affliction of an

sed gladiator erat: facit hoc illos Hyacinthos;   110
hoc pueris patriaeque, hoc praetulit illa sorori
atque viro. ferrum est quod amant: hic Sergius idem
accepta rude coepisset Veiento videri.
   Quid privata domus, quid fecerit Hippia, curas?
respice rivales divorum, Claudius audi   115
quae tulerit. dormire virum cum senserat uxor,
ausa Palatino tegetem praeferre cubili,
sumere nocturnos meretrix Augusta cucullos,
linquebat comite ancilla non amplius una,
et nigrum flavo crinem abscondente galero   120
intravit calidum veteri centone lupanar
et cellam vacuam atque suam. tunc nuda papillis
constitit auratis titulum mentita Lyciscae,
ostenditque tuum, generose Britannice, ventrem,
excepit blanda intrantes atque aera poposcit,   125
et resupina iacens multorum absorbuit ictus.

---

ever-trickling eye. But he was a gladiator: this it is that makes
Hyacinthi of them! This it was that she preferred to her boys,
and her country, and her sister, and her husband. It is the
steel that they love. This same Sergius, if he had received his
discharge, would have begun to appear a Veiento.

   Are you interested in the affairs of a private family, in the
doings of a Hippia? Look to the rivals of "the gods;" hear
what Claudius underwent. As soon as his wife had perceived that
her husband was sleeping, the imperial harlot, daring to prefer
a coarse bed-rug to her couch on the Palatine, and to put on a
nocturnal hood, used to leave with not more than one maid for
her companion. Then, with a yellow wig concealing her dark
hair, she entered a brothel, kept warm by an old curtain of
patchwork, and a cell vacant and devoted to her use. There
she took her stand, naked, with gilded nipples, having falsely
assumed the ticket of Lycisca, and exhibited the belly which
bore you, noble Britannicus. She received such as entered
caressingly, and asked for money; and, lying on her back, submitted to the embraces of many. Before long, the keeper of

mox lenone suas iam dimittente puellas
tristis abit, et, quod potuit, tamen ultima cellam
clausit, adhuc ardens rigidae tentigine vulvae,
et lassata viris nec dum satiata recessit,   130
obscurisque genis turpis fumoque lucernae
foeda lupanaris tulit ad pulvinar odorem.
hippomanes carmenque loquar coctumque venenum
privignoque datum? faciunt graviora coactae
imperio sexus minimumque libidine peccant.   135

    Optima sed quare Caesennia teste marito?
bis quingenta dedit: tanti vocat ille pudicam,
nec pharetris Veneris macer est aut lampade fervet;
inde faces ardent, veniunt a dote sagittae.
libertas emitur: coram licet innuat atque   140
rescribat, vidua est, locuples quae nupsit avaro.

    Cur desiderio Bibulae Sertorius ardet?
si verum excutias, facies non uxor amatur.

---

the brothel by this time dismissing his girls, reluctantly she
departed, and yet to the best of her power she was the last to
close her cell, still burning with the excitement of strong desire;
so, fatigued by her lovers, though not yet sated, she retired, and
foul with her dirty cheeks, and begrimed with the smoke of the
lamp, she bore the odour of the brothel to the imperial couch.
Shall I speak of magic potions and incantations and poison
prepared and administered to a stepson? They perpetrate still
graver crimes when urged by the empire of their sex: the sins
they commit through lust are the least.

    Then why is Caesennia the best of women on her husband's
showing? She brought him twice five hundred sestertia; such
is the price at which he calls her chaste, nor is he emaciated by
the quivers of Venus, nor does he burn with her torch; this is
the source at which his flames are lit, the arrows come from the
dowry. She buys her liberty; she may make signals in his
presence, and reply *to love-letters*: a rich woman who is married
to an avaricious man is *as good as* a single woman.

    Why does Sertorius burn with passion for Bibula? If you

tres rugae subeant et se cutis arida laxet,
fiant obscuri dentes oculique minores, 145
" collige sarcinulas," dicet libertus, " et exi !
iam gravis es nobis et saepe emungeris, exi
ocius et propera : sicco venit altera naso."
interea calet et regnat poscitque maritum
pastores et ovem Canusinam ulmosque Falernas, 150
quantulum in hoc ! pueros omnes, ergastula tota,
quodque domi non est sed habet vicinus ematur.
mense quidem brumae, quo iam mercator Iason
clausus et armatis obstat casa candida nautis,
grandia tolluntur crystallina, maxima rursus 155
murrina, deinde adamas notissimus et Bernices
in digito factus pretiosior; hunc dedit olim
barbarus incestae, dedit hunc Agrippa sorori,
observant ubi festa mero pede sabbata reges,
et vetus indulget senibus clementia porcis. 160

---

search out the truth, it is the face, not the wife, that is loved.
Let *but* three wrinkles make their appearance, and the dry skin
shrivel itself, let her teeth become black and her eyes smaller,
" Pack up your traps," the freedman will say, " and be off. You
are grown offensive to us, and you blow your nose *too* often ; be off
at once, and make haste. Another wife is coming with a dry nose."
Meanwhile she is fiery and imperious, and asks her husband for
shepherds and sheep from Canusium and Falernian elms—a
mere trifle this !—for all the boys *she sees,* for whole gangs of
slaves, and what is not in the house, and a neighbour has got,
must be bought *for her.* In the winter months, indeed, when
now *the fresco of* merchant Jason is hidden, and the white booth
shuts in the armed sailors, large crystal vases are carried off *by
her,* and again huge pieces of porcelain, and then a diamond of
great repute, made more precious *by having been worn* on the
finger of Berenice. This a barbarian *king* once gave to his
incestuous love. This Agrippa gave to his sister, where kings
observe their festive Sabbaths with naked feet, and long-
established clemency is indulgent to aged pigs.

Nullane de tantis gregibus tibi digna videtur?
sit formosa decens dives fecunda, vetustos
porticibus disponat avos, intactior omni
crinibus effusis bellum dirimente Sabina,
rara avis in terris nigroque simillima cygno,   · 165
quis ferat uxorem, cui constant omnia? malo,
malo Venusinam, quam te, Cornelia mater
Gracchorum, si cum magnis virtutibus affers
grande supercilium et numeras in dote triumphos.
tolle tuum, precor, Hannibalem victumque Syphacem   170
in castris et cum tota Carthagine migra!
"parce, precor, Paean, et tu depone sagittas;
nil pueri faciunt, ipsam configite matrem!"
Amphion clamat, sed Paean contrahit arcum.
extulit ergo greges natorum ipsumque parentem,   175
dum sibi nobilior Latonae gente videtur
atque eadem scrofa Niobe fecundior alba.
quae tanti gravitas, quae forma, ut se tibi semper

166. feret.

Does no woman, *then*, out of such large herds, appear to you
worthy? Let her be handsome, graceful, rich, fruitful; let her
distribute her ancient forefathers in her corridors; more chaste
than any of the Sabine women, who, with streaming locks,
decided the war—a rare bird upon earth, and very much resembling a black swan—who could bear a wife in whom all qualities
are conjoined? I prefer—*yes*, I prefer—a Venusian *country-
woman* to you, Cornelia, mother of the Gracchi, if, with your
great virtues, you bring your lofty pride and reckon your
triumphs in your dowry. Be off, I pray, with your Hannibal
and your Syphax conquered in the camp, and tramp with the
whole of your Carthage. "Be merciful, I pray you, Paean;
and do you, *Diana*, lay down your arrows. The boys are doing
nothing; transfix the mother herself!" Amphion cries; but
Paean bends his bow. So Niobe bore to their graves her herds
of children and their parent himself, while she seemed to herself
more noble than the race of Latona, and, at the same time, more

imputet ? huius enim rari summique voluptas
nulla boni, quoties animo corrupta superbo   180
plus aloes quam mellis habet.   quis deditus autem
usque adeo est, ut non illam, quem laudibus effert,
horreat inque diem septenis oderit horis ?

Quaedam parva quidem, sed non toleranda maritis.
nam quid rancidius, quam quod se non putat ulla   185
formosam, nisi quae de Tusca Graecula facta est,
de Sulmonensi mera Cecropis ? omnia Graece,
cum sit turpe magis nostris nescire Latine.
hoc sermone pavent, hoc iram gaudia curas,
hoc cuncta effundunt animi secreta.   quid ultra ?   190
concumbunt Graece.   donec tamen ista puellis,
tune etiam, quam sextus et octogesimus annus
pulsat, adhuc Graece ? non est hic sermo pudicus
in vetula.   quoties lascivum intervenit illud

185. num (Heinr) ; putet.   192. tunc etiam.

---

prolific than the white sow. What dignity, what beauty can
be of such great price, that she should always reckon herself
your creditor ? For all pleasure in these rare and consummate
advantages is *rendered* null, whenever, spoilt by her pride of
soul, she has more of the aloe than the honey. Who, rather, is
so utterly made over as not to loathe her whom he extols with
his praises, as not to hate her for seven hours in the day?
There are some things, small *in themselves*, it is true, but
intolerable to husbands. For what more nauseous than that
not one of them thinks herself beautiful, unless from a Tuscan
she has become a Greekling ; from a native of Sulmo, a pure
Athenian. Everything in Greek, whereas it is a greater disgrace
to our people to be ignorant of Latin. In this language they
give vent to their fears ; in this they pour forth their anger,
joys, cares—all the secrets of their souls. What more *can they
do ?* They embrace in the Greek fashion. Yet one may concede
such things to girls. But do you, too, whom your six-and-
eightieth year is buffeting, still speak Greek ? That language is
not decent in an old woman. How often does that wanton Ζωὴ

ζωὴ καὶ ψυχή! modo sub lodice relictis   195
uteris in turba. quod enim non excitet inguen
vox blanda et nequam ? digitos habet.   Ut tamen omnes
subsidant pennae, dicas haec mollius Haemo
quamquam et Carpophoro.   Facies tua computat annos.
   Si tibi legitimis pactam iunctamque tabellis   200
non es amaturus, ducendi nulla videtur
causa, nec est quare coenam et mustacea perdas,
labente officio crudis donanda, nec illud,
quod prima pro nocte datur, cum lance beata
Dacicus et scripto radiat Germanicus auro.   205
si tibi simplicitas uxoria, deditus uni
est animus, summitte caput cervice parata
ferre iugum : nullam invenies quae parcat amanti ;
ardeat ipsa licet, tormentis gaudet amantis
et spoliis. igitur longe minus utilis illi   210

197. digitos valet (Heinr).   198. pinnae.

καὶ ψυχή (*my life and soul!*) come in ! You use in the crowd
words you have just left under the counterpane. Whose passions,
indeed, would not be excited by the coaxing and naughty
expression ?   It seems to have fingers ; yet so that, for all that,
every one's pinions droop, though you speak these words more
softly than Haemus or Carpophorus.   Your face reckons up
your years !
   If you are not likely to love her who is engaged and united
to you by a lawful contract, there seems to be no reason for
marrying ; nor is there any object in your wasting a supper, and
the wedding-cakes which will have to be bestowed, at the close
of their attendance, on people *already* surfeited, or that *present*
which is given for the first night, when in the rich dish
"Dacicus" and "Germanicus" glitter on the inscribed gold
coin.   If yours is an uxorious simplicity, your soul is surrendered
to one person.   Bow down your head, with neck prepared to
bear the yoke ; you will find none to spare the man who loves
her.   Though she be enamoured herself, she delights in tormenting and plundering the loved one.   Therefore, a wife will be

uxor, quisquis erit bonus optandusque maritus.
nil umquam invita donabis coniuge, vendes
hac obstante nihil, nihil, haec si nolet, emetur;
haec dabit affectus, ille excludetur amicus
iam senior, cuius barbam tua ianua vidit.   215
testandi cum sit lenonibus atque lanistis
libertas et iuris idem contingat arenae,
non unus tibi rivalis dictabitur heres.
"pone crucem servo." "meruit quo crimine servus
supplicium? quis testis adest? quis detulit? audi;   220
nulla umquam de morte hominis cunctatio longa est."
"o demens, ita servus homo est? nil fecerit, esto:
hoc volo, sic iubeo, sit pro ratione voluntas."

   Imperat ergo viro, sed mox haec regna relinquit
permutatque domos et flammea conterit, inde   225
avolat et spreti repetit vestigia lecti.

---

far less advantageous to him who is likely to be a good and
desirable husband. You will give nothing away, at any time,
without the consent of your wife; you will sell nothing if she
opposes; nothing will be bought if she disapprove. She will
prescribe your regards. Yonder old friend will be denied
admittance, whose *youthful* beard your gate beheld. While
pimps and trainers have the liberty to make a will, and the
same amount of right is enjoyed by the arena, *the name of* more
than one rival will be dictated to you as a legatee. "Put up a
cross for the slave." "On what charge has the slave deserved
punishment? Who presents himself as a witness? Who has
informed against him? Hear *what he has to say!* No delay
is *too* long when the death of a man is in question." "O
driveller! so then a slave is a man? He has done nothing,
you say—granted! Such is my will, so I order it; my pleasure
must stand for a reason."

   She rules over her husband accordingly. But soon she leaves
these realms of hers, and changes her homes, and wears out her

ornatas paulo ante fores, pendentia linquit
vela domus et adhuc virides in limine ramos.
sic crescit numerus, sic fiunt octo mariti
quinque per autumnos, titulo res digna sepulcri.   230
    Desperanda tibi salva concordia socru.
illa docet spoliis nudi gaudere mariti,
illa docet missis a corruptore tabellis
nil rude nec simplex rescribere, decipit illa
custodes aut aere domat. tunc corpore sano   235
advocat Archigenen onerosaque pallia iactat;
abditus interea latet et secretus adulter,
impatiensque morae pavet et praeputia ducit.
scilicet exspectas ut tradat mater honestos
atque alios mores quam quos habet? utile porro   240
filiolam turpi vetulae producere turpem.
    Nulla fere causa est, in qua non femina litem

237. securus.   239. exspectes.   240. aut alios.

---

bridal-veils; thence she flies away and returns to seek again her
imprint in the bed she had spurned. She leaves the doors
ornamented *but* a little while before, the hanging draperies on
the house, and the boughs still green over the threshold. So
the number grows; so it is that eight husbands are manufactured
in five autumns—a thing worthy of an inscription on her tomb!
    You must give up all hope of concord while your mother-in-
law is alive. She it is who teaches how to delight in the spoils
of a helpless husband; she it is who teaches how to write no
ignorant nor innocent reply to notes sent by the seducer; she
deceives your spies, or overcomes them with a bribe; then,
though sound in health, she (*the daughter*) calls in Archigenes,
and tosses the bed-clothes as too heavy for her. Meanwhile,
the adulterer lies concealed, hidden away and all alone, and,
impatient of delay, is in a tremor of anticipation. Can you
expect, forsooth, that the mother will teach good morals, or any
others than her own? Besides, it is useful to a wicked old
woman to bring up her young daughter to be wicked *too*.
    There is scarce any cause in which a woman has not set the

moverit. accusat Manilia, si rea non est.
componunt ipsae per se formantque libellos,
principium atque locos Celso dictare paratae.   245
    Endromidas Tyrias et femineum ceroma
quis nescit? vel quis non vidit vulnera pali?
quem cavat assiduis sudibus scutoque lacessit,
atque omnes implet numeros, dignissima prorsus
florali matrona tuba, nisi si quid in illo   250
pectore plus agitat veraeque paratur arenae.
quem praestare potest mulier galeata pudorem,
quae fugit a sexu? vires amat. haec tamen ipsa
vir nollet fieri; nam quantula nostra voluptas!
quale decus, rerum si coniugis auctio fiat,   255
balteus et manicae et cristae crurisque sinistri
dimidium tegmen! vel si diversa movebit
proelia, tu felix ocreas vendente puella!

    248. rudibus (Lipsius).   257. tegimen.

---

suit going. Manilia is the prosecutrix, if she is not the de-
fendant. They themselves compose, unaided, and fashion
Plaints, prepared to dictate exordium and "points" to Celsus
himself.

    Who does not know the wrappers of Tyrian purple, and the
ointment for female use? Or who has not seen the wounds
inflicted on the training-post, which she pierces with perpetual
foil, and excites with her shield, while she goes through all her
exercises; a matron truly most worthy of the trumpet of the
Floralia, unless, indeed, she meditates something more in that
breast of hers, and is being prepared for a real arena. What
sense of shame can a woman exhibit who wears a helmet, and
flies from her sex? She loves strength. Yet this very woman
would be unwilling to be turned into a man; for how small, *in
comparison*, is our pleasure! What a pretty thing if an auction
of your wife's property were to take place—the belt, and
gauntlets, and crests, and a half covering for the left leg; or if
she takes to other sorts of fighting, happy fellow *you will be*,
with your young wife selling her greaves. These are the women

hac sunt quae tenui sudant in cyclade, quarum
delicias et panniculus bombycinus urit.   260
aspice quo fremitu monstratos perferat ictus,
et quanto galeae curvetur pondere, quanta
poplitibus sedeat, quam denso fascia libro,
et ride, positis scaphium cum sumitur armis.
dicite vos neptes Lepidi caecive Metelli,   '265
Gurgitis aut Fabii, quae ludia sumpserit umquam
hos habitus?   quando ad palum gemat uxor Asyli?
   Semper habet lites alternaque iurgia lectus,
in quo nupta iacet; minimum dormitur in illo.
tunc gravis illa viro, tunc orba tigride peior,   270
cum simulat gemitus occulti conscia facti,
aut odit pueros, aut ficta pellice plorat,
uberibus semper lacrimis semperque paratis
in statione sua, atque exspectantibus illam,
quo iubeat manare modo.   tu credis amorem,   275

---

who perspire under a robe of thin material, whose delicate
charms even a small rag of silk oppresses with heat.   See, with
what a cry she deals home the thrusts which have been shown
her; how she is bent beneath the great weight of her helmet,
what huge leggings, *bound* with what thick bark, are seated on
her knees—and laugh, when laying down her arms, she takes
up the chamber-pot.   Tell us, ye grand-daughters of Lepidus,
or of blind Metellus, or of Fabius Gurges, what gladiator's wife
ever assumed such attire as this?   When did the wife of Asylus
gasp at the training-post?
   The bed in which the bride lies is always the scene of quarrels
and mutual recriminations: there is very little sleep to be got
there.   Then is she a torment to her husband; then is she
worse than a tigress deprived of her young; when she counter-
feits groans, though conscious of her hidden guilt, or loathes the
slave-boys, or cries over a fictitious rival, with tears always
copious, and always ready at their station, and awaiting her
signal to flow in whatever way she orders them.   You think it
is *all* love; you are delighted with yourself then, you hedge-

tu tibi tunc curruca places fletumque labellis
exsorbes, quae scripta et quas lecture tabellas,
si tibi zelotypae retegantur scrinia moechae.
sed iacet in servi complexibus aut equitis.   dic,
dic aliquem, sodes, hic, Quintiliane, colorem.   280
" haeremus, dic ipsa."   " olim convenerat " inquit
" ut faceres tu quod velles, nec non ego possem
indulgere mihi.   clames licet et mare coelo
confundas, homo. sum."   nihil est audacius illis
deprensis : iram atque animos a crimine sumunt.   285
     Unde haec monstra tamen vel quo de fonte requiris ?
praestabat castas humilis fortuna Latinas
quondam, nec vitiis contingi parva sinebat
tecta labor somnique breves et vellere Tusco
vexatae duraeque manus ac proximus urbi   290
Hannibal et stantes Collina turre mariti.
nunc patimur longae pacis mala, saevior armis

276. uruca.   277. quot.   285. animum de crimine.   291. in turre.

---

sparrow, and dry her tears with your lips—*you* who would read
such letters and such billets-doux, if the desk of this jealous
adulteress were thrown open to you ! But she lies in the
embraces of a slave or a knight. Give us, give us, I pray you,
Quintilian, some colourable excuse in this case. "I am at a
loss. Give one yourself." "It had long since been agreed upon
between us," says she, "that you should do what you choose,
and that I too might please myself. You may clamour, if you
please, and confound sea with sky, I am a human being." There
is nothing more audacious than they are when caught in the act.
They derive fury and courage from their crime itself.

     Yet do you seek to know whence, or from what source, *came*
these prodigies? In days of yore, their humble fortune preserved the Latin women chaste, and their lowly roofs were kept
from the contamination of vice by toil, by short slumbers, by
hands galled and hardened with the Tuscan fleece, and Hannibal
close to the city, and their husbands standing *on guard* on the
Colline tower. Now we suffer the evils of long peace ; luxury,

luxuria incubuit victumque ulciscitur orbem.
nullum crimen abest facinusque libidinis, ex quo
paupertas Romana perit, hinc fluxit ad istos   295
et Sybaris colles, hinc et Rhodos et Miletos
atque coronatum et petulans madidumque Tarentum.
prima peregrinos obscena pecunia mores
intulit, et turpi fregerunt secula luxu
divitiae molles.   quid enim Venus ebria curat ?   300
inguinis et capitis quae sint discrimina, nescit
grandia quae mediis iam noctibus ostrea mordet,
cum perfusa mero spumant unguenta Falerno,
cum bibitur concha, cum iam vertigine tectum
ambulat et geminis exsurgit mensa lucernis.   305
i nunc et dubita qua sorbeat aera sanna
Tullia, quid dicat notae collactia Maurae,
Maura Pudicitiae veterem cum praeterit aram ;
noctibus hic ponunt lecticas, micturiunt hic
effigiemque deae longis siphonibus implent,   310

295. Indos, Istros.

---

more cruel than war, broods over us and avenges a conquered
world. No crime is wanting, or deed of lust, from the time
that Roman poverty came to an end ; henceforth Sybaris flowed
to these hills, and Rhodes and Miletus, and garlanded, saucy,
drunken Tarentum. Filthy money first brought in foreign
manners, and voluptuous wealth enervated the age with foul
luxury. For what does Venus in her cups care for ? She does
not know the difference between one part of the person and
another, who at very midnight bites huge oysters, when unguents
foam mixed with neat Falernian, when they drink out of the
perfume-jar, when the ceiling has begun to go round and round,
and the table rises up with its lamps doubled. Go now and
doubt with what a sneer Tullia snuffs the air, *or* what her foster-
sister says to the notorious Maura, when Maura passes by the
ancient altar of chastity. Here they set down their litters at
night, here they make water, and bedew the effigy of the
goddess with copious streams of moisture, and by turns indulge

inque vices equitant ac luna teste moventur,
inde domos abeunt; tu calcas luce reversa
coniugis urinam magnos visurus amicos.
nota bonae secreta deae, cum tibia lumbos
incitat et cornu pariter vinoque feruntur   315
attonitae crinemque rotant ululantque Priapum
maenades.   o quantus tunc illis mentibus ardor
concubitus! quae vox saltante libidine! quantus
ille meri veteris per crura madentia torrens!
lenonum ancillas posita Saufeia corona   320
provocat et tollit pendentis praemia coxae,
ipsa Medullinae fluctum crissantis adorat:
palmam inter dominas virtus natalibus aequat.
nil ibi per ludum simulabitur, omnia fient
ad verum, quibus incendi iam frigidus aevo   325
Laomedontiades et Nestoris hernia possit.
tunc prurigo morae impatiens, tunc femina simplex,

316. Priapo, Priapi, ululante Priapo.   324. tibi.

---

in their wanton practices, with the moon for a witness. Then
they go off home; you, when daylight has returned, meet with
traces of your wife, on your way to visit your great friends.
Notorious are the secret rites of Bona Dea, when the pipe stimu-
lates the loins, and the Maenades, inspired alike by the horn-
instrument and by wine, whirl their locks and howl out Priapus.
Oh, how great is then the sexual desire in these minds! What
a voice *is theirs* with the lust dancing *within them!* What a
torrent is that of old wine over their soaking legs! Saufeia, a
prize being proposed, challenges the brothel-keepers' girls, and
carries off the victory in the amatory contest. She herself
admires the lascivious motions of the wanton Medullina. Among
these great ladies, the prowess shown puts such a victory on an
equality with the glories of birth. There, nothing will be
feigned in sport; everything will be done to the life, by which
the son of Laomedon, already frozen with age, or the ruptured
Nestor might be fired. Then there is lechery impatient of
delay, then there is woman without any disguise. And a shout

ac pariter toto repetitus clamor ab antro :
" iam fas est; admitte viros ! " iam dormit adulter,
illa iubet sumpto iuvenem properare cucullo;   330
si nihil est, servis incurritur; abstuleris spem
servorum, venit et conductus aquarius; hic si
quaeritur et desunt homines, mora nulla per ipsam,
quominus imposito clunem summittat asello.
atque utinam ritus veteres et publica saltem   335
his intacta malis agerentur sacra ! sed omnes
noverunt Mauri atque Indi, quae psaltria penem
maiorem quam sunt duo Caesaris Anticatones,
illuc, testiculi sibi conscius unde fugit mus,
intulerit, ubi velari pictura iubetur,   340
quaecumque alterius sexus imitata figuram est.
et quis tunc hominum contemptor numinis ? aut quis
simpuvium ridere Numae nigrumque catinum
et Vaticano fragiles de monte patellas
ausus erat ? sed nunc ad quas non Clodius aras ?   345

328. it toto ; repetitur.   329. dormitat.   332. veniat, veniet.

---

is repeated in unison from the whole den, " Now is the appointed
time, admit the men." *If* her gallant is already asleep, she
orders the youth to hurry *thither*, with his hood on. If there
be none, they make a rush upon the slaves. Take away the
hope of slaves, and even a hired water-carrier makes his appearance. If such an one is sought *in vain*, and men fail, they will
fly to any expedient. And I would that at least our ancient
rites and public religious ceremonies were conducted free from
such scandals; but all the Moors and Indians know what
" female musician " introduced his person, larger than are two
Anticatones of Caesar, into that place, whence even a mouse,
conscious of being a male, runs away, where a picture is ordered
to be veiled in every case where it represents the form of the
opposite sex. Yet who of men was at that time a contemner of
divine power? or who had dared to laugh at the ladle of Numa,
or the dark earthenware dish, or the brittle vessels from the
Vatican hill? But now at what altars is there not a Clodius?

Audio quid veteres olim monentis amici.
"pone seram, cohibe." sed quis custodiet ipsos
custodes ? cauta est et ab illis incipit uxor.
iamque eadem summis pariter minimisque libido,
nec melior, silicem pedibus quae conterit atrum,   350
quam quae longorum vehitur cervice Syrorum.
  Ut spectet ludos, conducit Ogulnia vestem,
conducit comites sellam cervical amicas
nutricem et flavam, cui det mandata, puellam.
haec tamen argenti superest quodcumque paterni   355
levibus athletis et vasa novissima donat ;
multis res angusta domi, sed nulla pudorem
paupertatis habet, nec se metitur ad illum,
quem dedit haec posuitque modum. tamen utile quid sit
prospiciunt aliquando viri, frigusque famemque   360
formica tandem quidam expavere magistra ;
prodiga non sentit pereuntem femina censum,

I hear what you, my old friends, have long since been advising.
"Fasten the bolt, put her under restraint." But who is to keep
watch over the watchers themselves? The wife is cunning and
begins with them. And now there is the same wantonness in
the highest and in the lowest as well; nor is she better who
wears the dark stone pavement with her feet, than the one who
is carried on the heads of tall Syrians.

  In order to witness the games, Ogulnia hires a dress, hires
attendants, a sedan, a cushion, female friends, a nurse, and a
yellow-haired girl to give her orders to. Yet this woman gives
away whatever remains of the family plate and the last of her
vessels to smooth athletes. Many of them are in straitened
circumstances at home ; but none of them respects her poverty,
nor measures herself to the standard which it has allotted and
assigned her. Yet men do occasionally look forward to what
may be for their advantage, and some, with the ant for their
teacher, have at length felt a dread of cold and hunger. An
extravagant woman does not perceive that her fortune is wasting
away and, as though the coin would always sprout with fresh

ac velut exhausta redivivus pullulet arca
nummus et e pleno tollatur semper acervo,
non umquam reputant quanti sibi gaudia constent. 365
   Sunt quas eunuchi imbelles ac mollia semper
oscula delectent et desperatio barbae,
et quod abortivo non est opus ; illa voluptas
summa tamen, quod iam calida matura iuventa
inguina traduntur medicis, iam pectine nigro. 370
ergo spectatos ac iussos crescere primum
testiculos, postquam coeperunt esse bilibres,
tonsoris damno tantum rapit Heliodorus.
conspicuus longe cunctisque notabilis intrat
balnea, nec dubie custodem vitis et horti 375
provocat a domina factus spado. dormiat ille
cum domina, sed tu iam durum, Postume, iamque
tondendum eunucho Bromium committere noli.
   Si gaudet cantu, nullius fibula durat
vocem vendentis praetoribus, organa semper 380
in manibus, densi radiant testudine tota

365. reputat.   371. exspectatos.   379. dura est.

---

life from the exhausted strong-box, and there would always be
a full heap to take from, they never reckon what a great price
their pleasures cost them.

There are women whom unwarlike eunuchs, and kisses ever
effeminate, delight, and the despair of a beard, and the absence
of any need for abortives. Yet the height of their pleasure is
when a youth already glowing with manhood is submitted to
Heliodorus, who performs an operation to the loss of the barber
alone. Conspicuous from afar, and remarkable to all, he enters
the baths, and challenges without question the guardian of our
vines and gardens—made into an eunuch by his mistress. Let
him sleep with his mistress ; but do not you, Postumus, entrust
Bromius, by this time an adult and ready to have his locks
shorn, to the eunuch.

If she delights in singing, the fibula of no one who sells his
voice to the Praetor can last. Musical instruments are always

sardonyches, crispo numerantur pectine chordae,
quo tener Hedymeles operam dedit, hunc tenet, hoc se
solatur gratoque indulget basia plectro.
quaedam de numero Lamiarum ac nominis alti   385
cum farre et vino Ianum Vestamque rogabat,
an Capitolinam deberet Pollio quercum
sperare et fidibus promittere. quid faceret plus
aegrotante viro, medicis quid tristibus erga
filiolum? stetit ante aram, nec turpe putavit   390
pro cithara velare caput, dictataque verba
pertulit, ut mos est, et aperta palluit agna.
dic mihi nunc, quaeso, dic, antiquissime divum,
respondes his, Iane pater? magna otia coeli;
non est, quod video, non est quod agatur apud vos.   395
haec de comoedis te consulit, illa tragoedum
commendare volet, varicosus fiet haruspex.

> 392. protulit.   395. ut video; quid agatur.

---

in her hands; the numerous sardonyxes sparkle all over the
tortoise-shell; the chords are run over by the vibrating quill
with which soft Hedymeles performed: this she holds, with
this she solaces herself, and favours with kisses the dear plec-
trum. A lady of the order of the Lamiae, and of lofty name,
used to ask of Janus and Vesta, with meal and wine *offerings*,
whether Pollio ought to hope for the Capitoline oak-crown and
promise it to his lyre. What more could she have done if her
husband had been ill; what *more* if the physicians had looked
sad about her little son? She stood before the altar and thought
it no disgrace to veil her head for a harper, and went through
the words dictated to her, according to the usage, and turned
pale when the lamb was opened. Tell me now, I pray you, tell
me, most ancient of the gods, Father Janus, do you reply to
these people? There must be great leisure in heaven: there is
not, that I can see, there is not any business than can be trans-
acted among you *gods*. This woman consults you about comedians; another will be wanting to recommend a tragedian.
The soothsayer will become varicose.

Sed cantet potius, quam totam pervolet urbem
audax et coetus possit quam ferre virorum
cumque paludatis ducibus praesente marito   400
ipsa loqui recta facie strictisque mamillis.
haec eadem novit quid toto fiat in orbe,
quid Seres, quid Thraces agant, secreta novercae
et pueri, quis amet, quis diripiatur adulter.
dicet quis viduam praeguantem fecerit et quo   405
mense, quibus verbis concumbat quaeque, modis quot.
instantem regi Armenio Parthoque cometen
prima videt, famam rumoresque illa recentes
excipit ad portas, quosdam facit, isse Niphaten
in populos magnoque illic cuncta arva teneri   410
diluvio, nutare urbes, subsidere terras,
quocumque in trivio, cuicumque est obvia, narrat.
    Nec tamen id vitium magis intolerabile, quam quae

399. quae.   **401.** siccisque.   **404.** decipiatur.
                      413. hoc vitium.

But let her sing rather than that she should fly brazen-faced
through the whole city, and be able to support assemblages of
men, and speak in person to generals in their full-dress cloaks,
in the presence of her husband, with bold visage and breasts
unsheathed.   This same woman knows what is taking place all
over the world; what the Seres, what the Thracians are doing;
the secrets of the stepmother and the youth; who is in love,
what gallant is being struggled for.   She will tell you who got
a single woman with child, and in what month; with what
words every woman submits to caresses, and in how many ways.
She is the first to see the comet which threatens the Armenian
and Parthian king; she intercepts at the city gates the news
and the latest reports; some she invents; that the Niphates
has overwhelmed *whole* populations, and that all the country
there is occupied by a vast deluge, that cities are tottering, that
tracts of land are sinking down, she relates, in every cross-way,
to every one she meets.
    And yet this plague is not more intolerable than she who is

vicinos humiles rapere et concidere loris
exorata solet.   nam si latratibus alti   415
rumpuntur somni, "fustes huc ocius," inquit,
"afferte," atque illis dominum iubet ante feriri,
deinde canem.   gravis occursu, teterrima vultu,
balnea nocte subit, conchas et castra moveri
nocte iubet, magno gaudet sudare tumultu,   420
cum lassata gravi ceciderunt brachia massa,
callidus et cristae digitos impressit aliptes
ac summum dominae femur exclamare coegit.
convivae miseri interea somnoque fameque
urgentur; tandem illa venit rubicundula, totum   425
oenophorum sitiens, plena quod tenditur urna
admotum pedibus, de quo sextarius alter
ducitur ante cibum, rabidam facturus orexim.
dum redit et loto terram ferit intestino,
marmoribus rivi properant, aurata Falernum   430
pelvis olet; nam sic, tamquam alta in dolia longus

---

wont to seize her poor neighbours and cut them to pieces with
whips, in spite of their prayers. For if her sound slumbers are
broken by barkings, "Quick, bring the cudgels here," she says,
and she orders the owner to be first beaten with them, and then
his dog.   Terrible to meet, most awful in visage, she enters the
baths by night; she orders her oil-jars and camp *equipage* to be
moved by night; she delights to perspire in a great tumult,
when her arms have dropped wearied with the heavy dumb-
bells, and the cunning anointer has impressed his fingers on her
person, and has made the top of his mistress's leg smack.   In
the meanwhile, her wretched guests are tormented by sleepiness
and hunger.   At last she appears, all in a glow, thirsting for a
whole flagon, which is filled to the brim with a full measure of
three gallons, and put at her feet, and of this a second pint is
tossed off before her meal, to produce a ravenous appetite.   As
it returns and strikes the earth with the washings of her inside,
the rivulets run along the marble floor, the gilded pan smells of

deciderit serpens, bibit et vomit. ergo maritus
nauseat atque oculis bilem substringit opertis.

Illa tamen gravior, quae cum discumbere coepit,
laudat Virgilium, periturae ignoscit Elissae,   435
committit vates et comparat, inde Maronem
atque alia parte in trutina suspendit Homerum.
cedunt grammatici, vincuntur rhetores, omnis
turba tacet, nec causidicus nec praeco loquatur,
altera nec mulier: verborum tanta cadit vis,   440
tot pariter pelves ac tintinnabula dicas
pulsari. iam nemo tubas, nemo aera fatiget;
una laboranti poterit succurrere lunae.
non habeat matrona, tibi quae iuncta recumbit,
dicendi genus, aut curtum sermone rotato   445
torqueat enthymema, nec historias sciat omnes,
sed quaedam ex libris et non intelligat. odi
hanc ego, quae repetit volvitque Palaemonis artem,

Falernian; for she drinks and vomits just like a serpent that
has tumbled into a tall cask. So her husband turns sick, and
compresses his bile with closed eyes.

Yet she is *still* more offensive, who, as soon as she has taken
her seat at table, praises Virgil, forgives the doomed Elissa
(*Dido*), matches together poets, and compares them; on one
side, suspends Maro, and, on the other side, Homer in the
scales. Grammarians give way, teachers of rhetoric are beaten,
all the assemblage is silent, not even a lawyer nor a public-crier
may speak, nor *indeed* another woman; such a power of words
falls from her, you would say so many pans, so many bells were
being struck at the same time. Let no one henceforth fatigue
trumpets or brasses; single-handed she will be able to succour
the moon in labour. Let not the matron who shares your
marriage-bed possess "a style" of oratory, or hurl with well-
rounded speech a curtailed "enthymema," nor let her know all
histories, but let there be some things from books which she
even does not understand. I hate the woman who is *always*
referring back to and consulting the principles of Palaemon,

servata semper lege et ratione loquendi,
ignotosque mihi tenet antiquaria versus,   450
nec curanda viris opicae castigat amicae
verba; soloecismum liceat fecisse marito.
imponit fiuem sapiens et rebus honestis ;
nam quae docta nimis cupit et facunda videri,
crure tenus medio tunicas succingere debet,   455
caedere Silvano porcum, quadrante lavari.

   Nil non permittit mulier sibi, turpe putat nil,
cum virides gemmas collo circumdedit et cum
auribus extentis magnos commisit elenchos.
intolerabilius nihil est, quam femina dives.   460
interea foeda aspectu ridendaque multo
pane tumet facies aut pinguia Poppaeana
spirat, et hinc miseri viscantur labra mariti.
ad moechum veniunt lota cute.   quando videri

                    464. veniet.

---

always observing the *strict* law and rule of speech, and has by
heart, the female antiquarian, verses unknown to me, and
corrects the expressions of her female friend as barbarous, which
not even men would attend to.   Let a husband be allowed to
commit a solecism !   A wise person places a limit even to
things good *in themselves*.   For she who desires to appear too
learned and too eloquent should gird up a tunic to the middle of
her leg, sacrifice a pig to Silvanus, and bathe for a quadrans *at
the public baths*.
   There is nothing which a woman does not permit herself,
nothing which she thinks discreditable, when she has encircled
her neck with green gems, and when she has inserted huge
pearls in her stretched ears.   There is nothing more insufferable
than a rich woman.   Meanwhile, foul of aspect and ridiculous
her face is puffed out with a quantity of bread, or is redolent of
the greasy Poppaean paste, and by this the lips of her wretched
husband are glued.   They come to the lover with a clean skin.
When is she desirous of appearing handsome at home ?   It is

vult formosa domi ?   moechis foliata parantur,   465
his emitur quidquid graciles huc mittitis Indi.
tandem aperit vultum et tectoria prima reponit,
incipit agnosci, atque illo lacte fovetur,
propter quod secum comites educit asellas,
exsul Hyperboreum si dimittatur ad axem.   470
sed quae mutatis inducitur atque fovetur
tot medicaminibus coctaeque siliginis offas
accipit et madidae, facies dicetur an ulcus ?
   Est pretium curae penitus cognoscere, toto
quid faciant agitentque die.   si nocte maritus   475
aversus iacuit, periit libraria, ponunt
cosmetae tunicas, tarde venisse Liburnus
dicitur et poenas alieni pendere somni
cogitur, hic frangit ferulas, rubet ille flagello,
hic scutica, sunt quae tortoribus annua praestent.   480
verberat atque obiter faciem linit, audit amicas

474. **Est operae pretium.**   479. **flagellis.**

---

for her lovers that unguents are procured; for them is bought
whatever you, ye slender Indians, send hither.   At length she
opens out her face, and removes the first coverings; she begins
to be recognisable, and bathes in that milk, for the sake of
which she would take out she-asses as her suite, if she were
sent in exile to the Hyperborean regions.   But shall a thing
which is overlaid and fomented with so many different medica-
ments, and which receives poultices of boiled and wet flour, be
termed a face or a sore ?

   It is worth while to investigate closely what it is they are
doing and busying themselves about all day.   If at night her
husband has lain with his back to her, her female secretary is-
undone; the valets of the wardrobe have to take off their tunics,
the Liburnian is declared to have come late, and is made to pay
the penalty of another's sleep; one has switches broken on his
back, another grows red under the scourge, another under the
whip; there are women who pay annual salaries to the torturers.
She flogs, and meanwhile anoints her face, listens to her female

aut latum pictae vestis considerat aurum
et caedit, longi relegit transversa diurni
et caedit, donec lassis caedentibus "exi!"
intonet horrendum iam cognitione peracta.   485
praefectura domus Sicula non mitior aula.
nam si constituit solitoque decentius optat
ornari et properat iamque exspectatur in hortis
aut apud Isiacae potius sacraria lenae,
disponit crinem, laceratis ipsa capillis,   490
nuda humero Psecas infelix nudisque mamillis.
"altior hic quare cincinnus?" taurea punit
continuo flexi crimen facinusque capilli.
quid Psecas admisit? quaenam est hic culpa puellae,
si tibi displicuit nasus tuus? altera laevum   495
extendit pectitque comas et volvit in orbem.
est in concilio materna admotaque lanis

> 491. humeros; nudo humero (Rup. and Heinr.)
> 496. flectit.   497. consilio.   497. matrona.

---

friends, or examines the broad gold *border* of an embroidered
dress, and strikes, and reads again the crossed entries on her
large account-book, and strikes on, until, the strikers being
wearied out, "Begone!" she thunders, in a dreadful tone, the
inquisition being now at an end.

The government of her house is no milder than *that* of a
Sicilian court. For if she has made an assignation, and wishes
to be toiletted more becomingly than usual, and is in a hurry,
and is already expected in the gardens, or rather near the
chapels of the procuress Isis, unhappy Psecas arranges her hair,
with her own locks torn, with naked shoulder and naked
breasts. "Why is this curl too high?" Instantly the bull's
hide punishes the crime and guilt of a misplaced hair. What
has Psecas done? What is the girl's fault in this, if your own
nose is not to your taste? Another on the left draws out the
hair and combs it, and rolls it into a circle. In the council is
one who had belonged to her mother, who, having served her
time with the crisping-pin, has a rest, and has been removed to

emerita quae cessat acu ; sententia prima
huius erit, post hanc aetate atque arte minores
censebunt, tamquam famae discrimen agatur   500
aut animae.   tanta est quaerendi cura decoris,
tot premit ordinibus, tot adhuc compagibus altum
aedificat caput.   Andromachen a fronte videbis ;
post minor est, credas aliam.   cedo, si breve parvi
sortita est lateris spatium breviorque videtur   505
virgine Pygmaea, nullis adiuta cothurnis,
et levis erecta consurgit ad oscula planta ?
nulla viri cura interea nec mentio fiet
damnorum, vivit tamquam vicina mariti,
hoc solo propior, quod amicos coniugis odit   510
et servos, gravis est rationibus.
                              Ecce furentis
Bellonae matrisque deum chorus intrat et ingens
semivir, obsceno facies reverenda minori,
mollia qui rapta secuit genitalia testa

        501. tanti.   509. marito.   514. rupta.

---

the wool department : the first opinion will be given by her ;
after her, her inferiors in age and in art will vote as if a question
of reputation or life were at stake, so great is the trouble she takes
in quest of beauty ; with so many tiers does she load, with so
many continuous stories does she build up on high her head.
In front you will see Andromache ; behind she is shorter. You
would think her another person. Tell me *how it will be* if she
has received from nature but a scant dimension of small flank,
and without the aid of buskins seems shorter than a Pigmy
virgin, and must spring up lightly on tiptoe to be kissed. No
care for her husband all this time, nor will mention be made of
his losses ; she lives as though she were her husband's neighbour, in this alone nearer to him, that she hates her consort's
friends and his slaves, and is a drag upon his income.

  Behold ! the chorus of the frantic Bellona, and the mother
of the gods, makes its entrance, and the huge eunuch,—a face
to be revered by the lesser filthy ones,—who has long since cut

iam pridem, cui rauca cohors, cui tympana cedunt   515
plebeia et Phrygia vestitur bucca tiara.
grande sonat metuique iubet Septembris et Austri
adventum, nisi se centum lustraverit ovis
et xerampelinas veteres donaverit ipsi,
ut quidquid subiti et magni discriminis instat,   520
in tunicas eat et totum semel expiet annum.
hibernum fracta glacie descendet in amnem,
ter matutino Tiberi mergetur et ipsis
verticibus timidum caput abluet, inde superbi
totum regis agrum nuda ac tremebunda cruentis   525
crepet genibus, si candida iusserit Io;
ibit ad Aegypti finem calidaque petitas
a Meroe portabit aquas, ut spargat in aedem
Isidis, antiquo quae proxima surgit ovili.
credit enim ipsius dominae se voce moneri.   530
en animam et mentem, cum qua di nocte loquantur!

---

off his soft parts with a hurried potsherd, to whom the hoarse
troop, to whom the timbrels of the herd give place, and whose
cheek is covered with his Phrygian tiara. He talks big, and
bids her dread the approach of September and the south wind,
unless she shall have purified herself with a hundred eggs, and
shall have presented to himself her cast-off murrey-coloured
dresses, that whatever unforeseen or mighty peril is at hand
may pass into the tunics, and make expiation for the whole
year at once. She will descend into the wintry river, after
breaking the ice; she will plunge thrice in the morning Tiber,
and bathe her timid head in its very eddies; thence, naked and
shivering, she will crawl forth with bleeding knees over the
whole field of the proud king, if white Io has commanded her;
she will go to the extremity of Egypt, and bring water fetched
from hot Meroe, to sprinkle on the Temple of Isis, which rises
close to the ancient sheepfold. For she believes herself to be
admonished by the voice of the goddess herself—a pretty soul
and mind for the gods to hold converse with by night! So,

ergo hic praecipuum summumque meretur honorem,
qui grege linigero circumdatus et grege calvo
plangentis populi currit derisor Anubis.
ille petit veniam, quoties non abstinet uxor   535
concubitu sacris observandisque diebus,
magnaque debetur violato poena cadurco,
et movisse caput visa est argentea serpens.
illius lacrimae meditataque murmura praestant
ut veniam culpae non abnuat ansere magno   540
scilicet et tenui popano corruptus Osiris.
    Cum dedit ille locum, cophino foenoque relicto
arcanam Iudaea tremens mendicat in aurem,
interpres legum Solymarum et magna sacerdos
arboris ac summi fida internuntia coeli.   545
implet et illa manum, sed parcius ; aere minuto
qualiacumque voles Iudaei somnia vendunt.
spondet amatorem tenerum vel divitis orbi
testamentum ingens, calidae pulmone columbae
tractato, Armenius vel Commagenus haruspex ;   550

---

then, this is he who deserves the first and highest honour—
Anubis, who, surrounded by his linen-clad herd, and his bald-
headed herd, runs along mocking at the wailing people. He it
is that sues for pardon, as often as the wife does not abstain
from connection on days which are sacred and to be observed,
and a great penalty is owing for a violation of the sheets, and
the silver serpent has been seen to move its head ; his are the
tears and practised mumblings which ensure that Osiris will not
refuse his pardon to her fault, when bribed, forsooth, with a fat
goose and a thin sacrificial cake.

When he has given place, a shivering Jewess, laying aside
basket and hay, begs into her secret ear, interpreter of the laws
of Solyma, great priestess of the tree, and faithful ambassa-
dress from highest heaven ! She, too, fills her hand, but more
sparingly : for a minute coin the Jews sell you whatever kind
of dreams you wish. The soothsayer from Armenia or Comma-

pectora pullorum rimabitur, exta catelli,
interdum et pueri; faciet, quod deferat ipse.
   Chaldaeis sed maior erit fiducia; quidquid
dixerit astrologus, credent a fonte relatum
Hammonis, quoniam Delphis oracula cessant   555
et genus humanum damnat caligo futuri.
praecipuus tamen est horum, qui saepius exsul,
cuius amicitia conducendaque tabella
magnus civis obit et formidatus Othoni.
inde fides artis, sonuit si dextera ferro   560
laevaque, si longo castrorum in carcere mansit.
nemo mathematicus genium indemnatus habebit,
sed qui paene perit, cui vix in Cyclada mitti
contigit et parva tandem caruisse Scripho.
consulit ictericae lento de funere matris,   565
ante tamen de te Tanaquil tua, quando sororem

551. rimatur et.   559. formidandus.

---

gene guarantees a young lover, or a huge inheritance from some
childless rich man, after handling the bowels of a dove still
warm: he inspects the breasts of chickens and the entrails of a
puppy, sometimes of a boy too; he will do *deeds* which he himself will inform about.

   But in Chaldaeans the confidence will be still greater; whatever the astrologer has spoken they will believe to have been
brought back from the spring of Hammon, since at Delphi
the oracles are silent, and darkness as to the future is the
punishment of the human race.   The chief, however, of these
men is he who has been ofttimes an exile, through whose
friendship and venal tablets a great citizen, and one dreaded by
Otho, perished.   Thence comes faith in his art, if his right
hand and left have clanked with fetters, if he has remained a
long while in the camp-prison.   No astrologer who has not been
condemned will *be deemed to* have a genius, but *only* he who
has all but met his death, who has barely had the good fortune
to be sent to one of the Cyclades, and to be set free at last from
small Seriphus.   Your Tanaquil consults him about the tardy

efferat et patruos, an sit victurus adulter
post ipsam; quid enim maius dare numina possunt?
haec tamen ignorat quid sidus triste minetur
Saturni, quo laeta Venus se proferat astro,   570
qui mensis damnis, quae dentur tempora lucro;
illius occursus etiam vitare memento,
in cuius manibus, ceu pinguia sucina, tritas
cernis ephemeridas, quae nullum consulit et iam
consulitur, quae castra viro patriamque petente   575
non ibit pariter numeris revocata Thrasylli.
ad primum lapidem vectari cum placet, hora
sumitur ex libro; si prurit frictus ocelli
angulus, inspecta genesi collyria poscit.
aegra licet iaceat, capiendo nulla videtur   580
aptior hora cibo, nisi quam dederit Petosiris.
si mediocris erit, spatium lustrabit utrimque
metarum, et sortes ducet frontemque manumque

580. capiendi.   581. cibi.

---

approach of her jaundiced mother's death, yet, before that, about
you; when will she bury her sister and her uncles? will her
lover survive her? for what greater boon can the deities bestow?
Yet this woman ignores what Saturn's dismal planet portends,
in what constellation happy Venus presents herself, what month
is to be set down to losses, what seasons to gain. But with
that woman be mindful to shun even a chance meeting in whose
hands you perceive, like clammy amber, the well-worn calendars;
who consults no one, and is by this time herself consulted;
who, if her husband is going to the camp or his native place,
will not go with him if recalled by the calculations of Thrasyllus.
When it is her fancy to be carried as far as the first mile-stone,
the *lucky* hour is taken from a book; if the corner of her eye
itches when rubbed, she consults her horoscope before calling
for salve. Though she be lying sick, no time seems more suitable for taking food than that which Petosiris has directed.
If she be a common person, she will traverse the space on both
sides of the goals, and will draw lots, and will hold out her

praebebit vati crebrum poppysma roganti.
divitibus responsa dabunt Phryx augur et Indus   585
conductus, dabit astrorum mundique peritus
atque aliquis senior, qui publica fulgura condit.
plebeium in circo positum est et in aggere fatum.
quae nullis longum ostendit cervicibus aurum,
consulit ante phalas delphinorumque columnas,   590
an saga vendenti nubat caupone relicto.
    Hae tamen et partus subeunt discrimen et omnes
nutricis tolerant fortuna urgente labores,
sed iacet aurato vix ulla puerpera lecto.
tantum artes huius, tantum medicamina possunt,   595
quae steriles facit atque homines in ventre necandos
conducit.   gaude, infelix, atque ipse bibendum
porrige, quidquid erit; nam si distendere vellet
et vexare uterum pueris salientibus, esses

585. dabit; inde.   589. nudis.   596. sterilem.

---

face and hands to the seer who calls for a frequent smacking-
kiss. To the rich a Phrygian or Indian augur, hired *for the
purpose,* will give responses, or one experienced in the stars and
the sky, or some old man who buries the public thunderbolts.
The destiny of the plebeian is settled in the circus or at the
rampart. She who has no long golden ornaments to show on
her neck inquires in front of the pillars and the dolphin-bearing
columns whether she shall leave the tavern-keeper and marry
the clothesman.

    Yet these not only undergo the dangers of child-bearing, but
also support all the labours of nursing, to which their lot compels them : but scarce any woman lies in confinement on a gilded
bed. Such power have the arts, such power have the drugs of
her who produces sterility, and contracts for hire to slaughter
human beings in the womb. Rejoice, unhappy man, and yourself hand it *to your wife* to drink, whatever it may be ; for if
she chose to distend and torture her womb with leaping boys,
you would perhaps be the father of a blackamoor : before long,

Aethiopis fortasse pater, mox decolor heres 600
impleret tabulas numquam tibi mane videndus.

Transeo suppositos et gaudia votaque saepe
ad spurcos decepta locus, atque inde petitos
pontifices, Salios, Scaurorum nomina falso
corpore laturos.   stat Fortuna improba noctu 605
arridens nudis infantibus, hos fovet omnes
involvitque sinu, domibus tunc porrigit altis
secretumque sibi mimum parat, hos amat, his se
ingerit utque suos ridens producit alumnos.

Hic magicos affert cantus, hic Thessala vendit 610
philtra, quibus valeant mentem vexare mariti
et solea pulsare nates; quod desipis, inde est,
inde animi·caligo et magna oblivio rerum,
quas modo gessisti.   tamen hoc tolerabile, si non
et furere incipias, ut avunculus ille Neronis, 615

603. saepe petitos.   606. blandis.
609. semper producit.   611. valeat.

---

a dark-coloured heir would fill *the chief place in* your will, a
fellow you would not like to meet in the morning.

I pass over supposititious children, and the joys and vows *so*
often cheated at the muddy pools, and the high priests and
Salii thence obtained, destined to bear the names of the Scauri
in their counterfeit persons. Mischievous Fortune stands by
night smiling on the naked babes; all these she cherishes and
folds in her bosom: then she presents them to noble houses,
and prepares for herself a secret farce. These she loves, on these
she presses her attentions, and laughingly brings them on as her
own children.

This fellow brings magical incantations; this one sells Thes-
salian philtres, by which they may have the power to confuse the
mind of a husband, and beat his backside with a slipper. That
you drivel comes from this; thence comes haziness of mind and
entire forgetfulness of the actions you have just performed.
Yet this is endurable, if you do not begin to rave as well, like
that uncle of Nero for whom Caesonia made an infusion of the

cui totam tremuli frontem Caesonia pulli
infudit; quae non faciet quod principis uxor?
ardebant cuncta et fracta compage ruebant
non aliter quam si fecisset Iuno maritum
insanum.   minus ergo nocens erit Agrippinae   620
boletus, siquidem unius praecordia pressit
ille senis tremulumque caput descendere iussit
in coelum et longa manantia labra saliva;
haec poscit ferrum atque ignes, haec potio torquet,
haec lacerat mixtos equitum cum sanguine patres.   625
tanti partus equae, tanti una venefica constat!

 Oderunt natos de pellice; nemo repugnet,
nemo vetet, iam iam privignum occidere fas est.
vos ego, pupilli, moneo, quibus amplior est res,
custodite animas et nulli credite mensae;   630
livida materno fervent adipata veneno.
mordeat ante aliquis quidquid porrexerit illa

626. quanti una venefica; quantum.

---

whole forehead of a shivering foal. What woman will not do
what the Prince's wife did? All things were in flames and falling in ruin, with joints dissevered, not otherwise than if Juno
had made her husband mad. Less baneful, then, will be the
mushroom of Agrippina, inasmuch as that stopped the breath
of a single old man, and bade his trembling pate, and lips dis-
tilling long streams of saliva, to descend into heaven. The
former potion calls for sword and flames, the former causes
tortures and tears to pieces senators, mingled in the slaughter of
knights. So great is the cost of a mare's foal, so great that of
a single sorceress.

 Women hate children born of their husband's mistress:
nobody opposes that, nobody forbids it; long since it is lawful
to murder a stepson. You I warn, ye wards, who have a good
property, keep watch over your lives, and trust to no table:
the dainties which will make you livid burn with the maternal
poison. Let some one taste before you whatever is handed by
her who brought you forth: let your trembling tutor first sip

quae peperit, timidus praegustet pocula pappas.
fingimus haec altum satira sumente cothurnum
scilicet, et finem egressi legemque priorum   635
grande Sophocleo carmen bacchamur hiatu
montibus ignotum Rutulis coeloque Latino?
nos utinam vani! sed clamat Pontia "feci,
confiteor, puerisque meis aconita paravi,
quae deprensa patent. facinus tamen ipsa peregi."   640
tunc duos una, saevissima vipera, coena?
tunc duos? "septem, si septem forte fuissent."
    Credamus tragicis quidquid de Colchide saeva
dicitur et Procne. nil contra conor; et illae
grandia monstra suis audebant temporibus, sed   645
non propter nummos. minor admiratio summis
debetur monstris, quoties facit ira nocentem
hunc sexum; rabie iecur incendente feruntur
praecipites, ut saxa iugis abrupta, quibus mons

643. torva.

---

the wine-cup. Do we invent these things, forsooth, our satire
assuming the lofty buskin of tragedy, and, transgressing the
bounds and the laws of our predecessors, are we raving in the
deep tones of a Sophocles some mighty strain unknown to the
Rutulian hills and the sky of Latium? Ah! would that we
were unreal! But Pontia is crying out, "I did it, I confess,
and prepared aconite for my boys, which facts are discovered
and patent: at any rate I have accomplished the deed with my
own hand." You, then, fellest of vipers, *killed* two *children* at
one meal? You *killed* two? "*Aye;* seven, if there had chanced
to be seven *there.*"

    Let us believe all that is related by the tragic writers of the
fierce Colchian or Procne: I make no attempt to dispute it: and
these women, *no doubt*, were guilty of great prodigies of crime
in their day—but not for the sake of money. Less wonder is
due to the most monstrous acts, in cases where rage makes this
sex criminal: with fury consuming their vitals, they are borne
headlong, like rocks torn from the heights, from which the

subtrahitur clivoque latus pendente recedit.　　　　650
illam ego non tulerim, quae computat et scelus ingens
sana facit.　spectant subeuntem fata mariti
Alcestim et, similis si permutatio detur,
morte viri cupiant animam servare catellae.
occurrent multae tibi Belides atque Eriphylae　　　655
mane, Clytaemnestram nullus non vicus habebit.
hoc tantum refert, quod Tyndaris illa bipennem
insulsam et fatuam dextra laevaque tenebat;
at nunc res agitur tenui pulmone rubetae,
sed tamen et ferro, si praegustabit Atrides　　　660
Pontica ter victi cautus medicamina regis.

---

mountain is withdrawn, while its side recedes from the hanging
declivity. The woman I cannot endure is she who calculates
and commits a great crime in her full senses. They see, *at the
play,* Alcestis undergoing death for her husband, and if a similar
substitution were accorded them, they would wish, at the price
of a husband's death, to save the life of a lapdog. Many Belides
and Eriphylae will run up against you of a morning; no street
that will not have its Clytaemnestra. The only difference is
this, that the daughter of Tyndarus in question wielded a stupid
senseless axe with right and left hand; but nowadays the
business is done with the delicate lung of a toad—and yet with
the steel too, if *her* wary Atrides shall have tasted beforehand
some of the antidotes from Pontus of the thrice-conquered
king.

ET spes et ratio studiorum in Caesare tantum.
   solus enim tristes hac tempestate Camenas
respexit, cum iam celebres notique poetae
balneolum Gabiis, Romae conducere furnos
tentarent, nec foedum alii nec turpe putarent   5
praecones fieri, cum desertis Aganippes
vallibus esuriens migraret in atria Clio.
nam si Pieria quadrans tibi nullus in umbra
ostendatur, ames nomen victumque Machaerae,
et vendas potius commissa quod auctio vendit   10
stantibus, oenophorum tripodes armaria cistas,
Alcithoen Pacci, Thebas et Terea Fausti.
hoc satius, quam si dicas sub iudice " vidi,"
quod non vidisti.   faciant equites Asiani,
quamquam et Cappadoces faciant equitesque Bithyni,   15

       8. arca.

SATIRE VII.

THE hope, as well as the motive, of our studies is in Caesar
only, for he alone has regarded the Camenae, sorrowful in this
age, when celebrated and well-known poets have for some time
been trying to hire a small bath at Gabii or bakehouses at
Rome ; while others have not thought it base or dishonouring
to turn public criers, when, deserting the valleys of Aganippe,
hungry Clio has migrated to the auction-rooms. For if never
a farthing be exhibited to you in the Pierian shade, be content
with the name and calling of Machaera, and sell in preference
what a forced auction sells to the bystanders—a wine-jar, three-
legged tables, cupboards, chests, the " Alcithoe " of Paccius,
the " Thebes " and " Tereus " of Faustus. This is better than
for you to say before the judge, " I saw "—what you did not
see, though Asiatic knights may do it, and Cappadocian and

altera quos nudo traducit Gallia talo.
nemo tamen studiis indignum ferre laborem
cogetur posthac, nectit quicumque canoris
eloquium vocale modis laurumque momordit.
hoc agite, o iuvenes ! circumspicit et stimulat vos   20
materiamque sibi ducis indulgentia quaerit.
si qua aliunde putas rerum exspectanda tuarum
praesidia, atque ideo croceae membrana tabellae
impletur, lignorum aliquid posce ocius et quae
componis dona Veneris, Telesine, marito,   25
aut claude et positos tinea pertunde libellos.
frange miser calamos vigilataque proelia dele,
qui facis in parva sublimia carmina cella,
ut dignus venias hederis et imagine macra.
spes nulla ulterior ; didicit iam dives avarus   30
tantum admirari, tantum laudare disertos,
ut pueri Iunonis avem.   sed defluit aetas

22. spectanda.   23. crocea tabella.   25. conscribis.
28. Sella (Vales).   30. nam.

Bithynian knights, whom Gallo-Graecia exposes to view with
naked feet.   No one, however, will henceforth be compelled to
submit to labour unbecoming his studies, who sets the eloquence
of words to harmonious metres, and has chewed the bay.   Stick
to your work, young men ; the kind favour of the Emperor is
looking round and stimulating you, and seeking materials *for its
exercise.*   If you think that encouragement for your pursuits is
to be expected from any other quarter—and it is with that
view that the parchment in its yellow boards is being filled—
call for a trifle of firewood with all speed, and present what
you are composing, Telesinus, to the husband of Venus, or shut
up your books and let the worm perforate them where they lie.
Break your pens, poor wretch, and rub out the battles you have
spent your nights on, you who write sublime poems in a small
closet, that you may turn out worthy of the ivy *crown* and a
lean bust.   There is no hope beyond ; the stingy rich man has
long learnt only to admire, only to praise the learned, as boys

et pelagi patiens et cassidis atque ligonis.
taedia tunc subeunt animos, tunc seque suamque
Terpsichoren odit facunda et nuda senectus.   35
    Accipe nunc artes ne quid tibi conferat iste
quem colis, et Musarum et Apollinis aede relicta,
ipse facit versus atque uni cedit Homero
propter mille annos, et, si dulcedine famae
succensus recites, maculosas commodat aedes.   40
haec longe ferrata domus servire iubetur,
in qua sollicitas imitatur ianua portas.
scit dare libertos extrema in parte sedentes
ordinis et magnas comitum disponere voces.
nemo dabit regum, quanti subsellia constent   45
et quae conducto pendent anabathra tigillo
quaeque reportandis posita est orchestra cathedris.
nos tamen hoc agimus tenuique in pulvere sulcos

    40. Maculonus, Maculonis.   48. tenuesque.

---

do the bird of Juno. But the time of life is flowing by which
can bear *the fatigues of* the sea, and the helmet, and the spade.
Disgust then steals over the mind ; then old age, eloquent and
naked, hates itself and its own muse.

    Hear now the artful contrivances, not to bestow anything
upon you, of him whom you court, after having deserted the
Temple of the Muses and Apollo. The great man himself
makes verses, and yields to Homer alone, on account of his
thousand years ; and if, excited by the sweets of fame, you
recite, he lends you a dirty apartment. Yonder house, long
barred up, is ordered to serve your purpose, in which the door
resembles the gates of a city in a time of trouble. He knows
how to give you his freedmen, sitting at the extreme back of
the rows, and to dispose *about* the loud voices of his hangers-on.
But none of these rich men will give you what the benches
cost you, or the hired wooden seats, rising one above another,
which hang *from the walls*, and the orchestra, which is set with
chairs, which will have to be returned. Yet we work at these
things, and draw furrows in the soft dust, and turn up the sea-

ducimus et litus sterili versamus aratro.
nam si discedas, laqueo tenet ambitiosi 50
consuetudo mali, tenet insanabile multos
scribendi cacoethes et aegro in corde senescit.
sed vatem egregium, cui non sit publica vena,
qui nihil expositum soleat deducere, nec qui
communi feriat carmen triviale moneta, 55
hunc, qualem nequeo monstrare et sentio tantum,
anxietate carens animus facit, omnis acerbi
impatiens, cupidus silvarum aptusque bibendis
fontibus Aonidum.   neque enim cantare sub antro
Pierio thyrsumve potest contingere moesta 60
paupertas atque aeris inops, quo nocte dieque
corpus eget: satur est, cum dicit Horatius "euoe!"
quis locus ingenio, nisi cum se carmine solo
vexant et dominis Cirrhae Nysaeque feruntur
pectora vestra duas non admittentia curas? 65
magnae mentis opus nec de lodice paranda

50. ambitiosum.   58. avidusque.   65. nostra.

shore with sterile plough.   For if you try to get away, the
habit of the ambitious mischief holds you in a noose; the
incurable disease of writing holds many, and attains to old age
in the sickened heart.   But a poet above the herd, whose vein
is not of a vulgar kind, who is wont to spin nothing commonplace, nor to coin a trivial poem at the public mint, such an
one, whom I am unable to designate, and can only imagine, is
produced by a mind freed from anxiety, exempt from all *the*
bitterness *of life*, longing for the woods, and fitted to drink
from the fountains of the Aonides.   Nor, of a truth, can
poverty, sorrowful and without money, of which by night and
day the body stands in need, sing under the Pierian grotto,
or handle the thyrsus.   Horace is full, when he cries Euoe !
What place is there for genius, save when your breasts, not
admitting two cares, torment themselves with the poetical
strain alone, and are carried along by the lords of Cirrha and
Nysa?   It was the work of a great mind, and one not per-

attonitae, currus et equos faciesque deorum
aspicere et qualis Rutulum confundat Erinnys.
nam si Virgilio puer et tolerabile deesset
hospitium, caderent omnes a crinibus hydri,   70
surda nihil gemeret grave buccina. poscimus ut sit
non minor antiquo Rubrenus Lappa cothurno,
cuius et alveolos et laenam pignerat Atreus.
non habet infelix Numitor quod mittat amico,
Quintillae quod donet habet, nec defuit illi   75
unde emeret multa pascendum carne leonem
iam domitum; constat leviori bellua sumptu
nimirum, et capiunt plus intestina poetae.
contentus fama iaceat Lucanus in hortis
marmoreis, at Serrano tenuique Saleio   80
gloria quantalibet quid erit, si gloria tantum est?
curritur ad vocem iucundam et carmen amicae
Thebaidos, laetam cum fecit Statius urbem

69. desit.

---

plexed about the procuring of a blanket, to behold the chariots
and horses and faces of the gods, and in what shape Erinnys
appalled the Rutulian.   For if a slave and tolerable quarters
had been wanting to Virgil, all the snakes would have fallen
from her locks, the voiceless trumpet would have sounded no
deep tone.   We demand that Rubrenus Lappa should not fall
short of the buskin of the ancients, while his "Atreus" has
obliged him to pawn his sauce-boats and his cloak.   Numitor,
poor fellow, has nothing to send to a friend, but he has something to present to Quintilla; nor was he short of the where-
withal to buy a lion, and a tamed one too, to be fed with much
meat.   Doubtless the beast stands in at a lighter outlay, and a
poet's intestines are more capacious!   Content with his fame,
let Lucan repose in his gardens adorned with marbles; but to
Serranus and starving Saleius, what will be *the value of* ever so
much glory, if it be glory and nothing else?   There is a rush
to the delightful voice, and the strains of the welcome "Thebais,"
when Statius has made the city glad, and appointed a day *for*

promisitque diem : tanta dulcedine captos
afficit ille animos tantaque libidine vulgi   85
auditur ; sed cum fregit subsellia versu,
esurit, intactam Paridi nisi vendat Agaven.
ille et militiae multis largitur honorem,
semestri vatum digitos circumligat auro.
quod non dant proceres, dabit histrio.   tu Camerinos   90
et Bareas, tu nobilium magna atria curas ?
praefectos Pelopea facit, Philomela tribunos.
haud tamen invideas vati quem pulpita pascunt.
quis tibi Maecenas, quis nunc erit aut Proculeius
aut Fabius, quis Cotta iterum, quis Lentulus alter ?   95
tunc par ingenio pretium, tunc utile multis
pallere et vinum toto nescire Decembri.

    Vester porro labor fecundior, historiarum
scriptores ? petit hic plus temporis atque olei plus.
namque oblita modi millesima pagina surgit   100

    99. petitur plus.   100. nullo quippe modo.

---

reciting. So greatly does he charm their enthralled minds, and
with such eagerness on the part of the crowd is he listened to ;
but when he has made the benches resound with his verse, he
starves unless he sells his virgin "Agave" to Paris. He (*Paris*),
besides, confers upon many, military honours, and surrounds the
fingers of poets with the gold ring of *a* six months' *command.*
What the great do not give, a player will give. Do you devote
your attention to the Camerini and the Bareae and the spacious
halls of nobles?   "Pelopea" makes prefects; "Philomela,"
tribunes. Yet do not be angry with the poet whom the boards
feed. Who will be a Maecenas to you ? who will be, nowadays,
either a Proculeius or a Fabius ? who a Cotta over again ? who
a second Lentulus ? Then, there were rewards on a par with
genius ; then it was of service to many to grow pale, and to
ignore wine through the whole of December.

    Is your labour, again, more fruitful, ye writers of histories ?
This is one which demands more time and more *midnight* oil ;
for, oblivious of bounds, the thousandth page springs up for you

omnibus et multa crescit damnosa papyro ;
sic ingens rerum numerus iubet atque operum lex.
quae tamen inde seges, terrae quis fructus apertae ?
quis dabit historico, quantum daret acta legenti ?
  " Sed genus ignavum, quod lecto gaudet et umbra."   105
dic igitur, quid causidicis civilia praestent
officia et magno comites in fasce libelli ?
ipsi magna sonant, sed tunc cum creditor audit
praecipue, vel si tetigit latus acrior illo,
qui venit ad dubium grandi cum codice nomen.   110
tunc immensa cavi spirant mendacia folles
conspuiturque sinus ; veram deprendere messem
si libet, hinc centum patrimonia causidicorum,
parte alia solum russati pone Lacernae.
consedere duces, surgis tu pallidus Aiax   115
dicturus dubia pro libertate, bubulco
iudice.   rumpe miser tensum iecur, ut tibi lasso

101. talibus.   105. tecto.   112. verum.

all, and grows, ruinous from the quantity of paper. So the vast
number of events enjoins, and the conditions of these works.
Yet what is the harvest from all this ? what the fruit from the
ground that has been opened? Who will give an historian as
much as he would give to one to read the news of the day ?
  " But the race is an idle one, which delights in the couch and
the shade."   Say, then, what do their services to the citizens,
and the briefs which accompany them in a huge bundle, bring
in to the lawyers? They talk big, of themselves, but particularly when the creditor is listening, or if some one still more
eager than he has nudged them in the side, who comes to *sue
for* a doubtful debt with a large account-book.   Then *the
lawyer's* hollow bellows exhale enormous lies, and his breast is
all spluttered over.   If you wish to ascertain the real harvest,
put on one side the fortunes of a hundred lawyers, and on the
other that of the red *charioteer* Lacerna alone.   "The chiefs "
have taken their seats ; you rise a pale "Ajax," to speak for the
liberty *of your client*, which is disputed, with a neatherd for

figantur virides, scalarum gloria, palmae.
quod vocis pretium ? siccus petasunculus et vas
pelamydum, aut veteres, Afrorum epimenia, bulbi,⠀⠀⠀⠀⠀120
aut vinum Tiberi devectum, quinque lagenae
si quater egisti ; si contigit aureus unus,
inde cadunt partes ex foedere pragmaticorum.
Aemilio dabitur quantum libet, et melius nos
egimus. huius enim stat currus aeneus, alti⠀⠀⠀⠀⠀125
quadriiuges in vestibulis, atque ipse feroci
bellatore sedens curvatum hastile minatur
eminus et statua meditatur proelia lusca.
sic Pedo conturbat, Matho deficit, exitus hic est
Tongilli, magno cum rhinocerote lavari⠀⠀⠀⠀⠀130
qui solet et vexat lutulenta balnea turba
perque forum iuvenes longo premit assere Medos,
empturus pueros argentum murrina villas ;

---

judge. Burst, poor wretch, your strained vitals, that, when you
are spent, green palm branches may be put up for you, the glory
of your staircase ! What is the reward of your voice ? A dry
little flitch of bacon, and a jar of small thunny-fish, or some old
roots, the monthly allowance of African *slaves*, or wine brought
down the Tiber, five bottles if you have pleaded four times.
If a single gold piece has fallen to your happy lot, the shares
of the attorneys have to be deducted according to agreement.
Aemilius will get as much as he pleases, and *yet* we pleaded
better than he ; but then he has his chariot of bronze, and a
lofty team of four standing in his courtyard, and he himself
sitting on his fierce charger aims his bending lance threateningly
with his hand, and meditates fight in *the person of* his statue
with one eye closed. So it is that Pedo is bankrupt, Matho
fails ; this is the end of Tongillus, who is in the habit of bathing
with a large rhinoceros-horn, and who infests the baths with a
mud-stained crowd *of attendants*, and along the Forum presses
on the young Medes, *his bearers*, with long litter-pole, to buy
slaves, plate, porcelain, villas ; for his deceptive purple, with its

spondet enim Tyrio stlataria purpura filo.
et tamen est illis hoc utile, purpura vendit 135
causidicum, vendunt amethystina, convenit illis
et strepitu et facie maioris vivere census,
sed finem impensae non servat prodiga Roma.
fidimus eloquio? Ciceroni nemo ducentos
nunc dederit nummos, nisi fulserit annulus ingens. 140
respicit haec primum qui litigat, an tibi servi
octo, decem comites, an post te sella, togati
ante pedes. ideo conducta Paulus agebat
sardonyche, atque ideo pluris quam Cossus agebat,
quam Basilus. rara in tenui facundia panno. 145
quando licet Basilo flentem producere matrem?
quis bene dicentem Basilum ferat? accipiat te
Gallia vel potius nutricula causidicorum
Africa, si placuit mercedem imponere linguae.
Declamare doces? o ferrea pectora Vetti, 150

134. splendet. 139. ut redeant veteres. 149. ponere.

Tyrian tissue, gets him credit. And yet this is of service to
them: his purples puff the lawyer, his violet-coloured garments
puff him: it suits these people to live with the bustle and the
appearance of a larger fortune *than they have*. But prodigal
Rome observes no bounds in her expenditure. Do we trust to
eloquence? No one nowadays would give Cicero two hundred
sesterces, unless a huge ring glittered *on his finger*. The man
who goes to law first looks to this, whether you have eight
slaves, ten attendants, a sedan following you, clients in togas
before you. It was on this account that Paulus used to plead
with a hired sardonyx-*ring*, and on this account that he used to
plead for a higher fee than Cossus or than Basilus. Eloquence
is *held to be* rare under a threadbare garment. When is Basilus
allowed to produce *in court* a weeping mother? Who can
endure Basilus even though he speak well? Let Gaul receive
you, or rather Africa, the nursing-mother of lawyers, if you
have decided to put a price upon your tongue.

Do you teach declamation? Oh! iron *must be* the breast of

cum perimit saevos classis numerosa tyrannos !
nam quaecumque sedens modo legerat, haec eadem stans
perferet atque eadem cantabit versibus isdem.
occidit miseros crambe repetita magistros.
quis color et quod sit causae genus atque ubi summa   155
quaestio, quae veniant diversa parte sagittae,
nosse velint omnes, mercedem solvere nemo.
" mercedem appellas ? quid enim scio ? " culpa docentis
scilicet arguitur, quod laeva in parte mamillae
nil salit Arcadico iuveni, cuius mihi sexta   160
quaque die miserum dirus caput Hannibal implet,
quidquid id est de quo deliberat, an petat urbem
a Cannis, an post nimbos et fulmina cautus
circumagat madidas a tempestate cohortes.
" quantum vis stipulare, et protinus accipe quod do,   165
ut toties illum pater audiat."   haec alii sex
vel plures uno conclamant ore sophistae,

153. proferet ; idem (Iahn).   159. si laeva parte (Fulgent).

Vettius, when his numerous class destroys savage tyrants. For whatever he (*the boy*) has just read, seated, the very same things he will go through standing up, and will drawl forth the same things in the same verses. "Cabbage repeated" kills the wretched schoolmasters. What may be the colour *to be given* to a cause, to what class it belongs, where lies the principal issue, what shafts may come from the opposite side—all wish to know, but no one to come down with payment. "You claim payment? why, what do I know?" The fault is charged on the teacher, forsooth, that there is nothing beating on the left side of the breast of this Arcadian youth, whose dreadful "Hannibal" fills my wretched head every sixth day, whatever it is about which he deliberates, whether he shall march to the city from Cannae, or, made cautious after the storms and the thunderbolts, shall wheel round his soaked cohorts from the tempest. "Bargain for any sum you please, and forthwith take what I hand you, on condition that his *own* father hear him as many times." These things half a dozen or more sophists

et veras agitant lites raptore relicto;
fusa venena silent, malus ingratusque maritus,
et quae iam veteres sanant mortaria caecos.   170
ergo sibi dabit ipse rudem, si nostra movebunt
consilia, et vitae diversum iter ingredietur,
ad pugnam qui rhetorica descendit ab umbra,
summula ne pereat, qua vilis tessera venit
frumenti; quippe haec merces lautissima. tenta,   175
Chrysogonus quanti doceat vel Pollio quanti
lautorum pueros, artem scindens Theodori.
balnea sexcentis et pluris porticus, in qua
gestetur dominus, quoties pluit. anne serenum
exspectet spargatque luto iumenta recenti ?   180
hic potius, namque hic mundae nitet ungula mulae.
parte alia longis Numidarum fulta columnis
surgat et algentem rapiat coenatio solem.
quanticumque domus, veniet qui fercula docte

                    177. scindes (Iahn).

besides cry out together with one voice, and pursue real lawsuits,
leaving "the ravisher"; "outpoured poisons" are no longer
heard of, nor "the wicked and ungrateful husband," nor "the
drugs which restore to soundness old blind men."/Therefore,
he who descends to the fight from his scholastic seclusion, will
present himself with his own discharge, if my counsels can
move him, that the little sum may not be thrown away for
which the cheap corn-ticket is sold, since this is the richest
return *he gets.*/Inquire on what terms Chrysogonus, or on
what terms Pollio teaches the sons of rich men, ridiculing the
art of Theodorus. Their baths cost six hundred sestertia, and
still more the covered way for my lord to be driven about in
whenever it rains. Is he to wait for fine weather, and *then*
bespatter his steeds with the fresh mud ? *No;* here rather *let
him drive,* for here the hoof of his clean mule glistens. On the
other side, supported by tall columns of Numidian *marble,* let
his dining-room rear itself and catch the winter sun. However
great the cost of his house, there will be some one to arrange

componat, veniet qui pulmentaria condat. 185
hos inter sumptus sestertia Quintiliano,
ut multum, duo sufficient: res nulla minoris
constabit patri, quam filius.   unde igitur tot
Quintilianus habet saltus ? exempla novorum
fatorum transi.   felix et pulcher et acer, 190
felix et sapiens et nobilis et generosus
appositam nigrae lunam subtexit alutae,
felix orator quoque maximus et iaculator ;
et, si perfrixit, cantat bene.   distat enim quae
sidera te excipiant modo primos incipientem 195
edere vagitus et adhuc a matre rubentem.
si fortuna volet, fies de rhetore consul ;
si volet haec eadem, fies de consule rhetor.
Ventidius quid enim ? quid Tullius ? anne aliud quam
sidus et occulti miranda potentia fati ? 200
servis regna dabunt, captivis fata triumphos.

196. ex matre.   201. triumphum.

his table skilfully—there will be some one to concoct made-
dishes.   Amidst these lavish outlays, two sestertia, as a large
fee, will be *deemed* sufficient for Quintilian : no article costs a
father less than his *own* son.   "Whence, then, does Quintilian
possess so many pastures?"   Pass over examples of unprecedented good fortune.   The lucky man is handsome and bold ;
the lucky man is wise as well as noble and highly-born, and
sews on to his black shoe the crescent-shaped appendage *of a
senator*.   The lucky man is the greatest of orators and arguers
likewise ; even if he has got a cold, he declaims well.   For it
makes a difference what stars welcome you, just beginning to
utter your first cries, and still red from your mother.   If Fortune
shall will it, from a rhetorician you will become a consul; if
this same *Fortune* shall will it, from a consul you will become
a rhetorician.   For what was Ventidius? what Tullius?   Were
they anything else than *examples of* their star and the marvellous power of a hidden destiny?   The fates bestow kingdoms
on slaves and triumphs on captives.   Yet this lucky man is, at

felix ille tamen corvo quoque rarior albo.
poenituit multos vanae sterilisque cathedrae,
sicut Thrasymachi probat exitus atque Secundi
Carinatis: et hunc inopem vidistis, Athenae,   205
nil praeter gelidas ausae conferre cicutas.
di, maiorum umbris tenuem et sine pondere terram
spirantesque crocos et in urna perpetuum ver,
qui praeceptorem sancti voluere parentis
esse loco.   metuens virgae iam grandis Achilles   210
cantabat patriis in montibus; et cui non tunc
eliceret risum citharoedi cauda magistri ?
sed Rufum atque alios caedit sua quemque iuventus,
Rufum, qui toties Ciceronem Allobroga dixit.

   Quis gremio Enceladi doctique Palaemonis affert   215
quantum grammaticus meruit labor ? et tamen ex hoc
quodcumque est, minus est autem quam rhetoris aera,
discipuli custos praemordet Acoenonetus

              214. quem.   218. ἀκοινώνητος.

---

the same time, rarer than a white raven.   Many have grown
weary of the vain and profitless teacher's chair, as the end of
Thrasymachus proves, and that of Secundus Carinas: and you
beheld one in poverty, O Athens ! on whom you dared to bestow
nothing besides cold hemlock !   Ye gods ! *grant* to the shades
of our ancestors an earth light and without weight, and fragrant
crocuses, and perpetual spring in their urns, who willed that a
preceptor should hold the place of a revered parent.   Achilles,
already full-grown, sang on his paternal mountains in awe of
the rod ; and yet in whom, even then, would not the tail of the
harper-teacher have provoked a laugh ?   But now Rufus and
others are beaten, each of them by his own pupils : Rufus, who
has so often called Cicero "the Allobrogian !"

   Who brings to the lap of Enceladus or learned Palaemon as
much as their labour, as teachers of grammar, has merited ?
And yet from this sum, whatever it is (and it is less, at any
rate, than the rhetorician's pay), Acoenonetus, the pupil's peda-
gogue, takes a bite beforehand, and the steward breaks off *a slice*

et qui dispensat frangit sibi.   cede, Palaemon,
et patere inde aliquid decrescere, non aliter quam   220
institor hibernae tegetis niveique cadurci,
dummodo non pereat, mediae quod noctis ab hora
sedisti, qua nemo faber, qua nemo sederet
qui docet obliquo lanam deducere ferro ;
dummodo non pereat totidem olfecisse lucernas,   225
quot stabant pueri, cum totus decolor esset
Flaccus et haereret nigro fuligo Maroni.
rara tamen merces, quae cognitione tribuni
non egeat.   sed vos saevas imponite leges,
ut praeceptori verborum regula constet,   230
ut legat historias, auctores noverit omnes
tamquam ungues digitosque suos, ut forte rogatus,
dum petit aut thermas aut Phoebi balnea, dicat
nutricem Anchisae, nomen patriamque novercae
Archemori, dicat quot Acestes vixerit annos,   235
quot Siculus Phrygibus vini donaverit urnas.

for himself.   Yield, Palaemon, and suffer something to be abated
from it, just like the salesman of winter rugs and white quilts,
provided it be not pure waste that you have sat up from the
hour of midnight, at which no workman, no one would sit up,
who teaches how to card wool with the crooked iron ; provided
it be not pure waste that you have smelt as many lamps as there
were boys standing by, with their whole Flaccus discoloured,
and the smoke clinging to the blackened Maro.   Even then, rare
is the payment which does not require a decision of the tribune.
But do you *parents* impose severe laws, that the preceptor be
perfect in the rules of syntax, that he read all histories, know all
authors like his own nails and fingers ; that, asked at haphazard,
while he is repairing to the Thermae or the baths of Phoebus,
he should *be able to* tell you the nurse of Anchises, the name
and country of the stepmother of Archemorus ; that he should
tell you how many years Acestes lived—how many flagons of
wine the Sicilian *king* gave to the Phrygians.   Insist that he

exigite ut mores teneros ceu pollice ducat,
ut si quis cera vultum facit, exigite ut sit
et pater ipsius coetus, ne turpia ludant,
ne faciant vicibus. "non est leve tot puerorum   240
observare manus oculosque in fine trementes."
"haec," inquit, "cures; et cum se verterit annus
accipe victori populus quod postulat aurum!"

SATIRA VIII.

STEMMATA quid faciunt? quid prodest, Pontice, longo
   sanguine censeri, pictos ostendere vultus
maiorum et stantes in curribus Aemilianos
et Curios iam dimidios humerosque minorem
Corvinum et Galbam auriculis nasoque carentem?   5

4. humeroque.

---

mould their youthful morals, as it were with his thumb, just as
one fashions a face out of wax; insist that he be a father even
to the whole flock, that they may not play obscenely or adopt
dirty practices. "It is no light thing to watch the hands and
eyes, tremulous at the end, of so many boys." "You attend
to these things," says *the father*, "and when the year is turned,
receive *from me* as much gold as the people demands for a victor
in the circus."

SATIRE VIII.

WHAT do pedigrees avail? Of what advantage is it, Ponticus,
to be estimated by the antiquity of your race, and to exhibit the
painted countenances of your ancestors, and Aemiliani standing
in their chariots, and Curii now in halves, and Corvinus short of
his shoulders, and Galba wanting ears and a nose? What profit

quis fructus, generis tabula iactare capaci
Corvinum, posthac multa contingere virga
fumosos equitum cum dictatore magistros,
si coram Lepidis male vivitur ? effigies quo
tot bellatorum, si luditur alea pernox   10
ante Numantinos, si dormire incipis ortu
luciferi, quo signa duces et castra movebant ?
cur Allobrogicis et magna gaudeat ara
natus in Herculeo Fabius lare, si cupidus, si
vanus et Euganea quantumvis mollior agna,   15
si tenerum attritus Catinensi pumice lumbum
squalentes traducit avos, emptorque veneni
frangenda miseram funestat imagine gentem ?
tota licet veteres exornent undique cerae
atria, nobilitas sola est atque unica virtus.   20
Paulus vel Cossus vel Drusus moribus esto,
hos ante effigies maiorum pone tuorum,
praecedant ipsas illi te consule virgas.

---

is there in boasting of Corvinus on your capacious family-roll,
and, after him, in reaching, through many a bough, smoke-dried
Masters of the Horse and Dictators, if, in presence of the Lepidi,
one leads a bad life ?   To what purpose the effigies of so many
warriors, if the dice are being played all night long before the
Numantini ; if you begin to sleep *only* at the rising of Lucifer,
when they, in the command of armies, were moving their standards and their camps ?   Why should a Fabius, born in the
household of Hercules, plume himself on Allobrogici and the
great altar, if he be covetous, empty, and ever so much more
effeminate than a lamb of Euganea ; if, with soft loins, polished
by Catanian pumice-stone, he exposes to contempt his rugged
sires, and, a purchaser of poison, defiles his unhappy race by his
image, which will have to be broken up ?   Though ancient wax
images set off the whole of your halls in every direction, the
sole, the only nobility is virtue.   Be a Paulus or a Cossus or a
Drusus in your character ; put that before the effigies of your
ancestors ; let that go before the Fasces themselves, when you

prima mihi debes animi bona. sanctus haberi
iustitiaeque tenax factis dictisque mereris,   '   25
agnosco procerem ; salve, Gaetulice, seu tu
Silanus, quocumque alio de sanguine, rarus
civis et egregius patriae contingis ovanti,
exclamare libet, populus quod clamat Osiri
invento. quis enim generosum dixerit hunc qui   30
indignus genere et praeclaro nomine tantum
insignis ? nanum cuiusdam Atlanta vocamus,
Aethiopem cygnum, pravam extortamque puellam
Europen, canibus pigris scabieque vetusta
levibus et siccae lambentibus ora lucernae   35
nomen erit pardus tigris leo, si quid adhuc est
quod fremat in terris violentius. ergo cavebis
et metues ne tu sis Creticus aut Camerinus.
   His ego quem monui ? tecum est mihi sermo, Rubelli
Plaute. tumes alto Drusorum stemmate, tamquam   40

33. parvam.   38. ne tu sic.   40. Blande ; sanguine.

---

are Consul. First, you owe me the virtues of the soul. Do
you deserve in word and deed to be held an upright man of
unflinching integrity? I recognise the nobleman. All hail,
Gaeticulus, or if you be a Silanus, or from whatever other stock
you may come, you fall to the happy lot of your rejoicing country,
a rare and remarkable citizen. One is disposed to shout out
what the people shout when Osiris is found. For who would
call him noble that is unworthy of his race, and distinguished
only by an illustrious name? We call some one's dwarf Atlas ;
an Ethiopian, a swan ; a crooked deformed girl, Europe ; lazy
curs, hairless from inveterate mange, and licking the edges of a
dry lamp, have for names, "Panther," "Tiger," "Lion,"—or if
there be anything else which roars with greater fury in the
world. You will have to take care then, and fear lest you be
a Creticus or Camerinus *on the same principle*.
   Whom have I been admonishing in these words? My talk
is with you, Rubellius Plautus. You are puffed up with the
lofty pedigree of the Drusi, just as if you yourself had achieved

feceris ipse aliquid propter quod nobilis esses,
ut te conciperet quae sanguine fulget Iuli,
non quae ventoso conducta sub aggere texit.
" vos humiles," inquis, " vulgi pars ultima nostri,
quorum nemo queat patriam monstrare parentis,   45
ast ego Cecropides." vivas et originis huius
gaudia longa feras ! tamen ima plebe Quiritem
facundum invenies; solet hic defendere causas
nobilis indocti; veniet de plebe togata,
qui iuris nodos et legum aenigmata solvat.   50
hic petit Euphraten iuvenis domitique Batavi
custodes aquilas armis industrius ; at tu
nil nisi Cecropides truncoque simillimus hermae ;
nullo quippe alio vincis discrimine, quam quod
illi marmoreum caput est, tua vivit imago.   55
dic mihi, Teucrorum proles, animalia muta
quis generosa putet, nisi fortia ? nempe volucrem

57. putat.

something, on account of which you were noble, *and* to cause
you to be conceived by one who shines with the blood of Iulus,
and not one who weaves for hire under the windy rampart.
" You are nobodies," you say, " the dregs of our populace, of
whom not one could tell the birthplace of his parent. But I
am a Cecropid !" Long life to you, and long may you enjoy
the delights of such a descent; and yet, in this lowest herd,
you will chance to find an eloquent Roman. It is he who is
wont to plead the causes of the nobleman who is unlearned.
From the toga'd crowd will come one who will solve the knotty
points of law and enigmas of the statutes. This one hies to the
Euphrates when in his prime, and to the eagles that guard the
conquered Batavi, assiduous in arms ; while you are nothing
but a Cecropid, and most like a pedestal with Hermes' head,
since in no other point of difference have you the advantage
than *in the fact* that his head is of marble, and your image
is possessed of life. Tell me, descendant of the Teucri,
who thinks dumb animals "noble" unless they be stout ?

sic laudamus equum facili cui plurima palma
fervet et exsultat rauco victoria circo.
nobilis hic, quocumque venit de gramine, cuius   60
clara fuga ante alios et primus in aequore pulvis ;
sed venale pecus Corythae posteritas et
Hirpini, si rara iugo Victoria sedit.
nil ibi maiorum respectus, gratia nulla
umbrarum ; dominos pretiis mutare iubentur   65
exiguis, trito ducunt epiredia collo
segnipedes dignique molam versare Nepotis.
ergo ut miremur te, non tua, primum aliquid da
quod possim titulis incidere, praeter honores
quos illis damus ac dedimus quibus omnia debes.   70
    Haec satis ad iuvenem, quem nobis fama superbum
tradit et inflatum plenumque Nerone propinquo ;
rarus enim ferme sensus communis in illa
fortuna ; sed te censeri laude tuorum,

58. facile, facilis.   66. tritoque trahunt.

Assuredly we praise a horse as swift, on the ground that many
a palm *of triumph* glows for the easy winner, while victory
exults in the hoarse circus.   He is noble, from whatever pasture
he comes, whose speed is distinguished before the others, whose
dust is first on the plain.   But the descendants of Corytha and
Hirpinus are *but* cattle for sale if victory has sat rarely on their
yoke.   In their case there is no regard for ancestors, no favour
to be gained from shades ; they are forced to change their owners
for small prices ; they draw carts, with galled neck, slow of foot,
and worthy only to turn the mill of Nepos.   Therefore, that
we may admire you, and not yours, first give me something
which I may be able to inscribe among your titles besides those
honours which we give, and *always* have given, to those to whom
you owe everything.

    Enough on the youth whom fame reports to us as proud and
puffed up and full of his relationship to Nero.   Indeed, a sense
of what is due to others is commonly rare in that condition of
life.   But I should be loath, Ponticus, for you to be estimated

Pontice, noluerim sic ut nihil ipse futurae   75
laudis agas.   miserum est aliorum incumbere famae,
ne collapsa ruant subductis tecta columnis.
stratus humi palmes viduas desiderat ulmos.
esto bonus miles, tutor bonus, arbiter idem
integer.   ambiguae si quando citabere testis   80
incertaeque rei, Phalaris licet imperet ut sis
falsus et admoto dictet periuria tauro,
summum crede nefas animam praeferre pudori
et propter vitam vivendi perdere causas.
dignus morte perit, coenet licet ostrea centum   85
Gaurana et Cosmi toto mergatur aeno.
exspectata diu tandem provincia cum te
rectorem accipiet, pone irae frena modumque,
pone et avaritiae, miserere inopum sociorum.
ossa vides regum vacuis exsucta medullis.   90
respice quid moneant leges, quid curia mandet,

---

by the renown of your belongings, on the understanding that
you yourself should do nothing *worthy* of future renown.   It is
a wretched thing to lean for support on the reputation of others,
lest the roof should fall in ruin when the pillars are withdrawn.
The vine trailing on the ground longs in vain for the unwedded
elms.   Be a good soldier, a good guardian, an upright arbitrator ;
if ever you be summoned as a witness in a doubtful and uncertain matter, though Phalaris *himself* command you to speak false,
and dictate perjuries with his bull set by you, deem it the
height of impiety to prefer existence to honour, and for the sake
of *mere* life to sacrifice the objects of living.   He that deserves
death has perished *already*, though he sup on a hundred oysters
from Gaurus, and be plunged in a whole copper of Cosmus's
perfumes.   When, in the course of time, the province so long
expected shall receive you for its ruler, put a check and a limit
on your violence and on your avarice as well ; have mercy on
our indigent allies.   You see the *very* bones of kings sucked
dry, with the marrow extracted.   Bear in mind what the laws
enjoin, what the Senate orders, what great rewards await the

praemia quanta bonos maneant, quam fulmine iusto
et Capito et Numitor ruerint damnante senatu,
piratae Cilicum.   sed quid damnatio confert,
cum Pansa eripiat quidquid tibi Natta reliquit ?   95
praeconem, Chaerippe, tuis circumspice pannis,
iamque tace ; furor est post omnia perdere naulum.
non idem gemitus olim neque vulnus erat par
damnorum, sociis florentibus et modo victis.
plena domus tunc omnis et ingens stabat acervus   100
nummorum, Spartana chlamys, conchylia Coa,
et cum Parrhasii tabulis signisque Myronis
Phidiacum vivebat ebur, nec non Polycleti
multus ubique labor, rarae sine Mentore mensae.
inde Dolabellae atque hinc Antonius, inde   105
sacrilegus Verres ; referebant navibus altis
occulta spolia et plures de pace triumphos.
nunc sociis iuga pauca boum, grex parvus equarum

105. Dolabella est.   108. parva.

---

good, by how just a thunderbolt both Capito and Numitor were
crushed, those pirates of the Cilicians, when the Senate condemned them.   But what does their condemnation avail you,
provincial, if Pansa is to wrest away whatever Natta has left
you ? Look round you, Chaerippus, for one to cry your rags
for sale, and hold your tongue at once.   It is madness, after
everything *else,* to lose your passage-money *to Rome.*   There
was not the same groaning formerly, nor were the wounds
caused by spoliation as great, when our allies were *still* flourish-
ing, and but recently conquered.   Then every house was full,
and a huge pile of money was standing ; the Spartan shawl,
purple dresses from Cos, and, with the paintings of Parrhasius
and the statues of Myro, the ivory of Phidias seemed alive, and
Polycletus' handiwork, too, was everywhere in plenty ; there
were few tables without a Mentor.   Then here come Dolabellas,
and there Antony, and there sacrilegious Verres : they used to
carry back in lofty ships their hidden spoils, and a good many
trophies of triumphs won from peace.   Now, our allies will

et pater armenti capto eripietur agello,
ipsi deinde lares, si quod spectabile signum,   110
si quis in aedicula deus unicus.   haec etenim sunt
pro summis, nam sunt haec maxima.   despicias tu
forsitan imbelles Rhodios unctamque Corinthum
despicias merito ; quid resinata iuventus
cruraque totius facient tibi levia gentis ?   115
horrida vitanda est Hispania, Gallicus axis
Illyricumque latus ; parce et messoribus illis,
qui saturant urbem circo scenaeque vacantem.
quanta autem inde feres tam dirae praemia culpae,
cum tenues nuper Marius discinxerit Afros ?   120
curandum imprimis ne magna iniuria fiat
fortibus et miseris.   tollas licet omne quod usquam est
auri atque argenti, scutum gladiumque relinques
et iaculum et galeam ; spoliatis arma supersunt.

109. eripiatur.

---

have their few yokes of oxen, the small stock of brood-mares,
and the father of the herd, carried off from a captured farm,
and the very Lares afterwards, if there be any image worth
looking at, if there be any solitary divinity in the little shrine.
These things, indeed, stand for the highest prizes, for these are
the greatest *now to be got.* You despise, it may be, the unwarlike Rhodians, and perfumed Corinth. You despise them with
reason. What can resin-smeared youths, or the depilated legs
of a whole nation do to you? *But* rugged Spain must be
avoided, and the clime of Gaul and the Illyrian sea-board.
Spare, too, those harvesters who glut the city, giving its time
to the circus and the theatre. Moreover, what so great prizes
will you get from that quarter *in return* for so dreadful a crime,
seeing that Marius has recently stripped the impoverished Africans of their *very* girdles? You must take especial care that
no deep injury be inflicted on those who are brave as well as poor;
though you take from them all the gold and silver they have
anywhere, you will *still* leave them shield and sword, javelins
and helmet. To the plundered there still remain arms!

Quod modo proposui, non est sententia, verum   125
credite me vobis folium recitare Sibyllae.
si tibi sancta cohors comitum, si nemo tribunal
vendit acersecomes, si nullum in coniuge crimen,
nec per conventus et cuncta per oppida curvis
unguibus ire parat nummos raptura Celaeno,   130
tunc licet a Pico numeres genus, altaque si te
nomina delectant, omnem Titanida pugnam
inter maiores ipsumque Promethea ponas,
de quocumque voles proavum tibi sumito libro.
quod si praecipitem rapit ambitio atque libido,   135
si frangis virgas sociorum in sanguine, si te
delectant hebetes lasso lictore secures,
incipit ipsorum contra te stare parentum
nobilitas claramque facem praeferre pudendis.
omne animi vitium tanto conspectius in se   140
crimen habet, quanto maior qui peccat habetur.

125. verum est.   131. tu licet, tum licet.   133. pingas.

What I have just set forth is not a mere aphorism; believe that I am reciting to you a veracious leaf of the sibyl. If you have an upright suite of attendants, if no long-haired young favourite sells your judgments, if your wife is free from guilt, and is not preparing to go through the district courts and through all the towns to swoop upon the coins with crooked talons, like another Celaeno, then—albeit you reckon your descent from Picus, or, if lofty names delight you, though you place the whole array of the Titans among your forefathers, and Prometheus himself,—take to yourself a progenitor from whatever book you please. But—if ambition and lust hurry you on headlong, if you break rods in the blood of our allies, if you delight in axes blunted with an executioner tired out,—the nobility of your parents themselves begins to rise up against you, and to hold out a bright torch to *light up* your shameful deeds. Every vice of the soul carries with it a condemnation the more glaring the higher the standing of the person who sins. Of what use is it for you to brag about yourself to me, if you are in the

quo mihi te solitum falsas signare tabellas
in templis quae fecit avus statuamque parentis
ante triumphalem ? quo, si nocturnus adulter
tempora Santonico velas adoperta cucullo ?   145
Praeter maiorum cineres atque ossa volucri
carpento rapitur pinguis Lateranus, et ipse,
ipse rotam adstringit multo sufflamine consul,
nocte quidem, sed luna videt, sed sidera testes
intendunt oculos. finitum tempus honoris   150
cum fuerit, clara Lateranus luce flagellum
sumet et occursum numquam trepidabit amici
iam senis, ac virga prior annuet atque maniplos
solvet et infundet iumentis hordea lassis.
interea dum lanatas torvumque iuvencum   155
more Numae caedit Iovis ante altaria, iurat
solam Eponam et facies olida ad praesepia pictas.
sed cum pervigiles placet instaurare popinas,

147. Damasippus.   153. innuet.   155. robumque.

---

habit of setting your seal to forged wills in the temples your
grandfather built, and before the triumphal statue of your
parent? Of what use, if, as a nocturnal adulterer, you veil
your brows, concealed by a Santon cowl?

Past the ashes and bones of his ancestors fat Lateranus is
whirled in his rapid coach, and with his own hands—with his
own hands—a consul!—locks his wheel with the frequent drag-
chain; by night, it is true, but the moon sees him, but the stars
strain on him their eyes, witnesses *of the act*. When the time
of his magistracy is completed, Lateranus will take up his whip
in the bright light *of day*, and will never be frightened at meeting an elderly friend, but will be the first to salute him with his
whip, and will untie the trusses, and will administer the barley
to his tired steeds. All this time, while he sacrifices woolly
victims and a stalwart heifer, after the rite of Numa, before the
altar of Jove, he swears by Epona alone, and the faces painted
up over the stinking stalls. But when he is pleased to repair
again to the taverns open all night, the Syrophoenician, reeking

obvius assiduo Syrophoenix udus amomo
currit, Idumaeae Syrophoenix incola portae,   160
hospitis affectu dominum regemque salutat,
et cum venali Cyane succincta lagena.

   Defensor culpae dicet mihi " fecimus et nos
haec iuvenes." esto. desisti nempe, nec ultra
fovisti errorem. breve sit quod turpiter audes,   165
quaedam cum prima resecentur crimina barba,
indulge veniam pueris. Lateranus ad illos
thermarum calices inscriptaque lintea vadit
maturus bello, Armeniae Syriaeque tuendis
amnibus et Rheno atque Istro; praestare Neronem   170
securum valet haec aetas. mitte ostia, Caesar,
mitte, sed in magna legatum quaere popina.
invenies aliquo cum percussore iacentem,
permixtum nautis et furibus ac fugitivis,
inter carnifices et fabros sandapilarum   175

167. Damasippus.

---

with constant perfume, runs out to meet him, the Syrophoenician who comes from the gate of Idumaea ; with the eagerness
of a host he salutes him as my lord and king, and *with him*
bustling Cyane with her bottle for sale.

   An apologist for his fault will say to me, " We too did these
things when we were young." Granted ; but, of course, you
left them off, and did not longer indulge in your folly. Let
that be brief which you dare to your discredit ; there are some
offences which should be cut short with the first beard. Make
allowance for boys. *But* Lateranus goes to those drinking-
bouts at the baths, and those inscribed curtains *of the brothels,*
when *of an age* ripe for war, for guarding the rivers of Armenia
and Syria, the Rhine and the Danube. His is a time of life
which is good for assuring the safety of Nero. Send to the
mouths of the Tiber, Caesar, but seek for your general in some
large tavern. You will find him reclining with some cut-throat
or other, mixed up with sailors and thieves and runaway slaves,
among executioners and makers of cheap coffins, and the now

et resupinati cessantia tympana Galli.
aequa ibi libertas, communia pocula, lectus
non alius cuiquam, nec mensa remotior ulli.
quid facias talem sortitus, Pontice, servum ?
nempe in Lucanos aut Tusca ergastula mittas.   180
at vos, Troiugenae, vobis ignoscitis, et quae
turpia cerdoni, Volesos Brutumque decebunt.
quid si numquam adeo foedis adeoque pudendis
utimur exemplis, ut non peiora supersint ?
consumptis opibus vocem, Damasippe, locasti   185
sipario, clamosum ageres ut phasma Catulli ;
Laureolum velox etiam bene Lentulus egit,
iudice me dignus vera cruce.   nec tamen ipsi
ignoscas populo ; populi frons durior huius,
qui sedet et spectat triscurria patriciorum,   190
planipedes audit Fabios, ridere potest qui
Mamercorum alapas.   quanti sua funera vendant,

192. vulnera, munera (Dobree).

---

silent timbrel of the eunuch-priest lying on his back. There there
is equal liberty ; the drinking-cups are in common, no separate
couch, nor table set apart for any one.   What would you do,
Ponticus, if chance had made you the owner of a slave of such a
character ?   Of course you would send him to Lucania, or to the
Tuscan bridewells.   But you, ye Trojugenae, excuse yourselves,
and what would be disgraceful in a journeyman will become Volesi
or a Brutus !   What if we can never employ examples so foul
and so shameful that worse do not remain behind ?   Your fortune squandered, Damasippus, you let out your voice to the
stage, to act the noisy " ghost " of Catullus.   Nimble Lentulus
acted Laureolus, and well too ; in my judgment, worthy of a real
cross.   Nor yet can you excuse the populace itself : the sense of
shame must be very tough of that populace which sits and looks
at the treble buffooneries of patricians, listens to Fabii with
naked feet, which can laugh at the stage-slaps bestowed on the
Mamerci.   At what price they sell their lives, what matters ?

quid refert ? vendunt nullo cogente Nerone,
nec dubitant celsi praetoris vendere ludis.
finge tamen gladios inde atque hinc pulpita pone,   195
quid satius ? mortem sic quisquam exhorruit, ut sit
zelotypus Thymeles, stupidi collega Corinthi ?
res haud mira tamen citharoedo principe mimus
nobilis.   haec ultra quid erit, nisi ludus ? et illud
dedecus urbis habes, nec mirmillonis in armis,   200
nec clipeo Gracchum pugnantem aut falce supina,
damnat enim tales habitus, et damnat et odit,
nec galea faciem abscondit ; movet ecce tridentem,
postquam vibrata pendentia retia dextra
nequidquam effudit, nudum ad spectacula vultum   205
erigit et tota fugit agnoscendus arena.
credamus tunicae, de faucibus aurea cum se
porrigat et longo iactetur spira galero.

195. poni.   199. illic.   203. frontem.

They sell them with no Nero to compel them [nor do they
hesitate to sell them at the games of the praetor seated on
high].   Imagine, however, a violent death on one side, and
put the stage on the other.   Which is preferable ?   Is any one
so terrified at death as to become the "jealous husband" of
Thymele, *or* the fellow-player of Corinthus, "the heavy man" ?
Yet it is nothing wonderful, with an emperor as a harper, for a
nobleman to be an actor.   Beyond this what remains but the
gladiatorial show ?   And you have that disgrace to the city and
Gracchus fighting, not in the arms of a Mirmillo, nor with
shield or upraised short sword [for he condemns such an equip-
ment, both condemns and hates it] ; nor does he hide his face
in a helmet.   See ! he brandishes a trident ; after he has made
a false cast with the nets hanging from his poised right hand,
he raises his uncovered face to the spectators and flies—easily
to be recognised—right through the arena.   There is no mis-
taking the tunic, when it stretches with its gold *fringe* from his
neck, and the strings flutter from the tall cap.   So, then, the

ergo ignominiam graviorem pertulit omni
vulnere cum Graccho iussus pugnare secutor   210
  Libera si dentur populo suffragia, quis tam
perditus, ut dubitet Senecam praeferre Neroni?
cuius supplicio non debuit una parari
simia nec serpens unus nec culeus unus.
par Agamemnonidae crimen, sed causa facit rem   215
dissimilem; quippe ille deis auctoribus ultor
patris erat caesi media inter pocula, sed nec
Electrae iugulo se polluit aut Spartani
sanguine coniugii, nullis aconita propinquis
miscuit, in scena numquam cantavit Orestes,   220
Troica non scripsit. quid enim Verginius armis
debuit ulcisci magis, aut cum Vindice Galba?
quid Nero tam saeva crudaque tyrannide fecit?
haec opera atque hae sunt generosi principis artes,
gaudentis foedo peregrina ad pulpita cantu   225

223. quod.   225. saltu.

secutor suffered a disgrace worse than any wound in being
ordered to fight with Gracchus.
  If the right of free voting were granted to the people, who
so abandoned that he would hesitate to prefer Seneca to Nero?
for whose punishment not one ape *only,* nor one serpent, nor
one sack should have been prepared. The crime of Agamemnon's son was of a like kind; but the motive makes the case
different, inasmuch as he, at the instigation of the gods, was the
avenger of his own father, slaughtered in the midst of his wine-
cups; but he neither stained himself with the murder of Electra,
nor the blood of his Spartan wife. Orestes did not mix aconite
for any of his relations; he never sang on the stage; he did not
write "Troica." For what was there that Verginius ought
rather to have avenged with his arms, or Galba in conjunction
with Vindex? What did Nero achieve in *all* his savage and
cruel tyranny? These are the works, these are the accomplish-
ments of a high-born prince, delighting to prostitute himself by
disgraceful singing on a foreign stage, and to earn a Greek

prostitui Graiaeque apium meruisse coronae.
maiorum effigies habeant insignia vocis,
ante pedes Domiti longum tu pone Thyestae
syrma vel Antigones tu personam Menalippes
et de marmoreo citharam suspende colosso.   230
    Quid, Catilina, tuis natalibus atque Cethegi
inveniet quisquam sublimius ?   arma tamen vos
nocturna et flammas domibus templisque parastis,
ut Braccatorum pueri Senonumque minores,
ausi quod liceat tunica punire molesta.   235
sed vigilat consul vexillaque vestra coercet.
hic novus Arpinas, ignobilis et modo Romae
municipalis eques, galeatum ponit ubique
praesidium attonitis et in omni gente laborat.
tantum igitur muros intra toga contulit illi   240
nominis ac tituli, quantum non Leucade, quantum
Thessaliae campis Octavius abstulit udo

    233. paratis.   235. deceat.   239. in omni monte.
        241. in Leucade (sibi Leucade. Jahn).

---

parsley-wreath !   Let the effigies of your ancestors possess the
insignia of your vocal powers !   Before the feet of a Domitius
do you place the long train of Thyestes or Antigone, and the
mask of Menalippe, and suspend your harp on some colossal
statue of marble.

    What, O Catiline ! will any one find loftier than your birth
and that of Cethegus ?   And yet you prepared nocturnal arms
and flames for our houses and temples, as though you had been
sons of the Braccati, or descendants of the Senones, daring a
deed which it would be lawful to punish with the tunic of pitch.
But the Consul is on the watch, and restrains your bands. This
upstart from Arpinum, of no noble birth, and but recently a
municipal knight at Rome, posts everywhere an armed guard
for the terrified *inhabitants*, and labours on behalf of all our
populations. So it was that within the city walls the toga conferred upon him such a name and title as not from Leucas, *not*
from the plains of Thessalia, did Octavius carry off with his

caedibus assiduis gladio; sed Roma parentem,
Roma patrem patriae Ciceronem libera dixit.
Arpinas alius Volscorum in monte solebat   245
poscere mercedes, alieno lassus aratro;
nodosam post haec frangebat vertice vitem,
si lentus pigra muniret castra dolabra.
hic tamen et Cimbros et summa pericula rerum
excipit, et solus trepidantem protegit urbem,   250
atque ideo, postquam ad Cimbros stragemque volabant
qui numquam attigerant maiora cadavera corvi,
nobilis ornatur lauro collega secunda.
plebeiae Deciorum animae, plebeia fuerunt
nomina: pro totis legionibus hi tamen et pro   255
omnibus auxiliis atque omni pube Latina
sufficiunt dis infernis terraeque parenti;
pluris enim Decii, quam quae servantur ab illis.
ancilla natus trabeam et diadema Quirini
et fasces meruit regum ultimus ille bonorum.   260

---

sword reeking with continual slaughter. But Rome called
Cicero her parent; Rome *called him* the father of his country,
when she was free. Another native of Arpinum was wont on
the Volscian hills to work for hire, toiling at another's plough;
after that, he used to have the knotty vine-switch broken on his
head in case he was lazy with sluggish axe in fortifying the
camp. Yet this man takes upon himself the Cimbri, and the
most critical state of affairs, and single-handed protects the
trembling city. And, therefore—after the ravens, that had
never lighted upon larger carcases, flew to the slaughtered
Cimbri—his colleague, a nobleman, is decorated *only* with the
second laurel. The souls of the Decii were plebeian, their names
plebeian; yet these are an equivalent for whole legions, and for
all the auxiliaries, and for all the Latin youth, in the eyes of
the infernal gods and mother earth. For the Decii are of more
value than what is saved by them! One born of a female slave
won the trabea and the diadem and the fasces of Quirinus, *Ser-*
vius, that last of the good kings. They that were loosening the

prodita laxabant portarum claustra tyrannis
exsulibus iuvenes ipsius consulis et quos
magnum aliquid dubia pro libertate deceret,
quod miraretur cum Coclite Mucius et quae
imperii fines Tiberinum virgo natavit.   265
occulta ad patres produxit crimina servus
matronis lugendus; at illos verbera iustis
afficiunt poenis et legum prima securis.

    Malo pater tibi sit Thersites, dummodo tu sis
Acacidae similis Vulcaniaque arma capessas,   270
quam te Thersitae similem producat Achilles.
et tamen ut longe repetas longeque revolvas
nomen, ab infami gentem deducis asylo:
maiorum primus quisquis fuit ille tuorum,
aut pastor fuit aut illud quod dicere nolo.   275

---

betrayed bolts of the city-gates to the exiled tyrants were the
youthful sons of the Consul himself, the very men from whom
some great exploit on behalf of *still* doubtful liberty was to be
expected, such as Mucius in unison with Cocles might admire,
and the virgin who swam the Tiber, *then* the limit of our
empire. He that revealed to the senators the secret crime was
a slave, *one day* to be lamented by matrons, while stripes inflict
upon the others a just punishment, and the axe the first *that
was used under the reign* of laws.

    I would prefer that your father were Thersites, provided you
resemble Acacides, and can wield the arms of Vulcan's making,
than that Achilles should beget you in the likeness of Thersites.
And after all, from whatever distance you trace back, and from
whatever distance you unroll your name, you derive your family
from an ignoble repair. That first of your ancestors, whoever
he was, was either a shepherd, or something which I decline to
mention.

SATIRA IX.

SCIRE velim quare toties mihi, Naevole, tristis
occurras fronte obducta ceu Marsya victus.
quid tibi cum vultu, qualem deprensus habebat
Ravola, dum Rhodopes uda terit inguina barba ?
nos colaphum incutimus lambenti crustula servo.   5
non erat hac facie miserabilior Crepereius
Pollio, qui triplicem usuram praestare paratus
circuit et fatuos non invenit.   unde repente
tot rugae ? certe modico contentus agebas
vernam equitem, conviva ioco mordente facetus   10
et salibus vehemens intra pomeria natis.
omnia nunc contra, vultus gravis, horrida siccae
silva comae, nullus tota nitor in cute, qualem
Bruttia praestabat calidi tibi fascia visci,
sed fruticante pilo neglecta et squalida crura.   15

14. praestabat calidi circumlita fascia visci.

SATIRE IX.

I SHOULD wish to know, Naevolus, why you meet me so often,
looking sad, with clouded brow, like a vanquished Marsyas.
What business have you with a face such as Ravola had when
caught in the act of drivelling over the charms of Rhodope?
[We administer a thump to a slave who licks pastry.] Crepereius Pollio was not more pitiable than that countenance *of
yours;* he that went round prepared to offer treble interest and
found no dupes. Whence of a sudden so many wrinkles?
Assuredly you used to play the genteel buffoon, content with
little, a diner-out, humorous with your biting jokes, and lively
with your smart sayings of town production.   Everything is now
the reverse ; a dismal visage, a bristling thicket of dry hair, none
of that sleekness of the whole skin, such as the Bruttian plaster
of warm pitch used to insure you, but legs neglected and foul

quid macies aegri veteris, quem tempore longo
torret quarta dies olimque domestica febris ?
deprendas animi tormenta latentis in aegro
corpore, deprendas et gaudia ; sumit utrumque
inde habitum facies. igitur flexisse videris   20
propositum et vitae contrarius ire priori.
nuper enim, ut repeto, fanum Isidis et Ganymeden
Pacis, et advectae secreta palatia Matris
et Cererem—nam quo non prostat femina templo ?—
notior Aufidio moechus celebrare solebas,   25
quodque taces, ipsos etiam inclinare maritos.
  " Utile et hoc multis vitae genus, at mihi nullum
iude operae pretium, pingues aliquando lacernas,
munimenta togae, duri crassique coloris
et male percussas textoris pectine Galli   30
accipimus, tenue argentum venaeque secundae.

17. torquet.   22. Ganymedis (Valla).
25. scelerare.   26. quod taceo atque.

---

with sprouting hair. What means this emaciation *like that* of
a sick old man, whom, for a great while past, a quartan ague
parches, and a fever that has long since made its home in him ?
You can detect the torments of a mind concealed in a sick body,
just as you can detect its joys ; from this source, the face takes
either complexion. You seem, then, to have changed your
course of life, and to be going counter to your former habits.
For not long ago, as I remember, you used to frequent the sanc-
tuary of Isis, and the Ganymede of the temple of Peace, and the
secret palaces of the imported mother *of the gods*, and Ceres (for
in what temple does not woman prostitute herself ?) a more noted
adulterer than Aufidius, and—which you are silent about—*you
used* actually to corrupt the husbands themselves.

  "Even this kind of life is profitable to many, but to me there
has been no return for my labour from it. I receive at times
a coarse cloak, as a protection to my toga, of rough and rude
complexion, and clumsily stricken by the comb of the Gallic
weaver, *or* a thin piece of silver of inferior metal. The Fates

fata regunt homines, fatum est et partibus illis,
quas sinus abscondit.   nam si tibi sidera cessant,
nil faciet longi mensura incognita nervi,
quamvis te nudum spumanti Virro labello   35
viderit ed blandae assidue densaeque tabellae
sollicitent, αὐτὸς γὰρ ἐφέλκεται ἄνδρα κίναιδος.
quod tamen ulterius monstrum, quam mollis avarus?
' haec tribui, deinde illa dedi, mox plura tulisti,'
computat ac cevet.   ' ponatur calculus, adsint   40
cum tabula pueri, numera sestertia quinque
omnibus in rebus,'—numerentur deinde labores!
an facile et pronum est agere intra viscera penem
legitimum atque illic hesternae occurrere coenae?
servus erit minus ille miser, qui foderit agrum,   45
quam dominum.   sed tu sane tenerum et puerum te
et pulchrum et dignum cyatho coeloque putabas!
vos humili asseculae, vos indulgebitis umquam
cultori, iam nec morbo donare parati?
en cui tu viridem umbellam, cui sucina mittas   50

---

rule mankind.   There is a fate even in those parts which the
folds of the toga conceal.   For if the stars fail you, your manly
powers, though unprecedented, will do nothing for you, though
Virro, with watering lip, has seen you naked, and coaxing and
numerous billets-doux are constantly assailing you ; ' for a man
of his stamp draws on others.'   Yet what monster can surpass
an effeminate who is a miser?   ' This I bestowed on you, then
that I gave you, and soon after you had more.'   He reckons up
and acts the wanton.   ' Let the counters be set out ; let the lads
come here with the reckoning-table ; count out five sestertia in
all.'   Let my services be counted up afterwards !   Pray, is it an
easy matter, or in accordance with one's tastes, to minister to his
lusts ? . . .   But you, I suppose, thought yourself tender and a
boy, and handsome and worthy of the cup *of Jove* and of heaven.
Will you, *and such as you*, ever show favour to a humble hanger-
on or follower, when you are not even prepared to give on behalf
of your diseased taste ?   Here is a fellow for you to send a green

grandia, natalis quoties redit aut madidum ver
incipit et strata positus longaque cathedra
munera femineis tractat secreta kalendis !
dic, passer, cui tot montes, tot praedia servas
Appula, tot milvos intra tua pascua lassos ?   55
te Trifolinus ager fecundis vitibus implet
suspectumque iugum Cumis et Gaurus inanis ;
nam quis plura linit victuro dolia musto ?
quantum erat exhausti lumbos donare clientis
ingeribus paucis ! meliusne hic rusticus infans,   60
cum matre et casulis et collusore catello,
cymbala pulsantis legatum fiet amici ?
' improbus es, cum poscis,' ait.   sed pensio clamat
' posce !' sed appellat puer unicus, ut Polyphemi
lata acies, per quam sollers evasit Ulixes.   65
alter emendus erit, namque hic non sufficit, ambo

63. ais.

---

parasol to, or large pieces of amber, as often as his birthday
recurs, or when rainy spring commences, and, deposited in his
pillowed and long ladies' chair, he handles secret presents *sent
him* on the female kalends !

   "Tell me, you sparrow, for whom are you keeping so many
hills, so many Apulian farms, so many hawks wearied *in flying*
across your pastures? The territory of Trifolium enriches you
with its fruitful vines, and the heights looked up to by Cumae
and hollow Gaurus. For who seals up more casks of new wine
destined to a long life? How great a matter would it have
been to present the loins of your worn-out client with a few
acres ! Will it be better that this rustic child, with his mother,
and the hovels, and the little dog his playmate, should become
the inheritance of a cymbal-beating friend? 'You are an impudent fellow to beg,' he says ; but my house-rent cries out,
Beg ! but my slave calls out, a solitary one, like the big eye of
Polyphemus, by *putting out* which, crafty Ulysses made his
escape. Another *slave* will have to be bought, for this one is
not equal to his work ; both of them will have to be fed. What

pascendi. quid agam bruma spirante ? quid, oro,
quid dicam scapulis puerorum aquilone Decembri
et pedibus ? 'durate atque exspectate cicadas ?'
verum, ut dissimules, ut mittas cetera, quanto   70
metiris pretio, quod, ni tibi deditus essem
devotusque cliens, uxor tua virgo maneret ?
scis certe, quibus ista modis, quam saepe rogaris
et quae pollicitus. fugientem saepe puellam
amplexu rapui ; tabulas quoque ruperat et iam   75
signabat, tota vix hoc ego nocte redemi
te plorante foris. testis mihi lectulus et tu,
ad quem pervenit lecti sonus et dominae vox.
instabile ac dirimi coeptum et iam paene solutum
coniugium in multis domibus servavit adulter.   80
quo te circumagas ? quae prima aut ultima ponas ?
nullum ergo meritum est, ingrate ac perfide, nullum,
quod tibi filiolus vel filia nascitur ex me ?

      68. servorum mense.   **80. servabit.**

---

shall I do when winter is abroad? What, pray, what shall I
say to the shoulders and feet of my slaves in the north wind of
December? 'Bear up, and wait for the grasshoppers?' But
though you should disguise, though you should pass over my
other services, at what price do you estimate this, that unless I
had been your submissive and devoted client, your wife would
remain a virgin? You assuredly know in what ways, and how
often, you asked those services of me, and what you promised.
I caught in my embrace your young wife, who was often trying
to escape ; she had even broken her marriage tablets, and was
just signing *new ones.* I scarcely settled this matter in a whole
night, when you were blubbering outside the door. The bed is
my witness, and you, whom the sound of the bed reached, and
the voice of my lady. In many a household has an unstable
union, and one beginning to be broken up, and already well-
nigh dissolved, been preserved by a lover. Which way will you
turn yourself? what will you reckon first and what last? Is it
no service, then, you ungrateful and perfidious man, is it none,

tollis enim et libris actorum spargere gaudes
argumenta viri. foribus suspende coronas,   85
iam pater es, dedimus quod famae opponere possis,
iura parentis habes, propter me scriberis heres,
legatum omne capis nec non et dulce caducum;
commoda praeterea iungentur multa caducis,
si numerum, si tres implevero." iusta doloris,   90
Naevole, causa tui, contra tamen ille quid affert?
    " Negligit atque alium bipedem sibi quaerit asellum.
haec soli commissa tibi celare memento,
et tacitus nostras intra te fige querelas ;
nam res mortifera est inimicus pumice levis.   95
qui modo secretum commiserat, ardet et odit,
tamquam prodiderim quidquid scio, sumere ferrum,
fuste aperire caput, candelam apponere valvis
non dubitat; nec contemnas aut despicias, quod

---

that a little son or daughter is born to you by means of me?
For you rear them, and delight to spread abroad, through the
gazettes, proofs of your virility. Hang garlands over your doors,
you are a father now. I have given you something which you
may oppose to rumour; you have the privileges of a parent;
through me you can be written down as heir; you can take a
legacy in its entirety; aye, and a pleasant windfall as well.
Many advantages, besides, will be joined to the windfall if I
make up the number, if I make up three."

The cause of your grievance is a just one, Naevolus; but what
does he allege in return?

" He neglects me, and looks out for another two-legged ass for
himself. *All* this, which is intrusted to yourself alone, be mindful to keep secret, and in silence implant my complaints in your
breast, for an enemy who smoothes himself with pumice-stone is
a deadly thing. He that has just intrusted his secret *to me* rages
and hates me, just as though I had divulged whatever I know.
He does not hesitate to employ steel, to open one's head with a
cudgel, to apply a candle to one's doors. Nor should you make

his opibus numquam cara est annona veneni.   100
ergo occulta teges, ut curia Martis Athenis."
o Corydon, Corydon, secretum divitis ullum
esse putas? servi ut taceant, iumenta loquentur
et canis et postes et marmora.   claude fenestras,
vela tegant rimas, iunge ostia, tollite lumen   105
e medio, taceant omnes, prope nemo recumbat;
quod tamen ad cantum galli facit ille secundi,
proximus ante diem caupo sciet, audiet et quae
finxerunt pariter librarius archimagiri
carptores.   quod enim dubitant componere crimen   110
in dominos, quoties rumoribus ulciscuntur
baltea? nec deerit qui te per compita quaerat
nolentem et miseram vinosus inebriet aurem.
illos ergo roges quidquid paulo ante petebas
a nobis, taceant illi.   sed prodere maluut   115
arcanum, quam surrepti potare Falerni,

---

light of, or neglect, *the fact* that to these rich people the price of
poison is never *too* high.   So, then, keep these things *as* secret
as the court of Mars at Athens."

O Corydon, Corydon! do you think there can be any rich
man's secret? Though the slaves should hold their tongues,
the beasts of burden will talk, and the dog, and the gate-posts,
and the marbles.   Shut the windows, cover the chinks with
curtains, fasten the doors, remove the light, let all be silent, let
no one lie near the place, yet what he does at the second cock-
crowing the nearest tavern-keeper will know before day, and will
hear what the secretary and the head cooks and the carvers have
invented at the same time.   For what charge do they hesitate
to concoct against their masters, as often as they avenge their
strappings by lies? Nor will there be wanting *some* one who
will hunt you out against your will through the crossways, and
drench your miserable ear with his drunken tales.   Beg of
these, then, what you were asking of me a short while ago:
let them hold their tongues.   Why, they would rather publish

pro populo faciens quantum Saufeia bibebat.
vivendum recte est cum propter plurima, tum his
praecipue causis, ut linguas mancipiorum
contemnas, nam lingua mali pars pessima servi.   120
deterior tamen hic, qui liber non erit illis,
quorum animas et farre suo custodit et aere.

" Idiciro ut possim linguam contemnere servi,
utile consilium modo, sed commune dedisti ;
nunc mihi quid suades post damnum temporis et spes 125
deceptas ?   festinat enim decurrere velox
flosculus angustae miseraeque brevissima vitae
portio ; dum bibimus, dum serta unguenta puellas
poscimus, obrepit non intellecta senectus."
ne trepida, numquam pathicus tibi deerit amicus   130
stantibus et salvis his collibus, undique ad illos
conveniunt et carpentis et navibus omnes

118. tunc his.   120. nec lingua.
132. conveniunt.

a secret than swill as much stolen Falernian as Saufeia used
to drink when sacrificing for the people.   One should lead an
upright life, as well on very many *other* accounts, as also especially for this reason, that you may despise the tongues of your
slaves, for his tongue is the worst part of a bad slave.   Yet he
is worse still who is not free in respect of those whose lives he
preserves with his own bread and *his own* money.

[" That I may be able, therefore, to despise the tongue of my
slave.]   The advice you have just given is useful, but it is
general.   Now what do you recommend in my case, after the loss
of my time, and the disappointment of my hopes?   For the
short-lived blossom, and contracted span of our bounded and
miserable existence is hastening to an end.   While we are
drinking, while we are calling for garlands, perfumes, maidens,
old age steals up unperceived."

Don't be frightened.   You will never lack a pathic friend
while these hills are standing fast.   To them will converge from
every quarter, in carriages and in ships, all those who scratch

qui digito scalpunt uno caput.   altera maior
spes superest, tu tantum erucis imprime dentem.
   " Haec exempla para felicibus ; at mea Clotho   135
et Lachesis gaudent, si pascitur inguine venter.
o parvi nostrique Lares, quos thure minuto
aut farre et tenui soleo exorare corona,
quando ego figam aliquid, quo sit mihi tuta senectus
a tegete et baculo ? viginti millia fenus   140
pignoribus positis, argenti vascula puri,
sed quae Fabricius censor notet, et duo fortes
de grege Moesorum, qui me cervice locata
securum iubeant clamoso insistere circo.
sit mihi praeterea curvus caelator et alter   145
qui multas facies fingat cito.   sufficiunt haec,
quando ego pauper ero.   votum miserabile, nec spes
his saltem ; nam cum pro me Fortuna rogatur,

their heads with one finger.   You have still better prospects in
store for you : do you only imprint your teeth upon rocket.
   " Furnish these instructions to luckier men : my Clotho and
Lachesis are well pleased if my belly is fed by my trade.   O my
small, my own Lares ! whom I am wont to supplicate with a
trifle of frankincense, or meal, and a poor garland, when shall I
spear anything by which my old age may be secure from the
mat and staff *of the beggar ?*   Twenty thousand *sesterces* income
on mortgage, some small vases of silver, unchased, but such as
Fabricius the censor would condemn, and two stout fellows
of the Moesian herd, who, with their necks placed under me,
should bid me take up my position without apprehension in the
noisy circus.   I should like to have, besides, a graver bending
over his work, and another *slave* to mould me quickly a number
of casts : this must suffice, since I shall *still* be poor.   A pitiable wish, and yet there is no hope of even this ; for when
Fortune is invoked for me, she has stuck *into her ears* wax

affixit ceras illa de nave petitas,
quae Siculos cantus effugit remige surdo."   150

SATIRA X.

O MNIBUS in terris, quae sunt a Gadibus usque
   Auroram et Gangen, pauci dignoscere possunt
vera bona atque illis multum diversa, remota
erroris nebula. quid enim ratione timemus
aut cupimus? quid tam dextro pede concipis, ut te   5
conatus non poeniteat votique peracti ?
evertere domos totas optantibus ipsis
di faciles; nocitura toga, nocitura petuntur
militia; torrens dicendi copia multis
et sua mortifera est facundia, viribus ille   10

       7. operantibus.

---

fetched from that ship (*of Ulysses*) which escaped the Sicilian
syren-songs with its deaf rowers."

SATIRE X.

IN all the lands which exist, from Gades even to Aurora and
the Ganges, there are few who are able to distinguish between
real blessings and things widely opposite to them, when the
mist of error is removed. For what is it that we fear, or desire,
rationally? What *purpose* do you conceive so auspiciously that
you have not to regret your undertaking, and the accomplish-
ment of your wish? The favouring gods have destroyed whole
families by *granting* their own prayers; things destined to be
hurtful in peace are asked for, and things destined to be hurtful
in war. To many, a torrent-like abundance of speech and their
own eloquence is fatal: there was one who perished from pre-
suming on his strength and his wonderful arms. But more still

confisus periit admirandisque lacertis.
sed plures nimia congesta pecunia cura
strangulat et cuncta exsuperans patrimonia census,
quanto delphinis balaena Britannica maior.
temporibus diris igitur iussuque Neronis   15
Longinum et magnos Senecae praedivitis hortos
clausit, et egregias Lateranorum obsidet aedes
tota cohors; rarus venit in coenacula miles.
pauca licet portes argenti vascula puri,
nocte iter ingressus gladium contumque timebis   20
et motae ad lunam trepidabis arundinis umbram;
cantabit vacuus coram latrone viator.
prima fere vota et cunctis notissima templis
divitiae, crescant ut opes, ut maxima toto
nostra sit arca foro.   sed nulla aconita bibuntur   25
fictilibus; tunc illa time, cum pocula sumes
gemmata et lato Setinum ardebit in auro.

11. admirandusque.

---

are choked by their money heaped together with too much care,
and their property exceeding all *other* fortunes, by as much as a
British whale is larger than dolphins. Hence it was that in
a time of terror, and by the order of Nero, a whole cohort
surrounded *the house of* Longinus and the vast gardens of the
enormously wealthy Seneca, and besieged the splendid man-
sion of the Laterani. The soldier rarely comes into a garret.
Though you carry but a few small cups of unchased silver when
starting on a night-journey, you will be afraid of the sword and
the pike, and will tremble at the shadow of a reed moving in the
moonlight; *while* the traveller who has nothing upon him will
sing in the face of the robber. The first of prayers, commonly,
and the best known in all the temples, are for wealth, that our
money may increase, that our strong-box may be the largest in
the whole forum. But no aconite is drunk from earthenware;
then fear it when you take up jewelled cups, and the Setine
glows in the broad gold. Do you not, after this, approve *the
fact* that, of the sages, one used to laugh as often as he moved

iamne igitur laudas, quod de sapientibus alter
ridebat, quoties de limine moverat unum
protuleratque pedem, flebat contrarius auctor ?   30
sed facilis cuivis rigidi censura cachinni ;
mirandum est, unde ille oculis suffecerit humor;
perpetuo risu pulmonem agitare solebat
Democritus, quamquam non essent urbibus illis
praetexta et trabeae fasces lectica tribunal.   35
quid si vidisset praetorem curribus altis
exstantem et medio sublimem in pulvere circi
in tunica Iovis, et pictae Sarrana ferentem
ex humeris aulaea togae magnaeque coronae
tantum orbem, quanto cervix non sufficit ulla ?   40
quippe tenet sudans hanc publicus et, sibi consul
ne placeat, curru servus portatur eodem.
da nunc et volucrem sceptro quae surgit eburno,
illinc cornicines, hinc praecedentia longi
agminis officia et niveos ad frena Quirites,   45

29. a limine.   30. alter.   37. medii.

---

and advanced one foot over the threshold, and the opposite
authority used to weep? But easy to any one is the censure of
a sardonic laugh ; the wonder is whence that moisture could
have come in sufficient quantities to the eyes *of the other.*
Democritus used to shake his lungs with perpetual laughter,
though there did not exist in those cities the praetexta or
trabeae, or fasces, or litters, or a tribunal. What if he had
seen the Praetor standing up in his lofty chariot, and on high,
in the midst of the dust of the circus, in the tunic of Jove, and
wearing the Tyrian hangings of an embroidered toga *depending*
from his shoulders, and a huge crown of such a circumference
as no single neck is equal to?—seeing that the public slave
holds this, all in a sweat, and, lest the Consul should be *too
much* pleased with himself, rides in the same chariot. Add to
this the bird which rises from his ivory sceptre ; on that side
the trumpeters, on this the clients preceding him in long array,
and the Quirites *all* in white by his bridle, whom the dole buried

defossa in loculis quos sportula fecit amicos.
tum quoque materiam risus invenit ad omnes
occursus hominum, cuius prudentia monstrat
summos posse viros et magna exempla daturos
vervecum in patria crassoque sub aere nasci.   50
ridebat curas, nec non et gaudia vulgi,
interdum et lacrimas, cum fortunae ipse minaci
mandaret laqueum mediumque ostenderet unguem.

    Ergo supervacua aut perniciosa petuntur,
propter quae fas est genua incerare deorum.   55
quosdam praecipitat subiecta potentia magnae
invidiae; mergit longa atque insignis honorum
pagina; descendunt statuae restemque sequuntur.
ipsas deinde rotas bigarum impacta securis
caedit, et immeritis franguntur crura caballis.   60
iam strident ignes, iam follibus atque caminis
ardet adoratum populo caput, et crepat ingens

55. incerate (Madvig).

---

in their purses has made his friends. Even in his day he found
material for laughter in every encounter of human beings; he
whose wisdom shows that men the most eminent, and destined
to furnish lofty examples, may be born in the country of wethers
and under a dull sky. He used to laugh at the cares, and the
joys too, of the vulgar, sometimes even at their tears, since he
himself, when Fortune threatened him, would bid her be hanged,
and point the finger of scorn at her.

    So then superfluous or pernicious things are asked for, on
behalf of which it is our fate to wax the knees of the gods.
Some, their power, exposed to great envy, hurls down headlong; the long and illustrious record of their honours sinks
them; their statues come down and are dragged behind a rope.
Then the very wheels of their *triumphal* chariots are smashed
by the violent blows of the axe, and the legs of the innocent
horses are broken. Now the flames roar, now the head that
was worshipped by the people glows with the bellows and the
furnace, and great Sejanus crackles. Then out of the face

Seianus, deinde ex facie toto orbe secunda
fiunt urceoli pelves sartago matellae.
pone domi lauros, duc in Capitolia magnum   65
cretatumque bovem, Seianus ducitur unco
spectandus! gaudent omnes. "quae labra, quis illi
vultus erat! numquam, si quid mihi credis, amavi
hunc hominem; sed quo cecidit sub crimine? quisnam
delator? quibus indiciis, quo teste probavit?"   70
"nil horum, verbosa et grandis epistola venit
a Capreis." "bene habet, nil plus interrogo. sed quid
turba Remi?" "sequitur fortunam, ut semper, et odit
damnatos. idem populus, si Nurtia Tusco
favisset, si oppressa foret secura senectus   75
principis, hac ipsa Seianum diceret hora
Augustum. iam pridem, ex quo suffragia nulli
vendimus, effudit curas; nam qui dabat olim
imperium fasces legiones omnia, nunc se

---

which was second in the whole world are manufactured little
jugs, basins, frying-pans, chamber utensils. Hang up bays on
your house, lead into the Capitol the large bull whitened with
chalk. Sejanus is being dragged along by the hook, *such* a
sight! Every one is delighted. "What lips, and what an expression he had! Never, if you will believe me, did I like that
man." "But under what charge has he fallen? Who was the
informer? By what evidence, by what witnesses did he prove
the charge?" "Nothing of the sort. A verbose and lengthy
letter came from Capreae." "All right. I ask no more. But
what does the crowd of Remus *do?*" "It follows Fortune, as
it always does, and hates those who are condemned. This same
people, if Nurtia had favoured the Tuscan, if the old Emperor
had been fallen upon when off his guard, would at this very
hour be calling Sejanus, Augustus. Long ago, since we left off
selling our votes, it has cast away all *public* cares. For that
people which once upon a time used to bestow military command,
the fasces, legions, everything, now limits its desires, and

continet atque duas tantum res anxius optat,   80
panem et circenses." " perituros audio multos."
" nil dubium, magna est fornacula, pallidulus mi
Brutidius meus ad Martis fuit obvius aram.
quam timeo, victus ne poenas exigat Ajax
ut male defensus! curramus praecipites et,   85
dum iacet in ripa, calcemus Caesaris hostem."
" sed videant servi, ne quis neget et pavidum in ius
cervice obstricta dominum trahat."   hi sermones
tunc de Seiano, secreta haec murmura vulgi.
visne salutari sicut Seianus, habere   90
tantumdem, atque illi summas donare curules,
illum exercitibus praeponere, tutor haberi
principis angustâ Caprearum in rupe sedentis
cum grege Chaldaeo? vis certe pila, cohortes,
egregios equites et castra domestica.   quidni   95
haec cupias? et qui nolunt occidere quemquam,

88. astricta.   93. augusta.

anxiously longs for two things only—bread and the games of
the circus." " I hear that many are doomed to die." " Not a
doubt of it: the 'little furnace' is a capacious one. My friend
Brutidius met me at the altar of Mars, looking a trifle pale.
How I fear that 'worsted Ajax' will wreak vengeance, as having
been badly defended.   Let us run with all speed and trample
on the foe of Caesar while he *still* lies on the river bank."
" Aye, and let our slaves see *us do it*, that none may deny it,
and drag his trembling master to trial with a rope about his
neck."   Such were the remarks at that time about Sejanus,
such were the secret whispers of the populace.   Do you wish to
have court paid you like Sejanus? to possess as much *as he did*,
and to bestow on one the highest curule offices, to set another at
the head of armies, to be esteemed the guardian of the sovereign
seated on the narrow rock of Capreae with his pack of Chal-
deans? Of course you would like *to have* chief-centurionships,
cohorts, picked cavalry, the household troops.   Why should you
not desire these things?   Even those who do not wish to kill any

posse volunt.   sed quae praeclara et prospera tanti,
ut rebus laetis par sit mensura malorum ?
huius, qui trahitur, praetextam sumere mavis
an Fidenarum Gabiorumque esse potestas   100
et de mensura ius dicere, vasa minora
frangere pannosus vacuis aedilis Ulubris ?
ergo quid optandum foret] ignorasse fateris
Scianum ; nam qui nimios optabat honores
et nimias poscebat opes, numerosa parabat   105
excelsae turris tabulata, unde altior esset
casus et impulsae praeceps immane ruinae.
quid Crassos, quid Pompeios evertit, et illum,
ad sua qui domitos deduxit flagra Quirites ?
summus nempe locus nulla non arte petitus   110
magnaque numinibus vota exaudita malignis.
ad generum Cereris sine caede ac vulnere pauci
descendunt reges et sicca morte tyranni.

         97. tantum.   112. sanguine.

---

one wish to have the power to do it.   But what brilliant fortune, what prosperity, can be of such great value *as to be worth the condition* that the measure of misfortunes should be equal to the good luck ? Would you prefer to assume the praetexta of him who is being dragged along, or to be the magistrate of Fidenae or Gabii, and to pronounce decisions about measures, and to break up pots below the standard, a ragged aedile in empty Ulubrae ? You admit, then, Sejanus to have been ignorant of what would have been desirable *for him :* for he that desired too great honours, and asked for too much wealth, was preparing story upon story of a lofty tower from which his fall should be the greater, and frightful the headlong descent of the stricken ruin. What was it that destroyed the Crassi, what the Pompeys, and him that brought the Quirites in subjection under his lash ? Assuredly it was the highest position sought by every art, and their ambitious prayers heard' too well by the unkind deities. Few kings descend to Ceres' son-in-law without slaughter and wounds, few tyrants by a bloodless death.

Eloquium ac famam Demosthenis aut Ciceronis
incipit optare et totis quinquatribus optat,   115
quisquis adhuc uno partam colit asse Minervam,
quem sequitur custos angustae vernula capsae.
eloquio sed uterque perit orator, utrumque
largus et exundans leto dedit ingenii fons.
ingenio manus est et cervix caesa, nec umquam   120
sanguine causidici maduerunt rostra pusilli.
" o fortunatam natam me consule Romam !"
Antoni gladios potuit contemnere, si sic
omnia dixisset.   ridenda poemata malo,
quam te conspicuae, divina Philippica, famae,   125
volveris a prima quae proxima.   saevus et illum
exitus eripuit, quem mirabantur Athenae
torrentem et pleni moderantem frena theatri.
dis ille adversis genitus fatoque sinistro,
quem pater ardentis massae fuligine lippus   130

116. parcam (Heins).

Whoever pays his court to Minerva, purchased as yet by *only*
a single As, whom a little slave follows in charge of his small
satchel, begins to long, and longs all through the quinquatrian
holidays, for the eloquence and fame of a Demosthenes or a
Cicero.   Yet it was through their eloquence that both of these
orators perished : both of them the copious and overflowing
fount of their genius gave over to destruction.   It was genius
whose hand and neck were struck ; the tribunes have never
been moistened by the blood of an insignificant pleader.
"O fortunate Rome, born under my consulship !"   He might
have despised the swords of Antony, if all his utterances had
been like this.   I prefer these ridiculous poems to thee, divine
Philippic of distinguished fame, that art unrolled next to the first.
Him, too, a cruel end carried off, whom Athens used to admire
flowing like a torrent and moderating *as* with a curb the crowded
theatre.   With gods adverse and fate inauspicious was he born,
whom his father, blear-eyed with the soot of the glowing mass,

a carbone et forcipibus gladiosque parante
incude et luteo Vulcano ad rhetora misit.

 Bellorum exuviae, truncis affixa tropaeis
lorica et fracta de casside buccula pendens
et curtum temone iugum victaeque triremis   135
aplustre et summo tristis captivus in arcu
humanis maiora bonis creduntur. ad hoc se
Romanus Graiusque et barbarus induperator
erexit, causas discriminis atque laboris
inde habuit. tanto maior famae sitis est quam   140
virtutis ; quis enim virtutem amplectitur ipsam,
praemia si tollas ? patriam tamen obruit olim
gloria paucorum et laudis titulique cupido
haesuri saxis cinerum custodibus, ad quae
discutienda valent sterilis mala robora fici,   145
quandoquidem data sunt ipsis quoque fata sepulcris.
expende Hannibalem, quot libras in duce summo

137. ad haec se.

sent from the coals and pincers and sword-forging anvil and
dirty Vulcan to the teacher of rhetoric.

 The spoils of war, the cuirass affixed to the trunk-shaped
trophies, the cheek-piece hanging from the broken helmet, the
chariot shorn of its pole, the stern-ornament of the vanquished
trireme, the melancholy captive on the top of the arch, are held
to be greater than human blessings. / To this the Roman and
Greek and barbarian commander directs his efforts; thence he
gets the incentives for his dangers and his labours. So much
greater is the thirst for fame than for virtue; for who embraces
virtue *for* herself if you take away the rewards? Yet at times
the glory of a few has been the ruin of their country, the craving
for renown and an epitaph to cleave to the stones, guardians
of their ashes, which the mischievous strength of the barren
fig-tree has the power to rend asunder, inasmuch as sepul-
chres themselves have fates assigned them. Weigh Hannibal;
how many pounds will you find in the consummate general?

invenies ? hic est quem non capit Africa Mauro
percussa Oceano Niloque admota tepenti,
rursus ad Aethiopum populos altosque elephantos.   150
additur imperiis Hispania, Pyrenaeum
transilit.   opposuit natura Alpemque nivemque,
diducit scopulos et montem rumpit aceto.
iam tenet Italiam, tamen ultra pergere tendit.
" actum," inquit, " nihil est, nisi Poeno milite portas   155
frangimus et media vexillum pono Subura."
o qualis facies et quali digna tabella,
cum Gaetula ducem portaret bellua luscum !
exitus ergo quis est ? o gloria ! vincitur idem
nempe et in exsilium praeceps fugit atque ibi magnus 160
mirandusque cliens sedet ad praetoria regis,
donec Bithyno libeat vigilare tyranno.
finem animae, quae res humanas miscuit olim,
non gladii, non saxa dabunt, nec tela, sed ille

149. perfusa.   153. deducit, diduxit.

Yet this is he whom not *even* Africa can contain, beaten by the
Mauritanian ocean, and stretching to the warm Nile, and back
again to the nations of the Aethiopians and the tall elephants.
Spain is added to his rule ; he bounds across the Pyrenees ;
nature has opposed to him the Alps and their snows ; he severs
the rocks and cleaves the mountains with vinegar.   Already he
holds Italy ; yet he aims at proceeding further.   " Nothing has
been achieved," he says, " unless we force the city gates with
the soldiers of Carthage, and I plant my standard in the middle
of the Suburra."   Oh ! what a face, and what a picture it would
have been a subject for—a Gaetulian elephant carrying the one-
eyed General !   What, then, is his end ?   O glory !   This same
man is conquered, to be sure, and flies headlong into exile, and
there seats himself, a great and wonder-moving client, by the
palace of the king, till such time as it please his Bithynian
majesty to wake.   Not swords, not rocks, nor darts will put an
end to the existence which once embroiled all humanity, but

Cannarum vindex et tanti sanguinis ultor   165
annulus. i demens et saevas curre per Alpes,
ut pueris placeas et declamatio fias !
unus Pellaeo iuveni non sufficit orbis
aestuat infelix angusto limite mundi,
ut Gyari clausus scopulis parvaque Scripho ;   170
cum tamen a figulis munitam intraverit urbem,
sarcophago contentus erit. mors sola fatetur,
quantula sint hominum corpuscula. creditur olim
velificatus Athos et quidquid Graecia mendax
audet in historia, constratum classibus isdem   175
suppositumque rotis solidum mare, credimus altos
defecisse amnes epotaque flumina Medo
prandente, et madidis cantat quae Sostratus alis.
ille tamen qualis rediit Salamine relicta,
in Corum atque Eurum solitus saevire flagellis   180
barbarus, Aeolio numquam hoc in carcere passos,

---

that ring the avenger of Cannae, the punisher of so much blood-
shed.   Go, madman, and run over the savage Alps—to please
schoolboys and become *the subject of* a declamation !

One world is not enough for the young man of Pella ; the
poor fellow is restless in the narrow limits of the universe, as
though imprisoned by the rocks of Gyarus, or in small Seriphus.   When, however, he shall have entered the city fortified
by brickmakers, he will be content with a sarcophagus.   Death
alone discloses how diminutive are the puny bodies of men.
Athos is believed to have been once sailed over—and whatever
else lying Greece ventures on in the way of history ; *it is believed*
that the sea was bridged by these same fleets, and made solid and
passed over by wheels.   We believe that deep streams failed,
and that rivers were drunk dry by the Medes at their dinner,
and whatever Sostratus sings with moistened wings.   Yet in
what a guise did that famous barbarian return, after leaving
Salamis, who had been wont to rage with whips against Corus
and Eurus, that had never suffered this *treatment* in their Aeolian
cavern, who had bound the earth-shaker *Neptune* himself in

ipsum compedibus qui vinxerat Ennosigaeum!
mitius id sane, quod non et stigmate dignum
crederet.   huic quisquam vellet servire deorum!
sed qualis rediit? nempe una nave, cruentis   185
fluctibus ac tarda per densa cadavera prora.
has toties optata exegit gloria poenas!

"Da spatium vitae, multos da, Iuppiter, annos!"
hoc recto vultu solum hoc et pallidus optas.
sed quam continuis et quantis longa senectus   190
plena malis! deformem et tetrum ante omnia vultum
dissimilemque sui, deformem pro cute pellem,
pendentesque genas et tales aspice rugas,
quales, umbriferos ubi pandit Tabraca saltus,
in vetula scalpit iam mater simia bucca.   195
plurima sunt iuvenum discrimina, pulchrior ille
hoc, atque ille alio, multum hic robustior illo;
una senum facies, cum voce trementia membra

   183. quid? non et.   184. credidit.   198. labra.

---

chains! Surely it was merciful *on his part* that he did not
think him deserving of being branded into the bargain. Here
was a man whom any of the gods would have been glad to be
the slave of! But in what a guise did he return? With a
single ship, to be sure, the waves all bloody; his prow retarded
by the multitude of corpses.   Such penalties has prayed-for glory
oftentimes exacted!

Grant length óf life! grant, O Jupiter, many years! For
this alone you pray in health and in sickness; but how unre-
mitting and how great are the ills with which a long old age is
filled! Behold, first of all, the ugly and offensive face, unlike
itself; the ugly hide in place of skin, and the flabby cheeks and
the wrinkles, such as those which—there where Tabraca extends
its shade-bearing jungles—the mother ape scratches on her aged
jowl.   There are many points of difference between young men:
this one is handsomer than that, and he than another; one is
much sturdier than another.   Old men have but one aspect:
limbs trembling in unison with their voice, a pate that has

et iam leve caput madidique infantia nasi.
frangendus misero gingiva panis inermi;   200
usque adeo gravis uxori natisque sibique,
ut captatori moveat fastidia Cosso.
non eadem vini atque cibi torpente palato
gaudia; nam coitus iam longa oblivio, vel si
coneris, iacet exiguus cum ramice nervus   205
et, quamvis tota palpetur nocte, iacebit.
anne aliquid sperare potest haec inguinis aegri
canities? quid, quod merito suspecta libido est,
quae Venerem affectat sine viribus. / aspice partis
nunc damnum alterius; nam quae cantante voluptas, 210
sit licet eximius citharoedus, sitve Seleucus
et quibus aurata mos est fulgere lacerna?
quid refert, magni sedeat qua parte theatri,
qui vix cornicines exaudiet atque tubarum
concentus? clamore opus est, ut sentiat auris,   215

200. miseris.   202. moveant.   205. conetur.
214. exaudiat.

---

become smooth, the *second* infancy of a drivelling nose. The
wretched creature has to break his bread with a toothless gum.
To such an extent *is he* burdensome to his wife and children
and himself, as to excite the nausea even of the fortune-hunter
Cossus. His pleasure in wine and food is no longer the same,
through the torpor of his palate. ⌊Sexual connection has long
since been forgotten, or, if the attempt be made, despite every
effort, he will be powerless. Can this grey decrepitude of
sickly lust expect anything *else?* and, moreover, do we not look
with just suspicion on the lechery which affects sexual love,
without the power?⌋

Observe now the loss of another faculty. For what pleasure
has he in a musician, though he be a distinguished harpist, or
even a Seleucus, or one of those who are wont to glitter in a
gold-embroidered cloak? What matters it in what part of the
vast theatre he sits, who will scarce hear distinctly even the
horn-blowers or the concert of trumpets? It is necessary to

quem dicat venisse puer, quot nunciet horas.
praeterea minimus gelido iam in corpore sanguis
febre calet solá, circumsilit agmine facto
morborum omne genus, quorum si nomina quaeras,
promptius expediam quot amaverit Hippia moechos,   220
quot Themison aegros autumno occiderit uno,
quot Basilus socios, quot circumscripserit Hirrus
pupillos, quot longa viros exsorbeat uno
Maura die, quot discipulos inclinet Hamillus ;
percurram citius quot villas possideat nunc,   225
quo tondente gravis iuveni mihi barba sonabat.
ille humero, hic lumbis, hic coxa debilis, ambos
perdidit ille oculos et luscis invidet, huius
pallida labra cibum accipiunt digitis alienis.
ipse ad conspectum coenae diducere rictum   230
suetus, hiat tantum, ceu pullus hirundinis, ad quem
ore volat pleno mater ieiuna.   sed omni

226. iuvenis.   229. capiunt.   230. deducere.

---

bawl out, that his ear may catch who it is that his slave says
has called, *or* the hour of day which he announces.   Moreover,
the scanty blood in his now cold body warms with fever alone ;
all kinds of diseases dance round him in a troop.   If you should
ask their names, I could sooner tell off how many gallants
Hippia has been in love with, how many patients Themison has
killed in a single autumn, how many partners have been cheated
by Basilus, how many wards by Hirrus, how many men tall
Maura has connection with in a single day, how many pupils
Hamillus corrupts. I could more quickly run through the *list
of* villas now possessed by one under whose razor my heavy
beard used to sound when I was a young man. One is weak in
the shoulder, another in the loins, another in the hip ; another
has lost both his eyes, and envies the one-eyed ; another's bloodless lips receive their food from others' fingers.   The man who
was wont of his own accord to break into a broad grin at the
sight of his dinner, now gapes merely, like the young of a
swallow to whom his mother, *herself* fasting, flies with full beak.

membrorum damno maior dementia, quae nec
nomina servorum nec vultum agnoscit amici,
cum quo praeterita coenavit nocte, nec illos,   235
quos genuit, quos eduxit.   nam codice saevo
heredes vetat esse suos, bona tota feruntur
ad Phialen ;[tantum artificis valet halitus oris,
quod steterat multis in carcere fornicis annis.]
ut vigeant sensus animi, ducenda tamen sunt   240
funera natorum, rogus aspiciendus amatae
coniugis et fratris plenaeque sororibus urnae.
haec data poena diu viventibus, ut renovata
semper clade domus multis in luctibus inque
perpetuo moerore et nigra veste senescant.   245
rex Pylius, magno si quidquam credis Homero,
exemplum vitae fuit a cornice secundae.
felix nimirum, qui tot per secula mortem
distulit atque suos iam dextra computat annos,
quique novum toties mustum bibit. oro parumper   250

But worse than all bodily ailments is the idiocy which
recognises neither the names of his slaves, nor the face of the
friend with whom he dined last night, nor those whom he begot,
whom he brought up. For, by a cruel will, he prevents them
from being his heirs : all his property is conferred upon Phiale
[—such power has the breath of her dexterous mouth, which
had been stationed for many years in the cell of a brothel !]
Should the faculties of the mind retain their vigour, yet one has
to bury one's children, to contemplate the funeral pile of a beloved
wife or brother, and the urns full of one's sisters' *ashes.* This is
the penalty imposed on the long-lived, that, with ever-renewed
family losses, they should grow old in many griefs, in perpetual
mourning, and a garb of black.   The King of Pylos, if you give
any credit to great Homer, was an instance of *long* life, second only
to that of the crow. A happy man, without doubt, who has put off
death for so many generations, and already counts his own years
on his right hand, and has drunk so often of new-made wine.
I pray you listen a moment how much he himself complains of

attendas, quantum de legibus ipse queratur
fatorum et nimio de stamine, cum videt acris
Antilochi barbam ardentem, cum quaerit ab omni,
quisquis adest socius, cur haec in tempora duret,
quod facinus dignum tam longo admiserit aevo.   255
haec eadem Peleus, raptum cum luget Achillem,
atque alius, cui fas Ithacum lugere natantem.
incolumi Troia Priamus venisset ad umbras
Assaraci, magnis solemnibus, Hectore funus
portante ac reliquis fratrum cervicibus inter   260
Iliadum lacrimas, ut primos edere planctus
Cassandra inciperet scissaque Polyxena palla,
si foret exstinctus diverso tempore, quo non
coeperat audaces Paris aedificare carinas.
longa dies igitur quid contulit? omnia vidit   265
eversa et flammis Asiam ferroque cadentem.
tunc miles tremulus posita tulit arma tiara
et ruit ante aram summi Iovis, ut vetulus bos,

---

the decrees of fate, and of the too long thread of his life, when
he sees the blazing beard of brave Antilochus, when he asks of
all his friends who are present why he survives to these times,
what crime he has committed deserving of so long a life. Peleus
utters the same *complaint* when he mourns the loss of Achilles;
and that other whose fate it was to mourn the son of Ithaca
at sea.

Priam would have gone to the shade of Assaracus, with Troy
standing, with great solemnities, with Hector and all his brothers
carrying the bier on their shoulders, amidst the tears of the Trojan
women, so soon as Cassandra had begun to lead off the first wail-
ings, and Polyxena with rent mantle, if his life had been closed
at a different epoch, when Paris had not begun to build his daring
ships. What, then, did length of days confer upon him? He
saw everything overturned, and Asia falling by flame and sword.
Then, laying aside his tiara, he took up arms, a tremulous warrior, and fell before the altar of supreme Jove, like an aged ox,

qui domini cultris tenue et miserabile collum
praebet ab ingrato iam fastiditus aratro.   270
exitus ille utcumque hominis, sed torva canino
latravit rictu, quae post hunc vixerat, uxor.
festino ad nostros et regem transeo Ponti
et Croesum, quem vox iusti facunda Solonis
respicere ad longae iussit spatia ultima vitae.   275
exsilium et carcer Minturnarumque paludes
et mendicatus victâ Carthagine panis
hinc causas habuere.   quid illo cive tulisset
natura in terris, quid Roma beatius umquam,
si circumducto captivorum agmine et omni   280
bellorum pompa animam exhalasset opimam,
cum de Teutonico vellet descendere curru ?
provida Pompeio dederat Campania febres
optandas, sed multae urbes et publica vota
vicerunt: igitur fortuna ipsius et urbis   285
servatum victo caput abstulit.   hoc cruciatu

---

which, now at length despised by the ungrateful plough, proffers
his lean and wretched neck to his master's knife.   This, at any
rate, was the end of a human being; but his wife, who survived
him, barked savagely with the jaws of a bitch.

I hasten to our countrymen, and pass over the King of Pontus
and Croesus, whom the eloquent voice of just Solon bade to consider the last course in a long life. *Marius's* exile and prison,
and the marshes of Minturnae, and the bread begged for in
conquered Carthage, had their origin in this.   What would
Nature in all the earth, what would Rome, have ever borne
more blest than that citizen, if, after the array of captives had
been led their round, and all the pomp of war, he had exhaled
his triumphant soul when he was preparing to descend from his
Teutonic chariot ?   Foreseeing Campania had given Pompey a
fever he should have prayed for, but the multitude of cities
and the public prayers prevailed.   So then his own fortune
and that of the city deprived him, when vanquished, of the

Lentulus, hac poena caruit, ceciditque Cethegus
integer, et iacuit Catilina cadavere toto.
  Formam optat modico pueris, maiore puellis
murmure, cum Veneris fanum videt anxia mater,   290
usque ad delicias votorum. " cur tamen," inquit,
" corripias ? pulchra gaudet Latona Diana."
sed vetat optari faciem Lucretia qualem
ipsa habuit, cuperet Rutilae Virginia gibbum
accipere atque suam Rutilae dare. filius autem   295
corporis egregii miseros trepidosque parentes
semper habet. rara est adeo concordia formae
atque pudicitiae. sanctos licet horrida mores
tradiderit domus ac veteres imitata Sabinos,
praeterea castum ingenium vultumque modesto   300
sanguine ferventem tribuat natura benigna
larga manu—quid enim puero conferre potest plus
custode et cura natura potentior omni ?—

---

head they had *themselves* preserved. Lentulus escaped this
anguish, this indignity, and Cethegus perished unmutilated,
and Catiline lay with his corpse entire.
  The anxious mother, when she sees the shrine of Venus,
prays for beauty for her boys with a gentle murmur, with yet
a louder one for her girls, to the extent of making whimsical
prayers. " Yet why reprove me ?" she says ; " Latona delights
in the beauty of Diana." But Lucretia forbids such a face as
she herself had to be prayed for ; Virginia would wish to take
Rutila's hump, and give her own *face* to Rutila. Besides, a son
of very beautiful person always keeps his parents miserable and
trembling, so rare is the union of beauty with chastity. Though
the family, unsophisticated, and imitating the ancient Sabines,
has handed down *the tradition of* purity of morals ; moreover,
though liberal Nature with benignant hand bestow on him a
chaste mind, and a face hot with modest blood (for what more
can be conferred upon the boy by Nature, more powerful than
all guardians and all watchfulness ?), they are not allowed to

non licet esse viros; nam prodiga corruptoris
improbitas ipsos audet tentare parentes.   305
tanta in muneribus fiducia. (nullus ephebum
deformem saeva castravit in arce tyrannus,
nec praetextatum rapuit Nero loripedem nec
strumosum atque utero pariter gibboque tumentem.'
i nunc, et iuvenis specie laetare tui, quem   310
maiora exspectant discrimina. fiet adulter
publicus et poenas metuet quascumque maritis
iratis debet, nec erit felicior astro
Martis, ut in laqueos numquam incidat. exigit autem
interdum ille dolor plus quam lex ulla dolori   315
concessit; necat hic ferro, secat ille cruentis
verberibus, quosdam moechos et mugilis intrat.
sed tuus Endymion dilectae fiet adulter
matronae; mox cum dederit Servilia nummos,
fiet et illius, quam non amat; exuet omnem   320

304. viris, viro.

---

become men, for the prodigal iniquity of the corruptor dares to
tempt the parents themselves. So great is the confidence in
bribes! But no tyrant in his cruel stronghold has castrated a
deformed youth, nor did Nero ravish a youth who was club-
footed, or one that was scrofulous, and bulging out at the same
time with a paunch and a hump. Go now and delight in the
beauty of your boy, whom greater dangers await. He will
become an adulterer for public hire, and will *have to* fear whatever penalties he owes to enraged husbands; nor will his star
be luckier than that of Mars, even though he never fall into the
net. Moreover, that kind of wrath sometimes exacts more than
any law has conceded to wrath. One slays with the sword,
another cuts with bloody stripes; some adulterers have the
" mullet" applied to them. But your Endymion will become
the gallant of some married lady whom he loves. *Yes! and*
before long, when Servilia has bribed him, he will become also
the gallant of one whom he does not love. She will strip her-

corporis ornatum ; quid enim ulla negaverit udis
inguinibus, sive est haec Oppia, sive Catulla ?
deterior totos habet illic femina mores.)
" sed casto quid forma nocet ? " quid profuit immo
Hippolyto grave propositum, quid Bellerophonti ?   325
erubuit nempe haec, ceu fastidita, repulsa
nec Stheneboea minus quam Cressa excanduit, et se
concussere ambae. mulier saevissima tunc est,
cum stimulos odio pudor admovet. elige quidnam
suadendum esse putes cui nubere Caesaris uxor   330
destinat. optimus hic et formosissimus idem
gentis patriciae rapitur miser exstinguendus
Messalinae oculis. dudum sedet illa parato
flammeolo, Tyriusque palam genialis in hortis
sternitur, et ritu decies centena dabuntur   335
antiquo, veniet cum signatoribus auspex.

326. hac ceu fastidita repulsa (M. Haupt).

self of all her personal ornaments. For what will any woman
deny to her lusts, whether she be an Oppia or a Catulla? The
abandoned woman has all her character centred in this point.
But what harm will his beauty do to one who is chaste ? Nay,
rather, of what advantage was his stern resolve to Hippolytus,
or to Bellerophon? Of course she (*Phaedra*) blushed as though
she had been scorned ; nor was Stheneboea, when repulsed, less
inflamed than the Cretan woman ; and both of them roused
themselves *to vengeance*. Woman is then most savage when
shame adds stings to hate. Choose what advice you think
should be given to him whom the wife of Caesar determines
to marry. He, the best, and at the same time the handsomest, of the patrician race, is hurried, poor wretch, to
destruction by Messalina's eyes. Long since she is seated with
bridal veil prepared, and the nuptial couch *with its coverings* of
purple is openly made ready in the gardens, and ten hundred
thousand sesterces will be given after the ancient usage, and the
augur will come with those that are to sign *the contract*. These

haec tu secreta et paucis commissa putabas.
non nisi legitime vult nubere.   quid placeat, dic ;
ni parere velis, pereundum erit ante lucernas ;
si scelus admittas, dabitur mora parvula, dum res   340
nota urbi et populo contingat principis aures.
dedecus ille domus sciet ultimus.   interea tu
obsequere imperio, si tanti vita dierum
paucorum.   quidquid melius leviusque putaris,
praebenda est gladio pulchra haec et candida cervix.   345
   " Nil ergo optabunt homines ? " si consilium vis,
permittes ipsis expendere numinibus, quid
conveniat nobis·rebusque sit utile nostris.
nam pro iucundis aptissima quaeque dabunt di.
carior est illis homo quam sibi.   nos animorum   350
impulsu et caeca magnaque cupidine ducti
coniugium petimus partumque uxoris ; at illis

337. putabis.   339. pereundum est.   341. aurem.
                 347. permittas.

---

things you thought were secret, and intrusted *only* to a few !
No ; she will not be married but with the legal forms. Say
what your decision is.   Unless you are ready to obey her, you
will have to die before nightfall.   If you perpetrate the crime,
a tiny delay will be afforded you, till a business known to the
city and the people shall have reached the prince's ears ; he will
be the last to learn the disgrace of his house.   Meanwhile do
you obey *her* orders, if a few days' life be worth the price. *But,*
whatever you think the best and easiest *course,* that beautiful
and white neck of yours must be submitted to the sword !
   Are men, then, to pray for nothing ?   If you desire a counsel,
you will permit the deities themselves to estimate what may be
suitable for us, and of advantage to our interests.   For in place
of pleasant things, the gods will give us whatever shall be most
fitting.   Man is dearer to them than *he is* to himself.   We, led
by the impulse of our minds, and our blind and powerful desires,
ask for a wedded partner, and for offspring from our wives ; but

notum, qui pueri qualisque futura sit uxor.
ut tamen et poscas aliquid, voveasque sacellis
exta et candiduli divina tomacula porci, 355
orandum est ut sit mens sana in corpore sano.
fortem posce animum, mortis terrore carentem,
qui spatium vitae extremum inter munera ponat
naturae, qui ferre queat quoscumque labores,
nesciat irasci, cupiat nihil et potiores 360
Herculis aerumnas credat saevosque labores
et Venere et coenis et pluma Sardanapali.
monstro quod ipse tibi possis dare.   semita certe
tranquillae per virtutem patet unica vitae.
nullum numen habes, si sit prudentia, nos te, 365
nos facimus, Fortuna, deam coeloque locamus.

365. abest ; si adsit (Heinr).

they know what our boys and of what sort our wife will be.   If,
however, you must e'en ask for something, and vow to their
shrines entrails and the sacred mincemeat of a white pig, pray
that you may have a sound mind in a sound body; ask for a
strong soul, free from the fear of death, which reckons the final
stage of life as among the boons of Nature; which is able to
bear toils of every kind; which is incapable of anger; which
covets nothing; which deems the tribulations of Hercules and
his cruel labours preferable to *the joys of* Venus, to the banquets,
to the down of Sardanapalus.   I show you what you may confer
upon yourself; *for,* assuredly, the only path of a peaceful life
lies through virtue.   You have no divine power, O Fortune,
where prudence exists; it is we, we who make a goddess of you
and place you in heaven.

A TTICUS eximie si coenat, lautus habetur,
    si Rutilus, demens.   quid enim maiore cachinno
excipitur vulgi, quam pauper Apicius? omnis
convictus thermae stationes omne theatrum
de Rutilo. nam pum valida ac iuvenilia membra   5
sufficiunt galeae dumque ardens sanguine, fertur
non cogente quidem, sed nec prohibente tribuno,
scripturus leges et regia verba lanistae.
multos porro vides, quos saepe clusus ad ipsum
creditor introitum solet exspectare macelli,   10
et quibus in solo vivendi causa palato est.
egregius coenat meliusque miserrimus horum
et cito casurus iam perlucente ruina.
interea gustus elementa per omnia quaerunt,

6. ardent.

SATIRE XI.

IF Atticus dines sumptuously, he is considered a glorious fellow ;
if Rutilus *does so, he is considered* to be out of his mind.   For
what is received with greater laughter from the vulgar than a
pauper Apicius?   Every party—the baths, the places of public
resort—every theatre *is full* of Rutilus. For while his sturdy
and youthful limbs are equal to the helmet, and while he is
glowing with life-blood, he is impelled (not, indeed, on the
compulsion of the Tribune, but without being prevented by
him) to copy out the rules and imperious commands of the
trainer of gladiators. You see many, besides, whom the oft-
deceived creditor is wont to wait for at the very entrance to
the market, whose motive for living is in the palate alone. The
most hard-up of these fellows, destined soon to fall, with ruin
already lightening through him, dines the more sumptuously
and the more daintily. Meanwhile they search through all the

numquam animo pretiis obstantibus; interius si   15
attendas, magis illa iuvant, quae pluris emuntur.
ergo haud difficile est perituram arcessere summam
lancibus oppositis vel matris imagine fracta,
et quadringentis nummis condire gulosum
fictile: sic veniunt ad miscellanea ludi.   20
refert ergo, quis haec eadem paret; in Rutilo nam
luxuria est, in Ventidio laudabile nomen
sumit et a censu famam trahit. illum ego iure
despiciam, qui scit quanto sublimior Atlas
omnibus in Libya sit montibus, hic tamen idem   25
ignoret quantum ferrata distet ab arca
sacculus. e coelo descendit γνῶθι σεαυτόν,
figendum et memori tractandum pectore, sive
coniugium quaeras vel sacri in parte senatus
esse velis—neque enim loricam poscit Achillis   30
Thersites, in qua se traducebat Ulixes—

---

elements for relishes, the prices never standing in the way of
their inclination ; *nay,* if you look at it more closely, those
things please them more which are bought at a higher price.
Well, then, it is not difficult to obtain the sum destined to
be squandered, by pawning their dishes, or breaking up their
mother's bust, and to season the gluttonous platter with four
hundred sesterces. So it is they come to the hodge-podge of
the training-school.

It makes a difference, then, who it is that sets forth these
same *delicacies;* for in Rutilus this is extravagance ; in Ventidius, it assumes a creditable name, and derives its character
from the state of his fortune. I should despise the man, and
justly, who knows how much higher Atlas is than all the *other*
mountains in Libya; while he, the same man, does not know
how great a difference there is between a small *money*-bag and
an iron-bound strong-box. "Know thyself" descended from
heaven, to be implanted and revolved in the memory ; whether
you are seeking marriage or wishing to form part of the sacred
Senate (for not even Thersites claims the cuirass of Achilles, in

ancipitem seu tu magno discrimine causam
protegere affectas, te consule, dic tibi qui sis,
orator vehemens, an Curtius et Matho buccae.
noscenda est mensura sui spectandaque rebus   35
in summis minimisque, etiam cum piscis emetur,
ne mullum cupias, cum sit tibi gobio tantum
in loculis.   quis enim te, deficiente crumena
et crescente gula, manet exitus, aere paterno
ac rebus mersis in ventrem fenoris atque   40
argenti gravis et pecorum agrorumque capacem?
talibus a dominis post cuncta novissimus exit
annulus, et digito mendicat Pollio nudo.
non praematuri cineres, nec funus acerbum
luxuriae, sed morte magis metuenda senectus.   45
hi plerumque gradus. conducta pecunia Romae
et coram dominis consumitur; inde ubi paulum
nescio quid superest et pallet fenoris auctor,

38. culina.

---

which *even* Ulysses cut a doubtful figure), or whether you
aspire to defend a doubtful cause of great moment, consult
yourself; tell yourself what you are, a powerful orator or a
Curtius or Matho—*mere* cheeks. A man should know his own
measure, and consider it in the smallest as well as the greatest
matters; even in buying a fish, that you may not covet a mullet
when you have only got a gudgeon in your purse. For what
end awaits you, with your purse failing, while your gluttony is
increasing, with your paternal fortune and your effects sunk in
your belly, which can swallow up investments, and heavy plate,
and flocks and estates? From such masters as these, after
everything else, last of all the *knightly* ring takes its departure,
and Pollio begs with naked finger. It is not a premature
decease or an untimely grave, but old age, which should be
dreaded more than death by extravagance. These are mostly
the stages: the borrowed money is spent at Rome, and under
the very eyes of the lenders; then when a trifle, I know not
what, is left, and the usurer grows pale, they shift their quarters

qui vertere solum, Baias et ad ostrea currunt.
cedere namque foro iam non est deterius quam   50
Esquilias a ferventi migrare Subura.
ille dolor solus patriam fugientibus, illa
moestitia est, caruisse anno circensibus uno.
sanguinis in facie non haeret gutta, morantur
pauci ridiculum et fugientem ex urbe pudorem.   55
    Experiere hodie, numquid pulcherrima dictu,
Persice, non praestem vita vel moribus et re,
sed laudem siliquas occultus ganeo, pultes
coram aliis dictem puero, sed in aure placentas.
nam cum sis conviva mihi promissus, habebis   60
Evandrum, venies Tirynthius aut minor illo
hospes et ipse tamen contingens sanguine coelum,
alter aquis, alter flammis ad sidera missus.
fercula nunc audi nullis ornata macellis.
de Tiburtino veniet pinguissimus agro   65

49. ostia.   57. nec moribus.   58. si laudem.

---

and run to Baiae and the oysters. For to abscond from 'change is nowadays no more disgrace than to migrate to the Esquiline from the hot Suburra. This is the only grief of the fugitives from their country; this their *only* sorrow, to have missed the Circensian games for a single year. Not a particle of a blush remains in their face; few *seek to* detain modesty, become ridiculous and flying from the city.

You will *prove by* experience to-day, Persicus, whether these things which are so pretty to talk about are not carried out in my life, that is, in my conduct and in reality, and whether I praise pulse while in secret a glutton, calling out to my slave for porridge in the presence of others, for honey-cakes in private. For since you are my promised guest, you shall have *in me* an Evander; you shall come *like* the Tirynthian or the guest inferior to him, and who yet himself was connected by blood with heaven—the one sent to the stars by water, the other by fire. Now listen to the courses furnished by no public markets. From my farm at Tibur will come the well-fatted sucking-kid,

haedulus et toto grege mollior, inscius herbae,
necdum ausus virgas humilis mordere salicti,
qui plus lactis habet quam sanguinis, et montani
asparagi, posito quos legit villica fuso.
grandia praeterea tortoque calentia foeno   70
ova adsunt ipsis cum matribus, et servatae
parte anni, quales fuerant in vitibus, uvae,
Signinum Syriumque pirum, de corbibus isdem
aemula Picenis et odoris mala recentis,
nec metuenda tibi, siccatum frigore postquam   75
autumnum et crudi posuere pericula succi.
haec olim nostri iam luxuriosa senatus
coena fuit.   Curius parvo quae legerat horto,
ipse focis brevibus ponebat oluscula, quae nunc
squalidus in magna fastidit compede fossor,   80
qui meminit calidae sapiat quid vulva popinae.
sicci terga suis, rara pendentia crate,
moris erat quondam festis servare diebus

---

the tenderest of the whole flock, ignorant of herbage, that has
not yet ventured to nibble the twigs of the low willow-bed, who
has more milk *in him* than blood ; and mountain asparagus
which the bailiff's wife, laying down her spindle, has gathered.
Eggs of large size, besides, and warm from the twisted hay, are
here, with the very hens *that laid them*, and grapes preserved
for a part of the year just as they were upon the vines : the
Signian and the Syrian pear, *and*, from the same baskets, apples
rivalling those of Picenum, and fresh in smell, and which you
need not fear either, since they have parted with their autumn
crudeness (which has been dried out by the cold), and the perils
of the raw juice.

Such as this was once upon a time quite a luxurious dinner, *even*
for our Senate.   Curius used in person to place upon his scanty
fire the small pot-herbs which he had gathered in his little garden,
such as nowadays the squalid ditcher in heavy chains, who
calls to mind the flavour of dainties in the warm cookshop, turns
up his nose at.   It was part of the custom, of old, to keep for

et natalicium cognatis ponere lardum,
accedente nova, si quam dabat hostia, carne.   85
cognatorum aliquis titulo ter consulis atque
castrorum imperiis et dictatoris honore
functus ad has epulas solito maturius ibat,
erectum domito referens a monte ligonem.
cum tremerent autem Fabios durumque Catonem   90
et Scauros et Fabricios, postremo severos
censoris mores etiam collega timeret,
nemo inter curas et seria duxit habendum,
qualis in Oceani fluctu testudo nataret,
clarum Troiugenis factura et nobile fulcrum,   95
sed nudo latere et parvis frons aerea lectis
vile coronati caput ostendebat aselli,
ad quod lascivi ludebant ruris alumni.
tales ergo cibi, qualis domus atque supellex.

91. rigidique severos.

---

festival days the chines of dried bacon hanging from the wide-
barred frame, and to set before one's relations lard as a birthday
treat, with the addition of fresh meat, if there was a sacrificial
victim to supply any. One of these relatives, with the title of
thrice-consul, who had enjoyed the command in camps and the
dignity of dictator, would go somewhat earlier than usual to
such a feast as this, bearing off on his shoulder his spade from
the hill which he had been digging. Moreover, when men
trembled at the Fabii and rigid Cato and the Scauri and the
Fabricii, and when, in fine, the severe character of a censor was
feared even by his own colleague, no one thought it *a question*
to be included among his cares and serious concerns what sort
of tortoise was swimming in the ocean wave to make a conspicuous and noble bed for the Trojugenae. But on couches
with plain sides, and small, a front of bronze displayed the rude
head of an ass crowned *with a chaplet*, of which the saucy young
rustics used to make game. The food, then, was of a piece
with the house and the furniture.

tunc rudis et Graias mirari nescius artes   100
urbibus eversis praedarum in parte reperta
magnorum artificum frangebat pocula miles,
ut phaleris gauderet equus, caelataque cassis
Romuleae simulacra ferae mansuescere iussae
imperii fato, geminos sub rupe Quirinos,   105
ac nudam effigiem clipeo venientis et hasta
pendentisque dei perituro ostenderet hosti.
argenti quod erat solis fulgebat in armis.
ponebant igitur Tusco farrata catino;
omnia tunc quibus invideas si lividulus sis.   110
templorum quoque maiestas praesentior et vox
nocte fere media mediamque audita per urbem,
litore ab Oceani Gallis venientibus et dis
officium vatis peragentibus.   his monuit nos,
hanc rebus Latiis curam praestare solebat   115
fictilis et nullo violatus Iuppiter auro.

106. fulgentis.

In those days the soldier, untutored and incapable of admir-
ing the arts of Greece, when cities were overthrown, used to
break up the cups by great artists which he found in his share
of the booty, in order that his horse might exult in bridle ornaments, that his embossed helmet might exhibit the image of the
Romulean wild beast bidden to grow tame by the destiny of *our*
empire—and the twin Quirini under the rock, and the naked effigy
of the god coming with shield and spear and hanging *in the air*
—to the foe about to perish!   Whatever there was of silver
glittered on arms alone.   So they used to serve their porridge on
a platter of Tuscan ware: everything at that time was such as you
might envy, if you be a trifle given to jealousy.   The majesty of
the temples also was more present *to man*, and a voice was heard
about the middle of the night and through the middle of the city,
when the Gauls were coming from the ocean shore, and the gods
were discharging the functions of a prophet.   By such means did
Jupiter warn us, such care used he to bestow on the affairs of
Latium, when he was made of earthenware, and profaned by no

illa domi natas nostraque ex arbore mensas
tempora viderunt, hos lignum stabat in usus,
annosam si forte nucem deiecerat Eurus.
at nunc divitibus coenandi nulla voluptas,   120
nil rhombus, nil dama sapit, putere videntur
unguenta atque rosae, latos nisi sustinet orbes
grande ebur et magno sublimis pardus hiatu,
dentibus ex illis quos mittit porta Syenes
et Mauri celeres et Mauro obscurior Indus,   125
et quos deposuit Nabathaeo bellua saltu
iam nimios capitique graves. hinc surgit orexis,
hinc stomacho vires. nam pes argenteus illis,
annulus in digito quod ferreus. ergo superbum
convivam caveo, qui me sibi comparat et res   130
despicit exiguas. adeo nulla uncia nobis
est eboris, nec tessellae, nec calculus ex hac
materia, quin ipsa manubria cultellorum
ossea. non tamen his ulla umquam opsonia fiunt

128. bilis.

---

gold. Those times saw tables produced at home and from our
own trees: for these purposes there was timber stacked, if by
chance the east wind had thrown down an aged walnut-tree.
But now, for the rich, there is no pleasure in dining, the turbot, the venison have no flavour, perfumes and roses appear to
stink, unless the broad circumferences *of the tables* be supported
by massive ivory and a rampant leopard with gaping jaws, *made*
of those tusks which the gate of Syene sends *us*, and the active
Moors, and the Indian still darker than the Moor, which the
elephant has shed in a Nabathaean jungle, when *grown* too large
and burdensome to his head. Hence arises an appetite, hence
strength to the stomach, for a silver pedestal is to them what an
iron ring on their finger would be. So then I avoid a proud
guest who compares me with himself, and looks down upon
small means. So far am I from having an ounce of ivory—not
even little dice, nor a counter of that material—that the very
handles of my knives are of bone; yet no provisions are ever

raucidula, aut ideo peior gallina secatur.　　　　135
sed nec structor erit, cui cedere debeat omnis
pergula, discipulus Trypheri doctoris, apud quem
sumine cum magno lepus atque aper et pygargus
et Scythicae volucres et phoenicopterus ingens
et Gaetulus oryx hebeti lautissima ferro　　　　140
caeditur et tota sonat ulmea coena Subura.
nec frustum capreae subducere nec latus Afrae
novit avis noster, tirunculus ac rudis omni
tempore et exiguae furtis imbutus ofellae.
plebeios calices et paucis assibus emptos　　　　145
porriget incultus puer atque a frigore tutus ;
non Phryx aut Lycius, non a mangone petitus
quisquam erit, et magno: cum posces, posce Latine. ·
idem habitus cunctis, tonsi rectique capilli
atque hodie tantum propter convivia pexi.　　　　150
pastoris duri hic est filius, ille bubulci,

144. frustis.　　　　　　148. in magno.

made the least rancid by these, nor does a chicken cut up the
worse on that account.　Nor will there be a carver either, such
as the whole *carving*-school should yield to, a disciple of Professor Trypherus, at whose house, together with a large sow's
udder, the hare and the *wild*-boar, and the gazelle and phea-
sants, and the huge flamingo, and the Gaetulian wild-goat, a
most dainty supper made of elm, are cut up with blunt knives,
and resound through the whole Suburra.　Nor does my fellow
know how to purloin a slice of roe or the breast of a guinea-hen ;
a little tyro, untutored all his days, and initiated only in the
theft of a tiny collop.　My slave, unadorned and protected
from the cold, will hand *you* plebeian cups bought for a few
pence ; there will be no Phrygian or Lycian *slave*, nor any one
obtained from the dealer, and at a great price.　When you ask
for anything, ask in Latin.　All have the same attire, hair cut
short and straight, and only combed to-day on account of company.　One is the son of a hardy shepherd, another of a neatherd ; he sighs after his mother, whom he has not seen for a

suspirat longo non visam tempore matrem
et casulam et notos tristis desiderat haedos,
ingenui vultus puer ingenuique pudoris,
quales esse decet quos ardens purpura vestit,   155
nec pugillares defert in balnea raucus
testiculos, nec vellendas iam praebuit alas,
crassa nec opposito pavidus tegit inguina gutto.
hic tibi vina dabit diffusa in montibus illis
a quibus ipse venit, quorum sub vertice lusit;   160
namque una atque eadem est vini patria atque ministri.
forsitan exspectes ut Gaditana canoro
incipiat prurire choro plausuque probatae
ad terram tremulo descendant clune puellae—
spectant hoc nuptae iuxta recubante marito,   165
quod pudeat narrare aliquem praesentibus ipsis—
irritamentum Veneris languentis et acres
divitis urticae. maior tamen ista voluptas
alterius sexus; magis ille extenditur, et mox

---

long time, and mournfully regrets the little cottage and the well-
known kids—a boy of ingenuous face and ingenuous modesty,
such as it becomes those to be whom the bright purple clothes.
Nor does he carry into the baths the signs of his robust manhood,
nor has he already yielded his arm-pits to be plucked, nor has he
timidly to protect his person by the interposition of the oil-flask.
He, *such as he is*, will hand you wines bottled on the very hills
from which he himself comes, under whose summit he has played;
for the native country of the wine and the attendant is one and
the same.   Perhaps you may be expecting that a Gaditane *artiste*
will begin to wanton amid the tuneful choir, and that *dancing-
girls*, covered with applause, will curtsy to the ground with
quivering lips (brides, with their husbands reclining next them,
behold this *sight*, which any one would be ashamed to relate in
their presence), a provocative for languishing desire and sharp
incentives for the wealthy.   Yet this *sort of* pleasure is greater
in the case of the other sex, which is more worked upon, and
soon passion engendered through ears and eyes is set in motion.

auribus atque oculis concepta urina movetur.   170
non capit has nugas humilis domus. audiat ille
testarum crepitus cum verbis, nudum olido stans
fornice mancipium quibus abstinet, ille fruatur
vocibus obscenis omnique libidinis arte
qui Lacedaemonium pytismate lubricat orbem.   175
namque ibi fortunae veniam damus. alea turpis,
turpe et adulterium mediocribus; haec eadem illi
omnia cum faciunt, hilares nitidique vocantur.
nostra dabunt alios hodie convivia ludos,
conditor Iliados cantabitur atque Maronis   180
altisoni dubiam facientia carmina palmam.
quid refert tales versus qua voce legantur?
     Sed nunc dilatis averte negotia curis
et gratam requiem dona tibi, quando licebit
per totum cessare diem. non fenoris ulla   185
mentio, nec, prima si luce egressa reverti

170. paratur.

A humble household does not admit of this trumpery. Let
him listen to the clinking of castanets, accompanied by words
such as the slave girl, standing naked in the stinking brothel,
abstains from; let him enjoy the obscene language and all the
artifices of lechery, who lubricates the circles of his Laconian
marble floor by spitting *wine* over them; for, in that case, we
make allowance for his fortune. Gambling is disgraceful, and
adultery is disgraceful for common people. The others, when
they do all these same things, are called choice spirits and stylish
fellows. Our banquet to-day shall present other amusements.
The author of the Iliad shall be recited, and the strains of high-
sounding Maro, rendering the palm *of victory* a doubtful one.
What matters it with what voice such verses as these are read?
     But now, *at any rate*, your cares deferred, put aside business
matters, and treat yourself to a pleasant respite, since you will
be at liberty to idle through the whole day. *Let there be* no
mention whatever of interest *due*, nor let your wife stir up your

nocte solet, tacito bilem tibi contrahat uxor,
humida suspectis referens multicia rugis
vexatasque comas et vultum auremque calentem.
protinus ante meum quidquid dolet exue limen,　　　　190
pone domum et servos et quidquid frangitur illis
aut perit, ingratos ante omnia pone sodales.
interea Megalesiacae spectacula mappae,
Idaeum sollemne, colunt, similisque triumpho
praeda caballorum praetor sedet ac, mihi pace　　　　195
immensae nimiaeque licet si dicere plebis,
totam hodie Romam circus capit et fragor aurem
percutit, eventum viridis quo colligo panni.
nam si deficeret, maestam attonitamque videres
hanc urbem, veluti Cannarum in pulvere victis　　　　200
consulibus. spectent iuvenes, quos clamor et audax
sponsio, quos cultae decet assedisse puellae,
nostra bibat vernum contracta cuticula solem

195. praedo.

---

bile and make you silent, if she goes out at early dawn, and
is in the habit of returning at night, bringing back her light
dress wet with suspicious creases, and her hair tumbled,
and her face and ears red. At sight of my threshold, throw
off everything which annoys you; lay aside your household and your servants, and whatever is broken by them
or wasted : above all things, lay aside the ingratitude of your
friends. Meanwhile the people are frequenting the spectacle
of the Megalesian napkin, the Idaean solemnity, and, like one
triumphing, the Praetor sits, a prey to horseflesh; and—to beg
the pardon of the immense (and, if I may be allowed to say so,
overgrown) populace—the circus to-day contains the whole of
Rome, and a din strikes upon my ear from which I gather the
success of the green-jacket; for if it were to fail, you would see
this city sorrowing and awe-struck, as if the Consuls had been
vanquished in the dust of Cannae. Let the young men look on,
for whom the noise and bold betting and sitting by *some* smart
damsel are suitable ; let our dried-up skin imbibe the sun of

effugiatque togam. iam nunc in balnea salva
fronte licet vadas, quamquam solida hora supersit   205
ad sextam. facere hoc non possis quinque diebus
continuis, quia sunt talis quoque taedia vitae
magna : voluptates commendat rarior usus.

SATIRA XII.

NATALI, Corvine, die mihi dulcior haec lux,
    qua festus promissa deis animalia cespes
exspectat. niveam reginae ducimus agnam,
par vellus dabitur pugnanti Gorgone Maura,
sed procul extensum petulans quatit hostia funem   5
Tarpeio servata Iovi frontemque coruscat,
quippe ferox vitulus templis maturus et arae,

1. carior, clarior.   3. caedimus.

spring-time, and escape the toga. Even now you may go to
the bath without shame, although it wants a whole hour of the
sixth. You could not do this for five continuous days, because
the tedium even of such a life as this would be great. A rarer
experience of them enhances *one's* pleasures.

SATIRE XII.

SWEETER to me than my own birthday, Corvinus, is this day on
which the festal turf awaits the animals promised to the gods.
We are leading *to the sacrifice* a snow-white lamb for the Queen
of heaven; a like fleece will be given to her who fights *armed*
with the Mauritanian Gorgon; but the victim reserved for
Tarpeian Jove shakes in his wantonness the outstretched rope
and tosses his head—a wild steer, in truth, ripe for the temple
and the altar, and fit to be sprinkled with wine, who is already

spargendusque mero, quem iam pudet ubera matris
ducere, qui vexat nascenti robora cornu.
si res ampla domi similisque affectibus esset ; 10
pinguior Hispulla traheretur taurus et ipsa
mole piger nec finitima nutritus in herba,
laeta sed ostendens Clitumni pascua, sanguis
iret et a grandi cervix ferienda ministro,
ob reditum trepidantis adhuc horrendaque passi 15
nuper et incolumem sese mirantis amici.
nam praeter pelagi casus et fulminis ictus
evasit. densae coelum abscondere tenebrae
nube una subitusque antennas impulit ignis,
cum se quisque illo percussum crederet et mox 20
attonitus nullum conferri posse putaret
naufragium velis ardentibus. omnia fiunt
talia, tam graviter, si quando poetica surgit
tempestas. genus ecce aliud discriminis, audi

14. magno magistro (Serv.)   17. fulguris ictum.
23. quam quando.

---

ashamed to drain the teats of his mother, who butts the oaks
with his rising horn. If my personal means were ample, and
equal to my affections, a bull fatter than Hispulla should be
dragged along, one slow from his very bulk, and fed on no
neighbouring herbage, but, giving evidence of the rich pastures
of Clitumnus, the high-bred should go, with a neck that would
have to be struck by a burly sacrificer, on account of the return
of my friend still trembling, and who has just endured horrors,
and who wonders at finding himself alive.
    For besides the dangers of the sea, he escaped even the stroke
of lightning. Thick darkness concealed the heavens in one
cloud, and the sudden fire fell upon the yards ; when every one
thought himself struck by it, and thereupon, in a panic, deemed
that no shipwreck could be comparable to burning sails. Everything takes place in the same way, and just as disagreeably,
whenever a storm arises in poetry. Behold another kind of
danger ; listen and pity him again, though what follows belongs

et miserere iterum, quamquam sint cetera sortis   25
eiusdem, pars dira quidem, sed cognita multis
et quam votiva testantur fana tabella
plurima : pictores quis nescit ab Iside pasci ?
accidit et nostro similis fortuna Catullo.
cum plenus fluctu medius foret alveus et iam   30
alternum puppis latus evertentibus undis
arboris incertae, nullam prudentia cani
rectoris conferret opem, decidere iactu
coepit cum ventis, imitatus castora, qui se
eunuchum ipse facit, cupiens evadere damno   35
testiculi : adeo medicatum intelligit inguen.
" fundite, quae mea sunt," dicebat, " cuncta," Catullus,
praecipitare volens etiam pulcherrima, vestem
purpuream teneris quoque Maecenatibus aptam,
atque alias, quarum generosi graminis ipsum   40
infecit natura pecus, sed et egregius fons
viribus occultis et Baeticus adiuvat aer.

33. cum ferret.

to the same ill luck ; a portion dreadful indeed, but known to
many, and which a multitude of temples bear witness to with
their votive tablets. Who does not know that there are painters
who gain their living by Isis ? And a similar fortune befell our
Catullus. When the hold was full of water up to the middle,
and, now that the waves were heaving up each side alternately
of the stern of the crazy log, the skill of the hoary helmsman
could render no aid ; he began to compound with the winds by
throwing overboard *the cargo* in imitation of the beaver, who,
by his own act, makes himself a eunuch, hoping to escape by
the sacrifice of his testicles, so well does he understand the
medicinal properties of his parts. " Throw out everything that
belongs to me," Catullus kept saying, wishing to hurl overboard
the very choicest objects, a purple robe fitted even for effeminate
Maecenases, and others whose wool the nature of the generous
pasture has tinged, but also the exquisite springs by their hidden
properties and the air of Baetica contribute. He did not hesi-

ille nec argentum dubitabat mittere, lances
Parthenio factas, urnae cratera capacem
et dignum sitiente Pholo vel coniuge Fusci, 45
adde et bascaudas et mille escaria, multum
caelati, biberat quo callidus emptor Olynthi.
sed quis nunc alius, qua mundi parte, quis audet
argento praeferre caput rebusque salutem ?
non propter vitam faciunt patrimonia quidam, 50
sed vitio caeci propter patrimonia vivunt.
iactatur rerum utilium pars maxima, sed nec
damna levant. tunc adversis urgentibus illuc
decidit ut malum ferro summitteret, ac se
explicat angustum : discriminis ultima, quando 55
praesidia afferimus navem factura minorem.
i nunc, et ventis animam committe, dolato
confisus ligno, digitis a morte remotus
quatuor aut septem si sit latissima taeda ;

54. recidit ; hac re.

tate to throw overboard even his plate—platters made by
Parthenius, a bowl holding three gallons, and worthy of Pholus
when athirst, or even the wife of Fuscus ; add bascaudae into
the bargain, and a thousand meat-dishes, a quantity of chased
cups, out of which the cunning purchaser of Olynthus had
drunk. But who else nowadays, in any part of the world,
who ventures to prefer his life to his plate, and his safety to his
property? [Some men do not make fortunes for the sake of
living, but, blinded by a vice of nature, live for the sake of
making fortunes.] The greatest part of his necessaries is thrown
overboard, but not even do these sacrifices lighten *the ship.*
Then, under the pressure of danger, it came to this, that he
submitted his mast to the axe, and he extricates himself, though
crippled. *It must be* the extremity of danger when we apply
remedies which will take away part of the ship ! Go now and
commit your life to the winds, trusting to a hewn plank,
removed four inches from death, or seven if the deal be of the
thickest ; and then, together with your wallets and bread and

mox cum reticulis et pane et ventre lagenae   60
aspice sumendas in tempestate secures.
sed postquam iacuit planum mare, tempora postquam
prospera vectoris fatumque valentius curo
et pelago, postquam Parcae meliora benigna
pensa manu ducunt hilares et staminis albi   65
lanificae, modica nec multum fortior aura
ventus adest, inopi miserabilis arte cucurrit
vestibus extentis et, quod superaverat unum,
velo prora sua.   iam deficientibus austris,
spes vitae cum sole redit.   tunc gratus Iulo,   70
atque novercali sedes praelata Lavino,
conspicitur sublimis apex, cui candida nomen
scrofa dedit, laetis Phrygibus mirabile sumen,
et numquam visis triginta clara mamillis.
tandem intrat positas inclusa per aequora moles   75
Tyrrhenamque pharon porrectaque brachia rursum,
quae pelago occurrunt medio longeque relinquunt

61. accipe.

---

bulging flagon, see to *providing* hatchets to be used in case of a
storm.   But after the sea fell into a calm, after a lucky time *had
come* for the passengers, and Fate was mightier than Eurus and
the deep, after the Parcae were spinning kindlier piecework with
benign hand, blithe, and working their wool with white threads,
and the wind presented itself not much stronger than a moderate breeze, the prow drifted on pitiably with powerless shifts,
with clothes outspread and its foresail, which alone remained.
And now that the south wind was subsiding, hope of life returns
with the sunshine ; then the lofty peak is caught sight of, beloved
of Iulus, and preferred by him as a home to his stepmother's
Lavinium ; *the peak* to which the white sow gave its name, an
udder that excited the wonder of the rejoicing Phrygians, remarkable for what had never been seen *before*, thirty nipples.   At
length he reaches the moles built through the waters enclosed
between them and the Tuscan Pharos, and the arms stretching
back again, which run into the midst of the sea and leave Italy

Italiam—non sic igitur mirabere portus,
quos natura dedit—sed trunca puppe magister
interiora petit Baianae pervia cymbae   80
tuti stagna sinus, gaudent ubi vertice raso
garrula securi narrare pericula nautae.
   Ite igitur, pueri, linguis animisque faventes,
sertaque delubris et farra imponite cultris
ac molles ornate focos glebamque virentem.   85
iam sequar, et sacro, quod praestat, rite peracto
inde domum repetam, graciles ubi parva coronas
accipiunt fragili simulacra nitentia cera.
hic nostrum placabo Iovem Laribusque paternis
thura dabo atque omnes violae iactabo colores.   90
cuncta nitent, longos erexit ianua ramos
et matutinis operatur festa lucernis.
   Nec suspecta tibi sint haec, Corvine ; Catullus,
pro cuius reditu tot pono altaria, parvos

81. tunc stagnante sinu.

far behind ;—you would not, in fine, admire so much ports of
Nature's making ;—but with his disabled ship the skipper makes
for the inner still water of the safe basin, which a skiff from
Baiae could cross, where, with shaven crowns, the sailors, freed
from anxiety, delight in garrulous recitals of their perils.
   Go then, lads, keeping watch over your tongues and thoughts,
and place garlands on the shrines and meal on the knives, and
adorn the soft hearths and the green turf *altar*. I will follow
anon, and the sacrifice, which has the precedence, having been
duly performed, will thence return home where the little images
glistening with fragile wax receive their slender chaplets. Here
I will propitiate my own Jove, and will offer frankincense to
my paternal Lares, and will strew all the colours of the violet.
Everything is bright ; my festive door has put forth long boughs,
and is performing *its part in* the rite with *early* morning lamps.
   Nor let these things seem suspicious to you, Corvinus.
Catullus, for whose return I erect so many altars, has three

tres habet heredes.   libet exspectare quis aegram   95
et claudentem oculos gallinam impendat amico
tam sterili.   verum haec nimia est impensa, coturnix
nulla umquam pro patre cadet.   sentire calorem
si coepit locuples Gallita et Paccius orbi,
legitime fixis vestitur tota tabellis   100
porticus, exsistunt qui promittunt hecatomben,
quatenus hic non sunt nec venales elephanti,
nec Latio aut usquam sub nostro sidere talis
bellua concipitur, sed furva gente petita
arboribus Rutulis et Turni pascitur agro,   105
Caesaris armentum, nulli servire paratum
privato, siquidem Tyrio parere solebant
Hannibali et nostris ducibus regique Molosso
horum maiores ac dorso ferre cohortes,
partem aliquam belli et euntem in proelia turrim.   110
nulla igitur mora per Novium, mora nulla per Histrum
Pacuvium, quin illud ebur ducatur ad aras

---

little heirs.   I should like to see who would lay out a sick hen,
just closing her eyes, on so unprofitable a friend.   But of a truth
this would be too great an outlay ; not even a quail will ever be
sacrificed for one who is a father.   If rich Gallita has begun to
be sensible of fever, or Paccius—people who have no children—
the whole portico is clothed with votive tablets affixed in the
acknowledged way.   There are people who start up and promise
a hetacomb *of oxen*, since here there are no elephants even for
sale, nor *indeed* is such a huge beast generated in Latium or anywhere under our sky ; but procured from a swarthy nation, it
grazes in the Rutulian forests and the pastures of Turnus, the
herd of Caesar, prepared to serve no private individual, seeing
that their ancestors were wont to obey Tyrian Hannibal and
our generals and the Molossian king, and to bear on their backs
cohorts,—no trifling part of the fight,—and a tower that went
into battles.   It is no fault of Novius, then, no fault of Hister
Pacuvius, that that ivory is not led to the altars to fall a victim

et cadat ante Lares Gallitae victima, sola
tantis digna deis et captatoribus horum.
alter enim, si concedas mactare, vovebit   115
de grege servorum magna et pulcherrima quaeque
corpora, vel pueris et frontibus ancillarum
imponet vittas, et, si qua est nubilis illi
Iphigenia domi, dabit hanc altaribus, etsi
non sperat tragicae furtiva piacula cervae.   120
laudo meum civem, nec comparo testamento
mille rates; nam si Libitinam evaserit aeger,
delebit tabulas, inclusus carcere nassae,
post meritum sane mirandum, atque omnia soli
forsan Pacuvio breviter dabit, ille superbus   125
incedet victis rivalibus.   ergo vides quam
grande operae pretium faciat iugulata Mycenis.
vivat Pacuvius, quaeso, vel Nestora totum,
possideat quantum rapuit Nero, montibus aurum
exaequet, nec amet quemquam, nec ametur ab ullo!   130

before the Lares of Gallita, the only one worthy of such great
gods and those that court their favours.   Another *of these fellows*,
indeed, if you will consent to his making the sacrifice, will devote
the tallest and handsomest persons out of the flock of his slaves,
and will place *sacrificial* fillets on his slave-boys and the brows
of his maid-servants; and if by chance he has a marriageable
Iphigenia at home, he will give her to the altars, although he
does not expect the furtive substitution of the hind of the trage-
dians.   I praise my fellow-citizen, nor do I compare a thousand
ships to a will; for if the sick man escapes from Libitina, he
will cancel his will, caught in the grasp of the snare, after a
service so truly wonderful, and will perhaps summarily bestow
his all on Pacuvius as sole heir.   The latter will strut proudly
over his defeated rivals.   You see, then, what a great return for
his trouble the slaughter of the Mycenian maid may bring him.

May Pacuvius live, I pray, even to the full age of a Nestor; may
he possess as much as Nero plundered; may he pile his gold to the
height of mountains—and love no one, and be loved by none!

SATIRA XIII.

EXEMPLO quodcumque malo committitur, ipsi
　　displicet auctori.　prima est haec ultio, quod se
iudice nemo nocens absolvitur, improba quamvis
gratia fallaci praetoris vicerit urna.
quid sentire putas omnes, Calvine, recenti　　　　　　5
de scelere et fidei violatae crimine ? sed nec
tam tenuis census tibi contigit, ut mediocris
iacturae te mergat onus, nec rara videmus
quae pateris ; casus multis hic cognitus ac iam
tritus et e medio fortunae ductus acervo.　　　　　　10
ponamus nimios gemitus.　flagrantior aequo
non debet dolor esse viri, nec vulnere maior.
tu quamvis levium minimam exiguamque malorum
particulam vix ferre potes, spumantibus ardens

　　4. fallacis.　　　　13. laborum.

SATIRE XIII.

WHATEVER *act* is perpetrated *which serves* as a bad example, is
displeasing to its very author.　This is his first punishment—
that by his own verdict no offender is acquitted, though corrupt
favour may win in the Praetor's lying urn.　What do you suppose is the feeling of every one, Calvinus, respecting this recent
act of villany and crime of violated confidence ?　Besides, neither
is the fortune you are favoured with so slender that the weight
of a small loss should sink you, nor do we witness but seldom
what you are suffering.　This kind of mischance is familiar to
many, and commonplace by this time, and drawn from the mid-
heap of *the accidents of* fortune.　Let us lay aside excessive
laments ; the grief of a man should not be more vehement than
is reasonable, nor greater than the wound *received.*　You are
scarce able to bear the smallest and most trifling particle of ills,
however light, raging with your vitals in a foam, because your

visceribus, sacrum tibi quod non reddat amicus   15
depositum. stupet hacc, qui iam post terga reliquit
sexaginta annos, Fonteio consule natus ?
an nihil in melius tot rerum proficis usu ?
magna quidem, sacris quae dat praecepta libellis,
victrix fortunae sapientia ; ducimus autem   20
hos quoque felices, qui ferre incommoda vitae
nec iactare iugum vita didicere magistrá.
quae tam festa dies, ut cesset prodere furem
perfidiam fraudes atque omni ex crimine lucrum
quaesitum et partos gladio vel pyxide nummos ?   25
rari quippe boni, numero vix sunt totidem quot
Thebarum portae vel divitis ostia Nili.
nona aetas agitur, peioraque secula ferri
temporibus, quorum sceleri non invenit ipsa
nomen et a nullo posuit natura metallo.   30
nos hominum divumque fidem clamore ciemus,

18. proficit usus.   28. nunc aetas agitur.

---

friend does not restore to you a deposit that was sacred. Can
one be amazed at such things who has already left sixty years
behind his back, born in the consulship of Fonteius? or do you
profit nothing by so great an experience of the world? Great,
indeed, is philosophy, the conqueror of fortune, which sets forth
its precepts in sacred books; but we deem those happy, too,
who have learned to bear the incommodities of life, and not to
toss the yoke, with life *itself* for their teacher. What day so
holy that it fails to bring forth a thief, perfidy, frauds, and
profit obtained from every sort of crime, and money acquired
by the sword or the poison-box? For rare, indeed, are the
good; in number they are scarcely as many as the gates of
Thebes, or the mouths of the rich Nile. It is the ninth age
that we are passing through—times worse than the period of
iron, for whose wickedness Nature herself does not find a name,
and has given one from no metal. We are invoking the aid of
men and gods, with a clamour loud as that with which his vocal

quanto Faesidium laudat vocalis agentem
sportula. dic, senior bulla dignissime, nescis
quas habeat Veneres aliena pecunia ? nescis
quem tua simplicitas risum vulgo moveat, cum   35
exigis a quoquam ne peieret et putet ullis
esse aliquod numen templis araeque rubenti ?
quondam hoc indigenae vivebant more, priusquam
sumeret agrestem posito diademate falcem
Saturnus fugiens, tunc, cum virguncula Iuno   40
et privatus adhuc Idaeis Iuppiter antris,
nulla super nubes convivia coelicolarum,
nec puer Iliacus, formosa nec Herculis uxor
ad cyathos, et iam siccato nectare tergens
brachia Vulcanus Liparaea nigra taberna.   45
prandebat sibi quisque deus, nec turba deorum
talis ut est hodie, contentaque sidera paucis
numinibus miserum urgebant Atlanta minori
pondere. nondum aliquis sortitus triste profundi

---

hangers-on applaud Faesidius when he is pleading ! Tell me,
old man, most worthy of the child's boss, know you not what
charms are possessed by another's money ? know you not what
a laugh your simplicity will excite in the herd, when you require
of any one that he should not perjure himself, and should deem
that there is some divinity in any temples or *on* blood-red altar ?
Once upon a time the aborigines used to live in this fashion,
before Saturn in his flight took up the rustic sickle, after laying
down his diadem ; in the days when Juno was a little maiden,
and Jupiter still a private individual in the caves of Ida, *when*
there were no banquets of the celestials above the clouds, no
Trojan boy, nor beautiful wife of Hercules at the cups, with
Vulcan, after draining the nectar, wiping his arms black from
his Liparaean workshop. Each god used to dine by himself,
nor was the crowd of gods such as it is nowadays ; and the
heavens, contented with few divinities, pressed upon poor Atlas
with less weight. No one as yet had allotted to him the gloomy

imperium aut Sicula torvus cum coniuge Pluton,   50
nec rota nec Furiae nec saxum aut vulturis atri
poena, sed infernis hilares sine regibus umbrae.
improbitas illo fuit admirabilis aevo.
credebant hoc grande nefas et morte piandum,
si iuvenis vetulo non assurrexerat et si   55
barbato cuicumque puer, licet ipse videret
plura domi fraga et maiores glandis acervos.
tam venerabile erat praecedere quatuor annis,
primaque par adeo sacrae lanugo senectae.
nunc, si depositum non infitietur amicus,   60
si reddat veterem cum tota aerugine follem,
prodigiosa fides et Tuscis digna libellis,
quaeque coronata lustrari debeat agna.
egregium sanctumque virum si cerno, bimembri
hoc monstrum puero aut miranti sub aratro   65
piscibus inventis, et fetae comparo mulae,

54. credebant quo.   65. mirandis.

empire of the deep, nor was there a grim Pluto, with his Sicilian
wife, nor the wheel, nor the Furies, nor the rock, nor the
punishment of the black vulture; but merry shades without
infernal kings. Improbity was a marvel in that age. They
thought it a great impiety, and one to be expiated by death, if
a young man had not risen up before an old man, or a boy
before any one that had got a beard, although he himself might
see more wild strawberries in his home, and larger piles of
acorns. Such a claim to veneration was it to be senior by four
years; to such an extent was the first down on a par with
sacred old age. Nowadays, if a friend do not repudiate a
deposit, if he restore the old purse with all its rusty contents,
his good faith is a matter of prodigy, worthy of the Etruscan
books, and such as ought to be expiated by *the sacrifice of* a
garlanded lamb. If I see a man above the herd, of true probity,
I compare such a monster to a boy, half man, half beast, or fish
found under the astonished plough, or a pregnant mule ; *as much*

sollicitus, tamquam lapides effuderit imber
examenque apium longá consederit uvá
culmine delubri, tamquam in mare fluxerit amnis
gurgitibus miris et lactis vertice torrens.   70

    Intercepta decem quereris sestertia fraude
sacrilega? quid si bis centum perdidit alter
hoc arcana modo? maiorem tertius illá
summam, quam patulae vix ceperat angulus arcae?
tam facile et pronum est superos contemnere testes,   75
si mortalis idem nemo sciat. aspice quanta
voce neget, quae sit ficti constantia vultús.
per Solis radios Tarpeiaque fulmina iurat
et Martis frameam et Cirrhaei spicula vatis,
per calamos venatricis pharetramque puellae   80
perque tuum, pater Aegaei Neptune, tridentem;
addit et Herculeos arcus hastamque Minervae,
quidquid habent telorum armamentaria coeli.

70. vortice.

---

alarmed as though a rain-cloud had poured forth stones, or a
swarm of bees had settled in a long cluster on the summit of a
temple; as though a river had flowed into the sea with unnatural
eddies, and rushing on with a whirlpool of milk.

    You complain that ten sestertia have been wrested *from you*
by an impious fraud? What if another man has lost two hundred, privately deposited, in the same way? a third a still larger
sum than that, which the corner of his broad strong-box would
scarcely hold? So easy and natural is it to despise the witnesses
on high, if no mortal be acquainted with the matter. See with
what a loud voice he denies it, what the assurance of his made-
up countenance. He swears by the sun's rays, and the Tarpeian
thunderbolts, and the lance of Mars, and the darts of the seer-
god of Cirrha, by the arrows and the quiver of the Huntress-
Virgin, and by your trident, Neptune, father of the Aegaean.
He adds the bow of Hercules too, and the spear of Minerva, all
the weapons that the armouries of heaven contain! If indeed

si vero et pater est, " comedam," inquit " flebile nati
sinciput elixi Pharioque madentis aceto." 85
    Sunt in fortunae qui casibus omnia ponunt
et nullo credunt mundum rectore moveri,
natura volvente vices et lucis et anni,
atque ideo intrepidi quaecumque altaria tangunt.
est alius metuens ne crimen poena sequatur ; 90
hic putat esse deos et peierat, atque ita secum :
" decernat quodcumque volet de corpore nostro
Isis et irato feriat mea lumina sistro,
dummodo vel caecus teneam, quos abnego, nummos.
et phthisis et vomicae putres et dimidium crus 95
sunt tanti.   pauper locupletem optare podagram
nec dubitet Ladas, si non eget Anticyra nec
Archigene ; quid enim velocis gloria plantae
praestat et esuriens Pisaeae ramus olivae ?

       86. Sunt qui in fortunae jam casibus.

---

he be a father as well, " I will eat up," he says, " the wretched
head of my son, boiled and reeking with vinegar from Pharos, *if
I lie.*"
    There are those who range all things among the accidents of
fortune, and believe the universe to be moving on with no power
to guide it, Nature evolving the changes both of days and years ;
and so, without a tremor, they lay their hands on any altar.
There is another who fears that punishment will follow his
offence ; this man believes that there are gods, and *yet* he commits perjury, and *reasons* thus with himself—" Let Isis decree
what she pleases about my body, and strike my eyes with her
angry sistrum, so long as I can hold possession, even with the
loss of sight, of the moneys which I deny having received.
Even consumption and putrid abscesses and a shrivelled leg
are worth the price.   Let Ladas himself, if poor, not hesitate to
pray for the rich man's gout, if he does not stand in need of
Anticyra or Archigenes.   For what indeed does the glory of the
swift foot bring him in, or the hungry branch of the olive of Pisa ?

ut sit magna tamen certe lenta ira deorum est;   100
si curant igitur cunctos punire nocentes,
quando ad me venient? sed et exorabile numen
fortasse experiar; solet his ignoscere.   multi
committunt eadem diverso crimina fato;
ille crucem sceleris pretium tulit, hic diadema."   105
sic animum dirae trepidum formidine culpae
confirmant.   Tunc te sacra ad delubra vocantem
praecedit, trahere immo ultro ac vexare paratus.
nam cum magna malae superest audacia causae,
creditur a multis fiducia.   mimum agit ille,   110
urbani qualem fugitivus scurra Catulli;
tu miser exclamas, ut Stentora vincere possis,
vel potius quantum Gradivus Homericus: "audis,
Iuppiter, haec, nec labra moves, cum mittere vocem
debueras vel marmoreus vel aeneus? aut cur   115
in carbone tuo charta pia thura soluta

107. confirmat.   115. debueris.

And after all, though the wrath of the gods be great, assuredly
it is slow.   If, then, they make it their business to punish all
the guilty, when will they come to me?   Aye, and I may perchance find that the divinity is not inexorable; he is wont to
forgive these kinds of things.   Many men commit the same crimes
with different destinies.   One receives crucifixion as the price of
his villany, another a diadem."   Thus they harden their souls,
trembling with the fright caused by their dread offence.   Then,
when you summon him to the sacred shrine, he goes there before
you, aye, even ready of his own accord to drag you along and
harass you; for when great impudence comes to the aid of a
bad cause, it is taken by many for honest confidence.   He is
acting just such a farce as the runaway slave in witty Catullus.
You, poor man, cry out with a voice to beat a Stentor, or rather
as loud as the Gradivus of Homer, "Do you hear this, Jupiter,
and don't even move your lips when you ought to have spoken
out, though you had been of marble or bronze?   Or why on
your altar-fire do we place the incense of piety from the opened

ponimus et sectum vituli iecur albaque porci
omenta ? ut video, nullum discrimen habendum est
effigies inter vestras statuamque Vagelli."

Accipe quae contra valeat solatia ferre   120
et qui nec cynicos nec stoica dogmata legit
a cynicis tunica distantia, non Epicurum
suspicit exigui lactum plantaribus horti.
curentur dubii medicis maioribus aegri,
tu venam vel discipulo committe Philippi.   125
si nullum in terris tam detestabile factum
ostendis, taceo, nec pugnis caedere pectus
te veto nec planâ faciem contundere palmâ,
quandoquidem accepto·claudenda est ianua damno,
et maiore domús gemitu, maiore tumultu   130
planguntur nummi quam funera. nemo dolorem
fingit in hoc casu, vestem diducere summam
contentus, vexare oculos humore coacto:

132. in occasu.

---

paper, and the sliced liver of a calf, and the white entrails of a
pig? As far as I see, there is no distinction to be made between
your images and the statue of Vagellius."

Hear now what consolations on the other side even he may
have it in his power to bring, who has read neither the Cynics
nor the dogmas of the Stoics, differing from those of the Cynics
by a tunic *only*, who does not look up to Epicurus delighting in
the plants of his tiny garden. Let patients in a ticklish state
be attended by greater physicians : do you trust your vein even
to an apprentice of Philippus. If you can show no *other* such
detestable deed in the world, I hold my tongue, nor do I forbid
you to strike your breast with your fists, nor to beat your face
with flattened palm, since your doors must be closed, if you
have sustained a *real* loss, and money is bewailed with a greater
lamentation of the household and greater tumult than deaths.
Nobody feigns grief in such a contingency as this, *nor is* content
to tear the top *only* of his garment *nor* to torment his eyes with

ploratur lacrimis amissa pecunia veris.   .
sed si cuncta vides simili fora plena querela,   135
si decies lectis diversa parte tabellis
vana supervacui dicunt chirographa ligni,
arguit ipsorum quos littera gemmaque princeps
sardonychum, loculis quae custoditur eburnis,
te nunc delicias! extra communia censes   140
ponendum? qui tu gallinae filius albae,
nos viles pulli nati infelicibus ovis?
rem pateris modicam et mediocri bile ferendam,
si flectas oculos maiora ad crimina. confer
conductum latronem, incendia sulfure coepta   145
atque dolo, primos cum ianua colligit ignes.
confer et hos, veteris qui tollunt grandia templi
pocula adorandae robiginis et populorum
dona, vel antiquo positas a rege coronas.
haec ibi si non sunt, minor exstat sacrilegus, qui   150
radat inaurati femur Herculis et faciem ipsam

---

forced moisture. The loss of money is deplored with real tears.
But if you see all the courts full of like complaints, if, after their
bonds have been read over half a score of times from the opposite
side, people declare their notes-of-hand to be void and the tablets
worthless, when their own writing and their own seal, the
choicest of sardonyxes, which is kept in an ivory purse, convict
them—do you, after this, my fine fellow, think that you are to
be placed outside the common lot? How is it that you are the
offspring of a white hen, and we, vile chicks born from unlucky
eggs? You are suffering a small matter and one to be borne
with moderate choler, if you will turn your eyes towards greater
crimes. Compare the hired bandit, fires commenced with the
stealthy sulphur when the house-door concentrates the first
flames; compare those, too, who carry off from the ancient
temples huge cups of venerable rustiness, and the gifts of nations,
or crowns deposited by some king of old. If no such things
are there, there starts up a sacrilegious wretch on a smaller
scale, who will scrape the thigh of a gilded Hercules and the

Neptuni, qui bracteolam de Castore ducat:
an dubitet solitus totum conflare tonantem ?
confer et artifices mercatoremque veneni,
et deducendum corio bovis in mare, cum quo   155
clauditur adversis innoxia simia fatis.
haec quota pars scelerum, quae custos Gallicus urbis
usque a lucifero donec lux occidat, audit ?
humani generis mores tibi nosse volenti
sufficit una domus ; paucos consume dies, et   160
dicere te miserum, postquam illinc veneris, aude.
quis tumidum guttur miratur in Alpibus ? aut quis
in Meroe crasso maiorem infante mamillam ?
caerula quis stupuit Germani lumina, flavam
caesariem et madido torquentem cornua cirro ?   165
nempe quod haec illis natura est omnibus una.
ad subitas Thracum volucres nubemque sonoram
Pygmaeus parvis currit bellator in armis,

153. stolidus (H. Vales).

---

very face of Neptune, who will strip a thin leaf of gold from
Castor. Could he hesitate who is wont to melt down the
Thunderer entire ? Compare, too, the compounders and pur-
chasers of poison, and the man who deserving to be launched
into the sea in a bull's-hide, *the man* with whom an innocent
ape has the evil fortune to be shut up. How small a portion
these of the crimes which Gallicus, the guardian of the city,
listens to continuously from the rising of Lucifer till the sun
sets ! If you wish to know the habits of the human race, a
single house is enough. Spend a few days *there*, and dare to
call yourself miserable after you have come thence ! Who
marvels at goître in the Alps ? Who, in Meroe, at the breast
bigger than the coarse baby ? Who is astounded at the blue
eyes of the German, at his yellow hair, at his twisting its tufts
into a moistened curl ? Because, to be sure, this natural appearance is common to all of them. The Pigmy warrior runs in his
small panoply to the suddenly appearing birds of Thrace and the
resounding cloud *of cranes ;* before long no match for his foe, and

mox impar hosti raptusque per aera curvis
unguibus a saeva fertur grue.   si videas hoc   170
gentibus in nostris, risu quatiare ; sed illic,
quamquam eadem assidue spectentur proelia, ridet
nemo, ubi tota cohors pede non est altior uno.
   " Nullane periuri capitis fraudisque nefandae
poena erit ? " abreptum crede hunc graviore catena   175
protinus et nostro—quid plus velit ira ?—necari
arbitrio ; manet illa tamen iactura, nec umquam
depositum tibi sospes erit, sed corpore trunco
invidiosa dabit minimus solatia sanguis.
" at vindicta bonum vita iucundius ipsa."   180
nempe hoc indocti, quorum praecordia nullis
interdum aut levibus videas flagrantia causis :
quantulacumque adeo est occasio, sufficit irae.
Chrysippus non dicet idem nec mite Thaletis
ingenium dulcique senex vicinus Hymetto,   185
qui partem acceptae saeva inter vincla cicutae

---

snatched away through the air by its curved talons, he is carried
off by the savage crane.   If you saw this among our people you
would shake with laughter ; but there, though combats of the
same kind are continually being looked at, no one laughs, since
the whole cohort is not more than a foot high.
   " Shall there be no punishment, then, for the perjured man
and the impious fraud ? "   Suppose him to be dragged off in
the heaviest chains forthwith and put to death (what more can
rage desire ?) at our discretion, yet still that loss remains, nor
will your deposit be ever restored to you ; and a very little blood
from a headless corpse will give you *but* an odious consolation.
" But revenge is a blessing more enjoyable than life itself ! "
Of course the ignorant say so, whose breasts you see inflamed
sometimes by small causes, or none at all.   However trifling
the occasion be, it suffices for their ire.   Chrysippus will not
say the same, nor the gentle-souled Thales, nor the old man
who lived near sweet Hymettus, who would not have given his
accuser a portion of the hemlock which he received in his cruel

accusatori nollet dare. plurima felix
paulatim vitia atque errores exuit omnes,
prima docet rectum sapientia. quippe minuti
semper et infirmi est animi exiguique voluptas   190
ultio: continuo sic collige, quod vindicta
nemo magis gaudet quam femina. cur tamen hos tu
evasisse putes, quos diri conscia facti
mens habet attonitos et surdo verbere caedit
occultum quatiente animo tortore flagellum ?   195
poena autem vehemens ac multo saevior illis,
quas et Caedicius gravis invenit et Rhadamanthus
nocte dieque suum gestare in pectore testem.
Spartano cuidam respondit Pythia vates,
haud impunitum quondam fore, quod dubitaret   200
depositum retinere et fraudem iure tueri
iurando. quaerebat enim quae numinis esset
mens, et an hoc illi facinus suaderet Apollo ?
reddidit ergo metu, non moribus; et tamen omnem

---

bonds. Happy philosophy by degrees strips us of most of our
natural defects and all our errors *of judgment ;* she first teaches
what is right ; for surely vengeance is ever the pleasure of a
stunted and feeble and petty mind. *You may* infer this at once
from the fact that no one delights in vengeance more than a
woman. Yet why should you deem those to have escaped,
whom their mind, conscious of a dreadful deed, holds awe-
struck, and strikes with noiseless lash, while their tormenting
soul brandishes the hidden scourge ? Aye, it is a sharp punishment, and far more cruel than those which dread Caedicius and
Rhadamanthus invent, to carry about in one's bosom by night
and by day one's own witness. The Pythian priestess gave
answer to a certain Spartan that he should not in time to come
go unpunished for hesitating in *the matter of* retaining a deposit
and backing his fraud by an oath ; for he was asking what was
the mind of the deity, and whether Apollo counselled him this
bad deed. He made restoration, then, through fear, not through
principle ; and yet he furnished proof that every word from the

vocem adyti dignam templo veramque probavit　　205
exstinctus tota pariter cum prole domoque
et quamvis longa deductis gente propinquis.
has patitur poenas peccandi sola voluntas.
nam scelus intra se tacitum qui cogitat ullum,
facti crimen habet : cedo, si conata peregit ?　　210
perpetua anxietas nec mensae tempore cessat,
faucibus ut morbo siccis interque molares
difficili crescente cibo, sed vina misellus
exspuit, Albani veteris pretiosa senectus
displicet ; ostendas melius, densissima ruga　　215
cogitur in frontem, velut acri ducta Falerno.
nocte brevem si forte indulsit cura soporem
et toto versata toro iam membra quiescunt,
continuo templum et violati numinis aras
et, quod praecipuis mentem sudoribus urget,　　220
te videt in somnis, tua sacra et maior imago
humana turbat pavidum cogitque fateri.

　　　208. saeva voluptas.　　　　　213. Setina.

---

shrine was worthy of the temple and true, by being exterminated, together with all his children and house and his relatives, from however remote a *common* stock derived. Such penalties does the mere wish to sin suffer ; for he who meditates any secret wickedness within himself incurs the guilt of the deed. Say, what if he has accomplished his endeavours ? His perpetual anxiety does not cease even at meal times, when his jaws are dry as in a fever, and the unwelcome food swells between his grinders ; yet the wretch spits out wines ; old Alban of costly age is distasteful to him ; show him still better, yet a crowd of wrinkles is forced upon his brow, as though produced by sour Falernian. By night, if haply care has indulged him with a brief torpor, and his limbs tossed over the whole bed at last repose, forthwith he sees the temple and the altars of the insulted deity, and, what presses on his mind with special terrors, *he sees* you in his dreams ! Your image, supernatural and greater than human, disturbs the frightened wretch, and forces him to confess. These are they

hi sunt, qui trepidant et ad omnia fulgura pallent,
cum tonat, exanimes primo quoque murmure coeli,
non quasi fortuitus nec ventorum rabie, sed   225
iratus cadat in terras et iudicet ignis.
illa nihil nocuit, curâ graviore timetur
proxima tempestas, velut hoc dilata sereno.
praeterea lateris vigili cum febre dolorem
si coepere pati, missum ad sua corpora morbum   230
infesto credunt a numine, saxa deorum
haec et tela putant.   pecudem spondere sacello
balantem et Laribus cristam promittere galli
non audent; quid enim sperare nocentibus aegris
concessum ? vel quae non dignior hostia vita ?   235
mobilis et varia est ferme natura malorum.
cum scelus admittunt, superest constantia; quid fas
atque nefas, tandem incipiunt sentire peractis
criminibus.   tamen ad mores natura recurrit
damnatos, fixa et mutari nescia.   nam quis   240

223. fulmina.   225. fortuitu.

who tremble and turn pale at every flash of lightning; when it
thunders, frightened out of their wits at the very first grumblings
of the sky, as though not by chance, nor through the violence of
the winds, but in anger, the fire were falling on the earth and
judging them.   If that one has done them no harm, the next
storm is feared with graver anxiety, as though but deferred by
this lull.   Moreover, if they have begun to suffer from pain in
the side with watchful fever, they believe the disease to be sent
to their bodies by an angry deity; they think these things the
stones and missiles of the gods.   They dare not vow a bleating
sheep to the shrine, nor promise a cock's-comb to their Lares;
for what can the guilty sick be permitted to hope for? or what
victim is not more worthy of life?   Changeable and varying is
commonly the nature of bad men.   When they commit a wicked
act, they have resolution to back them up; what is right and
wrong they begin to perceive too late, when their crimes have
been completed.   Yet Nature runs back to her reprobate habits,

peccandi finem posuit sibi ? quando recepit
eiectum semel attrita de fronte ruborem ?
quisnam hominum est, quem tu contentum videris uno
flagitio ? dabit in laqueum vestigia noster
perfidus et nigri patietur carceris uncum   245
aut maris Aegaei rupem scopulosque frequentes
exsulibus magnis.   poena gaudebis amara
nominis invisi, tandemque fatebere laetus
nec surdum nec Tiresiam quemquam esse deorum.

SATIRA XIV.

PLURIMA sunt, Fuscine, et fama digna sinistra
    et nitidis maculam haesuram figentia rebus,
quae monstrant ipsi pueris traduntque parentes.
si damnosa senem iuvat alea, ludit et heres

2. maculam et rugam.

fixed and incapable of change.   For who has prescribed for
himself a limit to sinning ? or ever got back the sense of shame
once ejected from the hardened brow ?   Who among men is
there whom you have seen contented with a single crime ?
Our rogue will put his feet in the snare, and will endure the
hook of the dark prison, or a rock of the Aegaean Sea, and the
crags swarming with great exiles.   You will delight in the
bitter punishment of the hated man, and will at last joyfully
confess that none of the gods is either deaf or a Tiresias.

SATIRE XIV.

THERE are very many acts, Fuscinus, not only deserving a bad
name, but also fixing a lasting stain on things bright *by nature*,
which parents themselves show and teach to their boys.   If
baneful gambling delight the old man, his heir, *still* wearing his

bullatus parvoque eadem movet arma fritillo.　　5
nec melius de se cuiquam sperare propinquo
concedet iuvenis, qui radere tubera terrae,
boletum condire et eodem iure natantes
mergere ficedulas didicit nebulone parente
et cana monstrante gula.　cum septimus annus　　10
transierit puero, nondum omni dente renato,
barbatos licet admoveas mille inde magistros,
hinc totidem, cupiet lauto coenare paratu
semper et a magna non degenerare culina.
mitem animum et mores modicis erroribus aequos　　15
praecipit atque animas servorum et corpora nostra
materia constare putat paribusque elementis,
an saevire docet Rutilus, qui gaudet acerbo
plagarum strepitu et nullam Sirena flagellis
comparat, Antiphates trepidi Laris ac Polyphemus,　　20
tunc felix, quoties aliquis tortore vocato

　　11. puerum.　　　　13. cupient.

---

bulla, plays too, and brandishes the same weapons in his little
dice-box. Nor will the youth permit any of his relatives to
have better hopes of him, who has learnt to peel truffles, to
season a mushroom, and to dip beccaficos swimming in the same
sauce—a profligate parent and his hoary gluttony showing the
way. When his seventh year has passed over the boy, ere all
his teeth are born again, though you introduce a thousand
bearded masters from this quarter, and as many from that, he
will always want to dine in grand style, and not to degenerate
from a great cuisine. Does Rutilus preach a mild temper, and
a disposition indulgent to small faults? And does he think that
the souls of slaves and their bodies consist of the same material
as ours, and of like elements? or does he teach how to act
cruelly, when he delights in the harsh sound of stripes, and
deems no Syren comparable with the whip, the Antiphates and
Polyphemus of his trembling household—then, indeed, happy as
often as the torturer is summoned, and some one is branded with

uritur ardenti duo propter lintea ferro?
quid suadet iuveni laetus stridore catenae,
quem mire alliciunt inscripta ergastula, carcer
rusticus? exspectas ut non sit adultera Largae 　　　25
filia, quae numquam maternos dicere moechos
tam cito nec tanto poterit contexere cursu,
ut non ter decies respiret? conscia matri
virgo fuit, ceras nunc hac dictante pusillas
implet et ad moechum dat eisdem ferre cinaedis. 　　　30
sic natura iubet: velocius et citius nos
corrumpunt vitiorum exempla domestica, magnis
cum subeunt animos auctoribus. unus et alter
forsitan haec spernant iuvenes, quibus arte benigna
et meliore luto finxit praecordia Titan, 　　　35
sed reliquos fugienda patrum vestigia ducunt
et monstrata diu veteris trahit orbita culpae.
abstineas igitur damnandis. huius enim vel

33. subeant.

---

the burning iron on account of a couple of towels? What does
he inculcate on the youth who is pleased with the clanking of
chains, whom branded slaves and a country bridewell marvel-
lously delight? Do you expect that the daughter of Larga will
not be an adulteress, who could never tell off her mother's lovers
so quickly, nor string them together at such a pace, as not to have
to take breath thirty times? When a girl, she was her mother's
accomplice; now, at the dictation of the latter, she fills up her
own little tablets, and gives them to the same wretches to carry
to her lover. So nature orders; more rapidly and easily are we
corrupted by examples of vices when they are in our homes,
when they steal into our minds with great authority. Perhaps youths—here and there one—whose hearts the Titan has
fashioned with kindlier art and of a superior clay, may spurn
these habits, yet the rest are led on by the footprints of their
fathers, which should be shunned, and drawn into the track,
which has long been exhibited to them, of the old sin. You
should abstain, then, from things to be condemned; for there is,

una potens ratio est, ne crimina nostra sequantur
ex nobis geniti, quoniam dociles imitandis　　　40
turpibus ac pravis omnes sumus, et Catilinam
quocumque in populo videas quocumque sub axe,
sed nec Brutus erit Bruti nec avunculus usquam.
nil dictu foedum visuque haec limina tangat,
intra quae puer est. procul hinc, procul inde puellae　　45
lenonum et cantus pernoctantis parasiti.
maxima debetur puero reverentia. si quid
turpe paras, ne tu pueri contempseris annos,
sed peccaturo obsistat tibi filius infans.
nam si quid dignum censoris fecerit ira　　　50
quandoque et similem tibi se non corpore tantum
nec vultu dederit, morum quoque filius et qui
omnia deterius tua per vestigia peccet,
corripies nimirum et castigabis acerbo
clamore ac post haec tabulas mutare parabis!　　55
unde tibi frontem libertatemque parentis,

45. intra quae pater est.　　　　52. morum tibi filius.

---

at any rate, one reason that enjoins this, that those born of us
may not follow our crimes, since we are all of us docile in imitating what is base and depraved, and you may see a Catiline in any
nation, under any sky ; but there will be no nowhere a Brutus or
Brutus's uncle. Let nothing which is foul to be spoken, or to
be seen, touch this threshold inside which the boy is. Away
from here, away from there, panders, damsels, and songs of the
parasite making a night of it. The greatest respect is due to a
boy. If you are contemplating anything disgraceful, do not you
despise the boy's years ; but let your infant son be a check on
the sin you are about to commit. For if, some day or other, he
shall do anything to deserve the censor's displeasure, and shall
show himself like you, not in form merely, or in face, but *as being*
the offspring of your character, and one who exaggerates all your
sins *as he goes* along your footprints, no doubt you will find fault
with him, and reprove him with bitter outcry, and thereupon
prepare to alter your will! Whence your front *severe*, and license

cum facias peiora senex vacuumque cerebro
iam pridem caput hoc ventosa cucurbita quaerat?
hospite venturo, cessabit nemo tuorum.
" verre pavimentum, nitidas ostende columnas, 　　　60
arida cum tota descendat aranea tela,
hic leve argentum, vasa aspera tergeat alter,"
vox domini furit instantis virgamque tenentis.
ergo miser trepidas, ne stercore foeda canino
atria displiceant oculis venientis amici, 　　　65
ne perfusa luto sit porticus; et tamen uno
semodio scobis haec emendat servulus unus :
illud non agitas, ut sanctam filius omni
aspiciat sine labe domum vitioque carentem.
gratum est quod patriae civem populoque dedisti, 　　　70
si facis ut patriae sit idoneus, utilis agris,
utilis et bellorum et pacis rebus agendis.
plurimum enim intererit quibus artibus et quibus hunc tu

62. hic lavet argentum.

---

of a parent, when you, an old man, do worse things, and the
windy cupping-glass has long since been looking out for that
brainless head of yours?

When a guest is coming, none of your people will be idle.
" Sweep the pavement, uncover the bright columns, let the dry
spider come down with all its web, let one polish the plain
silver, another the embossed vessels," raves the voice of the
master, urging them on and wielding his switch. So then, poor
man, you are frightened lest your hall, fouled by the ordure of
a dog, offend the eyes of your friend when he comes; lest your
colonnade be splashed with mud; whereas a single little slave,
with a single half measure of sawdust, can set all right; and yet
you do not bestir yourself about this, that your son shall behold a
virtuous household without any taint and free from vice. It is a
subject for thanks that you have given a citizen to your country
and to the people, if you take care that he shall be serviceable
to the country, useful to her lands, useful in transacting the
affairs both of war and peace; for it will make a very great

moribus instituas.   serpente ciconia pullos
nutrit et inventa per devia rura lacerta ;   75
illi eadem sumptis quaerunt animalia pinnis.
vultur iumento et canibus crucibusque relictis
ad fetus properat partemque cadaveris affert ;
hic est ergo cibus magni quoque vulturis et se
pascentis, propria cum iam facit arbore nidos.   80
sed leporem aut capream famulae Iovis et generosae
in saltu venantur aves, hinc praeda cubili
ponitur ; inde autem cum se matura levarit
progenies stimulante fame, festinat ad illam
quam primum praedam rupto gustaverat ovo.   85
    Aedificator erat Cetronius, et modo curvo
litore Caietae, summa nunc Tiburis arce,
nunc Praenestinis in montibus alta parabat
culmina villarum Graecis longeque petitis

76. pennis.   83. levabit.

---

difference by what methods and moral discipline you train this
same *youth.* The stork feeds her young on snakes and lizards
found in sequestered fields ; they, when they have put on their
feathers, go in quest of the same animals. The vulture, quitting
the cattle and dogs and crosses, hastens to her brood and brings
them a portion of the carcass. This, consequently, is also the
food of the vulture when full-grown and feeding itself, *and*
when it has begun to build a nest on a tree of its own. But
the noble birds, the attendants of Jove, hunt after the hare or
the kid in the forest ; hence *comes* the prey which is served up
in their nest ; from this cause, also, when their offspring, grown
to maturity, lifts himself *on his wings,* under the stimulus of
hunger, he hastens to the same prey which he had first tasted
on breaking the egg.
    Cetronius was given to building, and at one time, on the
curved shore of Caieta, now on the highest summit of Tibur,
now on the hills of Praeneste, he reared the lofty roofs of his
villas with his marbles from Greece, and fetched from afar, sur-

marmoribus vincens Fortunae atque Herculis aedem,   90
ut spado vincebat Capitolia nostra Posides.
dum sic ergo habitat Cetronius, imminuit rem,
fregit opes ; nec parva tamen mensura relictae
partis erat: totam hanc turbavit filius amens,
dum meliore novas attollit marmore villas.   95
    Quidam sortiti metuentem sabbata patrem
nil praeter nubes et coeli numen adorant,
nec distare putant humana carne suillam,
qua pater abstinuit, mox et praeputia ponunt.
Romanas autem soliti contemnere leges   100
Iudaicum ediscunt et servant ac metuunt ius,
tradidit arcano quodcumque volumine Moses,
non monstrare vias eadem nisi sacra colenti,
quaesitum ad fontem solos deducere verpos.
sed pater in causa, cui septima quaeque fuit lux   105
ignava et partem vitae non attigit ullam.

---

passing the temples of Fortune and of Hercules as much as the
eunuch Posides surpassed our Capitols.   While, then, Cetronius
housed himself in this way, he diminished his property, he
impaired his fortune ; yet the amount of the portion left was by
no means small.   His insane son squandered the whole of this,
while he raised up new villas of still finer marble.
    Some, whose lot it has been to have a father paying respect
to sabbaths, worship nothing except the clouds and the divinity
of the sky, and think the flesh of swine, from which their father
abstained, does not differ from that of human beings ; before
long they even undergo circumcision.   Moreover, having been
wont to despise the laws of Rome, they make themselves
masters of, and observe and respect, the Jewish code, whatever
Moses has taught in his mystic volume ; not to show the way
except to one who practises the same rites ; to guide the cir-
cumcised alone to the sought-for well.   But the father is to
blame, to whom every seventh day was one of idleness, and was
connected with no part of *the duties of* life.

Sponte tamen iuvenes imitantur cetera, solam
inviti quoque avaritiam exercere iubentur.
fallit enim vitium specie virtutis et umbra,
cum sit triste habitu vultuque et veste severum,   110
nec dubie tamquam frugi laudatur avarus,
tamquam parcus homo et rerum tutela suarum
certa magis quam si fortunas servet easdem
Hesperidum serpens aut Ponticus. adde quod hunc de
quo loquor egregium populus putat acquirendi   115
artificem : quippe his crescunt patrimonia fabris :
sed crescunt quocumque modo maioraque fiunt
incude assidua semperque ardente camino.
et pater ergo animi felices credit avaros,
qui miratur opes, qui nulla exempla beati   120
pauperis esse putat. iuvenes hortatur ut illam
ire viam pergant et eidem incumbere sectae.
sunt quaedam vitiorum elementa ; his protinus illos

115. atque verendum.

Still, of their own accord, youths imitate the other vices ;
avarice alone they are bidden to practise, even against their
will. For this vice deceives by an appearance and shadow of
virtue, inasmuch as it is subdued in bearing, severe in countenance and attire, and the miser is praised unhesitatingly as a
frugal person, as an economical man, and a protector of his own
property, more sure than if the serpent of the Hesperides or that
of Pontus watched over these same possessions. Add that the
people deem him of whom I am speaking an extraordinary
master of the art of acquiring ; since patrimonies grow through
such workmen as these—aye, they grow by all kinds of ways,
and are made larger on an unceasing anvil and in a forge that
is always burning. So, then, the father too considers misers
to be happy in their disposition ; *he* who admires wealth, who
thinks there are no examples of a poor man who is blessed.
He exhorts his youths to continue on that road, and to stick to
the same school. There are certain elements of the vices ; with
these he imbues them at starting, and compels them to master

imbuit et cogit minimas ediscere sordes,
mox acquirendi docet insatiabile votum.   125
servorum ventres modio castigat iniquo
ipse quoque esuriens; neque enim omnia sustinet umquam
mucida caerulei panis consumere frusta,
hesternum solitus medio servare minutal
Septembri, nec non differre in tempora coenae   130
alterius conchem aestivam cum parte lacerti
signatam vel dimidio putrique siluro,
filaque sectivi numerata includere porri:
invitatus ad haec aliquis de ponte negabit.
sed quo divitias haec per tormenta coactas,   135
cum furor haud dubius, cum sit manifesta phrenesis,
ut locuples moriaris, egentis vivere fato?
interea pleno cum turget sacculus ore,
crescit amor nummi, quantum ipsa pecunia crevit,
et minus hanc optat qui non habet. ergo paratur   140
altera villa tibi, cum rus non sufficit unum,

131. aestivi.   137. egenti.   139. crescit.

---

the smallest meannesses; soon he teaches them the insatiable desire of acquiring. He punishes the bellies of his slaves with short measure, while he himself is hungry into the bargain; he can never, indeed, bear to consume even the whole of the musty fragments of his mildewed loaf; *he is* wont to keep yesterday's mincemeat in the middle of September, and to put off to another dinner-time the summer beans, sealed up with a bit of sea-lizard or half a putrid shad, and to shut in with them the shreds, after they have been counted, of cut leeks. A beggar from the bridge invited to such a meal would decline. But to what end riches heaped together through such tortures, when the madness is indubitable, the insanity manifest, of living the lot of the destitute that you may die wealthy? In the meanwhile, when the small bag is swollen with its mouth full, the love of money grows as much as the money itself has grown. The man who has none is less eager for it. So another country-house must be procured for you, since one estate does not suffice,

et proferre libet fines, maiorque videtur
et melior vicina seges ; mercaris et hanc et
arbusta et densa montem qui canet oliva.
quorum si pretio dominus non vincitur ullo,   145
nocte boves macri lassoque famelica collo
iumenta ad virides huius mittentur aristas,
nec prius inde domum quam tota novalia saevos
in ventres abeant, ut credas falcibus actum.
dicere vix possis quam multi talia plorent   150
et quot venales iniuria fecerit agros.
sed qui sermones, quam foede buccina famae !
" quid nocet haec ? " inquit " tunicam mihi malo lupini,
quam si me toto laudet vicinia pago
exigui ruris paucissima farra secantem."   155
scilicet et morbis et debilitate carebis,
et luctum et curam effugies, et tempora vitae
longa tibi post haec fato meliore dabuntur,

147. armenta ; mittuntur.   152. foedae.

---

and you like to extend your boundaries, and the neighbouring
corn-land seems *to you* larger and better *than your own ;* you
buy this too, and the plantations, and the hill which is white
with the mass of olives ; and if their owner will not yield to any
offer, your lean oxen, and famished cattle with weary necks, are
turned into his green sprouting corn by night, and do not go
thence home before the whole crop has found its way into their
ravenous bellies, so that one would think the work had been
done with sickles.   One can hardly tell how many people have
to lament such losses, or how many estates injurious treatment
has caused to be offered for sale.

  But what talk there will be !   How foully the trumpet of
rumour *will blow !*   " What harm does that do ? " he says.   " I
would rather, for my part, have a bean-shell than that the
neighbourhood in the whole district should praise me *on condition of my* reaping paltry crops off a small estate."   Of course,
then, you will be exempt from diseases and infirmity, and escape
grief and care ; and, after this, a long period of life will be

si tantum culti solus possederis agri,
quantum sub Tatio populus Romanus arabat.   160
mox etiam fractis aetate ac Punica passis
proelia vel Pyrrhum immauem gladiosque Molossos
tandem pro multis vix iugera bina dabantur
vulneribus.   merces haec sanguinis atque laboris
nullis visa umquam meritis minor aut ingratae   165
curta fides patriae.   saturabat glebula talis
patrem ipsum turbamque casae, qua feta iacebat
uxor et infantes ludebant quatuor, unus
vernula, tres domini; sed magnis fratribus horum
a scrobe vel sulco redeuntibus altera coena   170
amplior et grandes fumabant pultibus ollae.
nunc modus hic agri nostro non sufficit horto.
inde fere scelerum causae, nec plura venena
miscuit aut ferro grassatur saepius ullum
humanae mentis vitium quam saeva cupido   175

---

bestowed on you with a happier destiny, provided you are the
sole possessor of as much cultivated land as the Roman people
used to plough under Tatius.   Afterwards, even to men broken
by age, and who had been engaged in the Punic wars, and
against fierce Pyrrhus and the swords of the Molossians, at the
end, scarce two acres apiece were given in return for many
wounds.   This, the price of their blood and their toils, never
seemed to any of them less than their deserts, nor *did* their
country *seem* ungratefully wanting in its engagements.   A little
farm like this amply satisfied the father himself and the troop
in the cottage, where his wife was lying pregnant and four
children were playing, one a little house-slave, three of them
masters; while for the big brothers of these, on their return from
the trench or the furrow, there was a second larger supper
and huge earthen jars smoking with porridge.   Nowadays this
measure of land does not suffice for our garden.   Hence commonly
the incentives to crimes; nor is there any vicious propensity of
the human mind which has mingled more poisons, or attacks
more frequently with the poniard, than this fierce longing for

immodici census: nam dives qui fieri vult,
et cito vult fieri: sed quae reverentia legum,
quis metus aut pudor est umquam properantis avari?
" vivite contenti casulis et collibus istis,
o pueri!" Marsus dicebat et Hernicus olim   180
Vestinusque senex; " panem quaeramus aratro,
qui satis est mensis. laudant hoc numina ruris,
quorum ope et auxilio gratae post munus aristae
contingunt homini veteris fastidia quercus,
nil vetitum fecisse volet, quem non pudet alto   185
per glaciem perone tegi, qui summovet euros
pellibus inversis. peregrina ignotaque nobis
ad scelus atque nefas, quaecumque est, purpura ducit."
haec illi veteres praecepta minoribus: at nunc
post finem autumni media de nocte supinum   190
clamosus iuvenem pater excitat; " accipe ceras,
scribe, puer, vigila, causas age, perlege rubras
maiorum leges aut vitem posce libello.

---

an immoderate fortune; for he who wishes to become rich
wishes to become rich quickly too. But what respect for the
laws, what apprehension or sense of shame is there ever on the
part of the miser in his haste? " Live contented with these
your cottages and hills, my lads," the Marsian and Hernican and
Vestinian old man used to say in days of yore. " Let us seek
with our ploughs bread which suffices for our tables: this the
rustic deities approve, by whose aid and assistance, since the
gift of the welcome corn-blade, contempt for the old oak has
come upon mankind. He will not wish to do anything for-
bidden who is not ashamed to wear the high country boot
through the winter, who elbows away the east winds with skins
turned inside out. This foreign purple, unknown to us *before*,
whatever it is, leads to crime and impiety." Such were the
precepts of the elders of those days to their juniors; but now,
after the close of autumn, immediately upon midnight, the father,
with loud voice, calls up his reposing son. " Take your tablets,
write, boy, watch, plead causes, read over the red-lettered laws

sed caput intactum buxo naresque pilosas
annotet et grandes miretur Laelius alas.   195
dirue Maurorum attegias, castella Brigantum,
ut locupletem aquilam tibi sexagesimus annus
afferat, aut, longos castrorum ferre labores
si piget et trepidum solvunt tibi cornua ventrem
cum lituis audita, pares quod vendere possis   200
pluris dimidio, nec te fastidia mercis
ullius subeant ablegandae Tiberim ultra,
neu credas ponendum aliquid discriminis inter
unguenta et corium.   lucri bonus est odor ex re
qualibet.   illa tuo sententia semper in ore   205
versetur, dis atque ipso Iove digna poeta,
' unde habeas, quaerit nemo, sed oportet habere.'
hoc monstrant vetulae pueris repentibus assae,
hoc discunt omnes ante alpha et beta puellae."

199. trepido.   208. poscentibus assem.

of our ancestors, or ask for the centurion's switch in a petition.
But *mind and* let Laelius remark your head untouched by a
comb, your hairy nostrils, and your stalwart shoulders.   Destroy
the huts of the Moors, the forts of the Brigantes, that your
sixtieth year may bring you the lucrative 'eagle;' or, if it is
irksome to you to bear the protracted labours of the camp, and
the horns heard in company with the trumpets loosen your
disturbed bowels, procure something to sell for more than half
as much again, and don't let disgust for any *kind of* merchandise that must be relegated to the other side of the Tiber enter
your head, nor deem that there is any distinction to be drawn
between perfumes and hide.   The odour of lucre is good from
anything you please.   Let that sentiment, worthy of the gods
and of Jove himself as its poetical author, be always in your
mouth : 'By what means you have become possessed, no one
asks, but you need to possess.'   This, old dry-nurses teach to
boys before they can walk.   This every girl learns before her
Alpha and Beta."

talibus instantem monitis quemcumque parentum 210
sic possem affari. dic, o vanissime, quis te
festinare iubet ? meliorem praesto magistro
discipulum. securus abi, vinceris, ut Aiax
praeteriit Telamonem, ut Pelea vicit Achilles.
parcendum est teneris ; nondum implevere medullas 215
maturae mala nequitiae. cum pectere barbam
coeperit et longi mucronem admittere cultri,
falsus erit testis, vendet periuria summa
exigua Cereris tangens aramque pedemque.
elatam iam crede nurum, si limina vestra 220
mortifera cum dote subit. quibus illa premetur
per somnum digitis ! nam quae terraque marique
acquirenda putas, brevior via conferet illi :
nullus enim magni sceleris labor. " haec ego numquam
mandavi," dices olim, " nec talia suasi." 225
mentis causa malae tamen est et origo penes te ;

211. possum.   216. natirae.

Any parent whatever urging such instructions as these, I
would address in this wise—Say, most senseless of men, who
bids you be in *such* a hurry ? I warrant the disciple superior
to his master. Go your way, without fear ; you will be beaten,
just as Ajax outstripped Telamon, just as Achilles beat Peleus.
Young people should be spared. The evils of mature wickedness have not yet permeated his marrow. When he has begun to
comb his beard, and to apply the long razor's edge, he will be a
false witness, he will sell his false oaths for a trifle, while laying
his hand on the altar and foot of Ceres. Consider your daughter-
in-law as good as buried if she passes your threshold with a death-
bearing dowry. With what fingers will she be throttled in her
sleep ! For that *wealth* which you think must be acquired by
land and sea a shorter way will confer upon him, since there is
no trouble in *committing* a great crime. " I never enjoined
this," you will say some day, " nor counselled such things."
Nevertheless, the cause of this depravity of mind and its origin
are with you ; for whosoever has inculcated the love of a large

nam quisquis magni census praccepit amorem
et laevo monitu pueros producit avaros,
et qui per fraudes patrimonia conduplicare,
dat libertatem et totas effundit habenas   230
curriculo, quem si revoces, subsistere nescit
et te contempto rapitur metisque relictis.
nemo satis credit tantum delinquere, quantum
permittas; adeo indulgent sibi latius ipsi.
cum dicis iuveni stultum, qui donet amico,   235
qui paupertatem levet attollatque propinqui,
et spoliare doces et circumscribere et omni
crimine divitias acquirere, quarum amor in te,
quantus erat patriae Deciorum in pectore, quantum
dilexit Thebas, si Graecia vera, Menoeceus,   240
in quorum sulcis legiones dentibus anguis
cum clipeis nascuntur et horrida bella capessunt
continuo, tamquam et tubicen surrexerit una.

230. effudit.   241. quarum.

---

fortune, and by his sinister counsel brings up his boys to be
greedy for gain [and who . . . by fraud to double their patri-
monies], gives them their head, and abandons the whole reins
to the chariot: if you are for calling back *the youth*, he can't
stop, and is borne along in contempt of you, and leaving the
goal behind him. No one thinks it enough to transgress just
as much as you permit him : so surely do people indulge themselves more freely on their own account. When you tell a
young man that he is a fool who gives to his friend, who
relieves and raises up the poverty of his kinsman, you are likewise teaching him to rob, and to cheat, and to acquire by every
kind of crime those riches, the love of which in you is as great
as was that of their country in the breasts of the Decii, as great
as was the love of Menoeceus, if Greece speak truth, for the The-
bans, in whose furrows legions are born with shields from the
teeth of the serpent, and engage in terrible war forthwith, just
as if a trumpeter into the bargain had sprung up at the same
time with them : so you will see the fire, the sparks of which

ergo ignem, cuius scintillas ipse dedisti,
flagrantem late et rapientem cuncta videbis.   245
nec tibi parcetur misero, trepidumque magistrum
in cavea magno fremitu leo tollet alumnus.
nota mathematicis genesis tua ; sed grave tardas
exspectare colus ; morieris stamine nondum
abrupto.   iam nunc obstas et vota moraris,   250
iam torquet iuvenem longa et cervina senectus.
ocius Archigenen quaere atque eme quod Mithridates
composuit, si vis aliam decerpere ficum
atque alias tractare rosas.   medicamen habendum est,
sorbere ante cibum quod debeat et pater et rex.   255
    Monstro voluptatem egregiam, cui nulla theatra,
nulla aequare queas praetoris pulpita lauti,
si spectes quanto capitis discrimine constent
incrementa domus, aerata multus in arca
fiscus et ad vigilem ponendi Castora nummi,   260
ex quo Mars ultor galeam quoque perdidit et res

---

you yourself have furnished, flaming widely and seizing on
everything.   Nor will you, miserable wretch, be spared, and the
lion you have reared will carry off with a loud roar his trembling
master in his cage.   Your nativity may be known to the astro-
logers ; but it is tiresome to wait upon the tardy distaff : you
will die before your thread is broken off.   Already, as it is, you
stand in the way, and delay his wishes.   Already your long and
stag-like old age torments the young man.   Make haste, and
look up Archigenes, and purchase what Mithridates compounded,
if you wish to pluck another fig, or even to handle other roses.
You must get the antidote, which a father as well as a king
should imbibe before food.

    I can show you a surpassing amusement which you shall not
be able to match by any theatres or any stage-boards of the
sumptuous Praetor, if you *only* observe what a danger to life
these additions to one's fortune cost, this quantity of treasure
in the brass-bound strong-box, and the moneys to be deposited
with watchful Castor, ever since Mars the Avenger lost even his

non potuit servare suas.   ergo omnia Florae
et Cereris licet et Cybeles aulaea relinquas,
tanto maiores humana negotia ludi.
an magis oblectant animum iactata petauro   265
corpora quique solet rectum descendere funem,
quam tu, Corycia semper qui puppe moraris
atque habitas, coro semper tollendus et austro,
perditus ac vilis sacci mercator olentis,
qui gaudes pingue antiquae de litore Cretae   270
passum et municipes Iovis advexisse lagenas?
hic tamen ancipiti figens vestigia planta
victum illa mercede parat brumamque famemque
illa reste cavet; tu propter mille talenta
et centum villas temerarius.   aspice portus   275
et plenum magnis trabibus mare; plus hominum est iam
in pelago; veniet classis quocumque vocarit
spes lucri, nec Carpathium Gaetulaque tantum
aequora transiliet, sed longe Calpe relicta

270. pingui. ·

helmet, and could not take care of his own property. You may
desert, then, all the drop-scenes of Flora and Ceres and Cybele,
so much better plays are the doings of mankind. Can bodies pro-
jected from the petaurum, or he who is wont to descend the tight-
rope, furnish the mind with more entertainment than you who are
always remaining on your Corycian ship and dwelling, constantly
to be tossed by Corus and by Auster, the desperate and paltry
salesman of a smelling bag *of merchandise*, who delight in import-
ing rich raisin wine and wine-jars, the compatriots of Jove, from
the shore of ancient Crete? But he who plants his steps with
doubtful tread obtains his living at this price, and avoids cold
and hunger by that rope of his. You are foolhardy, for the
sake of a thousand talents and a hundred villas. Behold the
ports and the sea full of large ships! The greater part of mankind are now on the main; a fleet will come whithersoever the
hope of gain invites, and will not only bound over the Carpathian
and Gaetulian seas, but, leaving Calpe far behind, will hear the

audiet Herculeo stridentem gurgite solem. 280
grande operae pretium est, ut tenso folle reverti
inde domum possis tumidaque superbus aluta
Oceani monstra et iuvenes vidisse marinos.
non unus mentes agitat furor.   ille sororis
in manibus vultu Eumenidum terretur et igni, 285
hic bove percusso mugire Agamemnona credit
aut Ithacum.   parcat tunicis licet atque lacernis,
curatoris eget qui navem mercibus implet
ad summum latus et tabula distinguitur unda,
cum sit causa mali tanti et discriminis huius 290
concisum argentum in titulos faciesque minutas.
occurrunt nubes et fulgura, " solvite funem ! "
frumenti dominus clamat piperisve coempti
" nil color hic coeli, nil fascia nigra minatur,
aestivum tonat." infelix hac forsitan ipsa 295
nocte cadet fractis trabibus, fluctuque premetur

287. lacertis.

---

sun hissing in the Herculean waters. A grand equivalent for
your labour it is that you be able to return home thence with
distended purse and proud, with your swollen money-bag, to
have beheld the monsters of the ocean and the youths of the
sea. Not one madness *only* distracts *men's* minds. One, in
his sister's arms, is terrified by the faces and the torches
of the Eumenides; another, when he has struck the bull,
thinks it is Agamemnon or the Ithacan that is roaring.
Though he may spare his coats and his cloaks, the man is
in need of a guardian who fills his ship with merchandise
up to the very bulwarks, and is separated from the waves by
a plank, when the incentive to such great misery and such
danger as this is silver cut up into inscriptions and miniatures.
Clouds and lightning oppose him.   " Loosen the rope," shouts
the owner of the bought-up corn or pepper; " this colour of
the sky, this black belt *of cloud* threatens nothing. It is
only summer thunder." Unhappy wretch ! perchance this very
night he will fall with his timbers shattered, and will be sub-

obrutus et zonam laeva morsuque tenebit.
sed cuius votis modo non suffecerat aurum,
quod Tagus et rutila volvit Pactolus arena,
frigida sufficient velantes inguina panni   300
exiguusque cibus, mersa rate naufragus assem
dum rogat et picta se tempestate tuetur.
  Tantis parta malis cura maiore metuque
servantur.   misera est magni custodia census.
dispositis praedives hamis vigilare cohortem   305
servorum noctu Licinus iubet, attonitus pro
electro signisque suis Phrygiaque columna
atque ebore et lata testudine.   dolia nudi
non ardent cynici; si fregeris, altera fiet
cras domus, aut eadem plumbo commissa manebit.   310
sensit Alexander, testa cum vidit in illa
magnum habitatorem, quanto felicior hic, qui
nil cuperet, quam qui totum sibi posceret orbem,

---

merged and overwhelmed by the billows, clutching his girdle
with his left hand and his teeth. Moreover, he to whose wishes
but lately all the gold would not have sufficed which Tagus rolls
and Pactolus in its red sand, will have to be satisfied with the
rags covering his cold loins and scanty nourishment, while ship-
wrecked, his bark sunk, he begs for a copper, and maintains
himself by a painting of the storm.

  What has been earned through such great hardships has to be
guarded with still greater solicitude and fear. The custody of
a large fortune is *a* wretched *business*. The millionaire Licinus,
after disposing his water-buckets, orders a *whole* cohort of slaves
to keep watch by night, in a wild fright about his amber and
his statues and columns of Phrygian marble, and his ivory and
broad tortoise-shell. The tub of the naked cynic does not take
fire. If you break it, another home will be made to-morrow,
or the same one will remain, patched up with lead. Alexander
perceived, when he saw in that tub its great inhabitant, how
much happier he was who wished for nothing, than he who
demanded the whole world for himself, destined to undergo

passurus gestis aequanda pericula rebus.
nullum numen habes, si sit prudentia ; nos te,   315
nos facimus, Fortuna, deam. mensura tamen quae
sufficiat census, si quis me consulat, edam.
in quantum sitis atque fames et frigora poscunt,
quantum, Epicure, tibi parvis suffecit in hortis,
quantum Socratici ceperunt ante Penates.   320
numquam aliud natura, aliud sapientia dicit.
acribus exemplis videor te claudere. misce
ergo aliquid nostris de moribus, effice summam,
bis septem ordinibus quam lex dignatur Othonis.
haec quoque si rugam trahit extenditque labellum,   325
sume duos equites, fac tertia quadringenta.
si nondum implevi gremium, si panditur ultra,
nec Croesi fortuna umquam nec Persica regna
sufficient animo, nec divitiae Narcissi,
indulsit Caesar cui Claudius omnia, cuius   330
paruit imperiis uxorem occidere iussus.

315. abest.   316. te facimus.

---

perils equivalent to the exploits he achieved. You have no
divine power where prudence exists. It is we, we who make a
goddess of you, O Fortune ! However, if any one asks my
opinion as to what measure of property is sufficient, I will tell
you. To the extent that thirst and hunger and cold demand ;
as much as sufficed you in your small garden, Epicurus ; as
much as the home of Socrates contained before. Nature never
says one thing and philosophy another. Do I seem to confine
you by examples that are too severe? Throw in, then, something from our manners ; make up the sum which the law of
Otho regards as fitting for the Fourteen Rows. If this, too, produces a frown, and makes you pout your lip, take two knights'
fees—make it a third four hundred. If I have not yet filled
your lap, if it is spread out beyond this, not even the fortune of
Croesus nor the realms of Persia will ever satisfy your inclinations,
nor the riches of Narcissus, to whom Claudius Caesar gave up
everything, whose orders he obeyed when bidden to kill his wife.

QUIS nescit, Volusi Bithynice, qualia demens
  Aegyptus portenta colat ?   crocodilon adorat
pars haec, illa pavet saturam serpentibus ibin.
effigies sacri nitet aurea cercopitheci,
dimidio magicae resonant ubi Memnone chordae   5
atque vetus Thebe centum iacet obruta portis.
illic aeluros, hic piscem fluminis, illic
oppida tota canem venerantur, nemo Dianam.
porrum et caepe nefas violare et frangere morsu.
o sanctas gentes, quibus haec nascuntur in hortis   10
numina! lanatis animalibus abstinet omnis
mensa, nefas illic fetum iugulare capellae,
carnibus humanis vesci licet. attonito cum
tale super coenam facinus narraret Ulixes
Alcinoo, bilem aut risum fortasse quibusdam   15

7. caeruleos.

SATIRE XV.

WHO does not know, Volusius of Bithynia, what kinds of
monsters demented Egypt worships?   One part adores the
crocodile, another quakes before the ibis gorged with serpents.
The golden image of a sacred long-tailed ape glitters where the
magic chords resound from mutilated Memnon, and ancient
Thebes lies in ruin with her hundred gates.   There whole towns
venerate cats, here a river-fish, there a dog, *but* no one Diana.
It is impiety to violate and break with the teeth the leek and
the onion.   O holy races, to whom such deities as these are
born in their gardens !   Every table abstains from woolly
animals; it is impiety there to cut the throat of a young kid;
it is lawful to feed on human flesh.   When narrating such a
misdeed as this to the amazed Alcinous over their supper,
Ulysses had not improbably excited the anger or the laughter

moverat, ut mendax aretalogus. "in mare nemo
hunc abicit saeva dignum veraque Charybdi,
fingentem immanes Laestrygonas atque Cyclopas?
nam citius Scyllam vel concurrentia saxa
Cyaneas, plenos et tempestatibus utres   20
crediderim, aut tenui percussum verbere Circes
et cum remigibus grunnisse Elpenora porcis.
tam vacui capitis populum Phaeaca putavit?"
sic aliquis merito nondum ebrius et minimum qui
de Corcyraea temetum duxerat urna;   25
solus enim haec Ithacus nullo sub teste canebat.
nos miranda quidem, sed nuper consule Iunio
gesta super calidae referemus moenia Copti,
nos vulgi scelus et cunctis graviora cothurnis;
nam scelus, a Pyrrha quamquam omnia syrmata volvas, 30
nullus apud tragicos populus facit. accipe nostro
dira quod exemplum feritas produxerit aevo.

27. Junco.

---

of some *of the guests* as a lying babbler. "Will no one pitch
into the sea this fellow, who deserves a cruel Charybdis and a
real one, with his fictions of huge Laestrygones and Cyclopes?
For I would sooner believe in Scylla or the Cyanean rocks
clashing together, or the bladders full of stormy winds, or that
Elpenor was struck with a light blow of Circe, and grunted in
company with the crew turned into hogs. Did he suppose the
Phaeacian people to be so void of brains?" So some one *may
have spoken* with reason who was not yet drunk, who had
quaffed but very little wine from the Corcyraean bowl. For the
Ithacan was singing this alone, with no witness *to corroborate him*.
We shall recount things, marvellous it is true, but which were
only lately enacted in the consulship of Junius, above the walls
of sultry Coptos; we *shall recount* the crime of a *whole* populace,
and things surpassing in gravity all tragedies. For though you
turn over all tragic themes from the time of Pyrrha, nowhere in
the poets does a *whole* people commit a crime. Hear what a
sample dread barbarism has produced in our own age.

Inter finitimos vetus atque antiqua simultas,
immortale odium et numquam sanabile vulnus
ardet adhuc, Ombos et Tentyra. summus utrimque   35
inde furor vulgo, quod numina vicinorum
odit uterque locus, cum solos credat habendos
esse deos, quos ipse colit. sed tempore festo
alterius populi rapienda occasio cunctis
visa inimicorum primoribus ac ducibus, ne   40
laetum hilaremque diem, ne magnae gaudia coenae
sentirent, positis ad templa et compita mensis
pervigilique toro, quem nocte ac luce iacentem
septimus interdum sol invenit. horrida sane
Aegyptus, sed luxuria, quantum ipse notavi,   45
barbara famoso non cedit turba Canopo.
adde quod et facilis victoria de madidis et
blaesis atque mero titubantibus. inde virorum
saltatus nigro tibicine, qualiacumque
unguenta et flores multaeque in fronte coronae,   50

A long-standing and ancient grudge, an undying hatred, and
a wound that can never be healed, still rages between *two* neighbours, Ombi and Tentyra. On both sides there is the utmost fury
on the part of the vulgar, from this cause, that each locality
hates its neighbour's deities, since it thinks those alone should
be accounted gods whom it worships itself. At any rate, at a
festival of one nation, the occasion seemed to all the enemy's
chiefs and leaders one to be seized, in order to prevent their
enjoying a happy and merry day, when the tables are placed
before the temples and in the crossways, as also the couch that
knows no sleep, which lying *there* night and day, the seventh
sun sometimes finds. Egypt is savage, to be sure ; yet, in luxu-
riousness, as far as I myself have remarked, the barbarous crowd
does not yield to the notorious Canopus. Add that victory is
easy even, over those who are drunk and stuttering and reeling
with wine. On one side there were men dancing to a black
piper ; perfumes, such as they were, and flowers and chaplets in
plenty on their brows ; on the other, hatred with an empty

hinc iciunum odium.   sed iurgia prima sonare
incipiunt animis ardentibus ; haec tuba rixae.
dein clamore pari concurritur, et vice teli
saevit nuda manus.   paucae sine vulnere malae,
vix cuiquam aut nulli toto certamine nasus   55
integer.   aspiceres iam cuncta per agmina vultus
dimidios, alias facies et hiantia ruptis
ossa genis, plenos oculorum sanguine pugnos.
ludere se credunt ipsi tamen et pueriles
exercere acies, quod nulla cadavera calcent.   60
et sane quo tot rixantis millia turbae,
si vivunt omnes ? ergo acrior impetus, et iam
saxa inclinatis per humum quaesita lacertis
incipiunt torquere, domestica seditioni
tela, nec hunc lapidem quales et Turnus et Aiax,   65
vel quo Tydides percussit pondere coxam
Aeneae, sed quem valeant emittere dextrae
illis dissimiles et nostro tempore natae.

51. genuinum.   64. seditione.

---

stomach.   However, the first altercations begin to resound with
souls all on fire ; this is the trumpet of the fray.   Then, with a
like clamour, they charge each other, and in place of a weapon
rages the naked hand.   There are few cheeks without a wound ;
scarce any, or none, in the whole fight has a nose intact.   You
might see already, through all the ranks, mutilated countenances,
faces that were no longer the same, bones gaping through the
divided cheeks, fists covered with blood from the eyes.   Yet
they themselves think they are at play and engaged in a child's
fight, because they are trampling on no dead bodies ; and,
to be sure, to what purpose a fighting crowd of so many
thousands, if every one is to remain alive ?   So the onslaught
grows sharper, and now they begin to hurl stones, which
they have picked up with arms bent along the ground, the
familiar weapons of sedition ; no such stone, indeed, as those
which Turnus and Ajax *hurled*, or of the weight of that with
which Tydides struck Aeneas on the hip, but such as right

nam genus hoc vivo iam decrescebat Homero:
terra malos homines nunc educat atque pusillos,   70
ergo deus, quicumque aspexit, ridet et odit.
a diverticulo repetatur fabula.   postquam
subsidiis aucti, pars altera promere ferrum
audet et infestis pugnam instaurare sagittis;
terga fuga celeri praestantibus omnibus, instant   75
qui vicina colunt umbrosae Tentyra palmae.
labitur hinc quidam nimia formidine cursum
praecipitans, capiturque.   ast illum in plurima sectum
frusta et particulas, ut multis mortuus unus
sufficeret, totum corrosis ossibus edit   80
victrix turba; nec ardenti decoxit aeno
aut verubus, longum usque adeo tardumque putavit
exspectare focos, contenta cadavere crudo.
hic gaudere libet quod non violaverit ignem,
quem summa coeli raptum de parte Prometheus   85

75. **praestant instantibus Ombis.**

hands, unlike theirs, and produced in our time, have strength
to project; for that race was already degenerating in the days of
Homer.   The earth nowadays nurtures wicked and puny men,
so whatever god has seen them, laughs at and despises them.

From this digression let us go back to our story.   After being
strengthened by reinforcements, one side ventures to draw the
sword, and renew the fight with deadly arrows; those who
inhabit Tentyra, neighbouring on the shady palm-trees, press on
their opponents, all showing their backs in rapid flight.   On this
side one who through excessive fear was precipitating his pace,
falls, and is captured; whereupon the victorious crowd, after he
had been cut into a great number of morsels and small portions,
that one dead man might suffice for many, eats up the whole of
him and gnaws his very bones; they did not even cook him in
the seething caldron or on a spit, so very long and tedious did
they deem it to wait for a fire, contented *as they were* with the
raw carcass.   At this point we may rejoice that they did not
desecrate the fire, which Prometheus stole from highest heaven

donavit terris.   elemento gratulor et te
exsultare reor.   sed qui mordere cadaver
sustinuit, nil umquam hac carne libentius edit.
nam scelere in tanto ne quaeras et dubites an
prima voluptatem gula senserit; ultimus autem   90
qui stetit absumpto iam toto corpore, ductis
per terram digitis aliquid de sanguine gustat.
Vascones, haec fama est, alimentis talibus olim
produxere animas; sed res diversa, sed illic
fortunae invidia est bellorumque ultima, casus   95
extremi, longae dira obsidionis egestas.
huius enim, quod nunc agitur, miserabile debet
exemplum esse cibi, sicut modo dicta mihi gens
post omnes herbas, post cuncta animalia, quidquid
cogebat vacui ventris furor, hostibus ipsis   100
pallorem ac maciem et tenues miserantibus artus,
membra aliena fame lacerabant, esse parati

---

and gave to earth.   I congratulate the element, and I imagine
you are rejoiced.   However, he who can bring himself to taste
a corpse never eats anything with more pleasure than this kind
of flesh; for in *the matter of* a crime so great, do not ask or
doubt whether the first palate *only* experienced pleasure.   Why,
the very last of them who came up after the entire body had
been consumed, drew his fingers along the ground, and tasted
some of the blood.

The Vascones—so the story is—in days of yore protracted
their lives by such nutriment as this; but the case was different; but there you have the malice of Fortune, and the
extremities of war, the climax of adversity, the dreadful desti-
tution of a long siege.   For the instance we are now mentioning
of such food ought to excite pity, inasmuch as the people I have
just named, after every kind of herbage, after all their animals,
and whatever the fury of their empty bellies drove them to, *had
been eaten*, when their very enemies were pitying their pallor and
emaciation and wasted frames, tore in pieces, through famine,
the limbs of others, prepared to eat even their own.   What man

et sua. quisnam hominum veniam dare quisve deorum
viribus abnueret dira atque immania passis,
et quibus illorum poterant ignoscere manes,　　　　　　　105
quorum corporibus vescebantur? melius nos
Zenonis praecepta monent; nec enim omnia, quaedam
pro vita facienda putat: sed Cantaber unde
stoicus, antiqui praesertim aetate Metelli?
nunc totus Graias nostrasque habet orbis Athenas,　　　110
Gallia causidicos docuit facunda Britannos,
de conducendo loquitur iam rhetore Thule.
nobilis ille tamen populus, quem diximus, et par
virtute atque fide, sed maior clade, Saguntus
tale quid excusat: Maeotide saevior ara　　　　　　　　115
Aegyptus; quippe illa nefandi Taurica sacri
inventrix homines, ut iam quae carmina tradunt
digna fide credas, tantum immolat, ulterius nil
aut gravius cultro timet hostia. quis modo casus

104. ventribus, urbibus.

---

or what god could refuse his pardon to strong men who had
endured *such* dreadful and monstrous things, and whom the
very manes of those on whose bodies they were feeding might
have forgiven? The precepts of Zeno teach us better; he
thinks, not, indeed, that all things, but some *only*, may be done
for the sake of life. Yet how should the Cantabrian be a
Stoic, especially in the age of old Metellus? Now the whole
world has the Greek Athens and our own. Eloquent Gaul has
instructed the British lawyers; already Thule speaks of engaging
a teacher of rhetoric. Yet that noble people we have named,
and Saguntum their equal in courage and fidelity, their more
than equal in calamity, have an excuse to offer for a deed
of this kind. Egypt is more cruel than the altar of
Maeotis; since that Tauric inventress of the abominable
rite (if, at least, you believe what the poems tell us to be worthy
of faith) only immolates, the victim has nothing further or worse
to fear than the knife. What mischance even impelled these
men? What hunger so great, or arms threatening their ram-

impulit hos ? quae tanta fames infestaque vallo   120
arma coegerunt tam detestabile monstrum
audere ? anne aliam terra Memphitide sicca
invidiam facerent nolenti surgere Nilo ?
qua nec terribiles Cimbri nec Britones umquam
Sauromataeque truces aut immanes Agathyrsi,   125
hac saevit rabie imbelle et inutile vulgus,
parvula fictilibus solitum dare vela phaselis   .
et brevibus pictae remis incumbere testae.
nec poenam sceleri invenies, nec digna parabis
supplicia his populis, in quorum mente pares sunt   130
et similes ira atque fames. mollissima corda
humano generi dare se natura fatetur,
quae lacrimas dedit ; haec nostri pars optima sensus.
plorare ergo iubet causam dicentis amici
squaloremque rei, pupillum ad iura vocantem   135
circumscriptorem, cuius manantia fletu
ora puellares faciunt incerta capilli.

134. casum lugentis.

---

parts, compelled them to dare so detestable a monstrosity ?
Could they, if the land of Memphis had been dry, have offered
a greater insult to the Nile for refusing to rise ? Never have
even the terrible Cimbri, nor the Britons, nor the savage Sarmatians, nor the monstrous Agathyrsi raged with such fury as
this effeminate and useless rabble, accustomed to set their little
bits of snails in their boats of clay, and to bend over the short
oars of their painted shells. You can neither find a penalty for
such guilt, nor provide a punishment worthy of these tribes in
whose minds anger and hunger are on a par, and alike *in their
results*. Nature confesses that she gives the tenderest of hearts
to the human race, by giving them tears : this is the best part
of our sensations. She bids us then weep over the misfortune
of our sorrowing friend, the squalid appearance of one accused,
the ward summoning his despoiler to justice, whose girlish
locks render uncertain the *sex of the* face bedewed with tears.

naturae imperio gemimus, cum funus adultae
virginis occurrit vel terra clauditur infans
et minor igne rogi.   quis enim bonus et face dignus   140
arcana, qualem Cereris vult esse sacerdos,
ulla aliena sibi credat mala ? separat hoc nos
a grege mutorum, atque ideo venerabile soli
sortiti ingenium divinorumque capaces
atque exercendis capiendisque artibus apti   145
sensum a coelesti demissum traximus arce,
cuius egent prona et terram spectantia.   mundi
principio indulsit communis conditor illis
tantum animas, nobis animum quoque, mutuus ut nos
affectus petere auxilium et praestare iuberet,   150
dispersos trahere in populum, migrare vetusto
de nemore et proavis habitatas linquere silvas,
aedificare domos, Laribus coniungere nostris
tectum aliud, tutos vicino limine somnos

142. credit.   154. limite.

At nature's bidding we sigh when the funeral of an adult virgin
meets us, or an infant, too young for the fire of the pile, is
buried in the earth.   For what good man worthy of the mystic
torch, such an one as the priest of Ceres would have him to be,
can deem any misfortunes to be foreign to himself ?   This it
is that separates us from the herd of dumb creatures, and on
that account we alone have had allotted to us a reverential
spirit, are capable of containing divine things, and, fitted for
practising and apprehending the arts, have received, trans-
mitted to us from the heights of heaven, a moral sense, which
animals bending downwards, and looking to the earth, are
wanting in.   In the beginning of the world the common Creator
allowed them life only, to us a soul as well, that our mutual
regard might bid us seek aid and afford it, draw the scattered
ones into a community, migrate from the ancient grove, leave
the woods inhabited by our forefathers, build houses, join on to
our Lares another habitation, that united confidence might give
us slumbers secured by a neighbour's threshold, protect with

ut collata daret fiducia, protegere armis   155
lapsum aut ingenti nutantem vulnere civem,
communi dare signa tuba, defendier isdem
turribus atque una portarum clave teneri.
sed iam serpentum maior concordia.   parcit
cognatis maculis similis fera.   quando leoni   160
fortior eripuit vitam leo ? quo nemore umquam
exspiravit aper maioris dentibus apri ?
Indica tigris agit rabida cum tigride pacem
perpetuam, saevis inter se convenit ursis.
ast homini ferrum letale incude nefanda   165
produxisse parum est ; cum rastra et sarcula tantum
assueti coquere et marris ac vomere lassi
nescierint primi gladios extendere fabri ;
aspicimus populos, quorum non sufficit irae
occidisse aliquem, sed pectora brachia vultum   170
crediderint genus esse cibi.   quid diceret ergo
vel quo non fugeret, si nunc haec monstra videret

168. extundere, excudere (Serv.)

arms a citizen who has fallen or is staggering under a severe wound,
sound our war-signals on a common trumpet, be defended by the
same towers, be enclosed by one key for our gates.   But now
there is greater concord among serpents ; a wild beast of like
kind spares his kindred spots.   When did a stronger lion
deprive of his life another lion ?   In what forest did a boar
ever expire by the teeth of a larger boar ?   The Indian tigress
lives with *each* rabid tigress in perpetual peace ; savage bears
agree among themselves.   But to man it is not enough to have
beaten out the deadly weapon on the accursed anvil, though the
first smiths, accustomed to forge harrows and hoes only, and
wearied with *making* mattocks and ploughshares, knew not how
to hammer out swords ; we behold nations to whose fury it does
not suffice to have killed some one, but they think his breast,
arms, face to be a kind of meat.   What, then, would Pythagoras say, or, rather, whither would he not flee, if, nowadays,
he witnessed such horrors—he who abstained from all animals

Pythagoras, cunctis animalibus abstinuit qui
tamquam homine et ventri indulsit non omne legumen?

SATIRA XVI.

QUIS numerare queat felicis praemia, Galle,
    militiae? quod si subeuntur prospera castra,
me pavidum excipiat tironem porta secundo
sidere.   plus etenim fati valet hora benigni,
quam si nos Veneris commendet epistola Marti   5
et Samia genetrix quae delectatur arena.
    Commoda tractemus primum communia, quorum
haud minimum illud erit, ne te pulsare togatus
audeat, immo etsi pulsetur, dissimulet, nec
audeat excussos praetori ostendere dentes   10
et nigram in facie tumidis livoribus offam

11. et tumidam in facie nigris.

---

as though from a human being, and would not allow his stomach
even all kinds of vegetables?

SATIRE XVI.

WHO, O Gallus, can enumerate the prizes of happy soldiering?
But if, *in addition,* a fortunate corps is being entered, may its
gate receive me, a timorous recruit, under a favourable star.
For indeed the moment of a smiling fate is of more avail than
if we were recommended to Mars by an epistle of Venus, or his
mother who delights in the sands of Samos.

    Let us first treat of the advantages common to all *soldiers,* of
which this is not the least, that a civilian won't dare to beat
you; nay, though he be beaten *himself,* will conceal it and
won't dare to show the Praetor his teeth that have been
knocked out, and the lump on his face, black with swollen

atque oculum medico nil promittente relictum.
Bardaicus iudex datur haec punire volenti
calceus et grandes magna ad subsellia surae,
legibus antiquis castrorum et more Camilli 15
servato, miles ne vallum litiget extra
et procul a signis. iustissima centurionum
cognitio est igitur de milite, nec mihi deerit
ultio, si iustae defertur causa querelae.
tota cohors tamen est inimica, omnesque manipli 20
consensu magno efficiunt, curabilis ut sit
vindicta et gravior quam iniuria. dignum erit ergo
declamatoris mulino corde Vagelli,
cum duo crura habeas, offendere tot caligas, tot
millia clavorum. quis tam procul absit ab urbe 25
praeterea? quis tam Pylades molem aggeris ultra
ut veniat? lacrimae siccentur protinus, et se
excusaturos non sollicitemus amicos,

21. officiunt; curabitis ut sit.   22. vindicta gravior.

---

bruises, and the eye still left to him, but about which the
doctor will make no promise. Those who wish to get redress
for these things have a *centurion's* big boot assigned them for a
judge, and *a pair of* huge calves under a stout bench, the ancient
military law and the rule of Camillus being observed, that the
soldier is not to be a party to a suit outside the trenches or at a
distance from the standards. Most just, therefore, is the juris-
diction of the centurions over the soldier, nor will my revenge
fail me if a cause in which the complaint is just be brought
before them. But the whole cohort are your enemies, and all
the maniples with great unanimity manage that your redress
shall be such as you shall care for, and worse than the *original*
injury. It would be worthy, then, of the ranter Vagellius, with
his mulish understanding, when you have *only* two legs, to
offend so many thick boots, so many thousands of hob-nails.
Moreover, who would absent himself such a distance from town?
who is such a Pylades as to come beyond the rampart-mound?
Let our tears be dried forthwith, and let us not trouble our

" da testem " iudex cum dixerit, audeat ille,
nescio quis, pugnos qui vidit, dicere " vidi,"   30
et credam dignum barba dignumque capillis
maiorum.   citius falsum producere testem
contra paganum possis, quam vera loquentem
contra fortunam armati contraque pudorem.

Praemia nunc alia atque alia emolumenta notemus   35
sacramentorum.   convallem ruris aviti
improbus aut campum mihi si vicinus ademit
et sacrum effodit medio de limite saxum,
quod mea cum patulo coluit puls annua libo,
debitor aut sumptos pergit non reddere nummos,   40
vana supervacui dicens chirographa ligni,
exspectandus erit, qui lites inchoet, annus
totius populi.   sed tunc quoque mille ferenda
taedia, mille morae : toties subsellia tantum
sternuntur, tum facundo ponente lacernas   45

39. vetulo.

---

friends, who are sure to excuse themselves. When the judge
has said, " Produce your witness," let the man, whoever he
be, who saw the fisticuffs, say, " I saw them," and I shall deem
him worthy of the beard and worthy of the locks of our ancestors. You could more readily produce a false witness against
a civilian than one to speak the truth against the fortune and
against the honour of a soldier.

Let us note now other prizes and other advantages of military
life. If a rascally neighbour has robbed me of a valley or a
field of my paternal estate, and has dug up from the middle of
the boundary-line, the sacred stone which my porridge has
yearly honoured, together with a broad cake, or a debtor per-
sists in not repaying the monies he has received, declaring his
note-of-hand void and the tablets worthless, I shall have to wait
a whole year, *the time* requisite for making *even* a beginning of
the lawsuits of an entire people. But even then a thousand
worries, a thousand delays have to be borne ; so often the seats
are merely cushioned ; then, while eloquent Caedicius is taking

Caedicio et Fusco iam micturiente, parati
digredimur, lentaque fori pugnamus arena.
ast illis, quos arma tegunt et balteus ambit,
quod placitum est ipsis praestatur tempus agendi,
nec res atteritur longo suflamine litis.   50
  Solis praeterea testandi militibus ius
vivo patre datur; nam quae sunt parta labore
militiae, placuit non esse in corpore census,
omne tenet cuius regimen pater.   ergo Coranum
signorum comitem castrorumque aera merentem   55
quamvis iam tremulus captat pater.   hunc labor aequus
provehit et pulchro reddit sua dona labori.
ipsius certe ducis hoc referre videtur,
ut qui fortis erit sit felicissimus idem,
ut laeti phaleris omnes et torquibus omnes—   60

---

off his cloak, and Fuscus has just gone out for another purpose,
though all prepared, we must take our departure, and *so* we
fight on the dilatory arena of the Forum. But to those who
wear armour and are girded with a belt, their own chosen time
for suing is insured, nor is their property ground down by the
tardy drag-chain of a lawsuit.

Moreover, to soldiers alone is accorded the right of making a
will in a father's life-time : for it has seemed good that what
has been acquired by the labours of military life should not
form part of the bulk of the property of which the father holds
the entire disposal.   So that Coranus, while following the
standards and in receipt of army pay, is courted by his own
father, though now trembling with age.   His labours duly performed, advance the former, and he pays back its gifts to honest
labour.   Certainly this seems to be to the interest of the general
himself, that whoever shows himself brave should also be
most fortunate, that all, rejoicing in trappings and collars—

END OF VOL. I.

PRINTED BY BALLANTYNE, HANSON AND CO.,
EDINBURGH AND LONDON